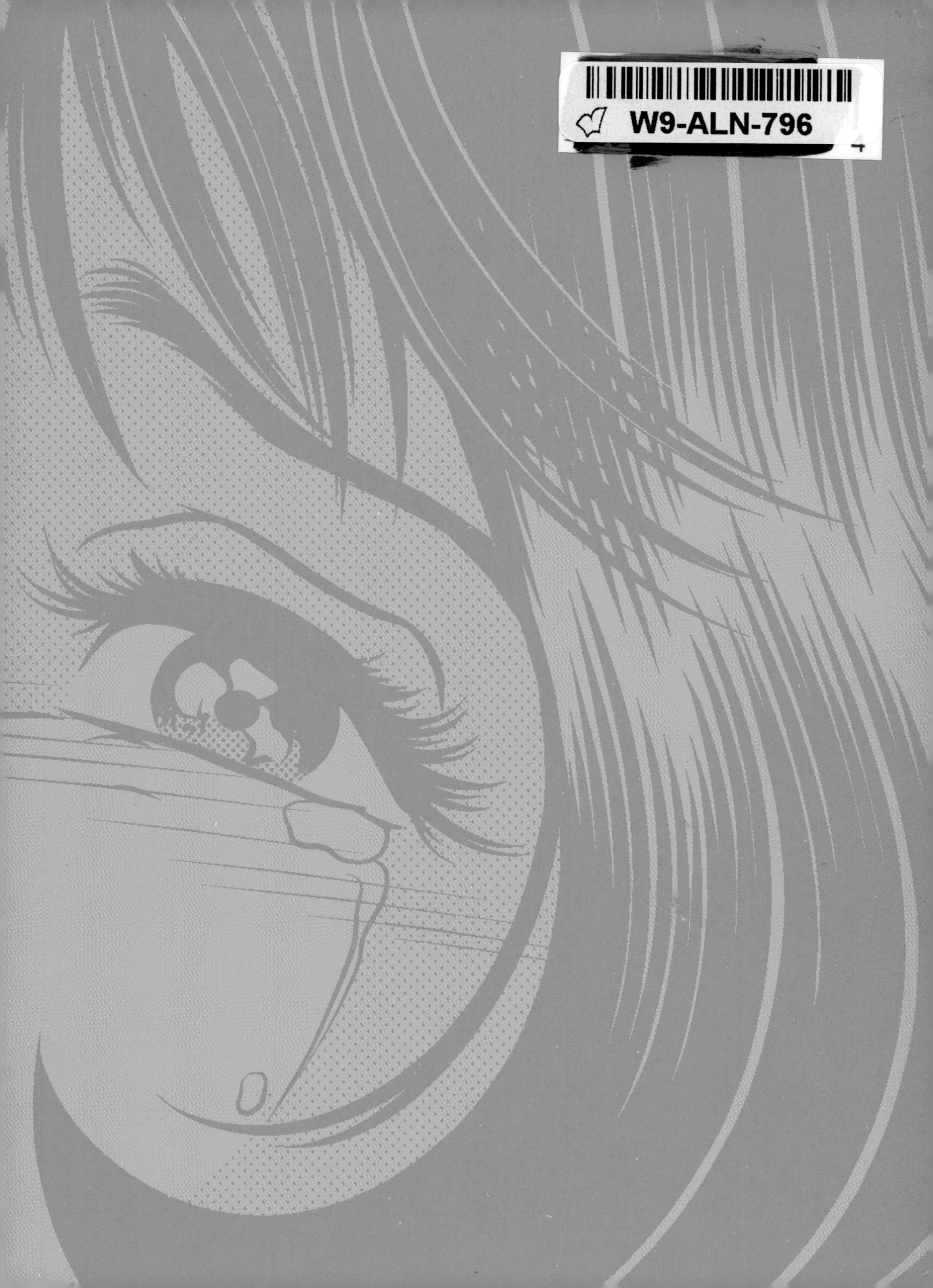

Adventures

Mauricio

#2
WE FOUGHT EACH OTHER AS KIDS... NOW WE'RE IN LOVE?!

charmZ
NEW YORK

Monica

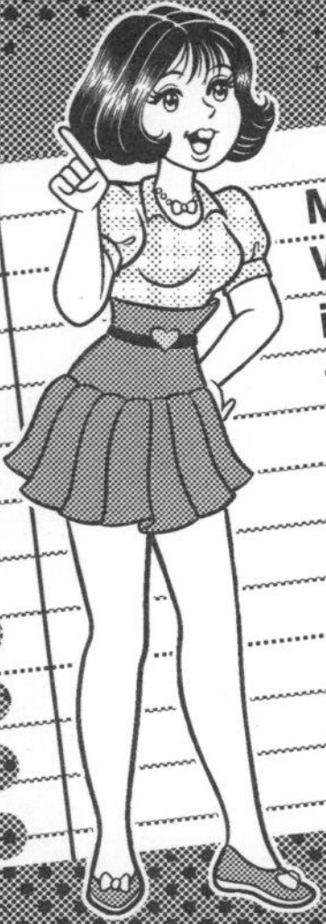

Monica is a sweet, happy, buck-toothed, teenage girl. When she was younger, she was known for being intolerant of disrespect and always stood up for her friends. That is, unless Jimmy-Five and Smudge would cause her trouble, then Monica would bash them with her favorite plush blue bunny, Samson! Still, occasionally, she does her classic bunny bashings as a teen, but has chilled out when it comes to Jimmy-Five, who has been catching her attention a lot more lately. Monica is the leader of the gang because of her honest and charisma-tic—and powerful—personality.

J-Five

Jimmy-Five, or J-Five, has always been picked on for his speech impediment. He used to lisp, which caused him to switch letters around, such as r's for w's, when he would speak. He has grown out of that as a teen, unless he's nervous, which typically happens around a certain girl. He also was picked on because of the five strands of hair he had on his head, which have all sort of filled out as a teen. Still, J-Five is sometimes made fun of for his hair, but he doesn't let it get to him as much anymore! When J-Five was young, he would often try to steal Monica's blue bunny from her and attempt to take over as leader of the gang with his questionable schemes. J-Five is no longer focused on being head of the gang as much as he's focused on being close with his friends, and closer to one friend in particular…

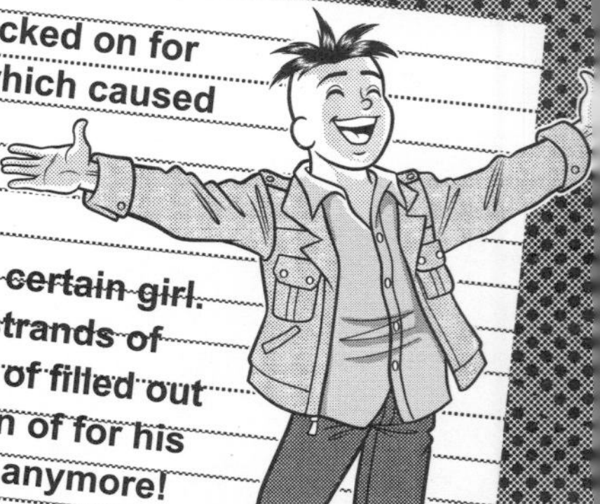

Smudge

Smudge has never liked water and prefers his messy and dirty lifestyle over showers, rain, swimming, or even drinking water any day, but he's warmed up to taking showers as a teen… sort of. He cleans up sometimes mainly because the opinion of girls has started to matter to him, unlike when he was a kid. Smudge loves sports, especially skateboarding and soccer because of how radical they are. He also loves comics, and shares this love with his best friend, J-Five! Smudge is kind of the "handyman" of the gang, always helping his friends in times of need but typically also messing everything up.

Maggy

Maggy is Monica's best friend, always having her back and being there for her in good times and bad. Maggy is also a huge lover of cats. Maggy has always had a voracious appetite, mostly eating watermelons but never discriminating against any other food put in front of her. Maggy is more conscious of what she eats now… perhaps a little too much. She is virtually obsessed with proper nutrition, sports, and exercise instead of eating anything she sees.

#2 "We Fought Each Other as Kids...Now We're in Love?!"

Characters, Story, and Illustration created by MAURICIO DE SOUSA
ZAZO AGUIAR, MARCELA CURAC RUSSI, and FELIPPE BARBIERI—Cover Artists
MAURICIO DE SOUSA, MARINA TAKEDA E SOUSA, PETRA LEÃO—Script
DENIS Y. OYAFUSO, JOSÉ APARECIDO CAVALCANTE, LINO PAES, ROBERTO M. PEREIRA—Pencils
MAURO SOUZA, ZAZO AGUILAR—Illustrations
CRISTINA H. ANDO, JAIME PODAVIN, ROSANA G. VALIM, TATIANA M. SANTOS, VIVIANE YAMABUCHI,
and WELLINGTON DIAS—Inks
MARCELO CASSARO—Lettering
A. MAURICIO SOUSA NETO—Finishes
JAE HYUNG WOO, FÁBIO ASADA, MARCELO KINA, MARIA JÚLIA S. BELLUCCI—Colorists
MARIA DE FÁTIMA A. CLARO—Art Coordination
SANDRO ANTONIO DA SILVA—Script Supervisor
ALICE K. TAKEDA—Executive Director
SIDNEY GUSMAN—Editorial Planner
ÍVANA MELLO, SOLANGE M. LEMES—Original editors
PECCAVI TRANSLATIONS—Original Translations

Special thanks to LOURDES GALIANO, RODRIGO PAIVA, MÔNICA SOUSA, and MAURICO DE SOUSA

JEFF WHITMAN—Editor, Production
KARR ANTUNES—Editorial Intern
JIM SALICRUP
Editor-in-Chief

Charmz is an imprint of Papercutz.
PB ISBN: 978-1-5458-0216-8
HC ISBN: 978-1-5458-0217-5

Printed in China
January 2019

Charmz books may be purchased for business or promotional use.
For information on bulk purchases please contact Macmillan
Corporate and Premium Sales Department at
(800) 221-7945 x5442

Distributed by Macmillan
First Charmz Printing

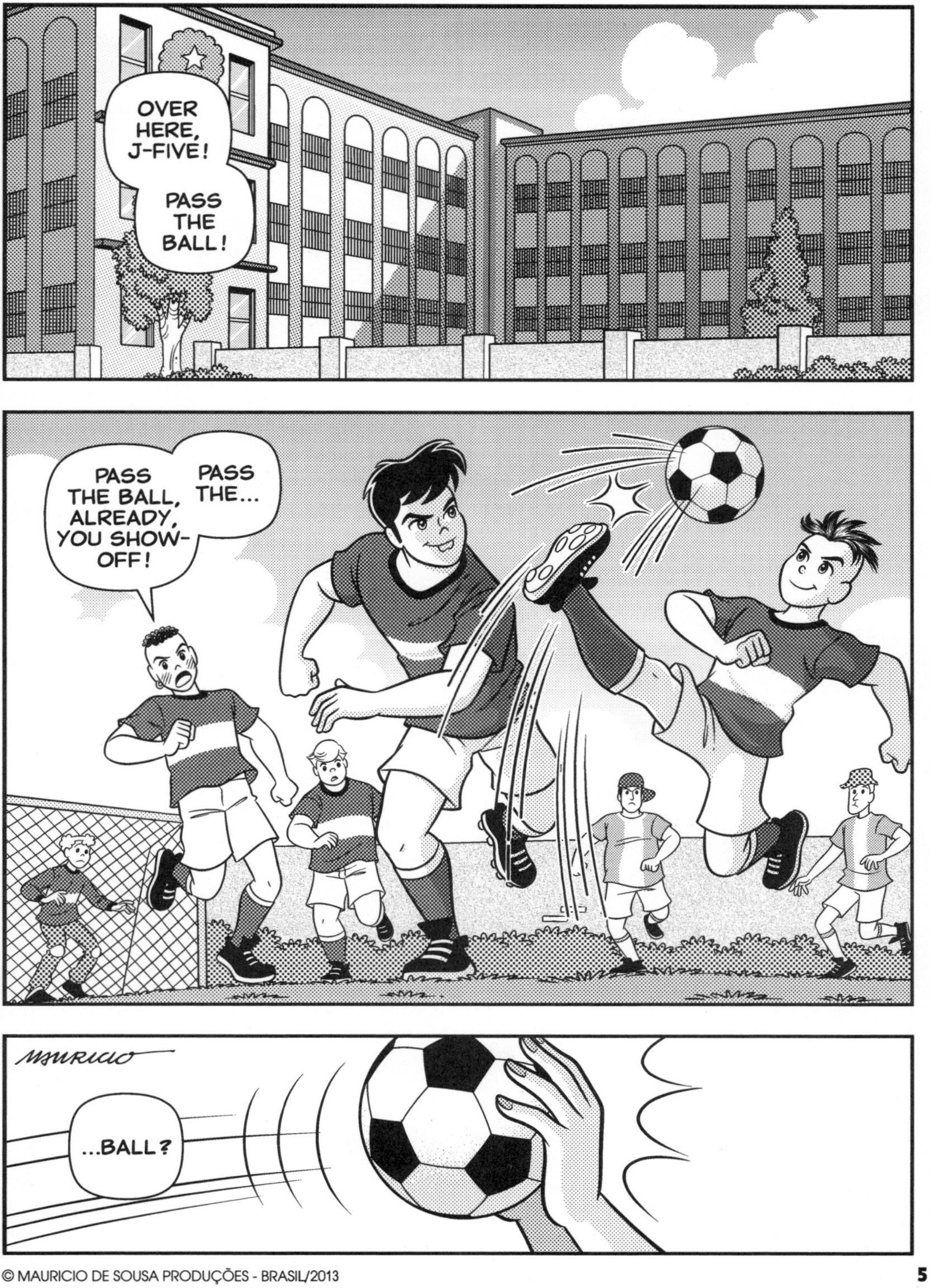

OVER HERE, J-FIVE!
PASS THE BALL!
PASS THE BALL, ALREADY, YOU SHOW-OFF!
PASS THE...
...BALL?

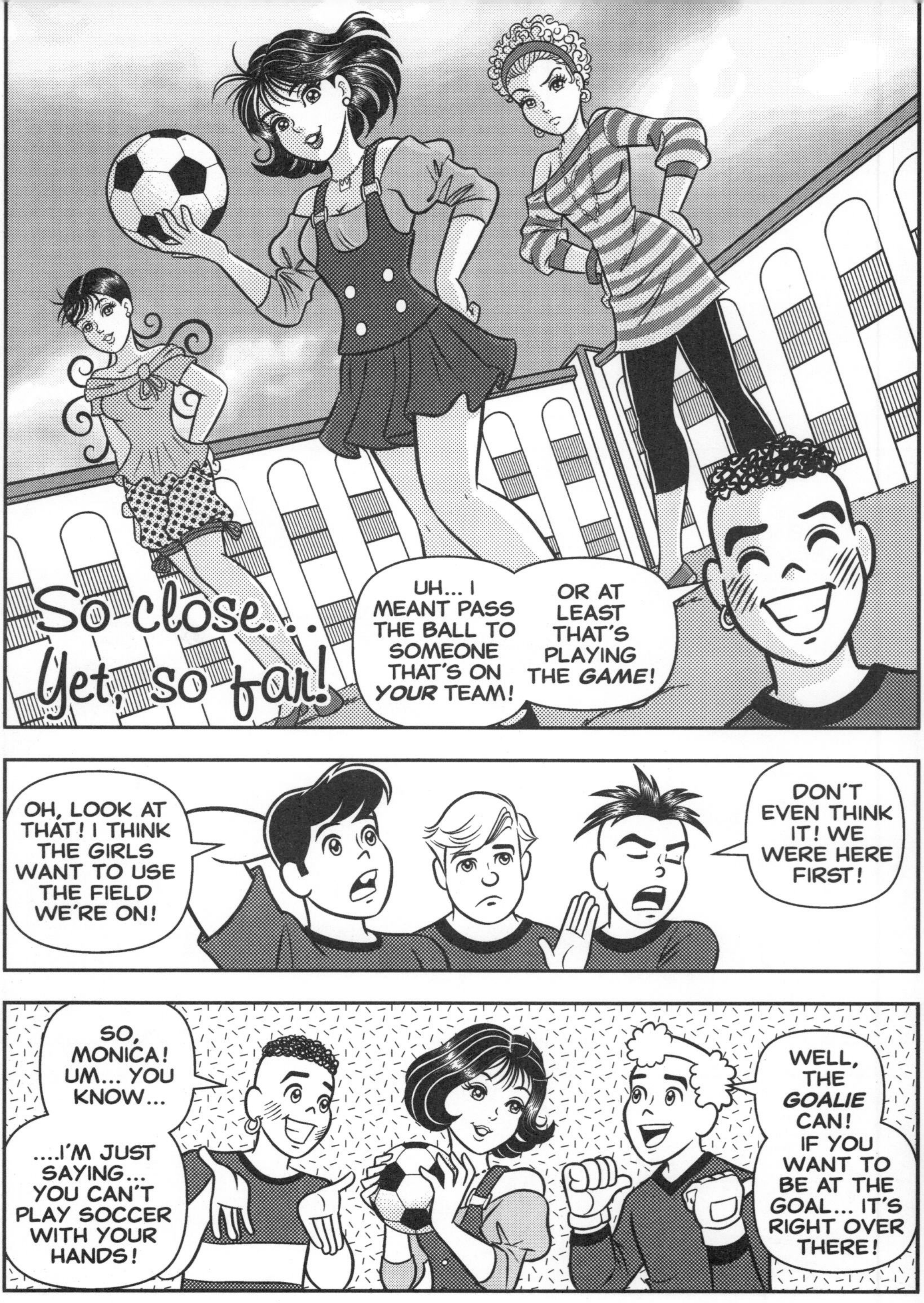
So close... Yet, so far!
UH... I MEANT PASS THE BALL TO SOMEONE THAT'S ON *YOUR* TEAM!
OR AT LEAST THAT'S PLAYING THE *GAME*!
OH, LOOK AT THAT! I THINK THE GIRLS WANT TO USE THE FIELD WE'RE ON!
DON'T EVEN THINK IT! WE WERE HERE FIRST!
SO, MONICA! UM... YOU KNOW...
....I'M JUST SAYING... YOU CAN'T PLAY SOCCER WITH YOUR HANDS!
WELL, THE *GOALIE* CAN!
IF YOU WANT TO BE AT THE GOAL... IT'S RIGHT OVER THERE!

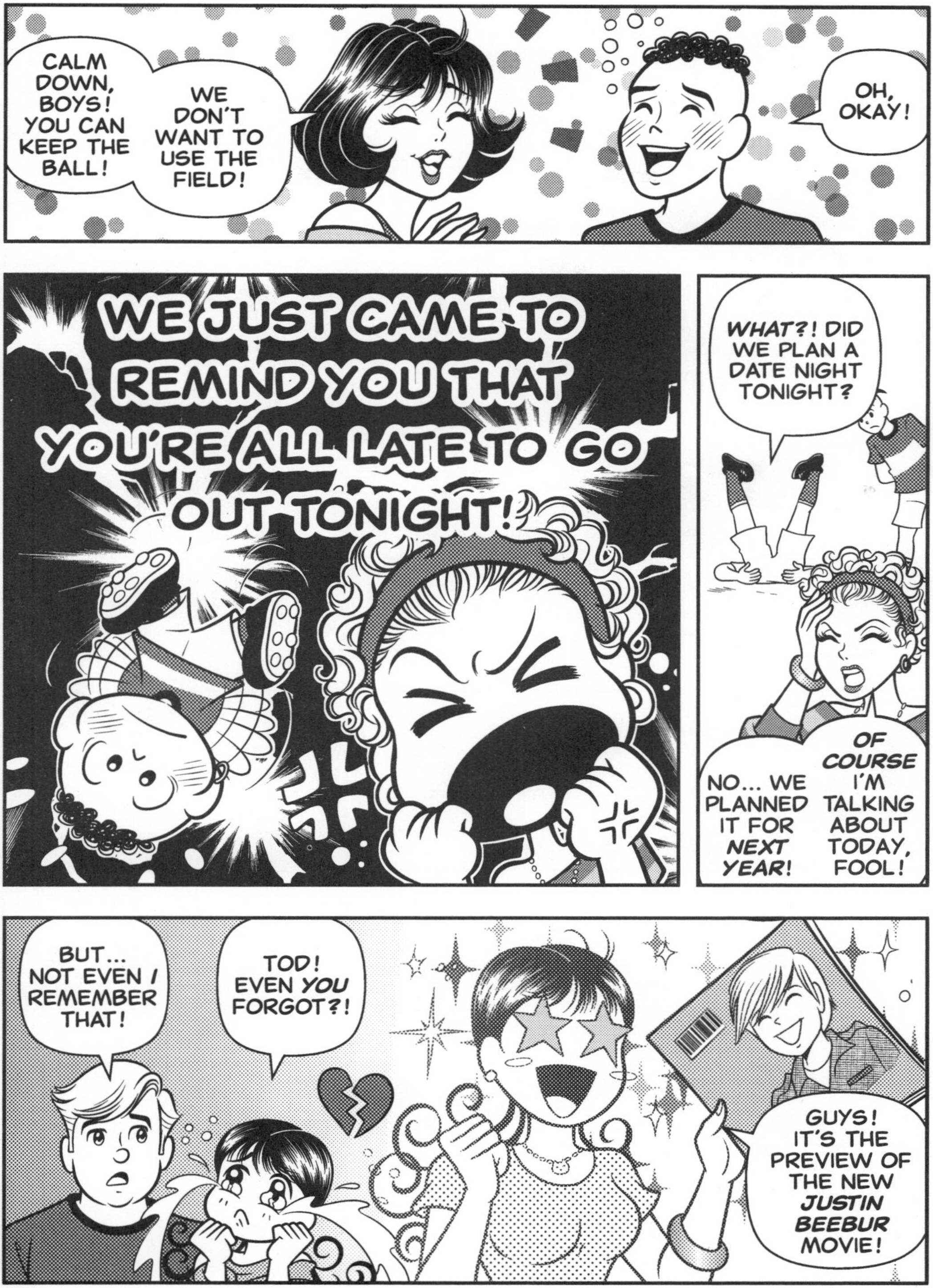
CALM DOWN, BOYS! YOU CAN KEEP THE BALL!
WE DON'T WANT TO USE THE FIELD!
OH, OKAY!
WE JUST CAME TO REMIND YOU THAT YOU'RE ALL LATE TO GO OUT TONIGHT!
WHAT?! DID WE PLAN A DATE NIGHT TONIGHT?
NO... WE PLANNED IT FOR *NEXT YEAR*!
OF COURSE I'M TALKING ABOUT TODAY, FOOL!
BUT... NOT EVEN *I* REMEMBER THAT!
TOD! EVEN *YOU* FORGOT?!
GUYS! IT'S THE PREVIEW OF THE NEW *JUSTIN BEEBUR* MOVIE!

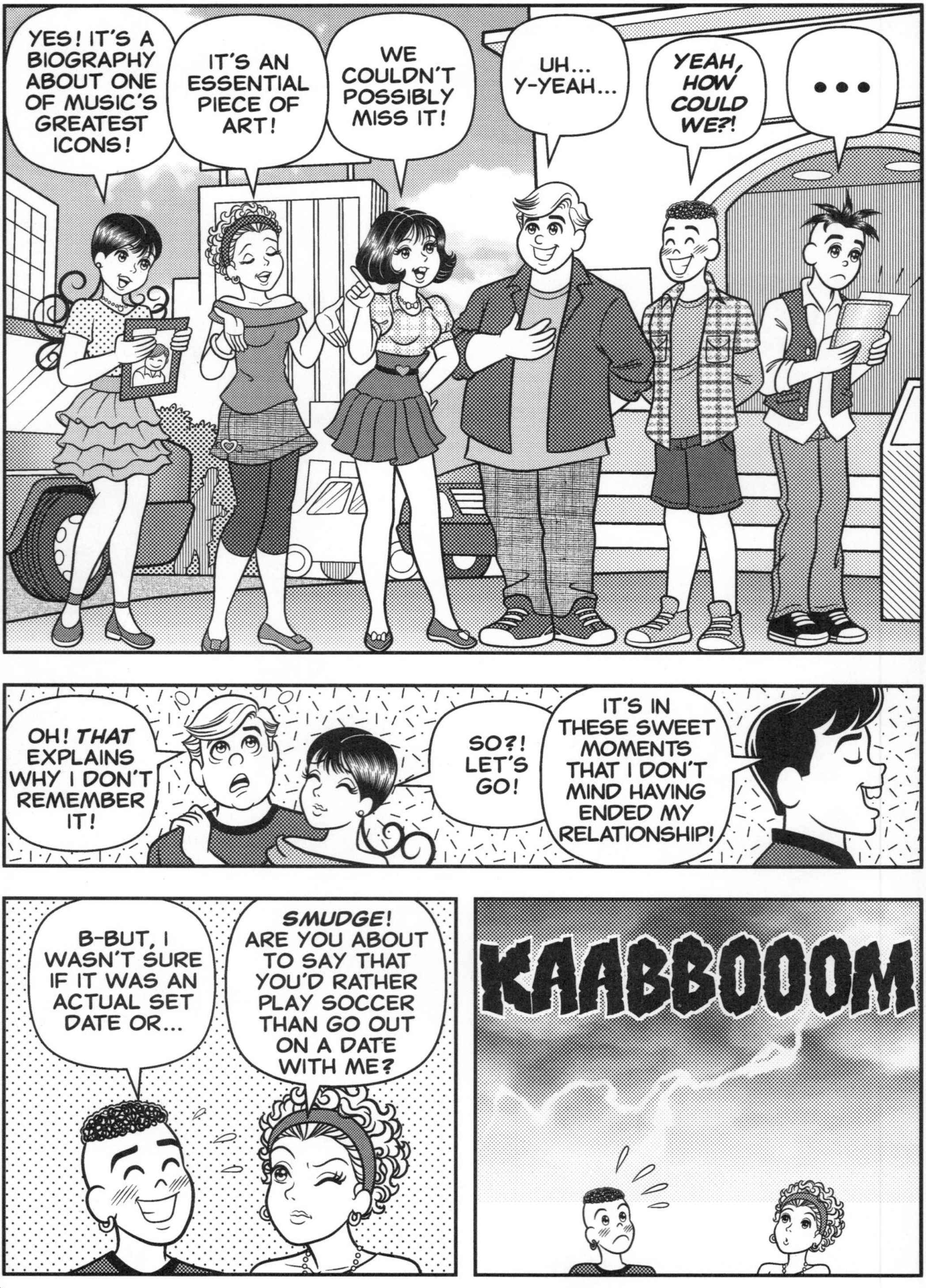
YES! IT'S A BIOGRAPHY ABOUT ONE OF MUSIC'S GREATEST ICONS!
IT'S AN ESSENTIAL PIECE OF ART!
WE COULDN'T POSSIBLY MISS IT!
UH... Y-YEAH...
YEAH, HOW COULD WE?!
• • •
OH! *THAT* EXPLAINS WHY I DON'T REMEMBER IT!
SO?! LET'S GO!
IT'S IN THESE SWEET MOMENTS THAT I DON'T MIND HAVING ENDED MY RELATIONSHIP!
B-BUT, I WASN'T SURE IF IT WAS AN ACTUAL SET DATE OR...
SMUDGE! ARE YOU ABOUT TO SAY THAT YOU'D RATHER PLAY SOCCER THAN GO OUT ON A DATE WITH ME?
KAABBOOOM

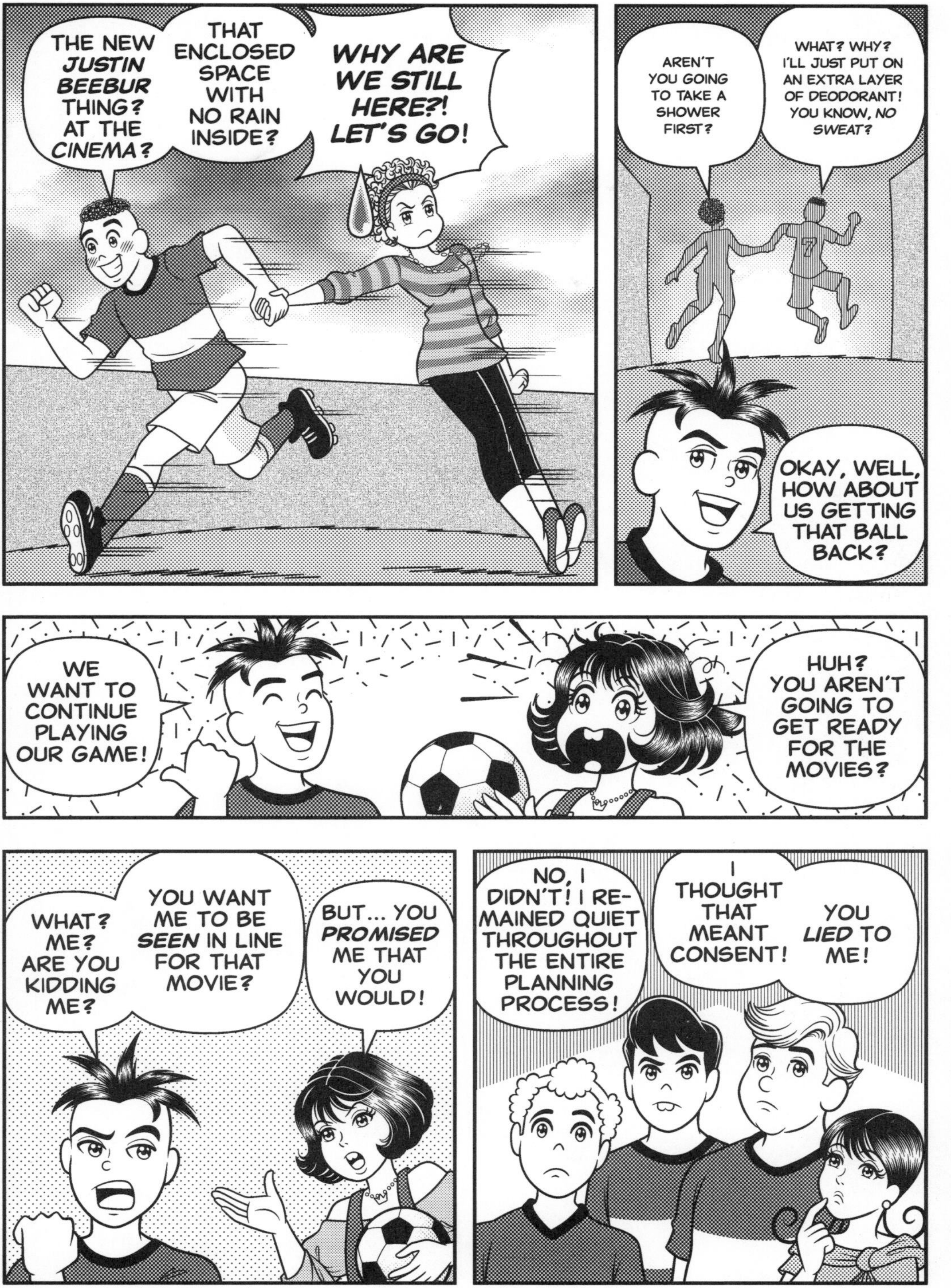
THE NEW JUSTIN BEEBUR THING? AT THE CINEMA?
THAT ENCLOSED SPACE WITH NO RAIN INSIDE?
WHY ARE WE STILL HERE?! LET'S GO!
AREN'T YOU GOING TO TAKE A SHOWER FIRST?
WHAT? WHY? I'LL JUST PUT ON AN EXTRA LAYER OF DEODORANT! YOU KNOW, NO SWEAT?
OKAY, WELL, HOW ABOUT US GETTING THAT BALL BACK?
WE WANT TO CONTINUE PLAYING OUR GAME!
HUH? YOU AREN'T GOING TO GET READY FOR THE MOVIES?
WHAT? ME? ARE YOU KIDDING ME?
YOU WANT ME TO BE SEEN IN LINE FOR THAT MOVIE?
BUT... YOU PROMISED ME THAT YOU WOULD!
NO, I DIDN'T! I RE-MAINED QUIET THROUGHOUT THE ENTIRE PLANNING PROCESS!
I THOUGHT THAT MEANT CONSENT!
YOU LIED TO ME!

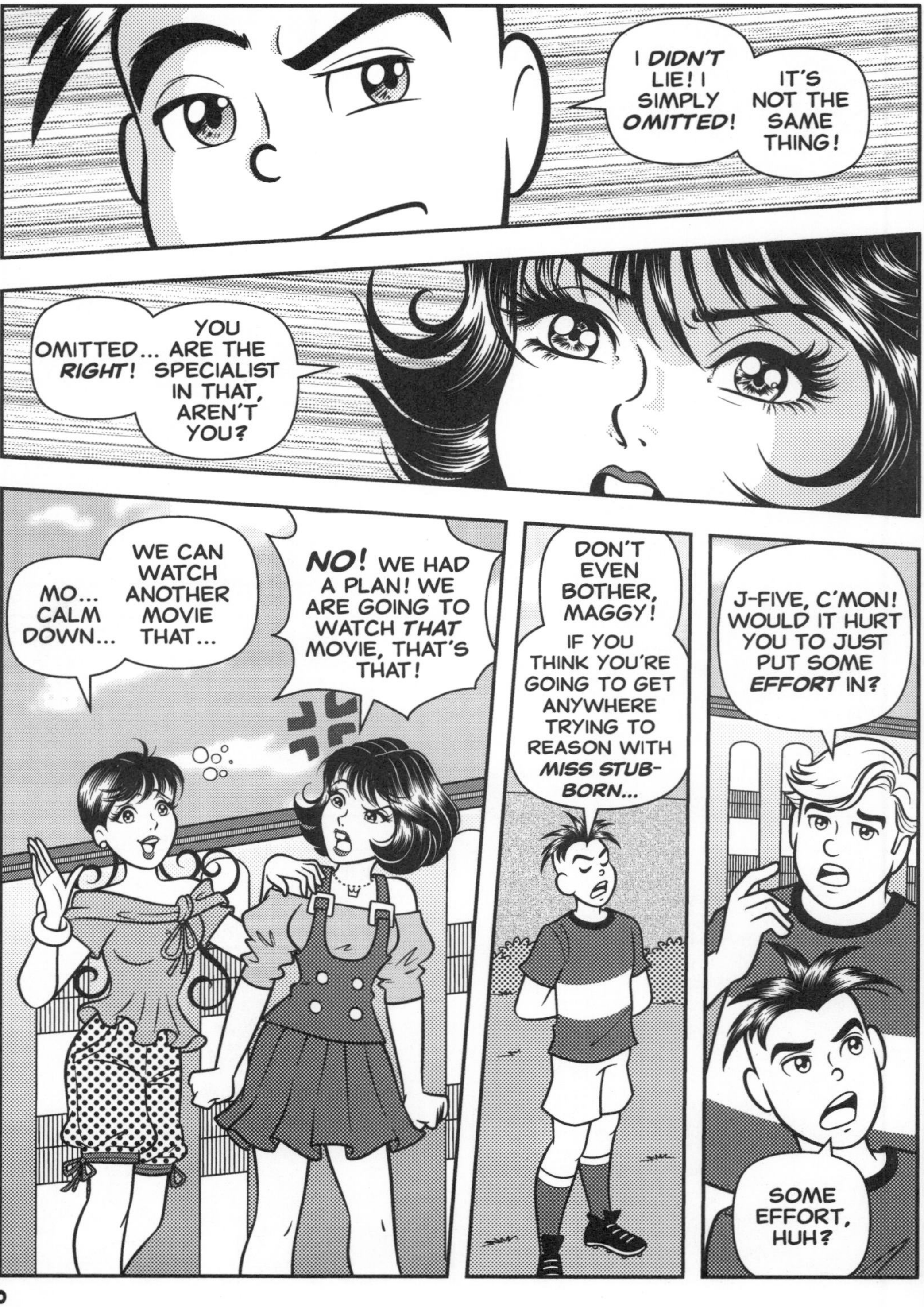
I *DIDN'T* LIE! I SIMPLY *OMITTED*!
IT'S NOT THE SAME THING!
OMITTED... RIGHT!
YOU ARE THE SPECIALIST IN THAT, AREN'T YOU?
MO... CALM DOWN...
WE CAN WATCH ANOTHER MOVIE THAT...
NO! WE HAD A PLAN! WE ARE GOING TO WATCH *THAT* MOVIE, THAT'S THAT!
DON'T EVEN BOTHER, MAGGY!
IF YOU THINK YOU'RE GOING TO GET ANYWHERE TRYING TO REASON WITH *MISS STUB-BORN...*
J-FIVE, C'MON! WOULD IT HURT YOU TO JUST PUT SOME *EFFORT* IN?
SOME EFFORT, HUH?

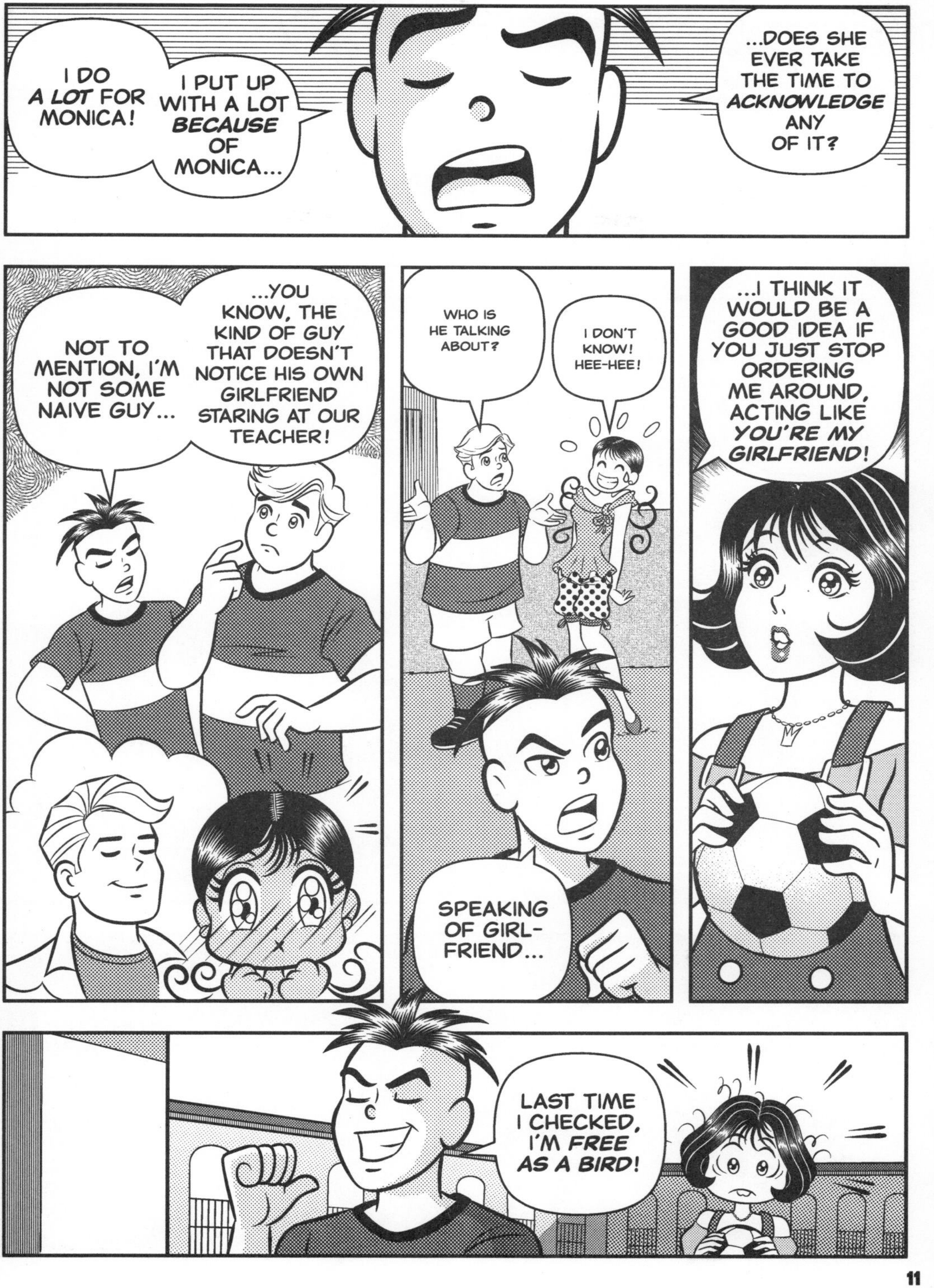
I DO A *LOT* FOR MONICA!
I PUT UP WITH A LOT *BECAUSE* OF MONICA...
...DOES SHE EVER TAKE THE TIME TO *ACKNOWLEDGE* ANY OF IT?
NOT TO MENTION, I'M NOT SOME NAIVE GUY...
...YOU KNOW, THE KIND OF GUY THAT DOESN'T NOTICE HIS OWN GIRLFRIEND STARING AT OUR TEACHER!
WHO IS HE TALKING ABOUT?
I DON'T KNOW! HEE-HEE!
SPEAKING OF GIRL-FRIEND...
...I THINK IT WOULD BE A GOOD IDEA IF YOU JUST STOP ORDERING ME AROUND, ACTING LIKE *YOU'RE MY GIRLFRIEND*!
LAST TIME I CHECKED, I'M *FREE AS A BIRD*!

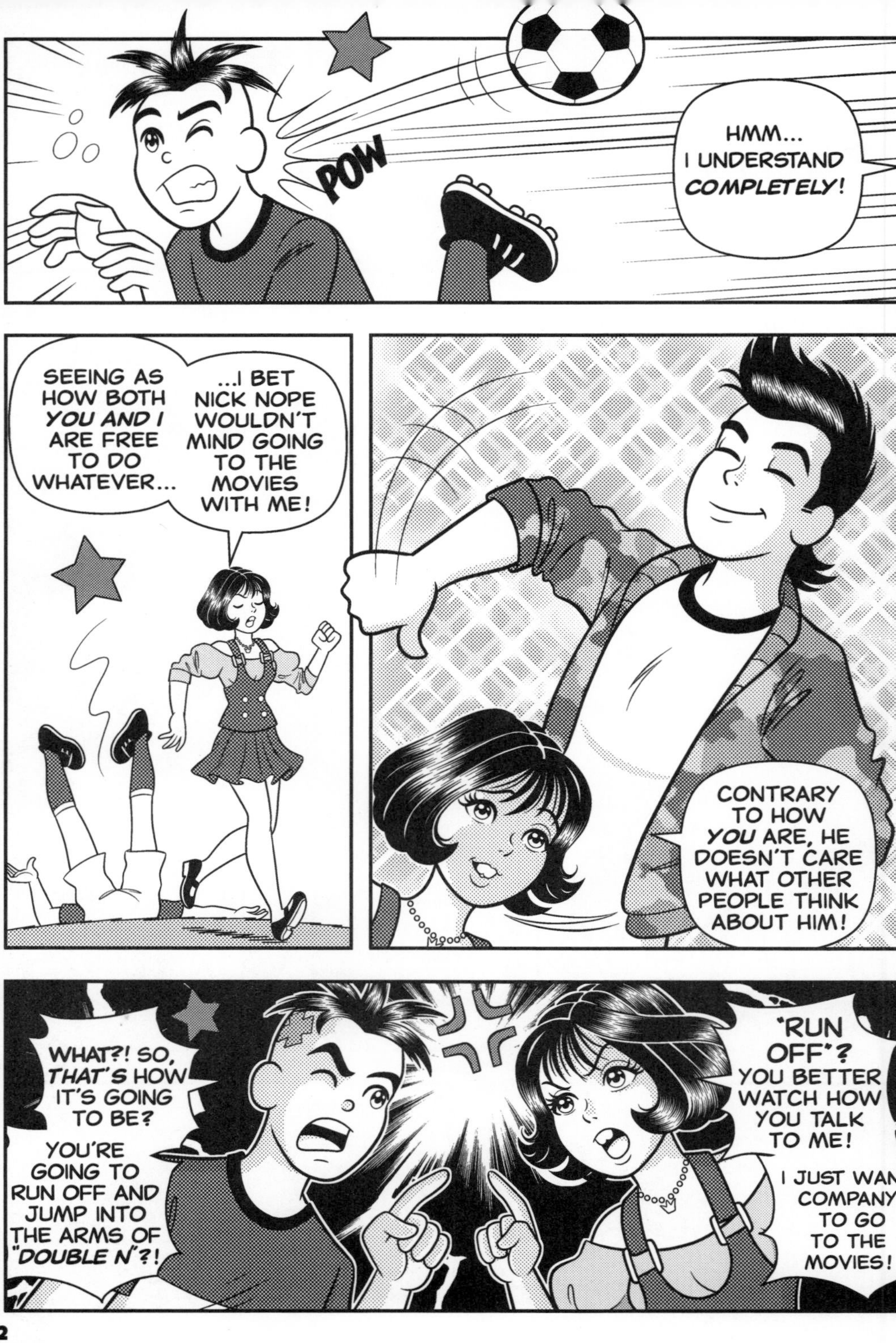
POW
HMM... I UNDERSTAND COMPLETELY!
SEEING AS HOW BOTH YOU AND I ARE FREE TO DO WHATEVER...
...I BET NICK NOPE WOULDN'T MIND GOING TO THE MOVIES WITH ME!
CONTRARY TO HOW YOU ARE, HE DOESN'T CARE WHAT OTHER PEOPLE THINK ABOUT HIM!
WHAT?! SO, THAT'S HOW IT'S GOING TO BE?
YOU'RE GOING TO RUN OFF AND JUMP INTO THE ARMS OF "DOUBLE N"?!
"RUN OFF"? YOU BETTER WATCH HOW YOU TALK TO ME!
I JUST WANT COMPANY TO GO TO THE MOVIES!

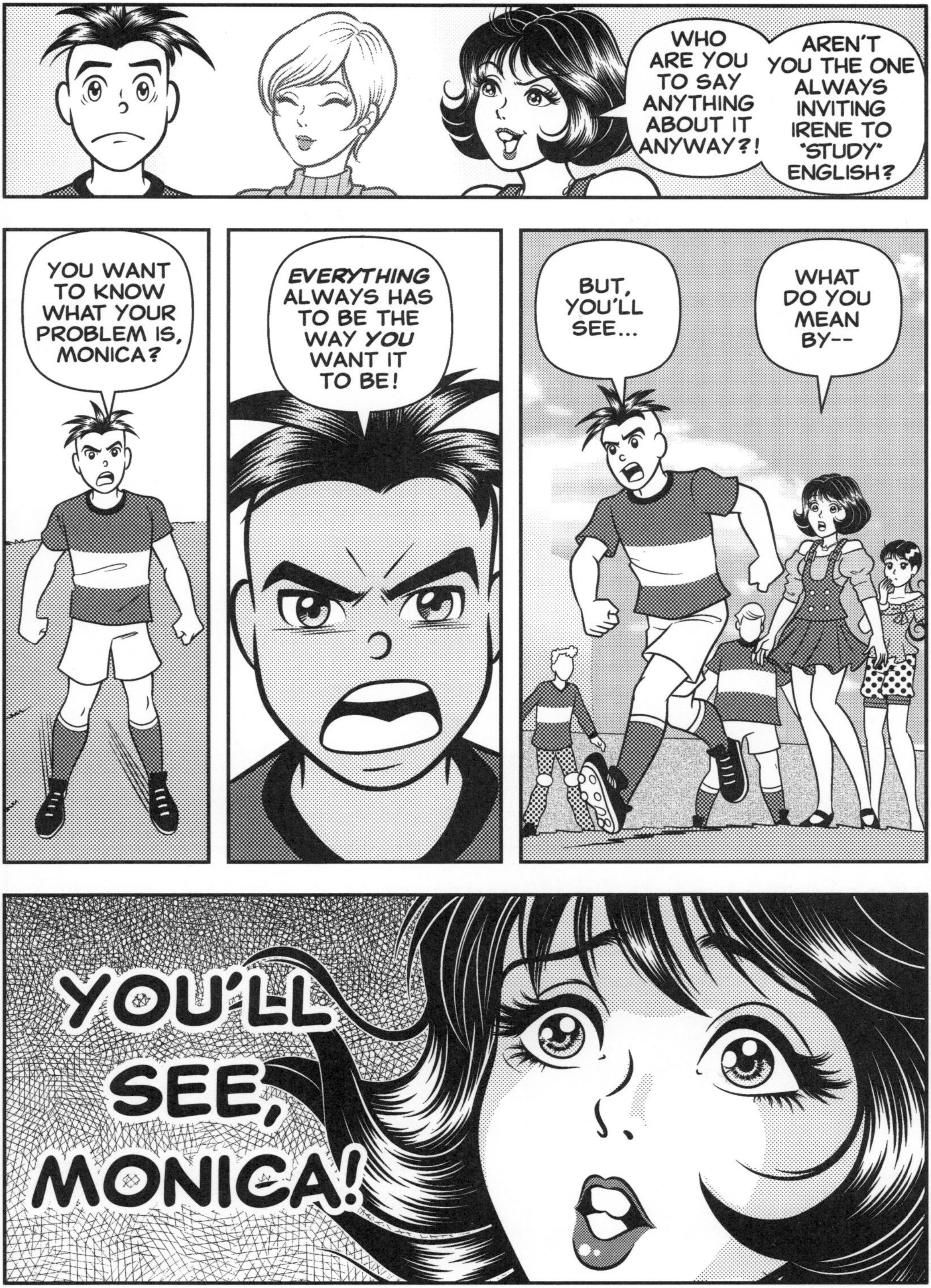
WHO ARE YOU TO SAY ANYTHING ABOUT IT ANYWAY?!
AREN'T YOU THE ONE ALWAYS INVITING IRENE TO "STUDY" ENGLISH?
YOU WANT TO KNOW WHAT YOUR PROBLEM IS, MONICA?
EVERYTHING ALWAYS HAS TO BE THE WAY *YOU* WANT IT TO BE!
BUT, YOU'LL SEE...
WHAT DO YOU MEAN BY--
YOU'LL SEE, MONICA!

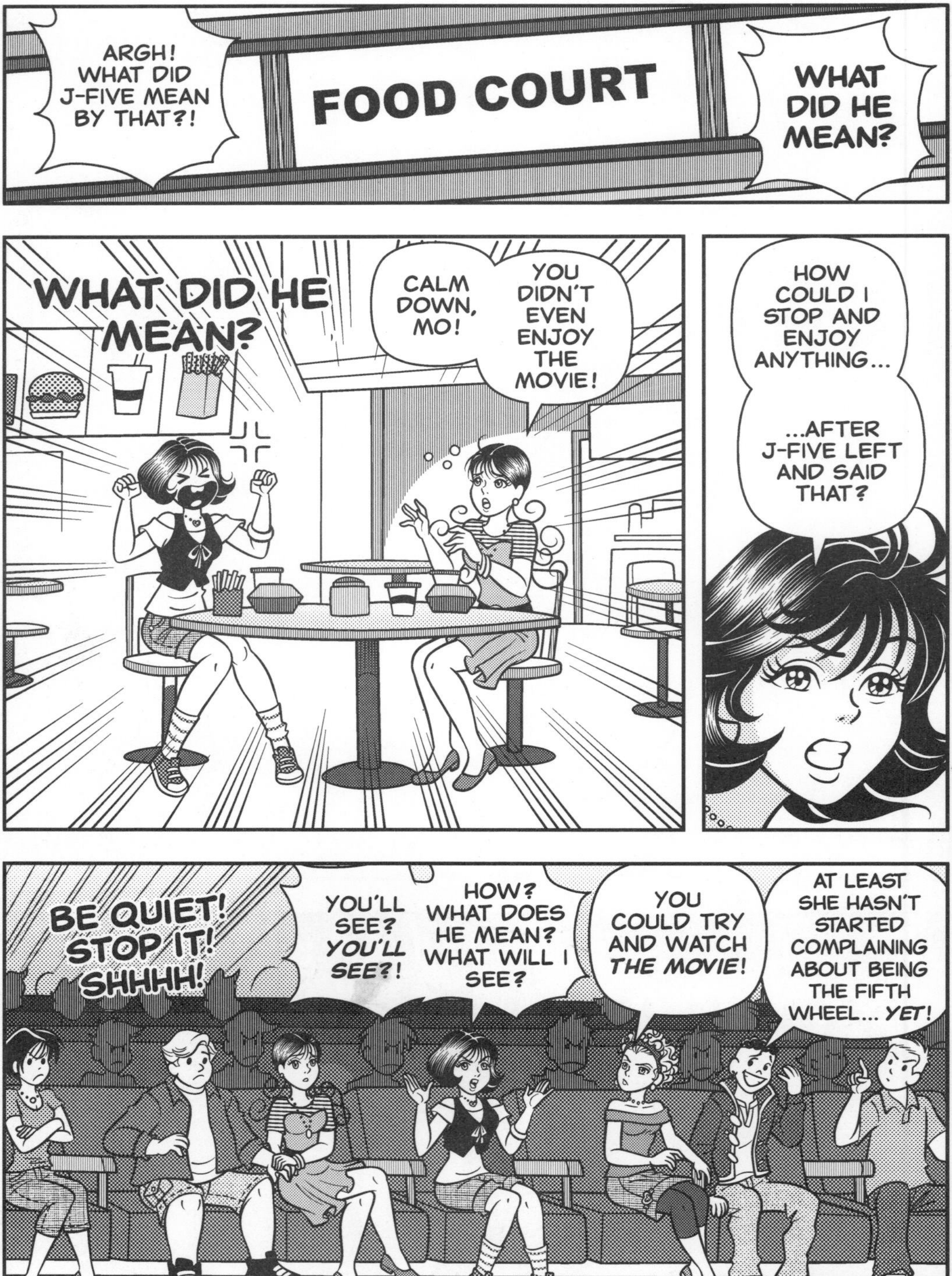
ARGH! WHAT DID J-FIVE MEAN BY THAT?!
FOOD COURT
WHAT DID HE MEAN?
WHAT DID HE MEAN?
CALM DOWN, MO!
YOU DIDN'T EVEN ENJOY THE MOVIE!
HOW COULD I STOP AND ENJOY ANYTHING...
...AFTER J-FIVE LEFT AND SAID THAT?
BE QUIET! STOP IT! SHHHH!
YOU'LL SEE? *YOU'LL SEE?!*
HOW? WHAT DOES HE MEAN? WHAT WILL I SEE?
YOU COULD TRY AND WATCH *THE MOVIE*!
AT LEAST SHE HASN'T STARTED COMPLAINING ABOUT BEING THE FIFTH WHEEL... *YET*!

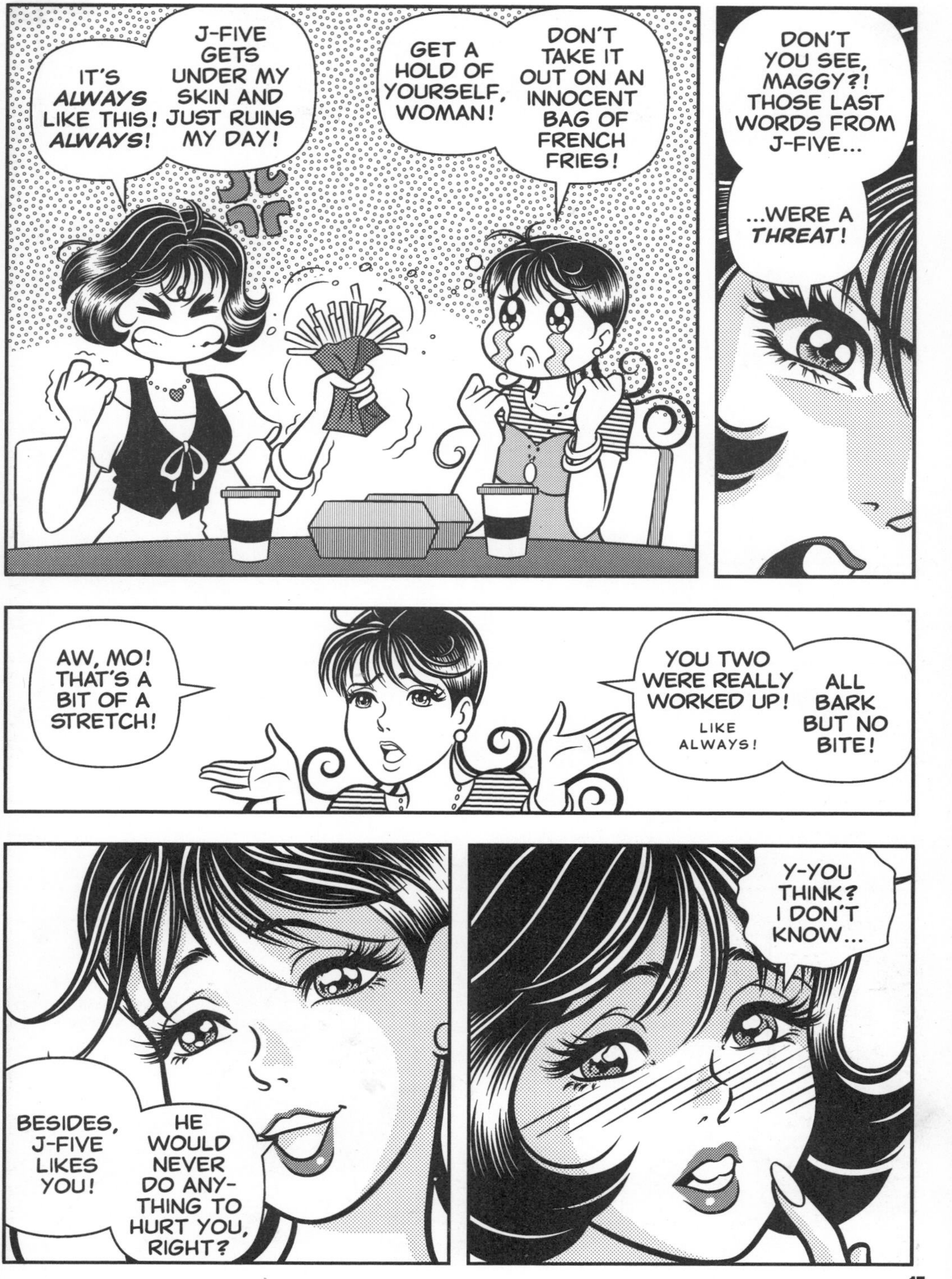
IT'S ALWAYS LIKE THIS! ALWAYS!
J-FIVE GETS UNDER MY SKIN AND JUST RUINS MY DAY!
GET A HOLD OF YOURSELF, WOMAN!
DON'T TAKE IT OUT ON AN INNOCENT BAG OF FRENCH FRIES!
DON'T YOU SEE, MAGGY?! THOSE LAST WORDS FROM J-FIVE...
...WERE A THREAT!
AW, MO! THAT'S A BIT OF A STRETCH!
YOU TWO WERE REALLY WORKED UP!
LIKE ALWAYS!
ALL BARK BUT NO BITE!
BESIDES, J-FIVE LIKES YOU!
HE WOULD NEVER DO ANY-THING TO HURT YOU, RIGHT?
Y-YOU THINK? I DON'T KNOW...

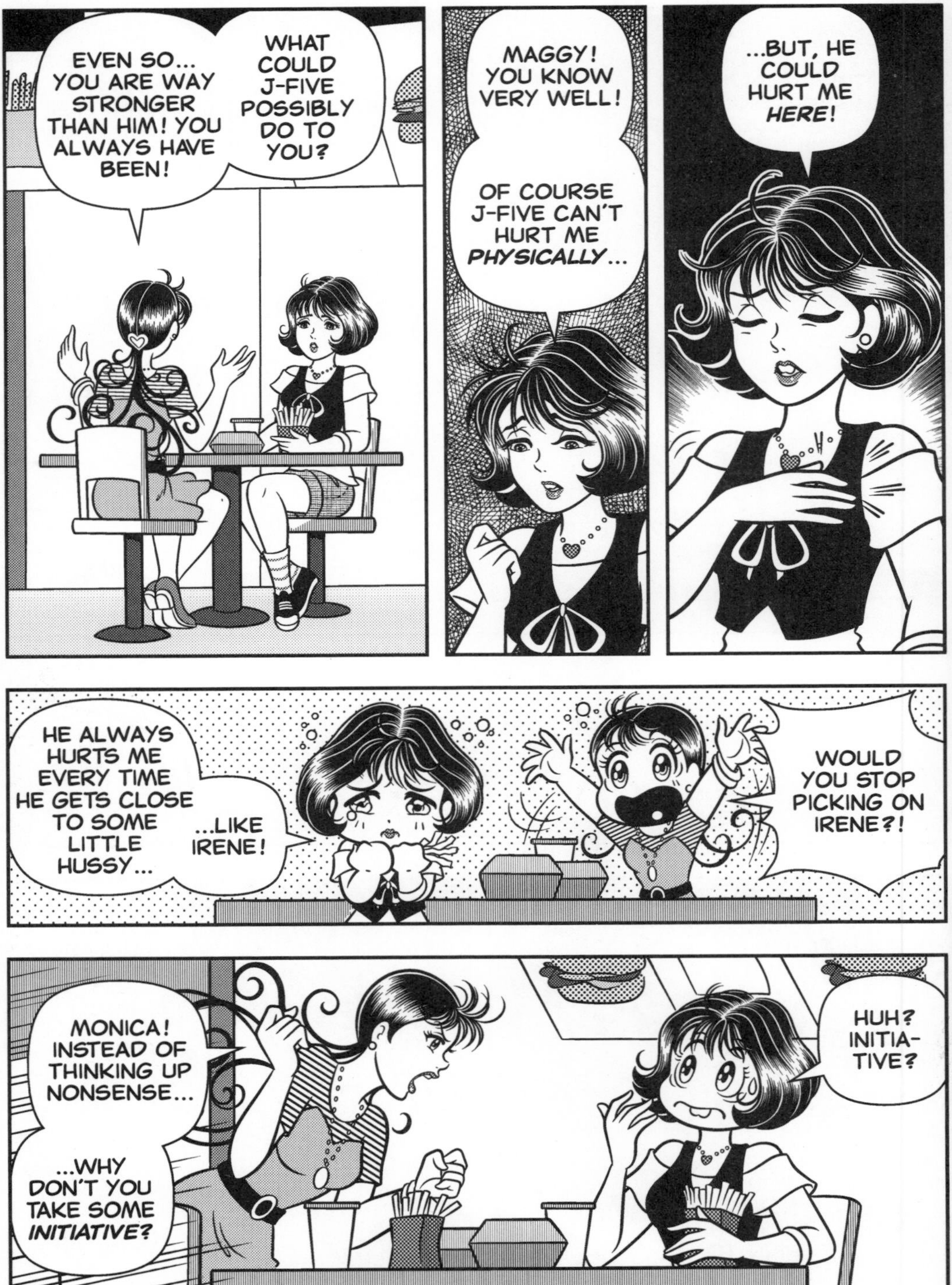
EVEN SO... YOU ARE WAY STRONGER THAN HIM! YOU ALWAYS HAVE BEEN!
WHAT COULD J-FIVE POSSIBLY DO TO YOU?
MAGGY! YOU KNOW VERY WELL!
OF COURSE J-FIVE CAN'T HURT ME *PHYSICALLY*...
...BUT, HE COULD HURT ME *HERE*!
HE ALWAYS HURTS ME EVERY TIME HE GETS CLOSE TO SOME LITTLE HUSSY...
...LIKE IRENE!
WOULD YOU STOP PICKING ON IRENE?!
MONICA! INSTEAD OF THINKING UP NONSENSE...
...WHY DON'T YOU TAKE SOME *INITIATIVE*?
HUH? INITIA-TIVE?

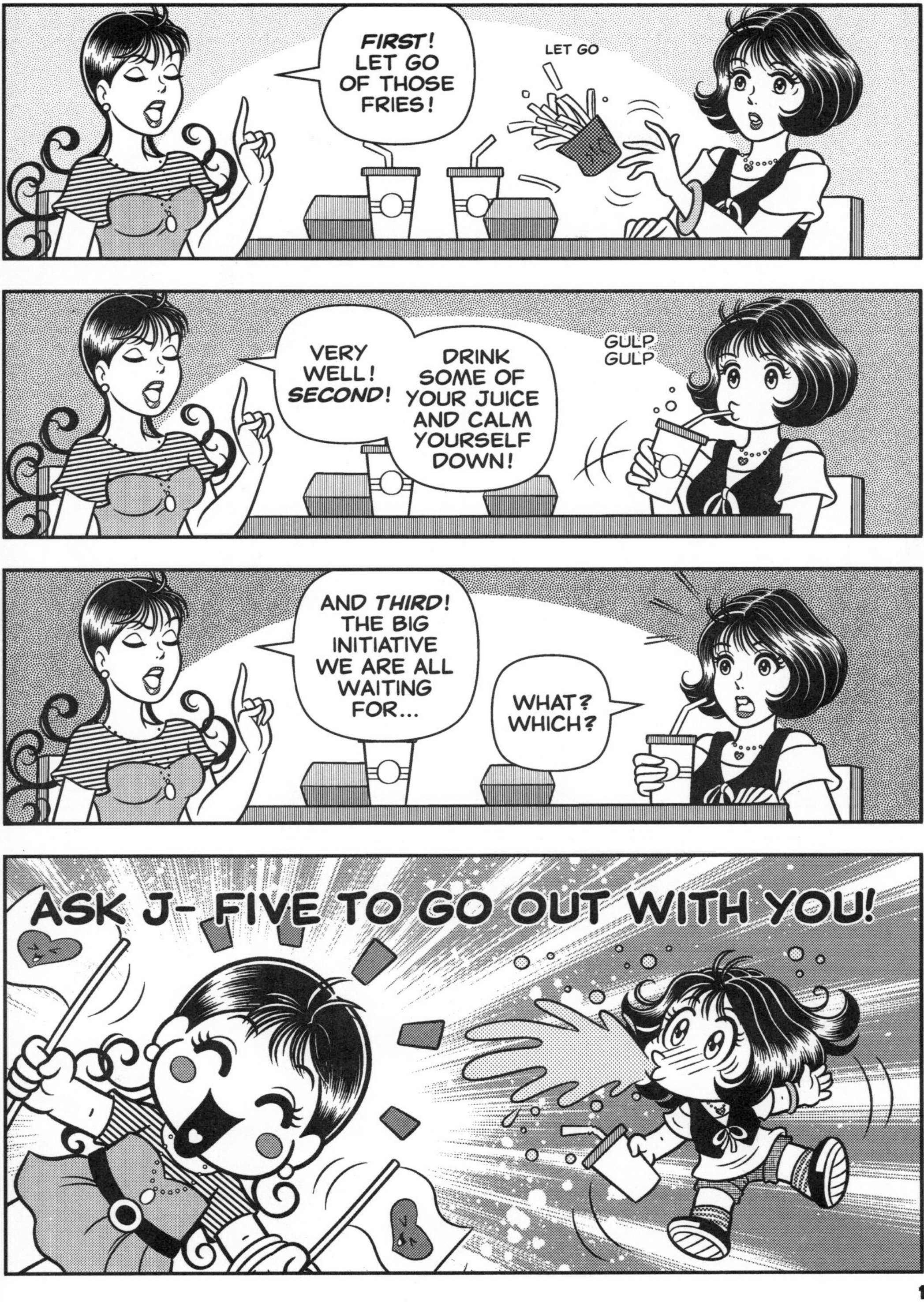
FIRST! LET GO OF THOSE FRIES!
LET GO
VERY WELL! SECOND!
DRINK SOME OF YOUR JUICE AND CALM YOURSELF DOWN!
GULP GULP
AND THIRD! THE BIG INITIATIVE WE ARE ALL WAITING FOR...
WHAT? WHICH?
ASK J- FIVE TO GO OUT WITH YOU!

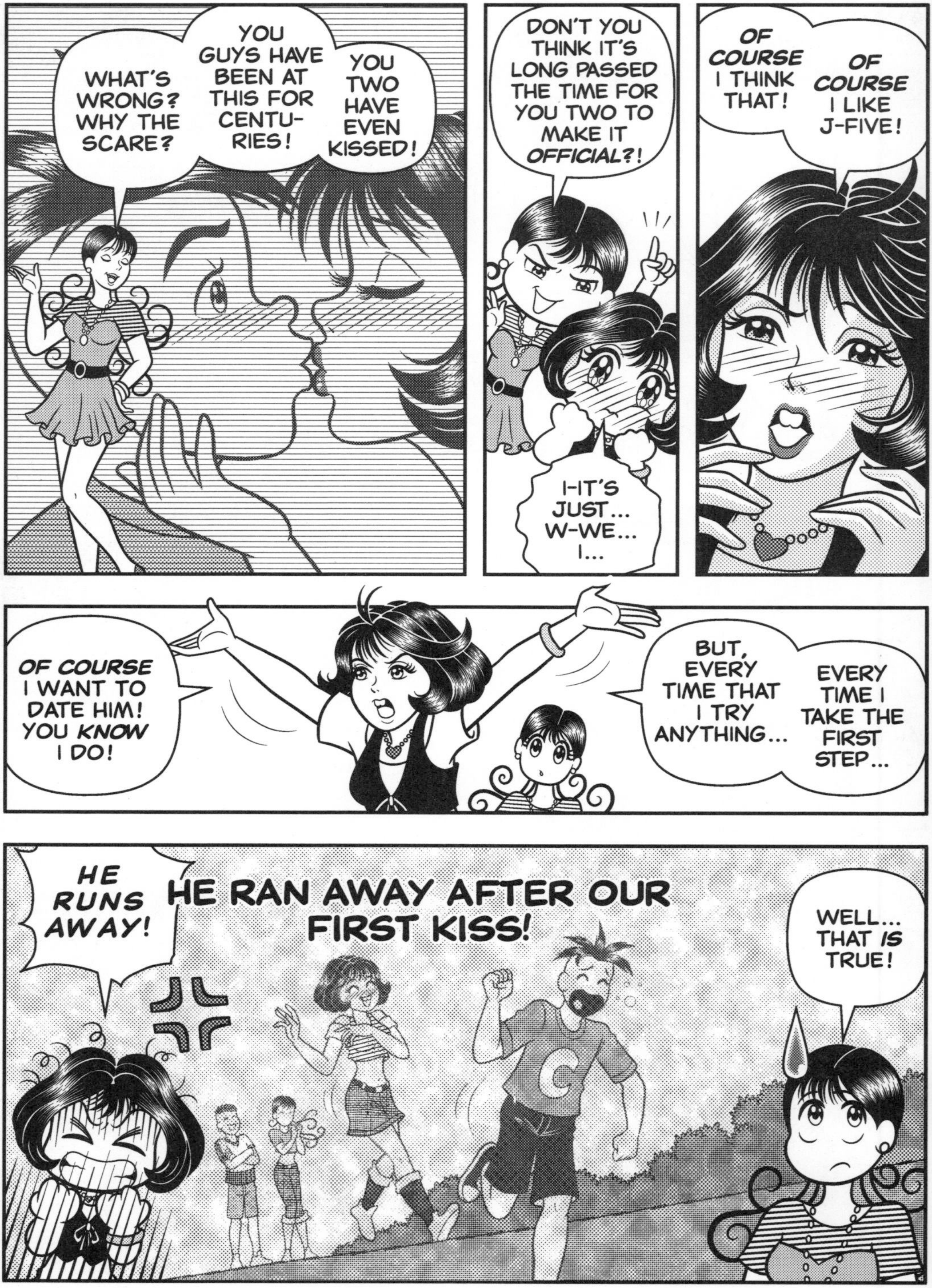
WHAT'S WRONG? WHY THE SCARE?
YOU GUYS HAVE BEEN AT THIS FOR CENTU-RIES!
YOU TWO HAVE EVEN KISSED!
DON'T YOU THINK IT'S LONG PASSED THE TIME FOR YOU TWO TO MAKE IT *OFFICIAL*?!
I-IT'S JUST... W-WE... I...
OF COURSE I THINK THAT!
OF COURSE I LIKE J-FIVE!
OF COURSE I WANT TO DATE HIM! YOU *KNOW* I DO!
BUT, EVERY TIME THAT I TRY ANYTHING...
EVERY TIME I TAKE THE FIRST STEP...
HE RUNS AWAY!
HE RAN AWAY AFTER OUR FIRST KISS!
WELL... THAT *IS* TRUE!

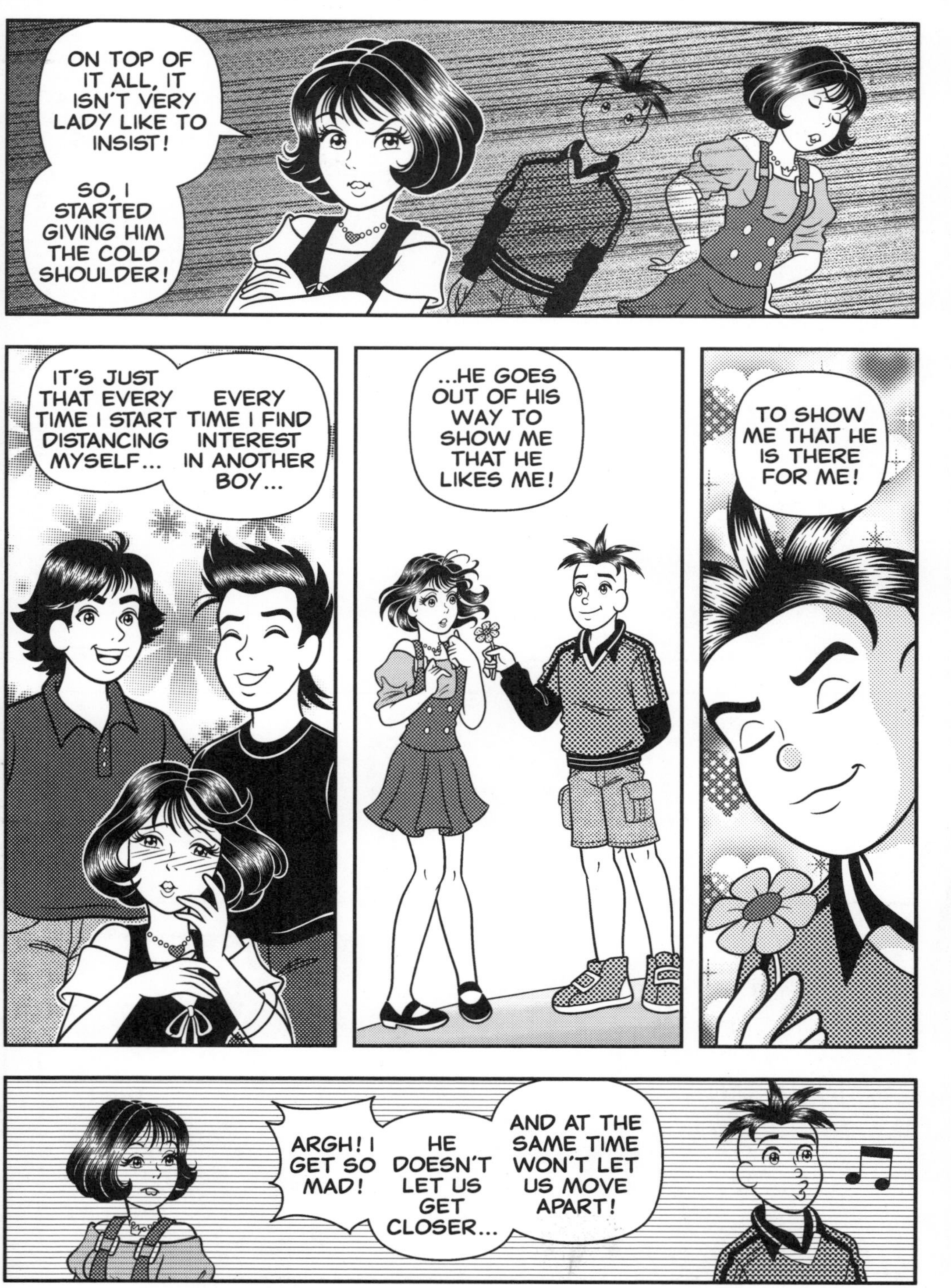
ON TOP OF IT ALL, IT ISN'T VERY LADY LIKE TO INSIST!
SO, I STARTED GIVING HIM THE COLD SHOULDER!
IT'S JUST THAT EVERY TIME I START DISTANCING MYSELF...
EVERY TIME I FIND INTEREST IN ANOTHER BOY...
...HE GOES OUT OF HIS WAY TO SHOW ME THAT HE LIKES ME!
TO SHOW ME THAT HE IS THERE FOR ME!
ARGH! I GET SO MAD!
HE DOESN'T LET US GET CLOSER...
AND AT THE SAME TIME WON'T LET US MOVE APART!

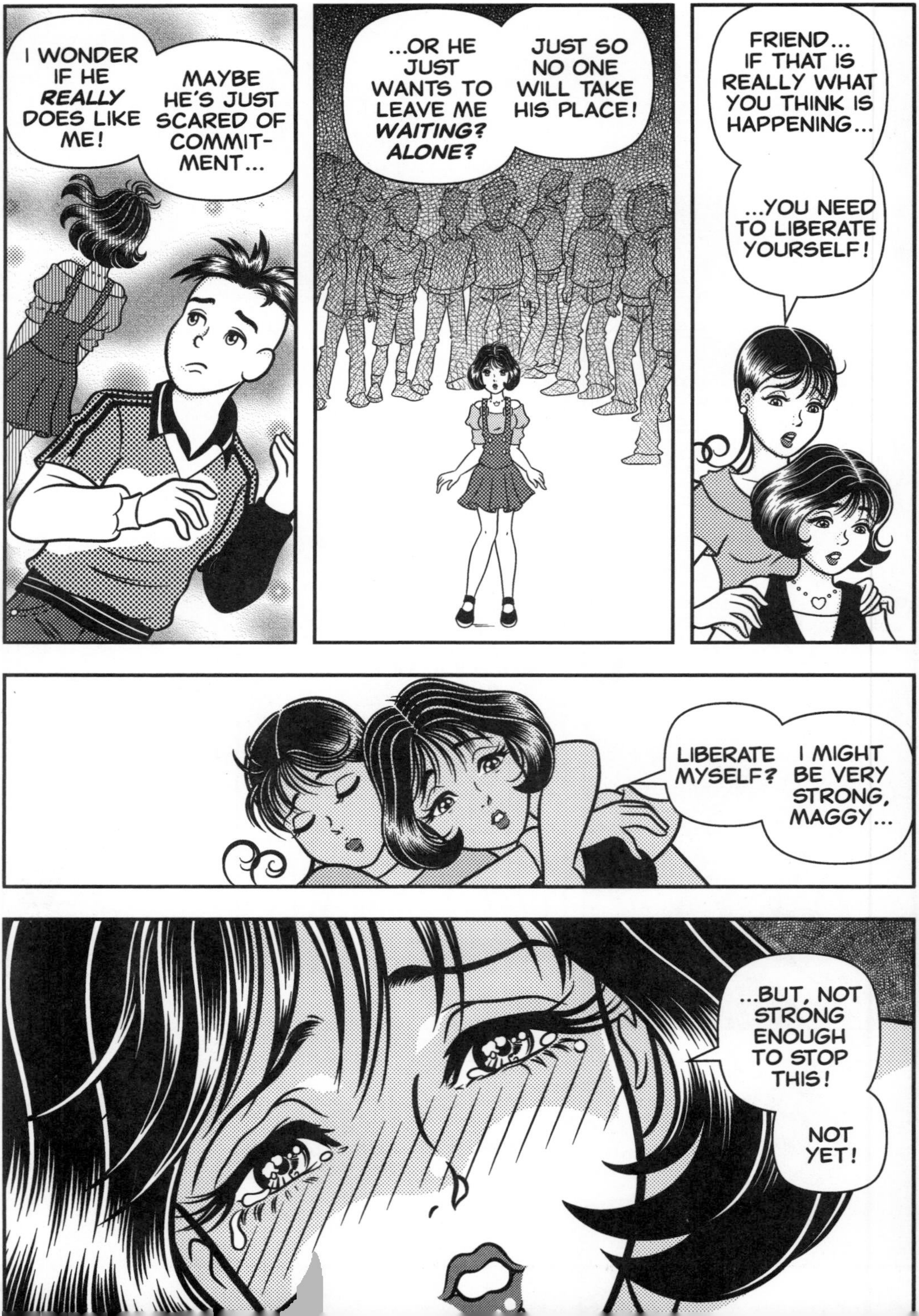
I WONDER IF HE *REALLY* DOES LIKE ME!
MAYBE HE'S JUST SCARED OF COMMIT-MENT...
...OR HE JUST WANTS TO LEAVE ME *WAITING? ALONE?*
JUST SO NO ONE WILL TAKE HIS PLACE!
FRIEND... IF THAT IS REALLY WHAT YOU THINK IS HAPPENING...
...YOU NEED TO LIBERATE YOURSELF!
LIBERATE MYSELF?
I MIGHT BE VERY STRONG, MAGGY...
...BUT, NOT STRONG ENOUGH TO STOP THIS!
NOT YET!

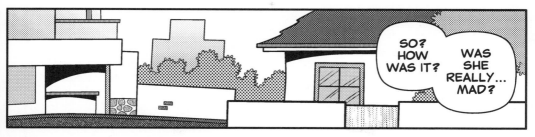

SO? HOW WAS IT? WAS SHE REALLY... MAD?

DON'T REMIND ME! EVERYONE LEFT AS SOON AS THE MOVIE WAS OVER! ONLY MAGGY STUCK AROUND AFTER!

TRUTH BE TOLD, I THINK IT WAS BECAUSE SHE HAD HER EYES ON THE SANDWICH MONICA WAS EATING...

To go out... or to give up?

DUDE, C'MON, REAL TALK!

ALL THAT STUFF YOU SAID TO MONICA WAS A LITTLE BIT HARSH, RIGHT?

DON'T YOU START, SMUDGE! YOU WEREN'T EVEN THERE!

GOSSIP TRAVELS FAST, BRO!

THE *WHOLE WORLD* NOW KNOWS YOU "DISSED" MONICA!

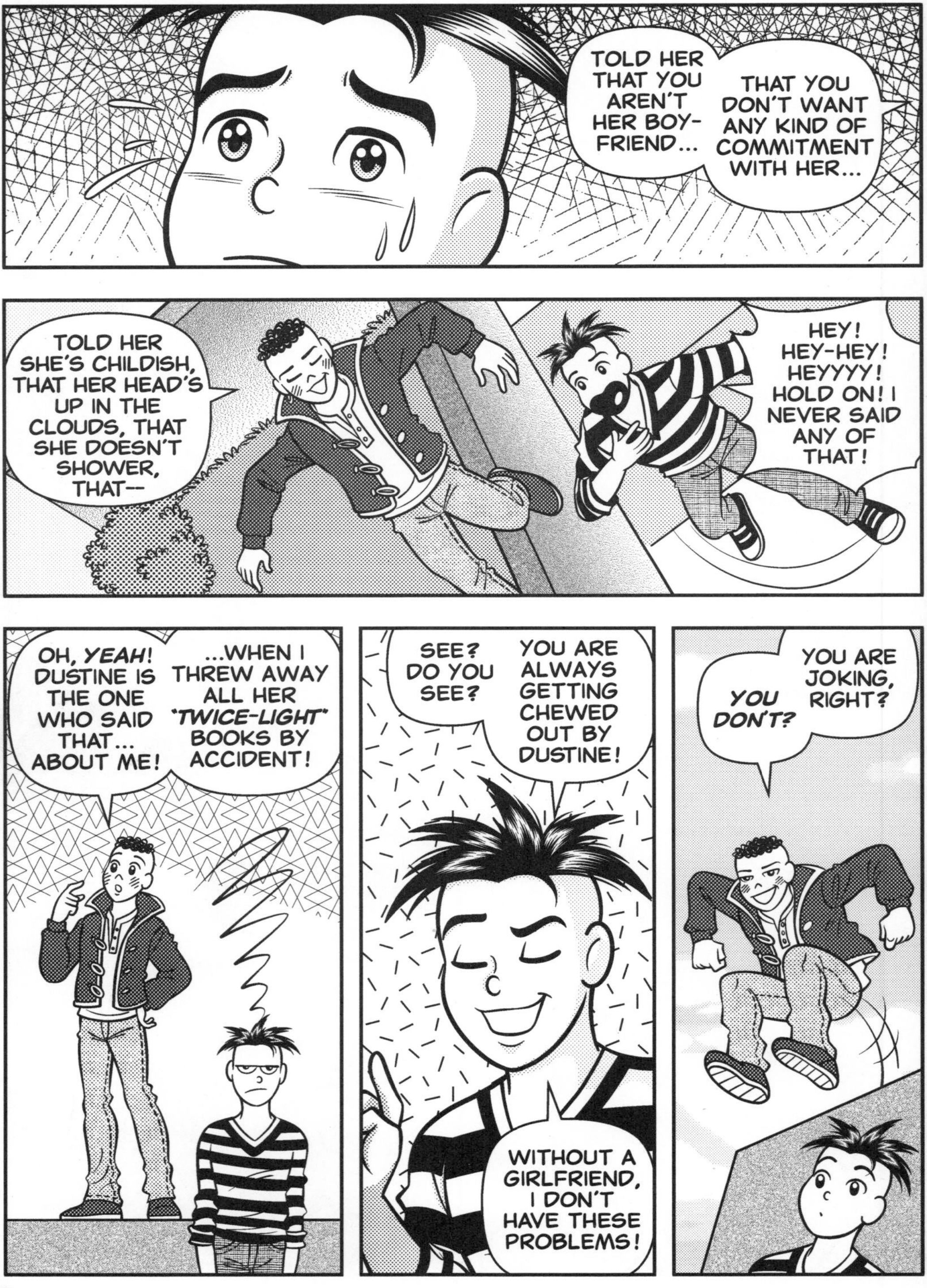
TOLD HER THAT YOU AREN'T HER BOY-FRIEND...
THAT YOU DON'T WANT ANY KIND OF COMMITMENT WITH HER...
TOLD HER SHE'S CHILDISH, THAT HER HEAD'S UP IN THE CLOUDS, THAT SHE DOESN'T SHOWER, THAT--
HEY! HEY-HEY! HEYYYY! HOLD ON! I NEVER SAID ANY OF THAT!
OH, *YEAH*! DUSTINE IS THE ONE WHO SAID THAT... ABOUT ME!
...WHEN I THREW AWAY ALL HER *"TWICE-LIGHT"* BOOKS BY ACCIDENT!
SEE? DO YOU SEE?
YOU ARE ALWAYS GETTING CHEWED OUT BY DUSTINE!
WITHOUT A GIRLFRIEND, I DON'T HAVE THESE PROBLEMS!
YOU ARE JOKING, RIGHT?
YOU DON'T?

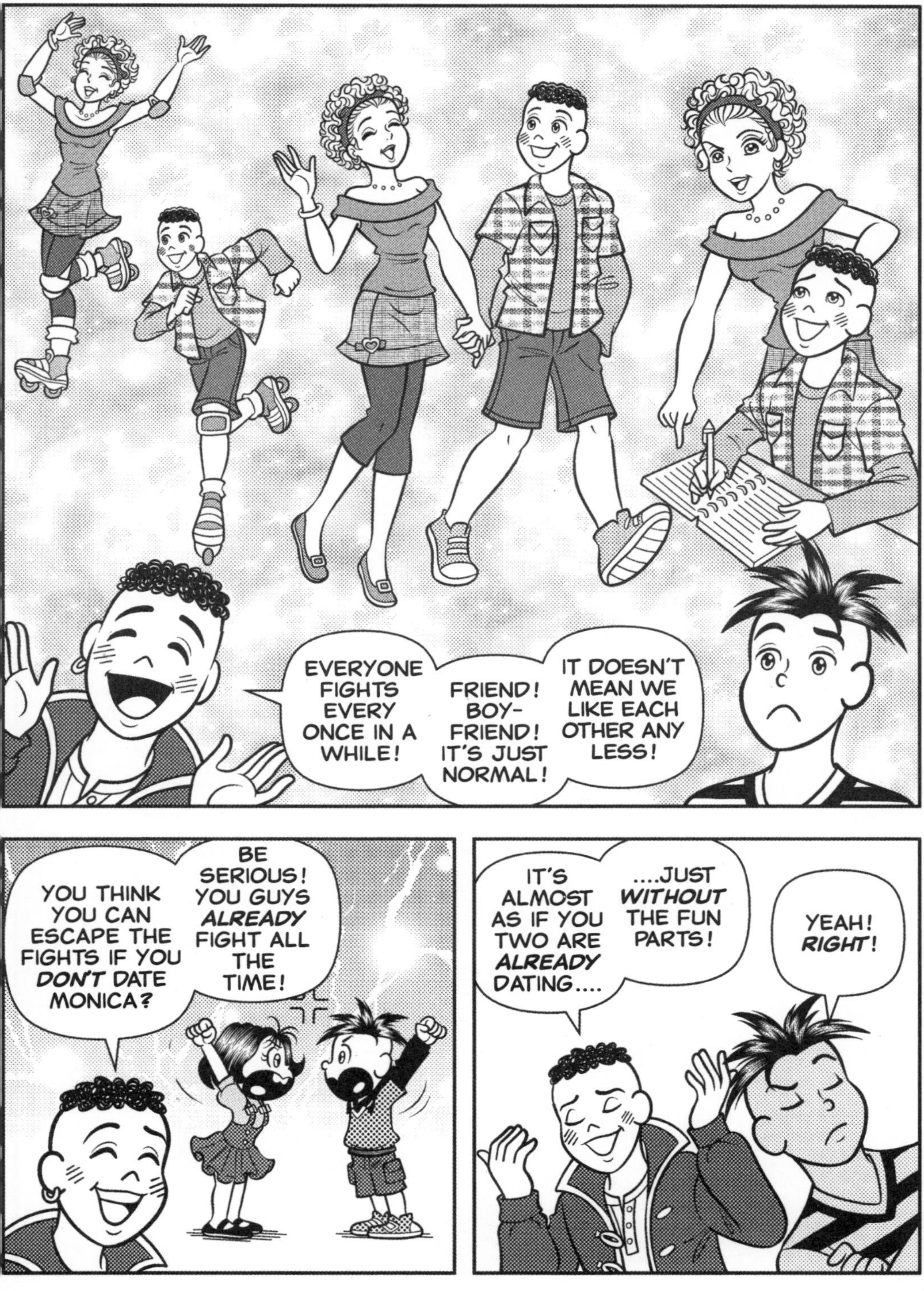
EVERYONE FIGHTS EVERY ONCE IN A WHILE!
FRIEND! BOY-FRIEND! IT'S JUST NORMAL!
IT DOESN'T MEAN WE LIKE EACH OTHER ANY LESS!
YOU THINK YOU CAN ESCAPE THE FIGHTS IF YOU *DON'T* DATE MONICA?
BE SERIOUS! YOU GUYS *ALREADY* FIGHT ALL THE TIME!
IT'S ALMOST AS IF YOU TWO ARE *ALREADY* DATING....
....JUST *WITHOUT* THE FUN PARTS!
YEAH! *RIGHT*!

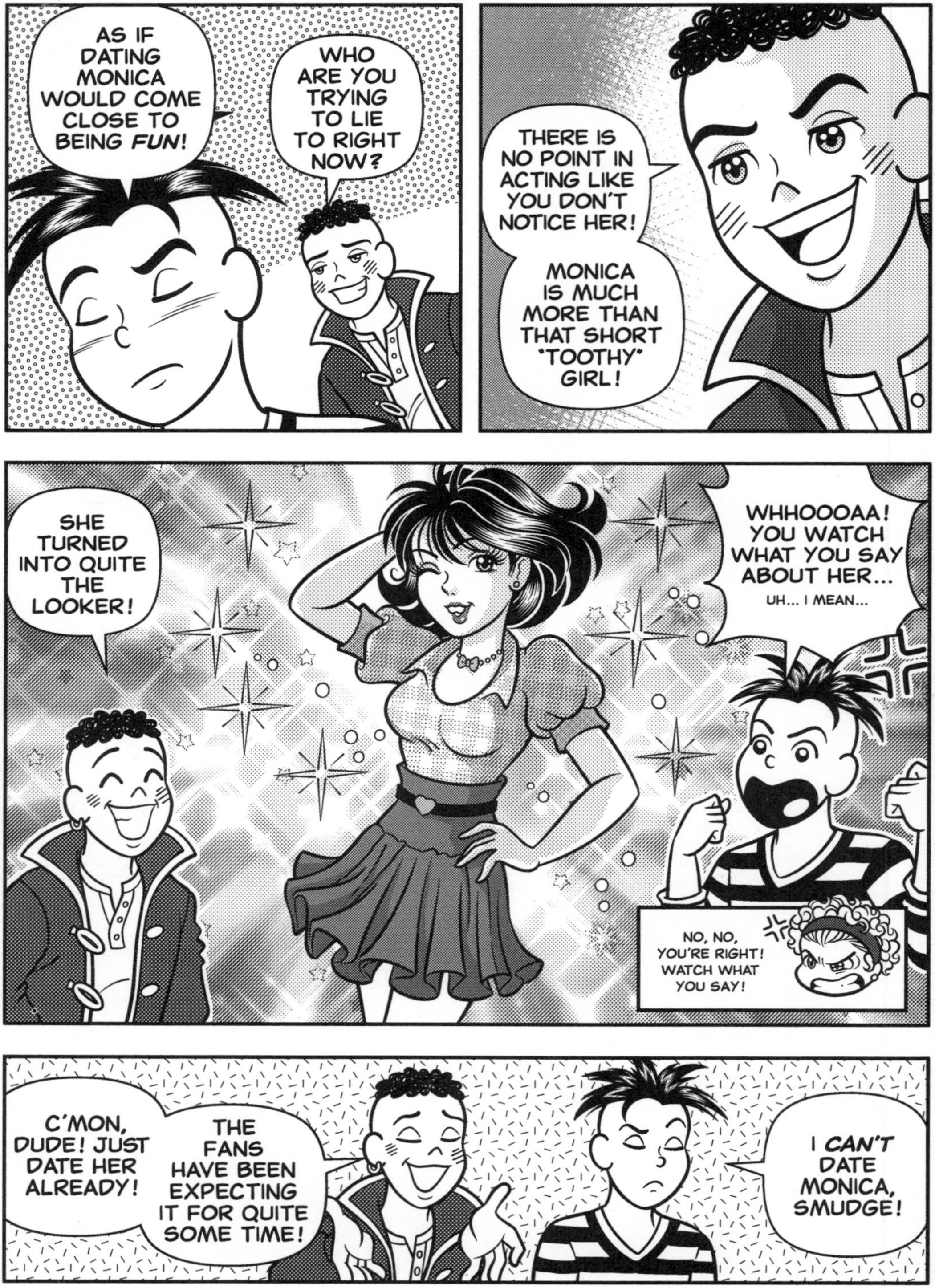

AS IF DATING MONICA WOULD COME CLOSE TO BEING *FUN*!
WHO ARE YOU TRYING TO LIE TO RIGHT NOW?
THERE IS NO POINT IN ACTING LIKE YOU DON'T NOTICE HER!
MONICA IS MUCH MORE THAN THAT SHORT "TOOTHY" GIRL!
SHE TURNED INTO QUITE THE LOOKER!
WHHOOOAA! YOU WATCH WHAT YOU SAY ABOUT HER...
UH... I MEAN...
NO, NO, YOU'RE RIGHT! WATCH WHAT YOU SAY!
C'MON, DUDE! JUST DATE HER ALREADY!
THE FANS HAVE BEEN EXPECTING IT FOR QUITE SOME TIME!
I *CAN'T* DATE MONICA, SMUDGE!

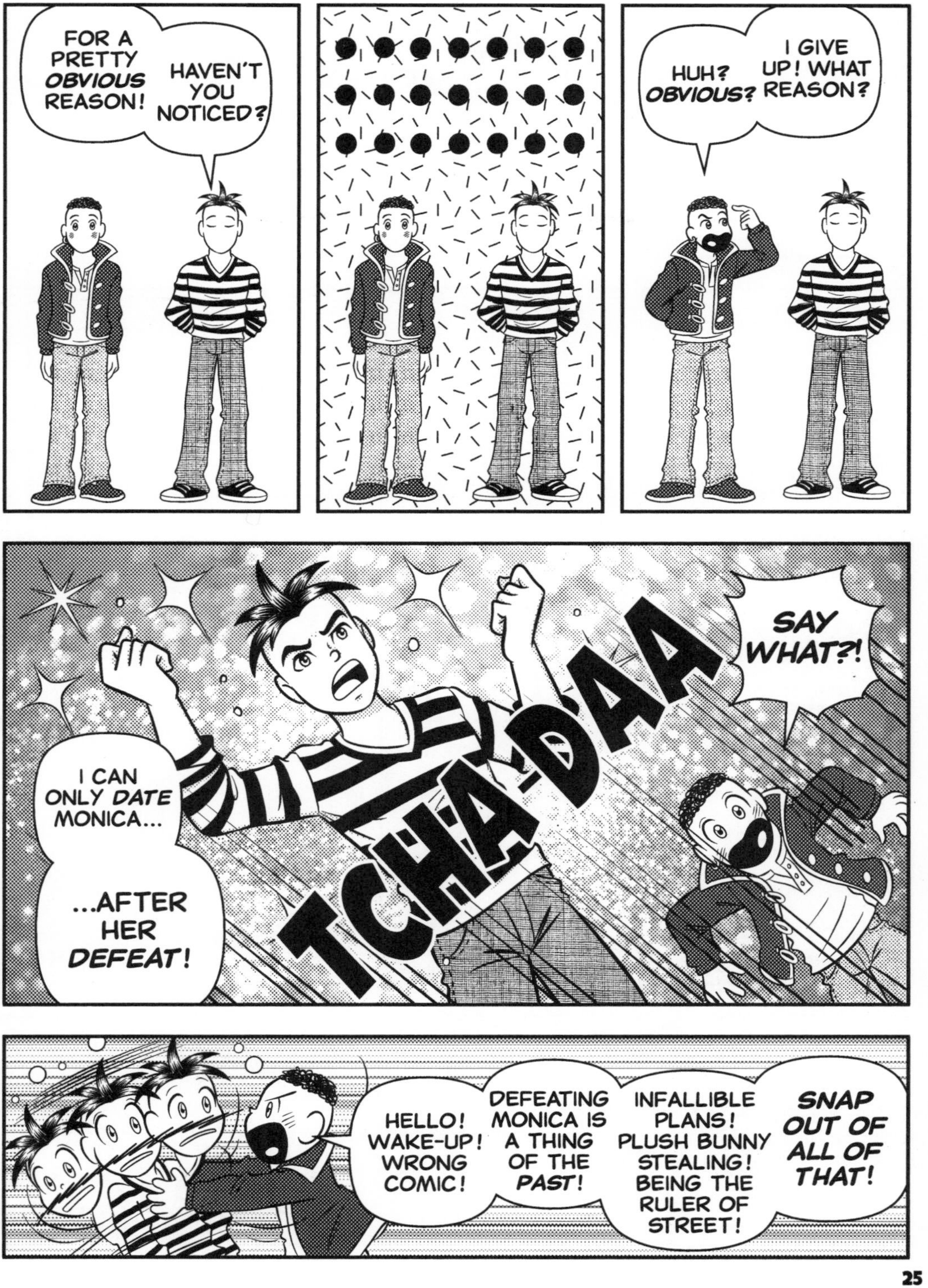
FOR A PRETTY OBVIOUS REASON!
HAVEN'T YOU NOTICED?
HUH? OBVIOUS?
I GIVE UP! WHAT REASON?
I CAN ONLY DATE MONICA...
...AFTER HER DEFEAT!
TCHA-DAA
SAY WHAT?!
HELLO! WAKE-UP! WRONG COMIC!
DEFEATING MONICA IS A THING OF THE PAST!
INFALLIBLE PLANS! PLUSH BUNNY STEALING! BEING THE RULER OF STREET!
SNAP OUT OF ALL OF THAT!

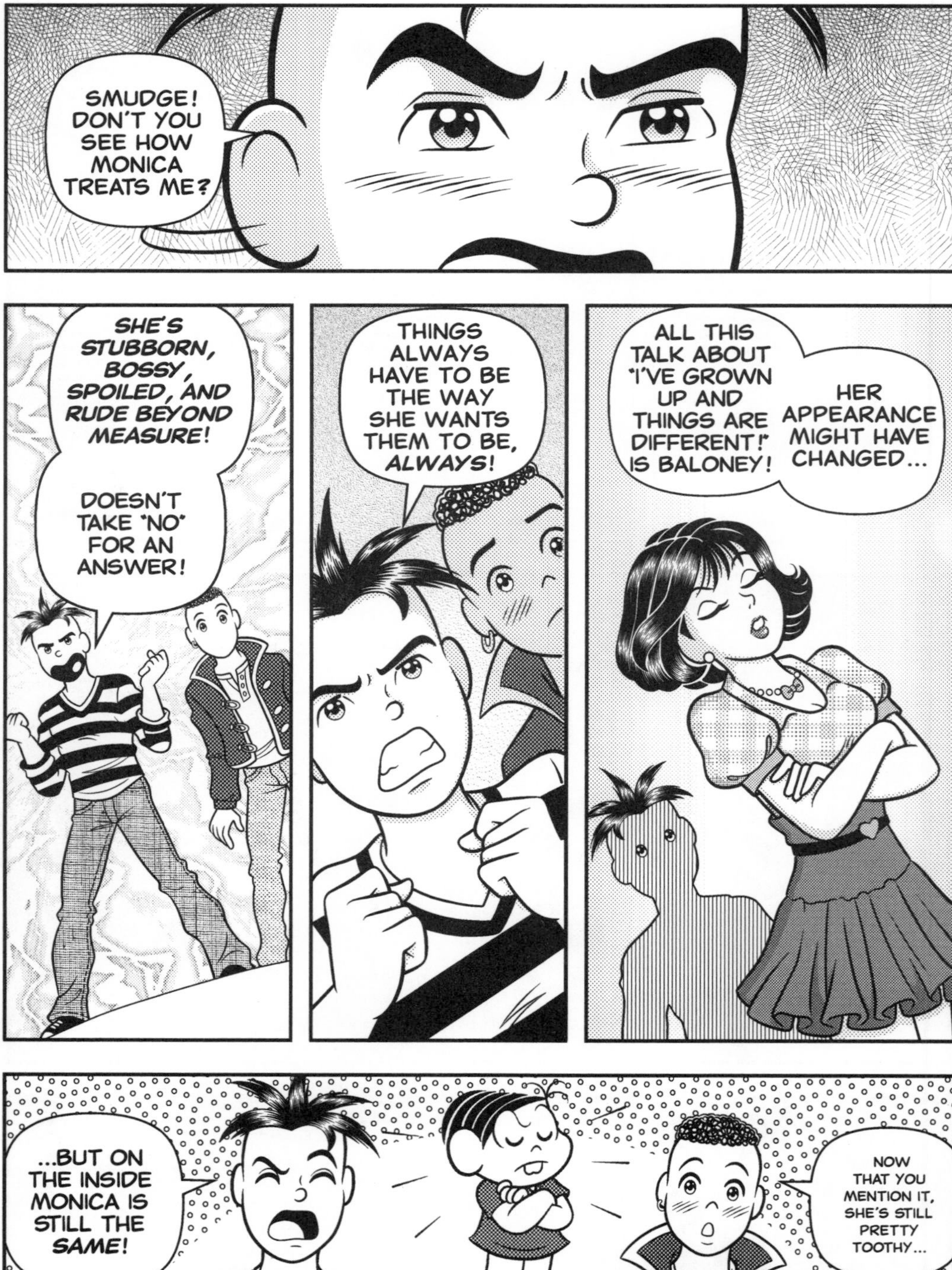
SMUDGE! DON'T YOU SEE HOW MONICA TREATS ME?
SHE'S STUBBORN, BOSSY, SPOILED, AND RUDE BEYOND MEASURE!
DOESN'T TAKE "NO" FOR AN ANSWER!
THINGS ALWAYS HAVE TO BE THE WAY SHE WANTS THEM TO BE, ALWAYS!
ALL THIS TALK ABOUT "I'VE GROWN UP AND THINGS ARE DIFFERENT!" IS BALONEY!
HER APPEARANCE MIGHT HAVE CHANGED...
...BUT ON THE INSIDE MONICA IS STILL THE SAME!
NOW THAT YOU MENTION IT, SHE'S STILL PRETTY TOOTHY...

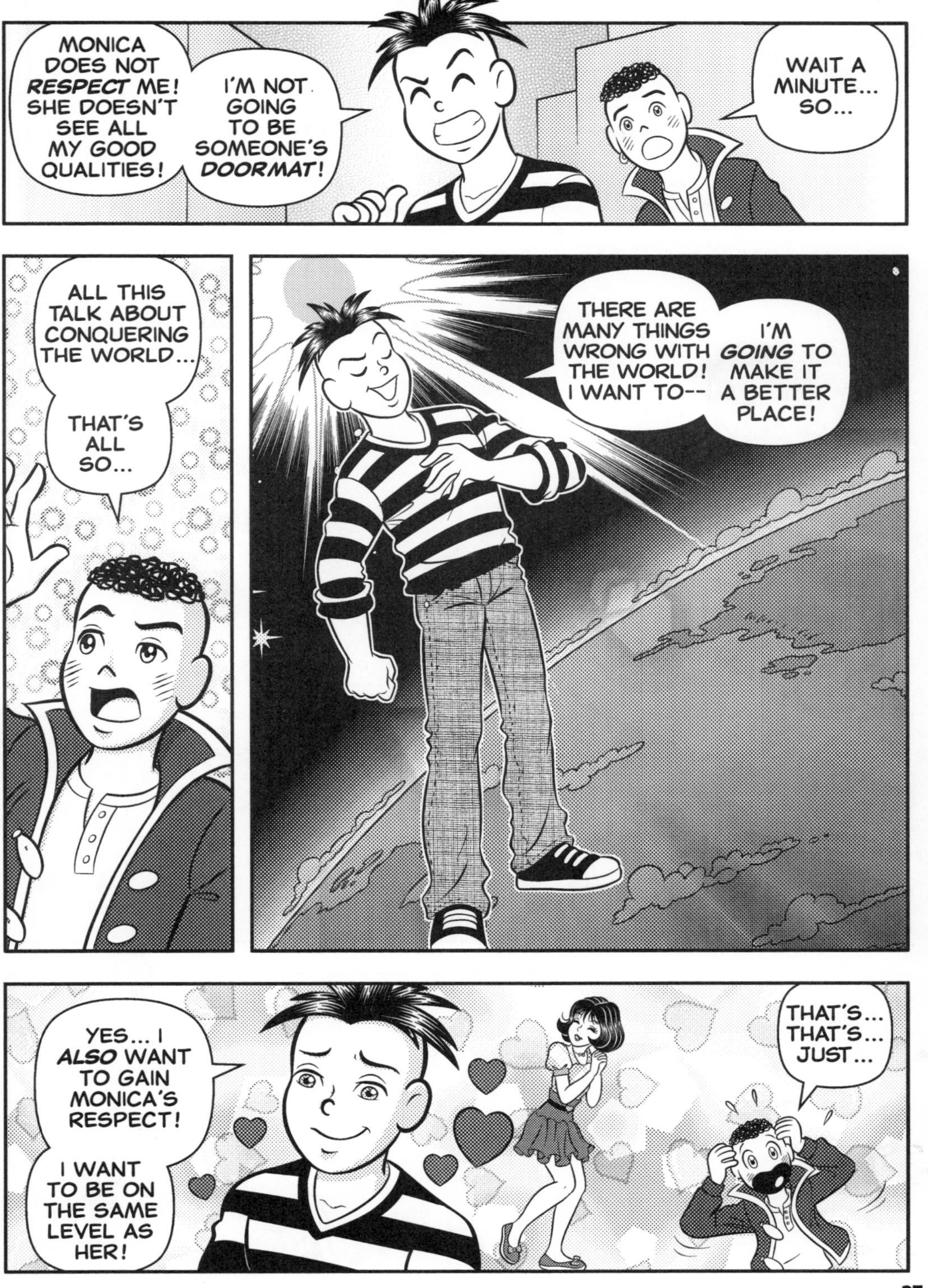

MONICA DOES NOT *RESPECT* ME! SHE DOESN'T SEE ALL MY *GOOD* QUALITIES!
I'M NOT GOING TO BE SOMEONE'S *DOORMAT*!
WAIT A MINUTE... SO...
ALL THIS TALK ABOUT CONQUERING THE WORLD...
THAT'S ALL SO...
THERE ARE MANY THINGS WRONG WITH THE WORLD! I WANT TO--
I'M *GOING* TO MAKE IT A BETTER PLACE!
YES... I *ALSO* WANT TO GAIN MONICA'S RESPECT!
I WANT TO BE ON THE SAME LEVEL AS HER!
THAT'S... THAT'S... JUST...

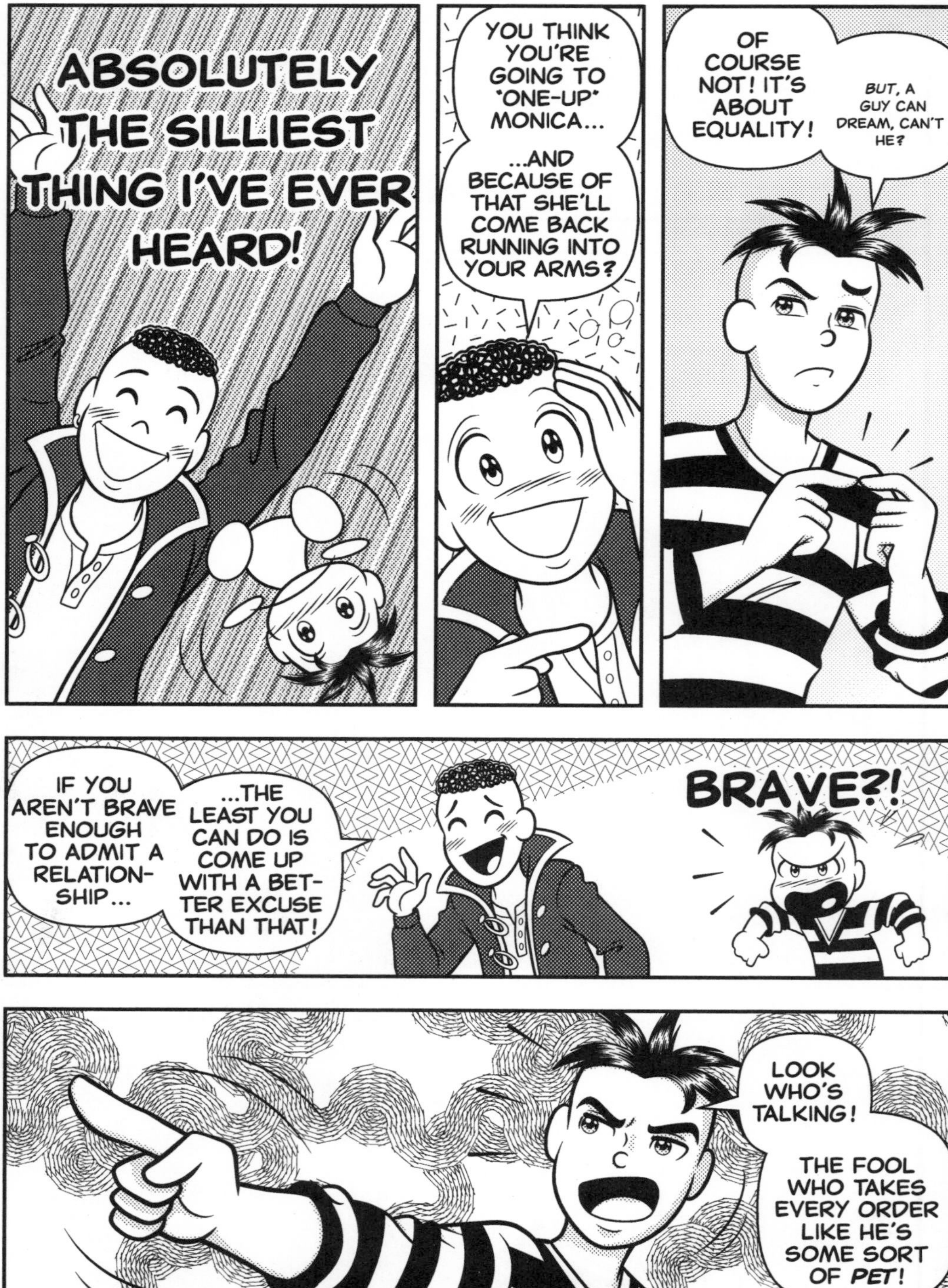
ABSOLUTELY THE SILLIEST THING I'VE EVER HEARD!
YOU THINK YOU'RE GOING TO "ONE-UP" MONICA...
...AND BECAUSE OF THAT SHE'LL COME BACK RUNNING INTO YOUR ARMS?
OF COURSE NOT! IT'S ABOUT EQUALITY!
BUT, A GUY CAN DREAM, CAN'T HE?
IF YOU AREN'T BRAVE ENOUGH TO ADMIT A RELATION-SHIP...
...THE LEAST YOU CAN DO IS COME UP WITH A BET-TER EXCUSE THAN THAT!
BRAVE?!
LOOK WHO'S TALKING!
THE FOOL WHO TAKES EVERY ORDER LIKE HE'S SOME SORT OF *PET*!

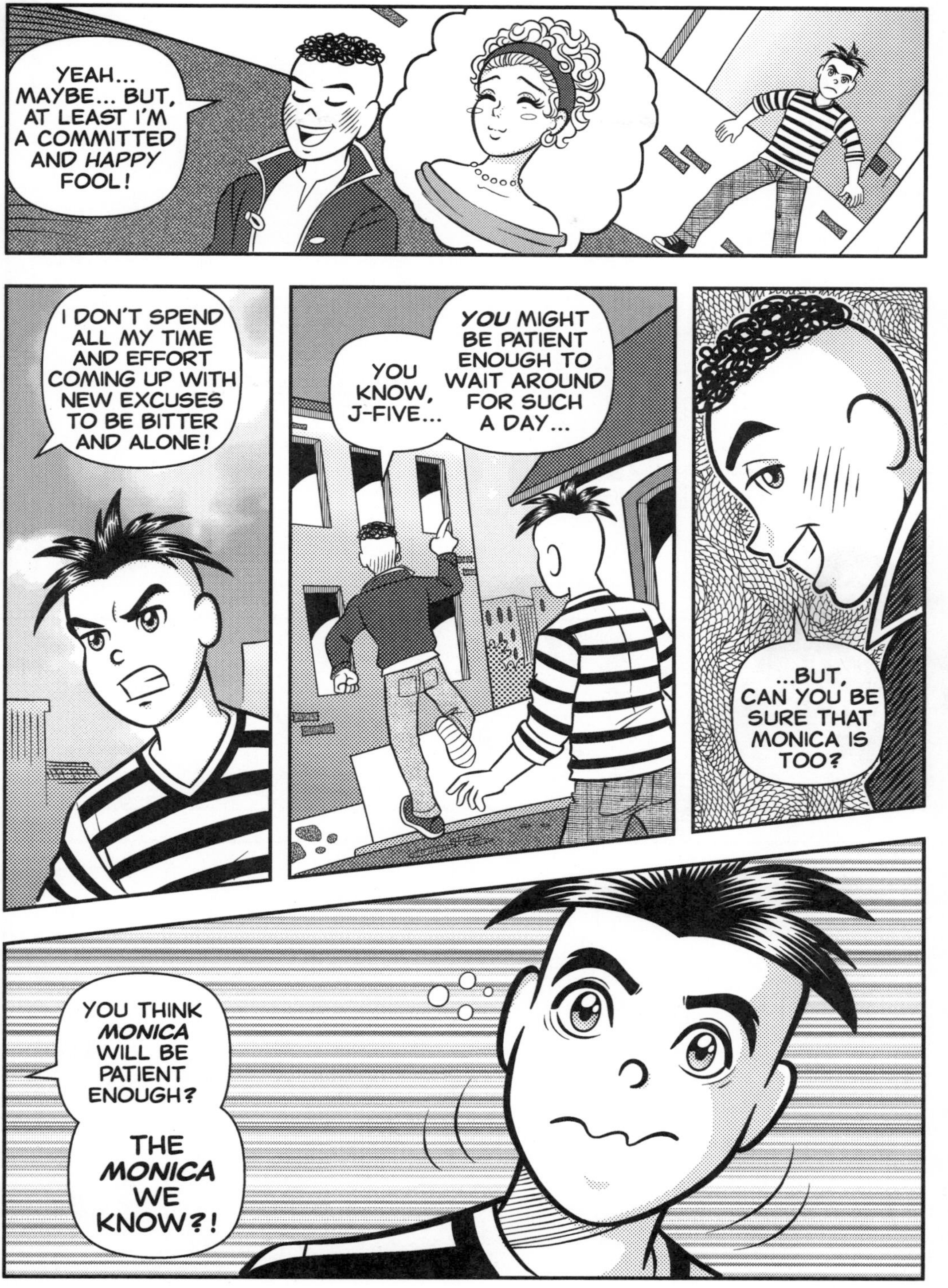

YEAH... MAYBE... BUT, AT LEAST I'M A COMMITTED AND HAPPY FOOL!
I DON'T SPEND ALL MY TIME AND EFFORT COMING UP WITH NEW EXCUSES TO BE BITTER AND ALONE!
YOU KNOW, J-FIVE...
YOU MIGHT BE PATIENT ENOUGH TO WAIT AROUND FOR SUCH A DAY...
...BUT, CAN YOU BE SURE THAT MONICA IS TOO?
YOU THINK MONICA WILL BE PATIENT ENOUGH?
THE MONICA WE KNOW?!

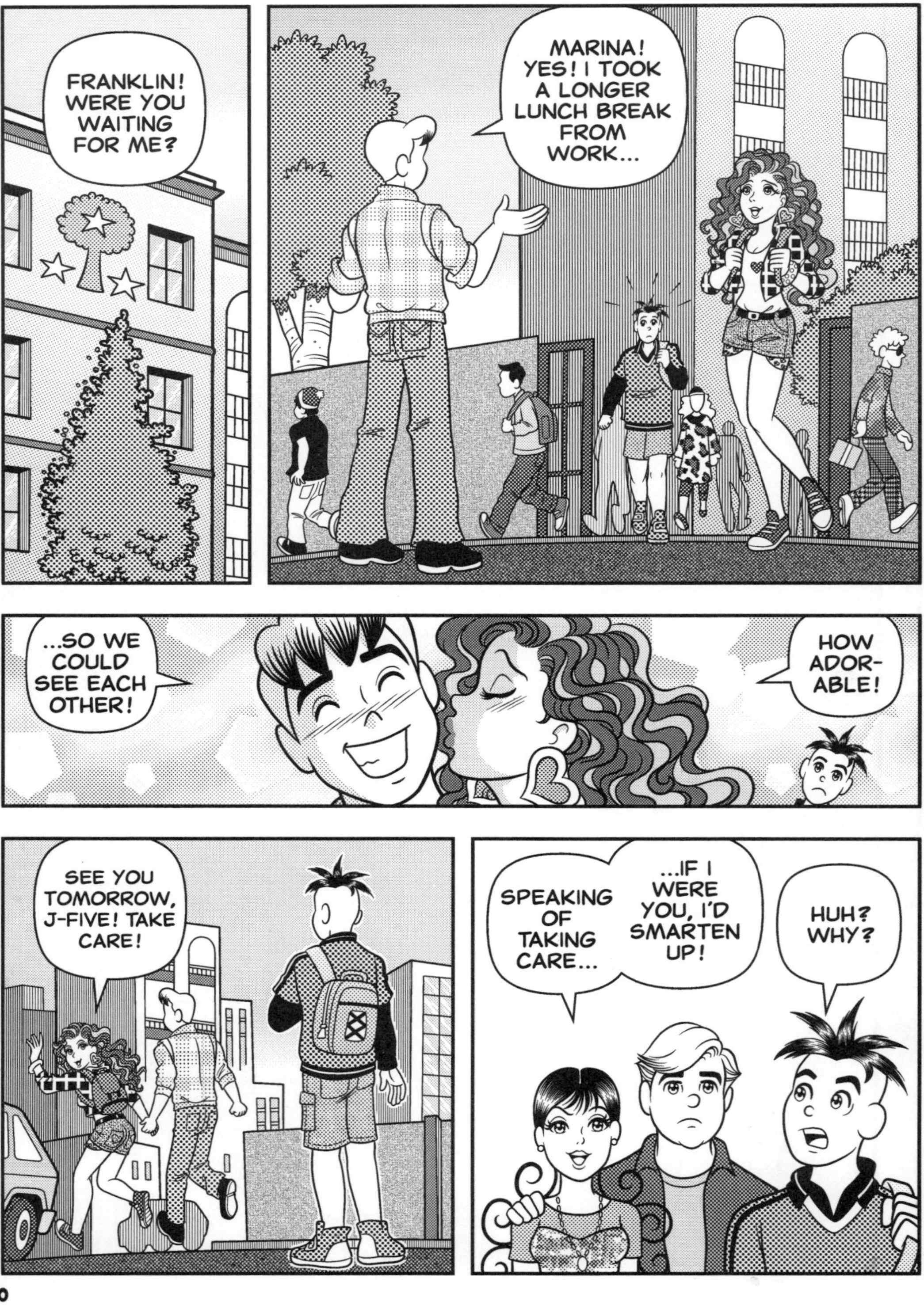
FRANKLIN! WERE YOU WAITING FOR ME?
MARINA! YES! I TOOK A LONGER LUNCH BREAK FROM WORK...
...SO WE COULD SEE EACH OTHER!
HOW ADOR-ABLE!
SEE YOU TOMORROW, J-FIVE! TAKE CARE!
SPEAKING OF TAKING CARE...
...IF I WERE YOU, I'D SMARTEN UP!
HUH? WHY?

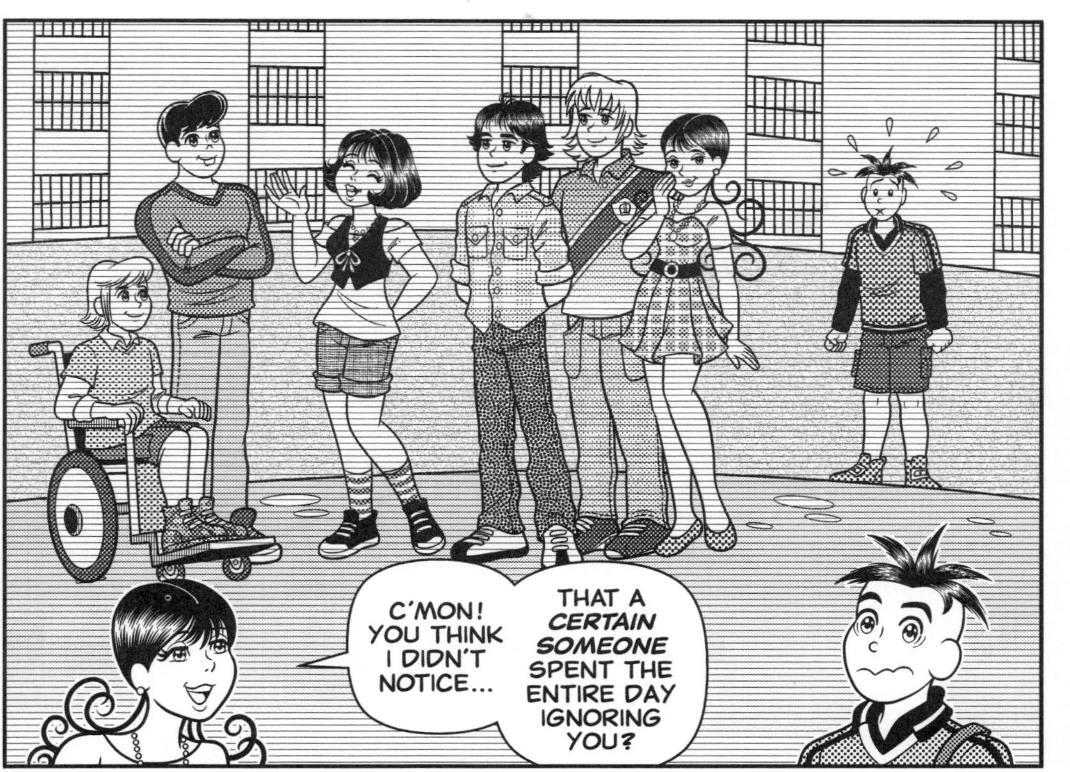
C'MON! YOU THINK I DIDN'T NOTICE...
THAT A *CERTAIN SOMEONE* SPENT THE ENTIRE DAY IGNORING YOU?

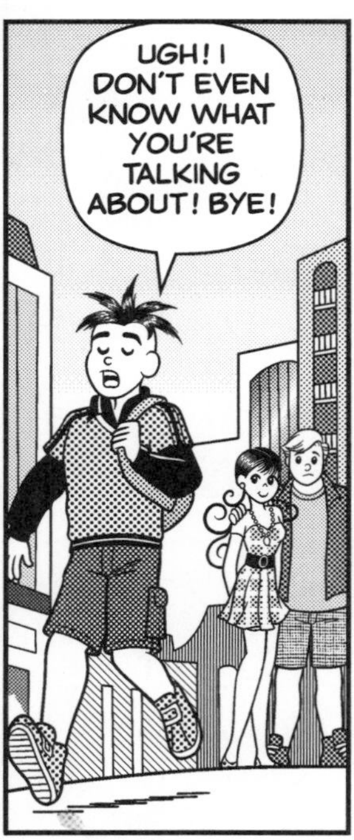
UGH! I DON'T EVEN KNOW WHAT YOU'RE TALKING ABOUT! BYE!

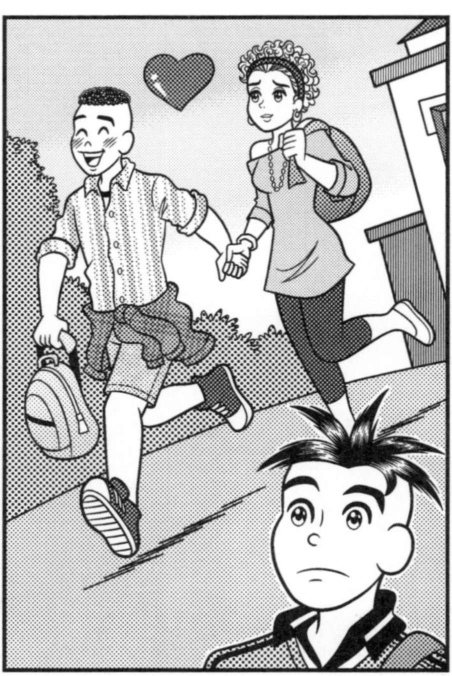

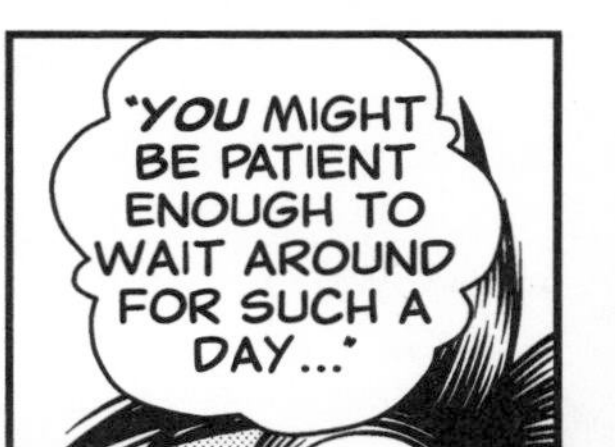
"*YOU* MIGHT BE PATIENT ENOUGH TO WAIT AROUND FOR SUCH A DAY..."
"...BUT, CAN YOU BE SURE THAT MONICA IS TOO?"

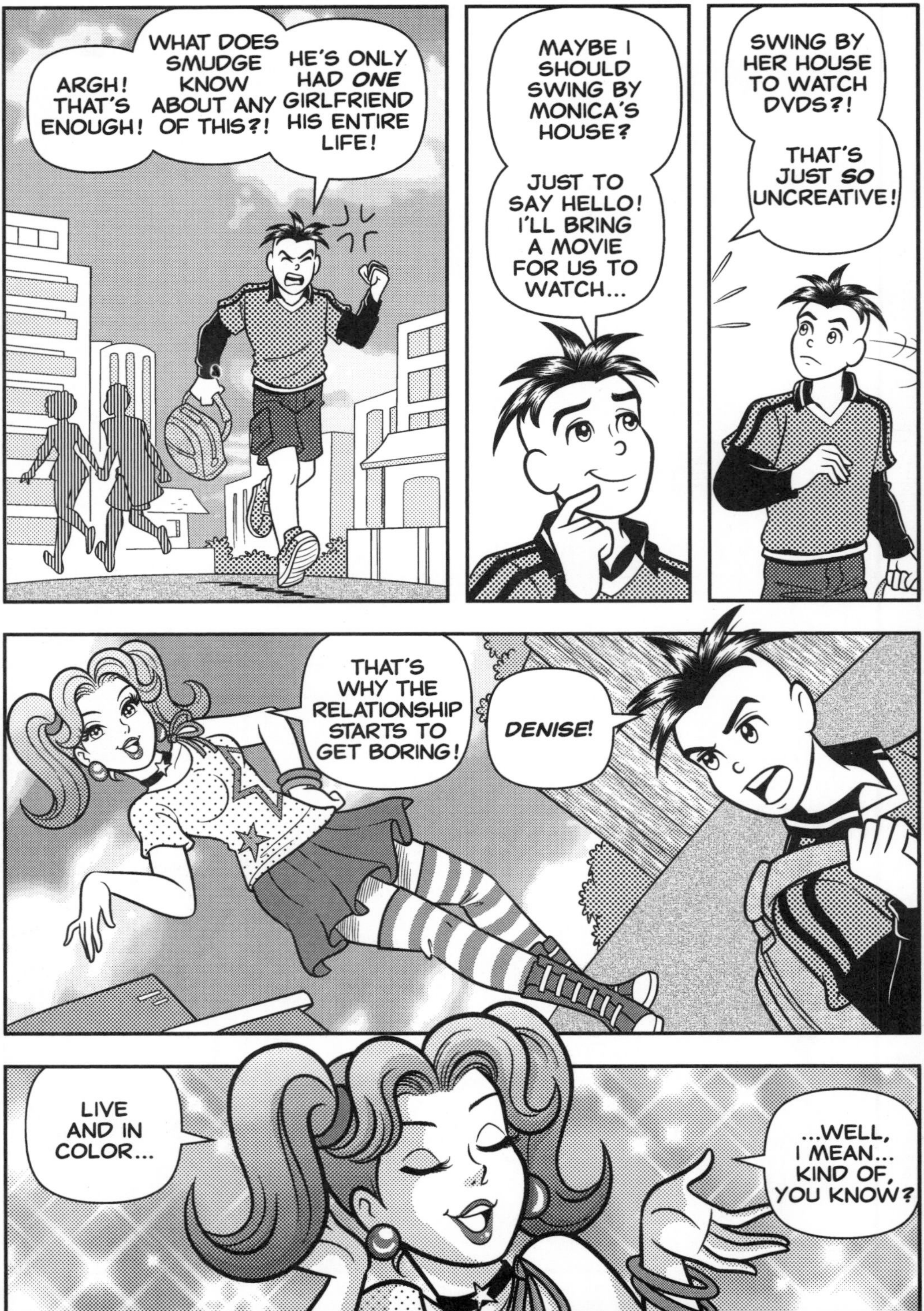

ARGH! THAT'S ENOUGH!
WHAT DOES SMUDGE KNOW ABOUT ANY OF THIS?!
HE'S ONLY HAD *ONE* GIRLFRIEND HIS ENTIRE LIFE!
MAYBE I SHOULD SWING BY MONICA'S HOUSE?
JUST TO SAY HELLO! I'LL BRING A MOVIE FOR US TO WATCH...
SWING BY HER HOUSE TO WATCH DVDS?!
THAT'S JUST *SO* UNCREATIVE!
THAT'S WHY THE RELATIONSHIP STARTS TO GET BORING!
DENISE!
LIVE AND IN COLOR...
...WELL, I MEAN... KIND OF, YOU KNOW?

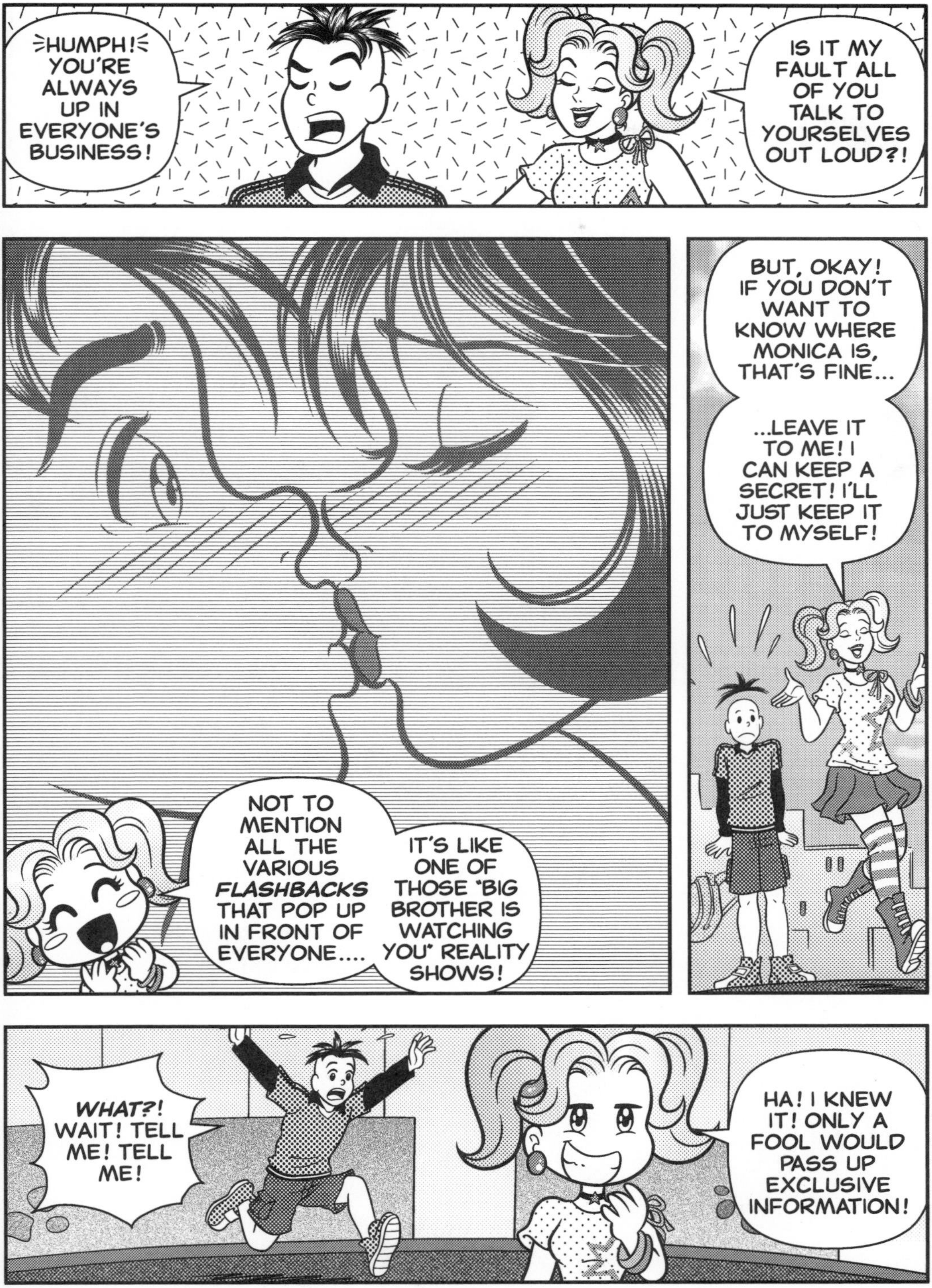
HUMPH! YOU'RE ALWAYS UP IN EVERYONE'S BUSINESS!
IS IT MY FAULT ALL OF YOU TALK TO YOURSELVES OUT LOUD?!
NOT TO MENTION ALL THE VARIOUS FLASHBACKS THAT POP UP IN FRONT OF EVERYONE....
IT'S LIKE ONE OF THOSE "BIG BROTHER IS WATCHING YOU" REALITY SHOWS!
BUT, OKAY! IF YOU DON'T WANT TO KNOW WHERE MONICA IS, THAT'S FINE...
...LEAVE IT TO ME! I CAN KEEP A SECRET! I'LL JUST KEEP IT TO MYSELF!
WHAT?! WAIT! TELL ME! TELL ME!
HA! I KNEW IT! ONLY A FOOL WOULD PASS UP EXCLUSIVE INFORMATION!

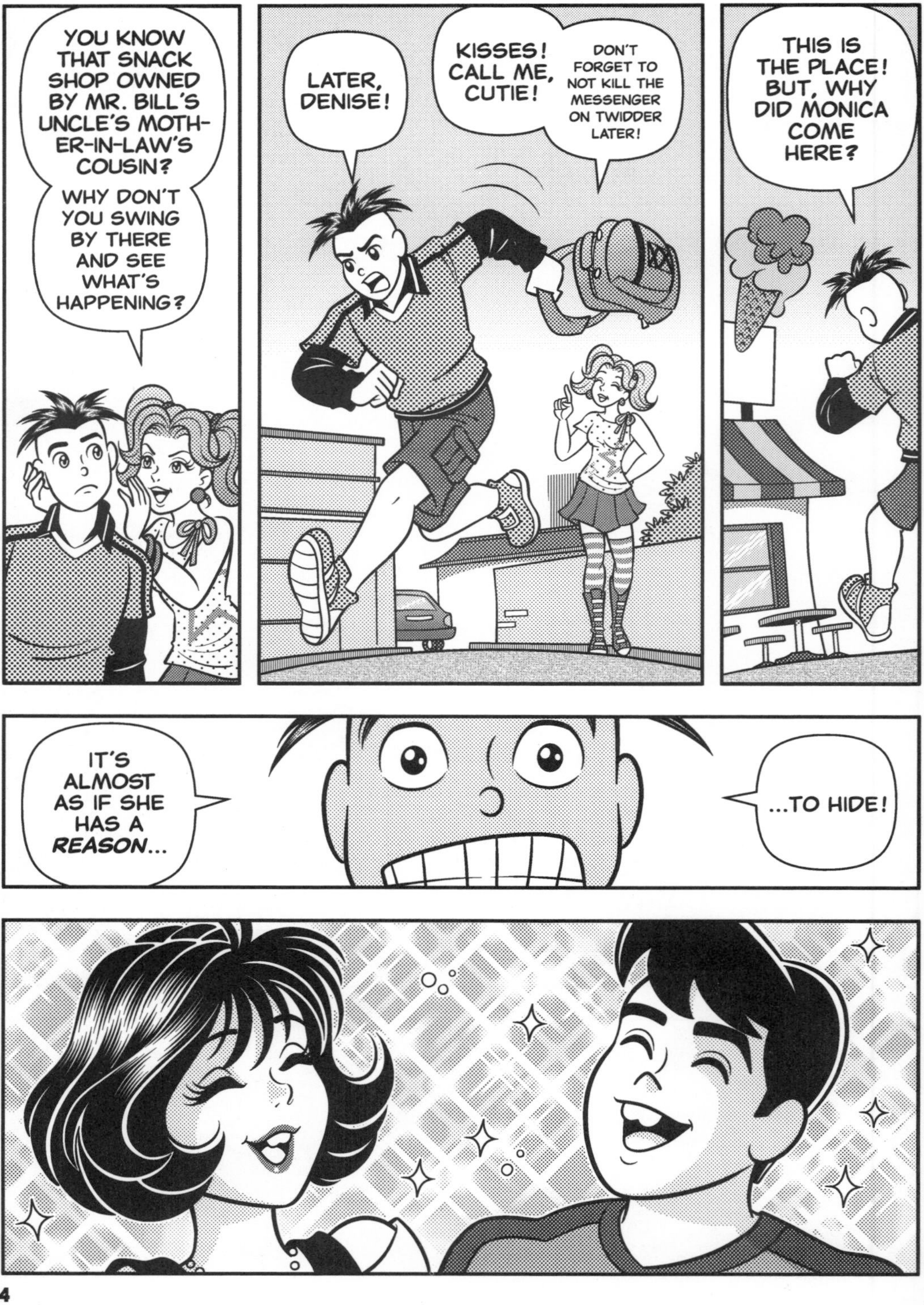
YOU KNOW THAT SNACK SHOP OWNED BY MR. BILL'S UNCLE'S MOTHER-IN-LAW'S COUSIN?
WHY DON'T YOU SWING BY THERE AND SEE WHAT'S HAPPENING?
LATER, DENISE!
KISSES! CALL ME, CUTIE!
DON'T FORGET TO NOT KILL THE MESSENGER ON TWIDDER LATER!
THIS IS THE PLACE! BUT, WHY DID MONICA COME HERE?
IT'S ALMOST AS IF SHE HAS A *REASON*...
...TO HIDE!

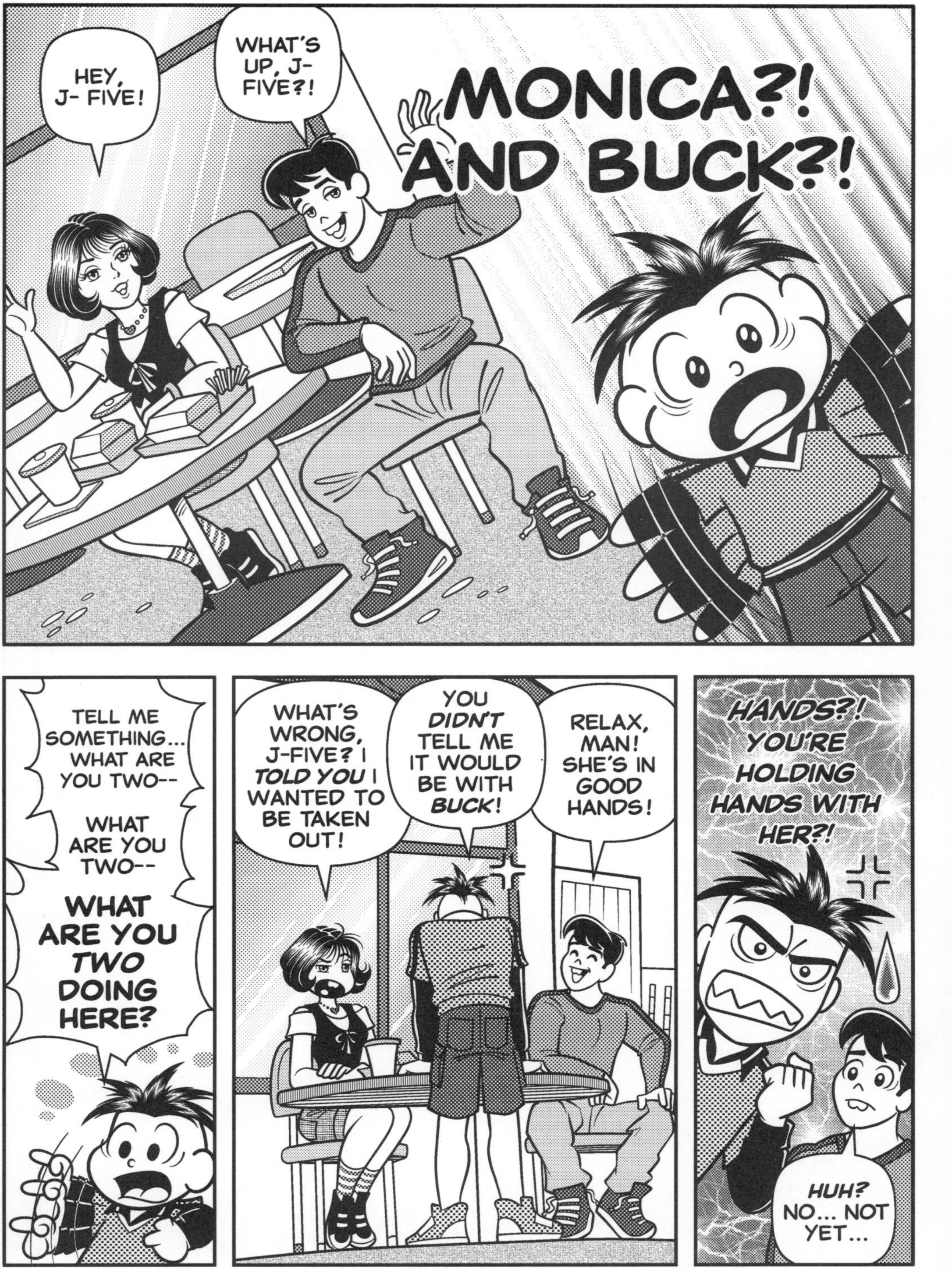
HEY, J- FIVE!
WHAT'S UP, J- FIVE?!
MONICA?! AND BUCK?!
TELL ME SOMETHING... WHAT ARE YOU TWO-- WHAT ARE YOU TWO-- **WHAT ARE YOU *TWO* DOING HERE?**
WHAT'S WRONG, J-FIVE? I *TOLD YOU* I WANTED TO BE TAKEN OUT!
YOU *DIDN'T* TELL ME IT WOULD BE WITH *BUCK*!
RELAX, MAN! SHE'S IN GOOD HANDS!
HANDS?! YOU'RE HOLDING HANDS WITH HER?!
HUH? NO... NOT YET...

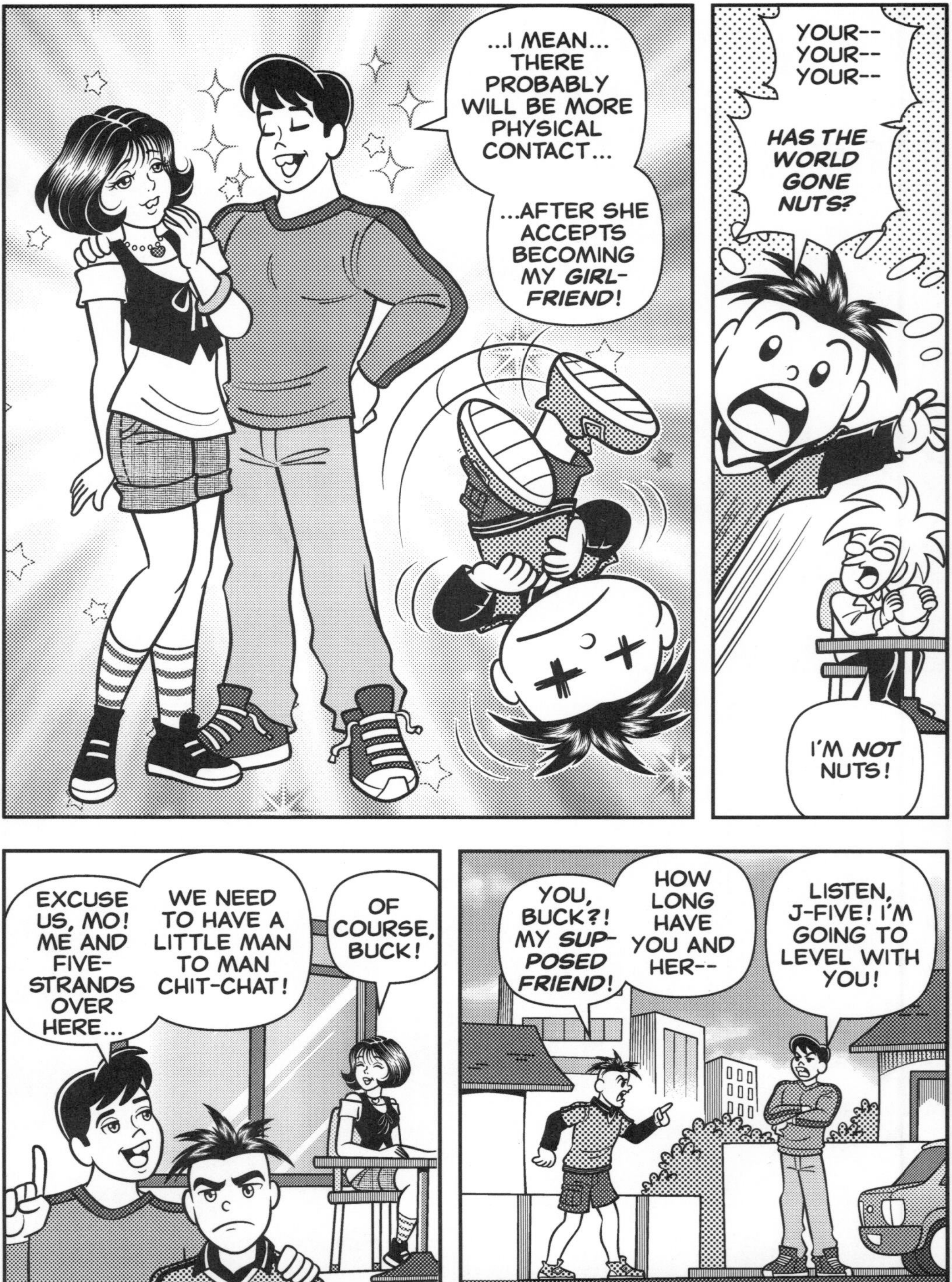
...I MEAN... THERE PROBABLY WILL BE MORE PHYSICAL CONTACT...
...AFTER SHE ACCEPTS BECOMING MY GIRL-FRIEND!
YOUR-- YOUR-- YOUR--
HAS THE WORLD GONE NUTS?
I'M NOT NUTS!
EXCUSE US, MO! ME AND FIVE-STRANDS OVER HERE...
WE NEED TO HAVE A LITTLE MAN TO MAN CHIT-CHAT!
OF COURSE, BUCK!
YOU, BUCK?! MY SUP-POSED FRIEND!
HOW LONG HAVE YOU AND HER--
LISTEN, J-FIVE! I'M GOING TO LEVEL WITH YOU!

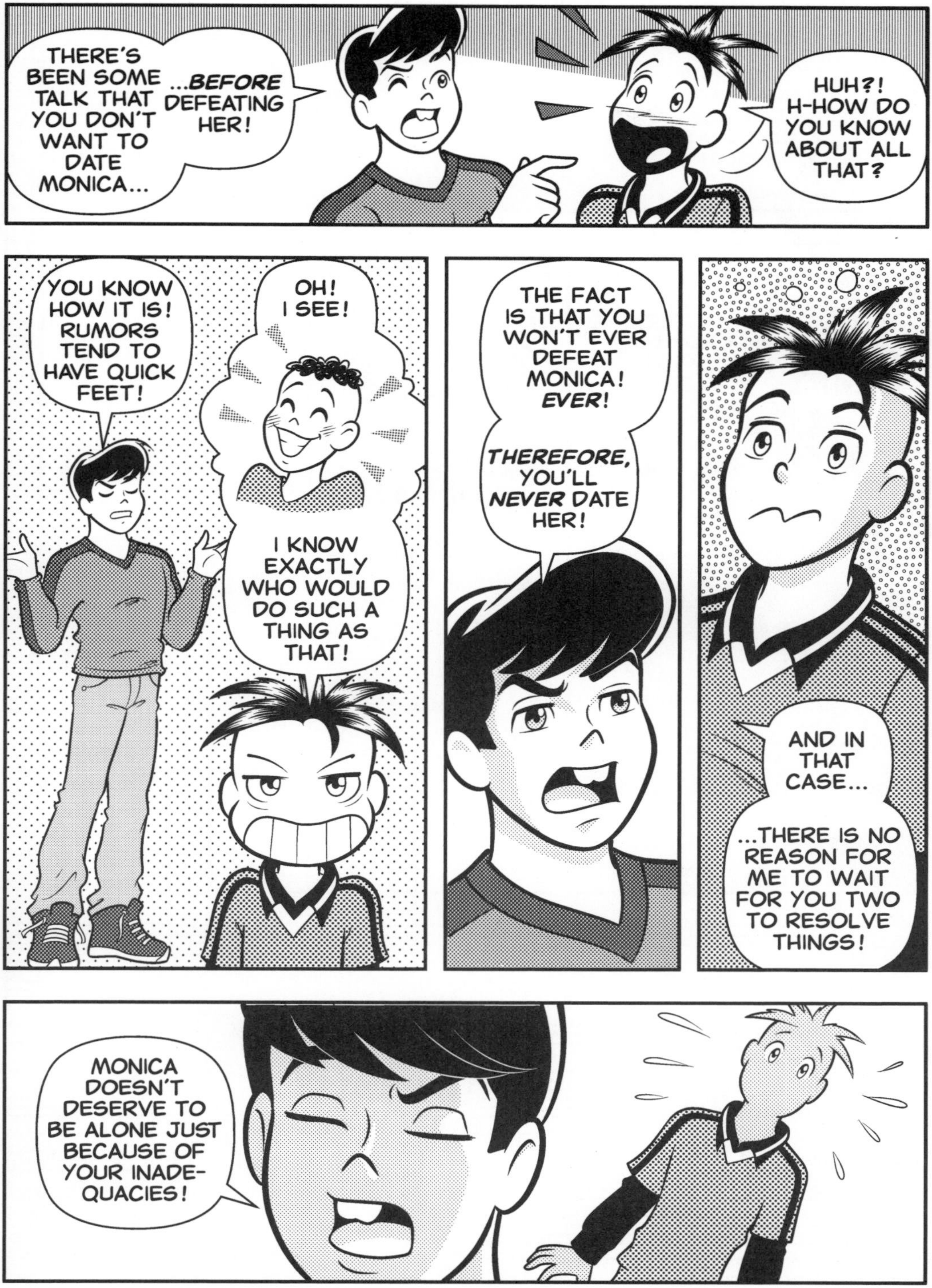
THERE'S BEEN SOME TALK THAT YOU DON'T WANT TO DATE MONICA...
...BEFORE DEFEATING HER!
HUH?! H-HOW DO YOU KNOW ABOUT ALL THAT?
YOU KNOW HOW IT IS! RUMORS TEND TO HAVE QUICK FEET!
OH! I SEE!
I KNOW EXACTLY WHO WOULD DO SUCH A THING AS THAT!
THE FACT IS THAT YOU WON'T EVER DEFEAT MONICA! EVER!
THEREFORE, YOU'LL NEVER DATE HER!
AND IN THAT CASE...
...THERE IS NO REASON FOR ME TO WAIT FOR YOU TWO TO RESOLVE THINGS!
MONICA DOESN'T DESERVE TO BE ALONE JUST BECAUSE OF YOUR INADE-QUACIES!

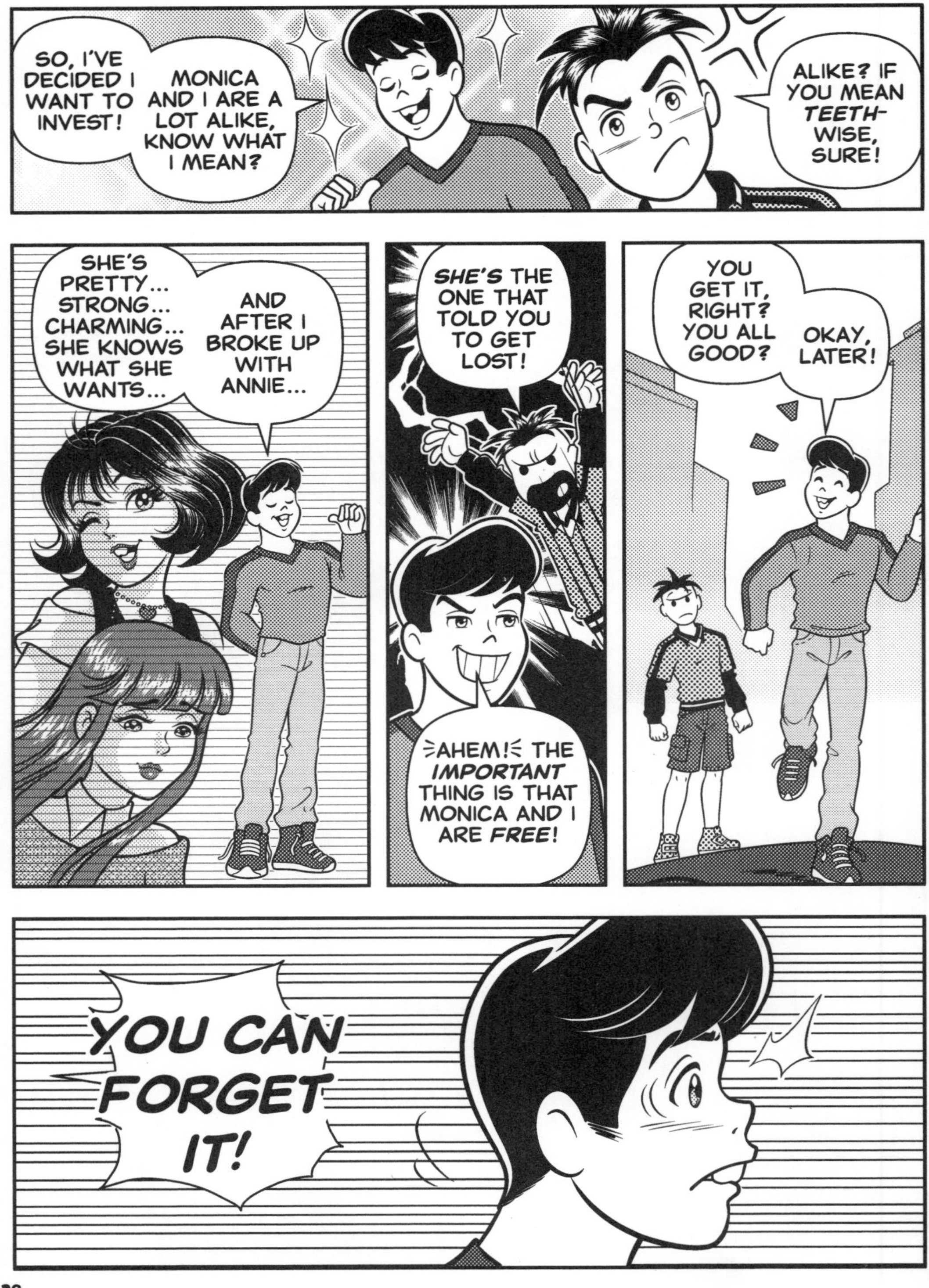
SO, I'VE DECIDED I WANT TO INVEST!
MONICA AND I ARE A LOT ALIKE, KNOW WHAT I MEAN?
ALIKE? IF YOU MEAN TEETH-WISE, SURE!
SHE'S PRETTY... STRONG... CHARMING... SHE KNOWS WHAT SHE WANTS...
AND AFTER I BROKE UP WITH ANNIE...
SHE'S THE ONE THAT TOLD YOU TO GET LOST!
AHEM! THE IMPORTANT THING IS THAT MONICA AND I ARE FREE!
YOU GET IT, RIGHT? YOU ALL GOOD?
OKAY, LATER!
YOU CAN FORGET IT!

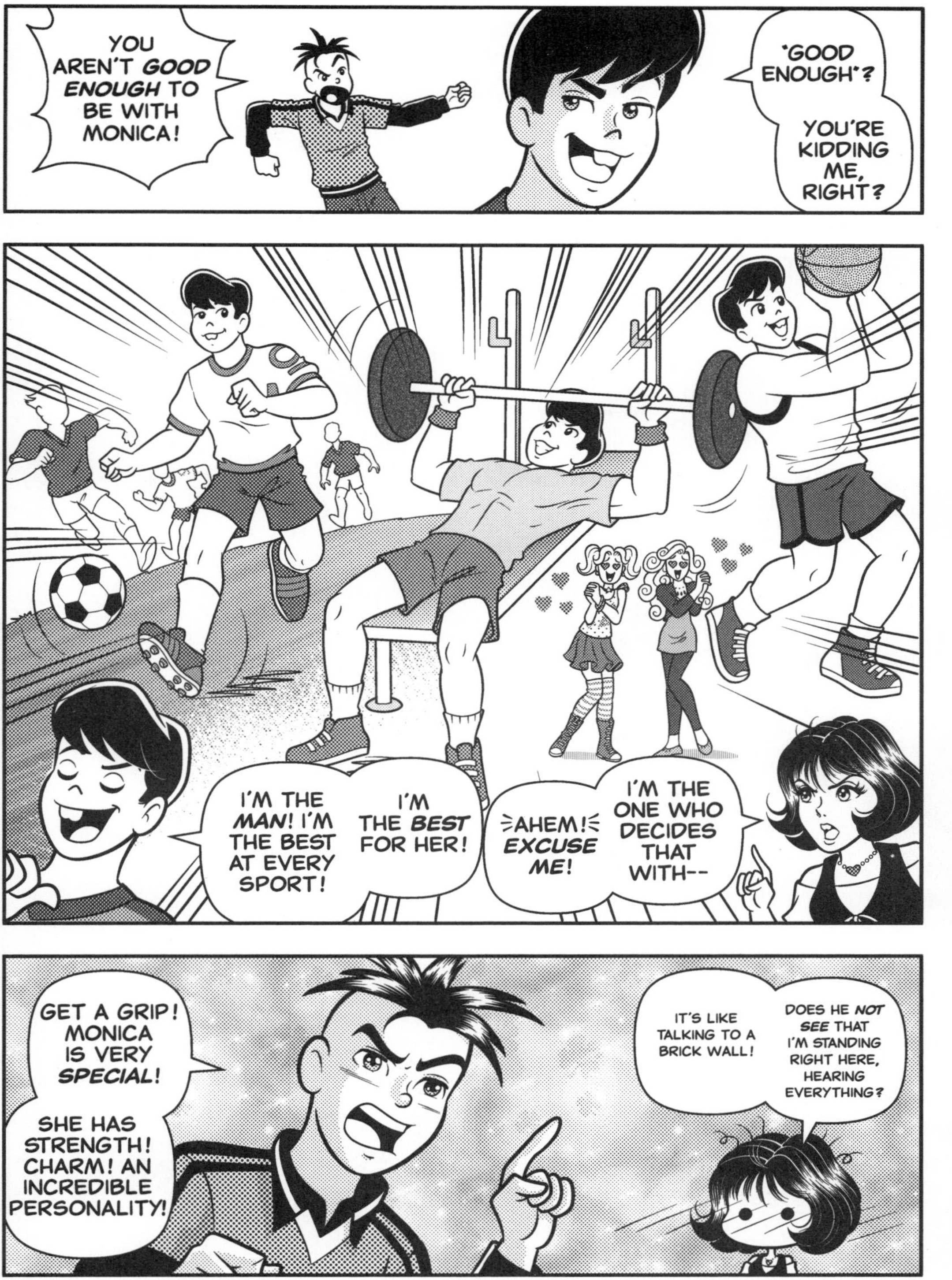
YOU AREN'T GOOD ENOUGH TO BE WITH MONICA!
"GOOD ENOUGH"?
YOU'RE KIDDING ME, RIGHT?
I'M THE MAN! I'M THE BEST AT EVERY SPORT!
I'M THE BEST FOR HER!
AHEM! EXCUSE ME!
I'M THE ONE WHO DECIDES THAT WITH--
GET A GRIP! MONICA IS VERY SPECIAL!
SHE HAS STRENGTH! CHARM! AN INCREDIBLE PERSONALITY!
IT'S LIKE TALKING TO A BRICK WALL!
DOES HE NOT SEE THAT I'M STANDING RIGHT HERE, HEARING EVERYTHING?

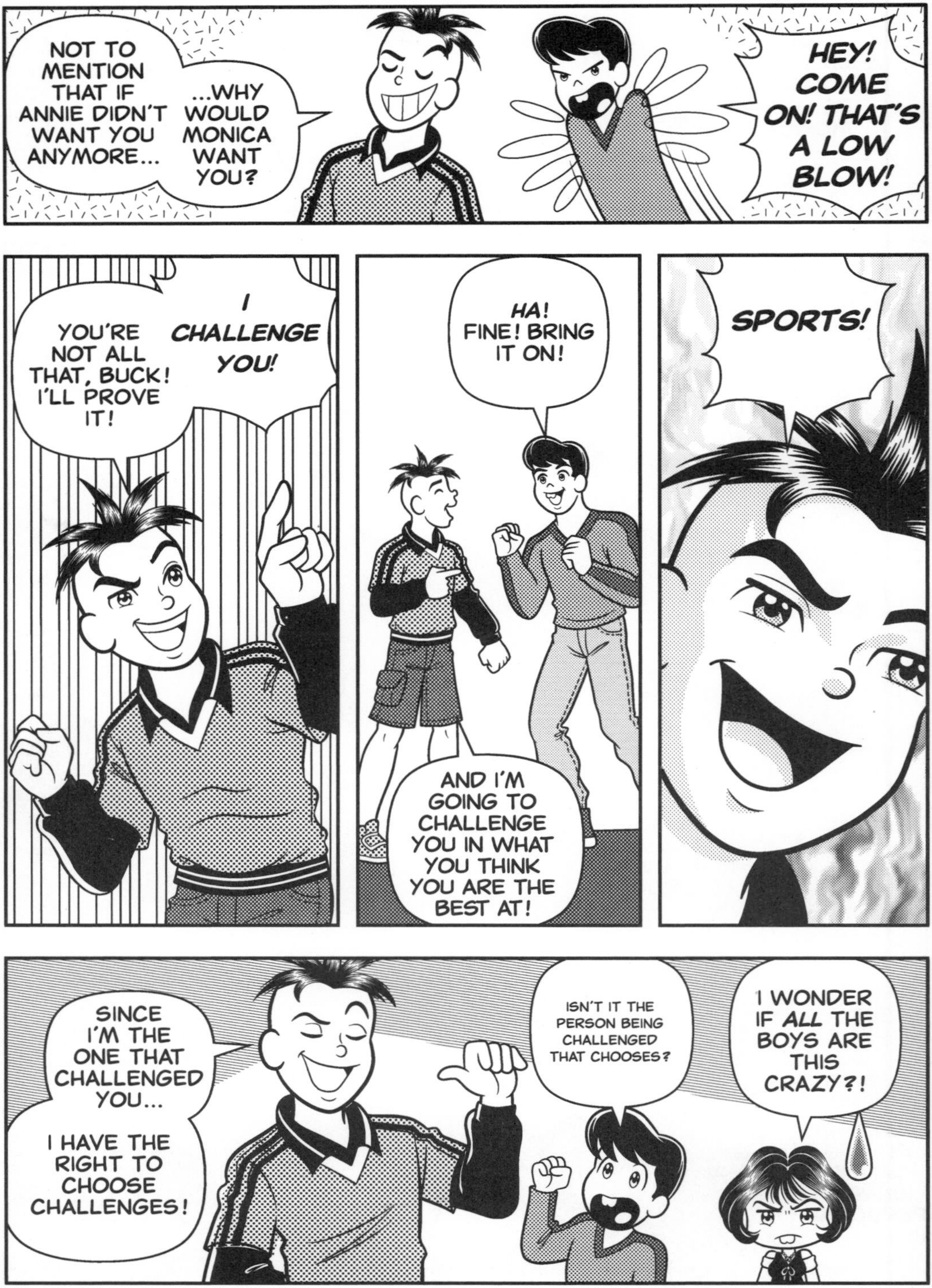
NOT TO MENTION THAT IF ANNIE DIDN'T WANT YOU ANYMORE...
...WHY WOULD MONICA WANT YOU?
HEY! COME ON! THAT'S A LOW BLOW!
YOU'RE NOT ALL THAT, BUCK! I'LL PROVE IT!
I CHALLENGE YOU!
HA! FINE! BRING IT ON!
AND I'M GOING TO CHALLENGE YOU IN WHAT YOU THINK YOU ARE THE BEST AT!
SPORTS!
SINCE I'M THE ONE THAT CHALLENGED YOU...
I HAVE THE RIGHT TO CHOOSE CHALLENGES!
ISN'T IT THE PERSON BEING CHALLENGED THAT CHOOSES?
I WONDER IF ALL THE BOYS ARE THIS CRAZY?!

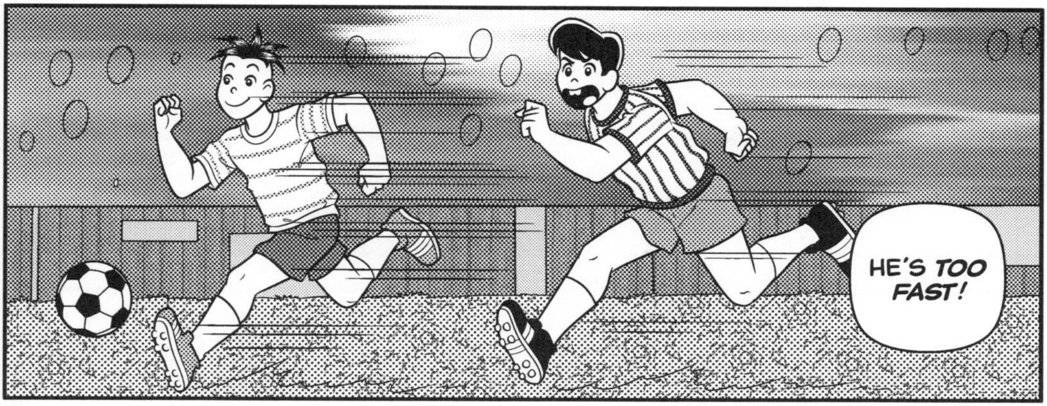
HE'S *TOO FAST*!

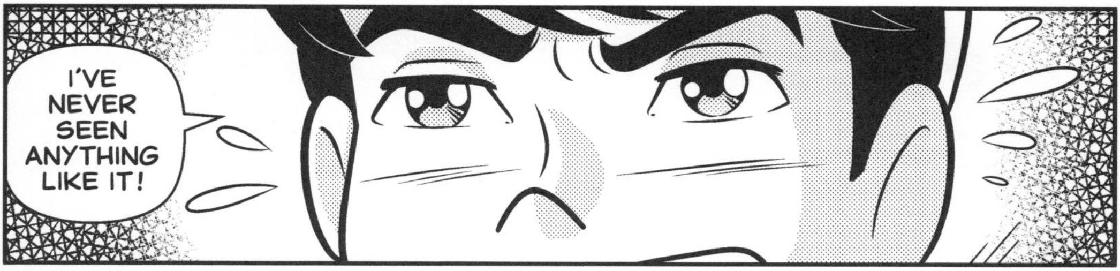
I'VE NEVER SEEN ANYTHING LIKE IT!

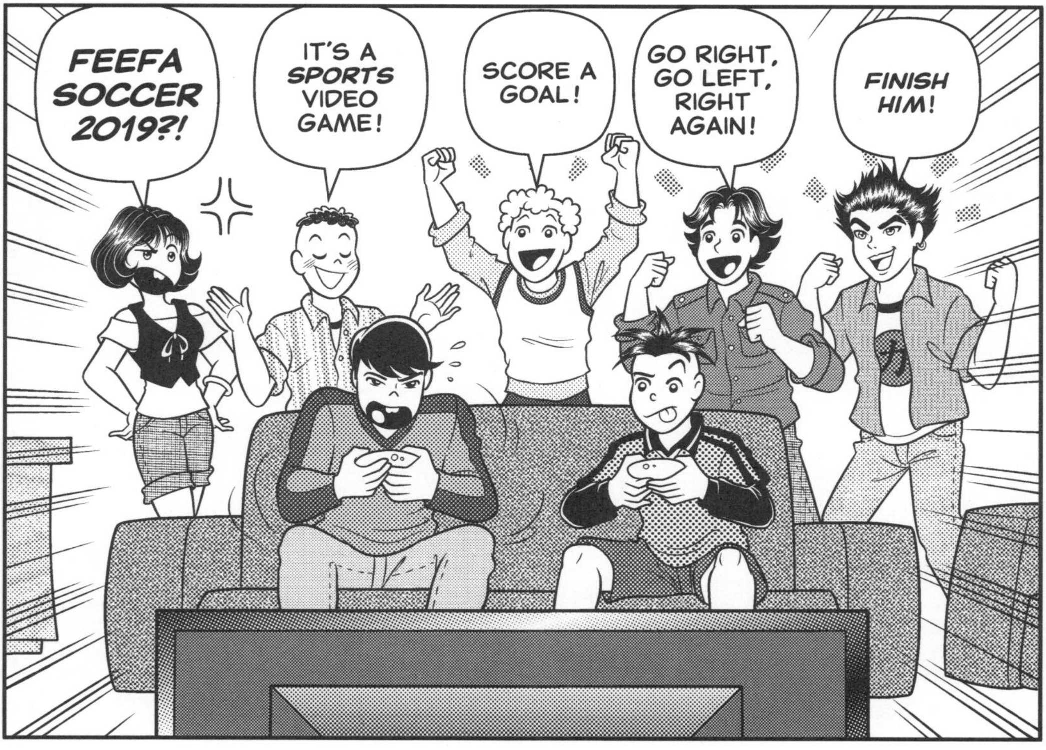
FEEFA SOCCER 2019?!
IT'S A *SPORTS* VIDEO GAME!
SCORE A GOAL!
GO RIGHT, GO LEFT, RIGHT AGAIN!
FINISH HIM!

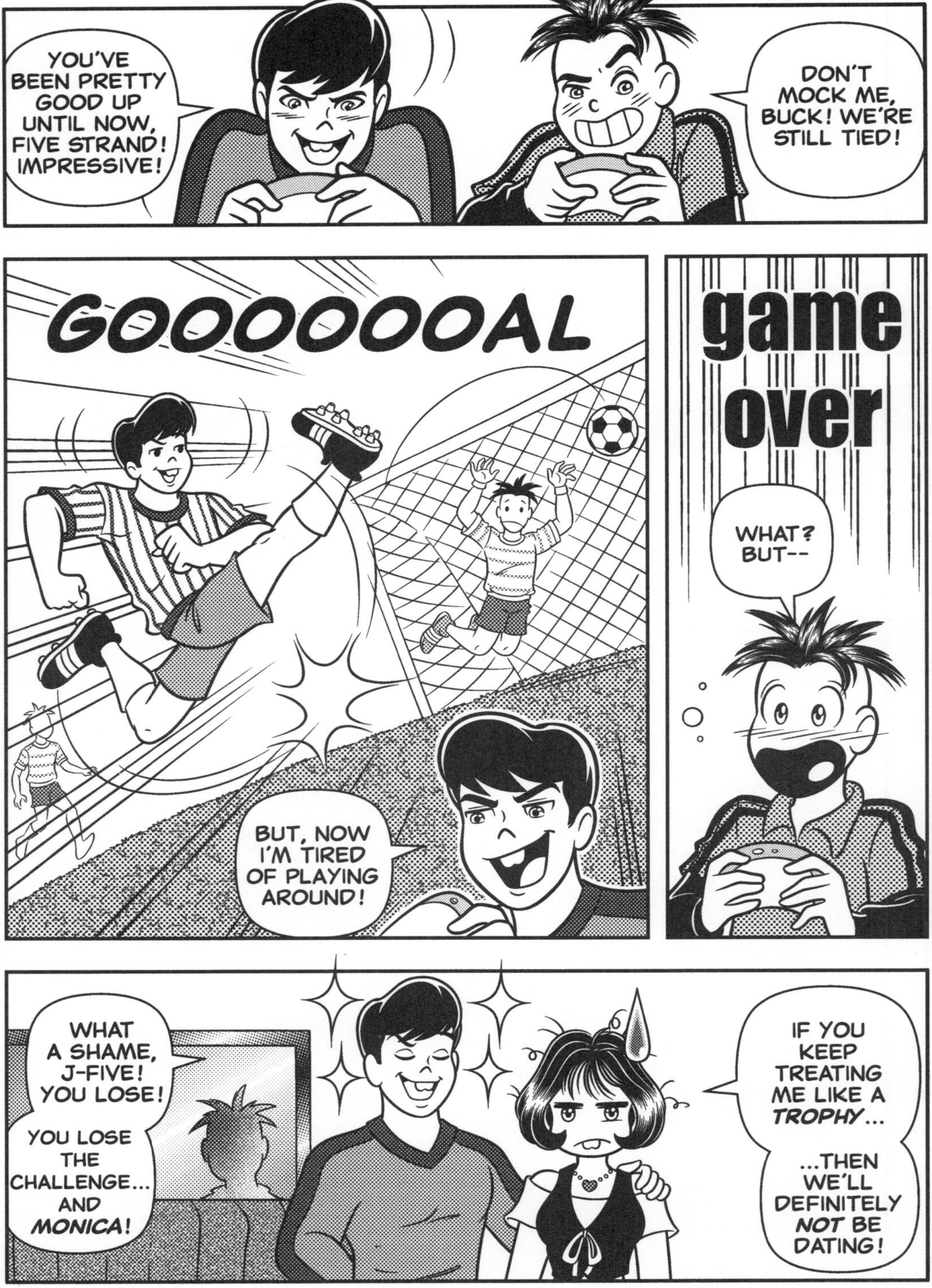
YOU'VE BEEN PRETTY GOOD UP UNTIL NOW, FIVE STRAND! IMPRESSIVE!
DON'T MOCK ME, BUCK! WE'RE STILL TIED!
GOOOOOOAL
BUT, NOW I'M TIRED OF PLAYING AROUND!
game over
WHAT? BUT--
WHAT A SHAME, J-FIVE! YOU LOSE!
YOU LOSE THE CHALLENGE... AND *MONICA*!
IF YOU KEEP TREATING ME LIKE A *TROPHY*...
...THEN WE'LL DEFINITELY *NOT* BE DATING!

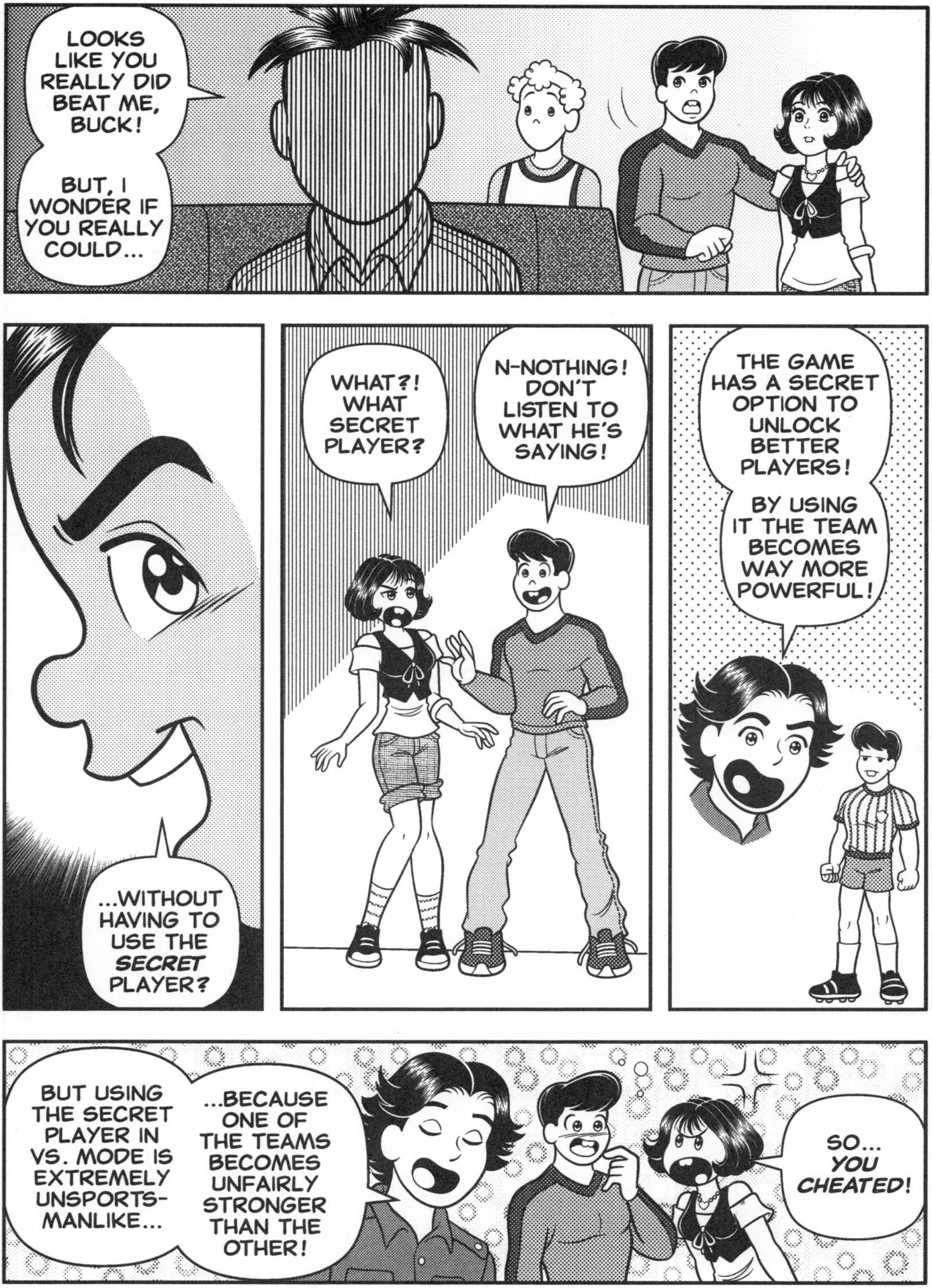
LOOKS LIKE YOU REALLY DID BEAT ME, BUCK!
BUT, I WONDER IF YOU REALLY COULD...
...WITHOUT HAVING TO USE THE *SECRET* PLAYER?
WHAT?! WHAT SECRET PLAYER?
N-NOTHING! DON'T LISTEN TO WHAT HE'S SAYING!
THE GAME HAS A SECRET OPTION TO UNLOCK BETTER PLAYERS!
BY USING IT THE TEAM BECOMES WAY MORE POWERFUL!
BUT USING THE SECRET PLAYER IN VS. MODE IS EXTREMELY UNSPORTS-MANLIKE...
...BECAUSE ONE OF THE TEAMS BECOMES UNFAIRLY STRONGER THAN THE OTHER!
SO... *YOU CHEATED!*

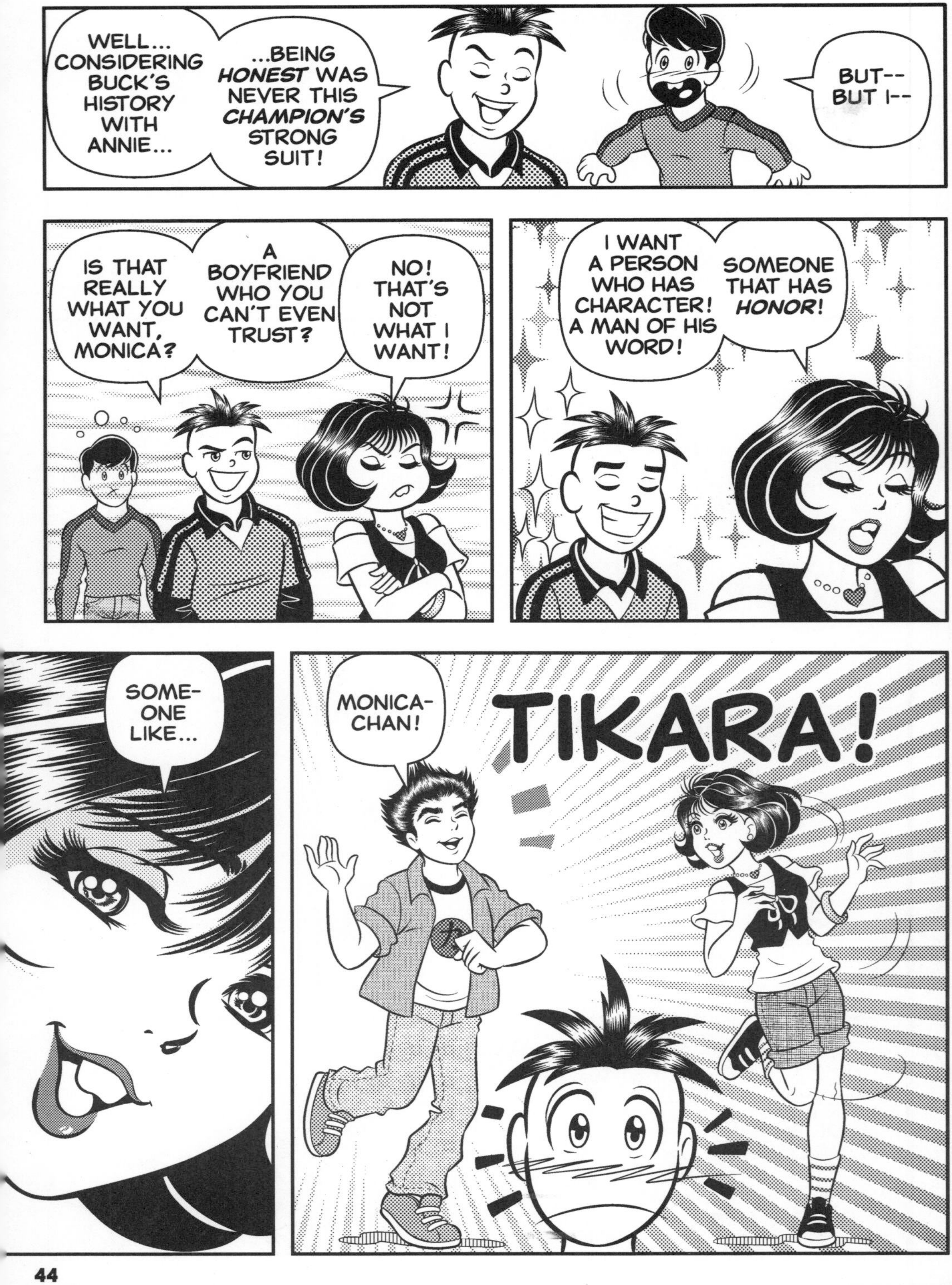
WELL... CONSIDERING BUCK'S HISTORY WITH ANNIE...
...BEING *HONEST* WAS NEVER THIS *CHAMPION'S* STRONG SUIT!
BUT-- BUT I--
IS THAT REALLY WHAT YOU WANT, MONICA?
A BOYFRIEND WHO YOU CAN'T EVEN TRUST?
NO! THAT'S NOT WHAT I WANT!
I WANT A PERSON WHO HAS CHARACTER! A MAN OF HIS WORD!
SOMEONE THAT HAS *HONOR*!
SOME-ONE LIKE...
MONICA-CHAN!
TIKARA!

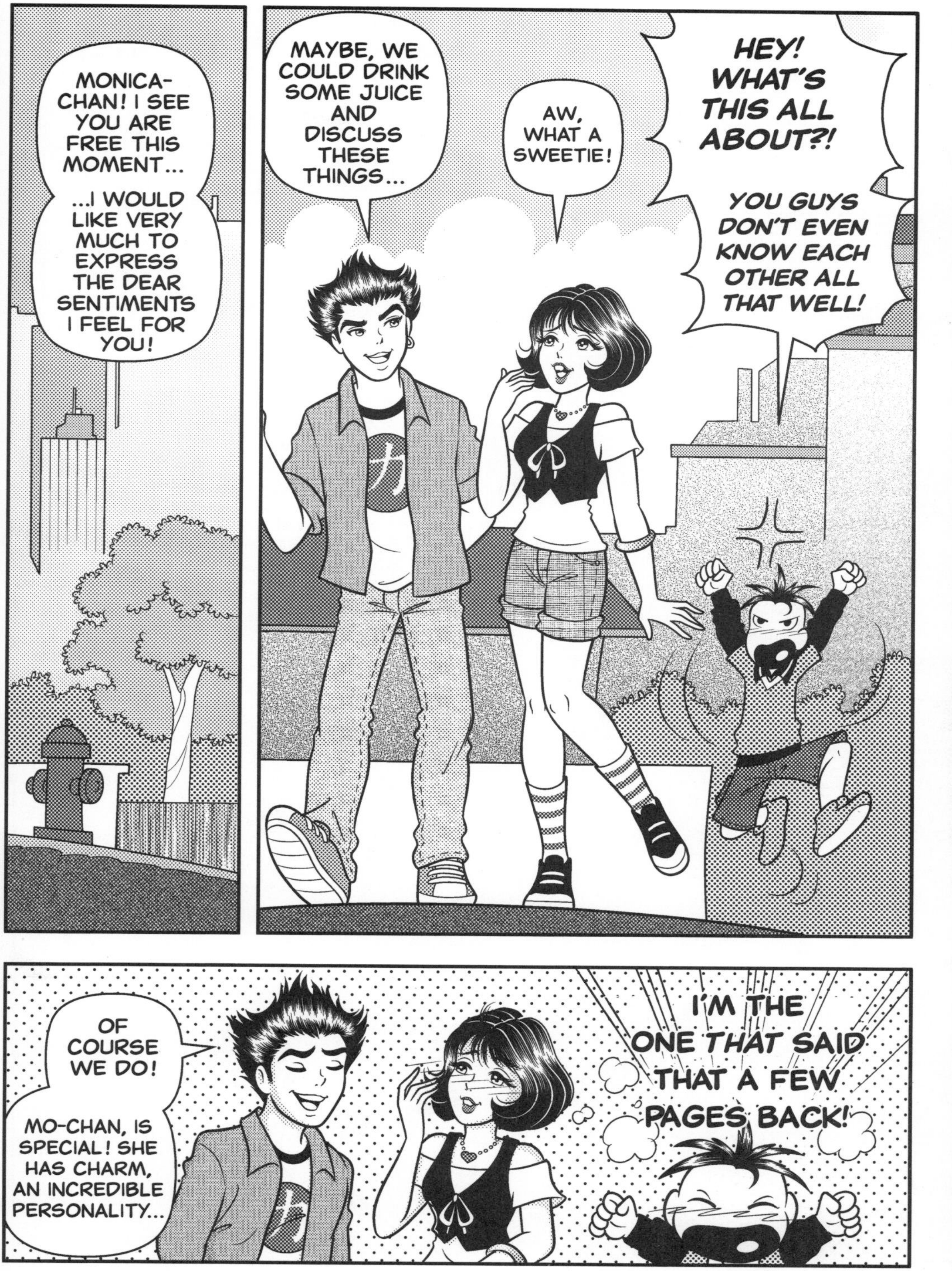

MONICA-CHAN! I SEE YOU ARE FREE THIS MOMENT...
...I WOULD LIKE VERY MUCH TO EXPRESS THE DEAR SENTIMENTS I FEEL FOR YOU!
MAYBE, WE COULD DRINK SOME JUICE AND DISCUSS THESE THINGS...
AW, WHAT A SWEETIE!
HEY! WHAT'S THIS ALL ABOUT?!
YOU GUYS DON'T EVEN KNOW EACH OTHER ALL THAT WELL!
OF COURSE WE DO!
MO-CHAN, IS SPECIAL! SHE HAS CHARM, AN INCREDIBLE PERSONALITY...
I'M THE ONE THAT SAID THAT A FEW PAGES BACK!

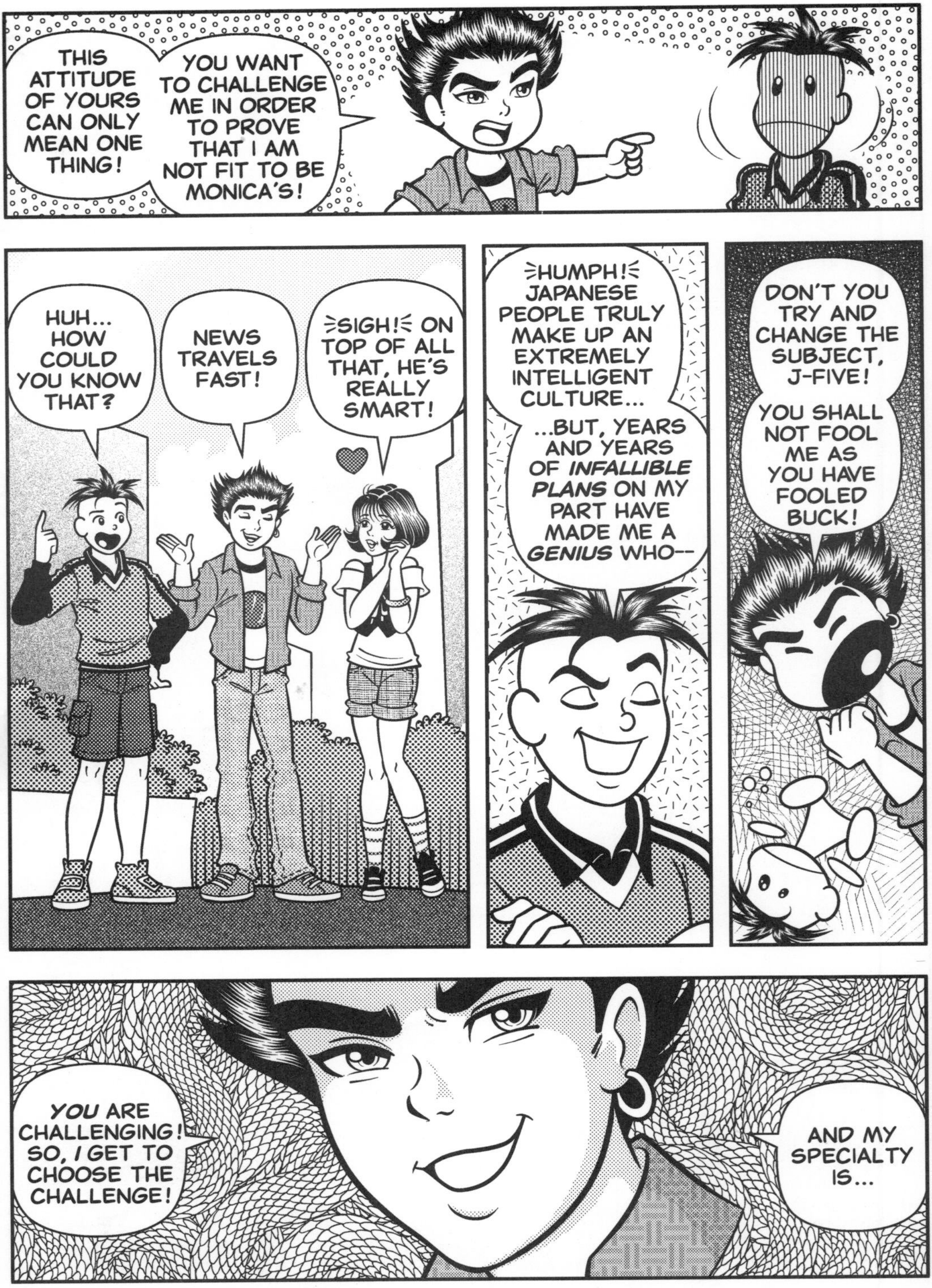
THIS ATTITUDE OF YOURS CAN ONLY MEAN ONE THING!
YOU WANT TO CHALLENGE ME IN ORDER TO PROVE THAT I AM NOT FIT TO BE MONICA'S!
HUH... HOW COULD YOU KNOW THAT?
NEWS TRAVELS FAST!
SIGH! ON TOP OF ALL THAT, HE'S REALLY SMART!
HUMPH! JAPANESE PEOPLE TRULY MAKE UP AN EXTREMELY INTELLIGENT CULTURE...
...BUT, YEARS AND YEARS OF *INFALLIBLE PLANS* ON MY PART HAVE MADE ME A *GENIUS* WHO--
DON'T YOU TRY AND CHANGE THE SUBJECT, J-FIVE!
YOU SHALL NOT FOOL ME AS YOU HAVE FOOLED BUCK!
YOU ARE CHALLENGING! SO, *I* GET TO CHOOSE THE CHALLENGE!
AND MY SPECIALTY IS...

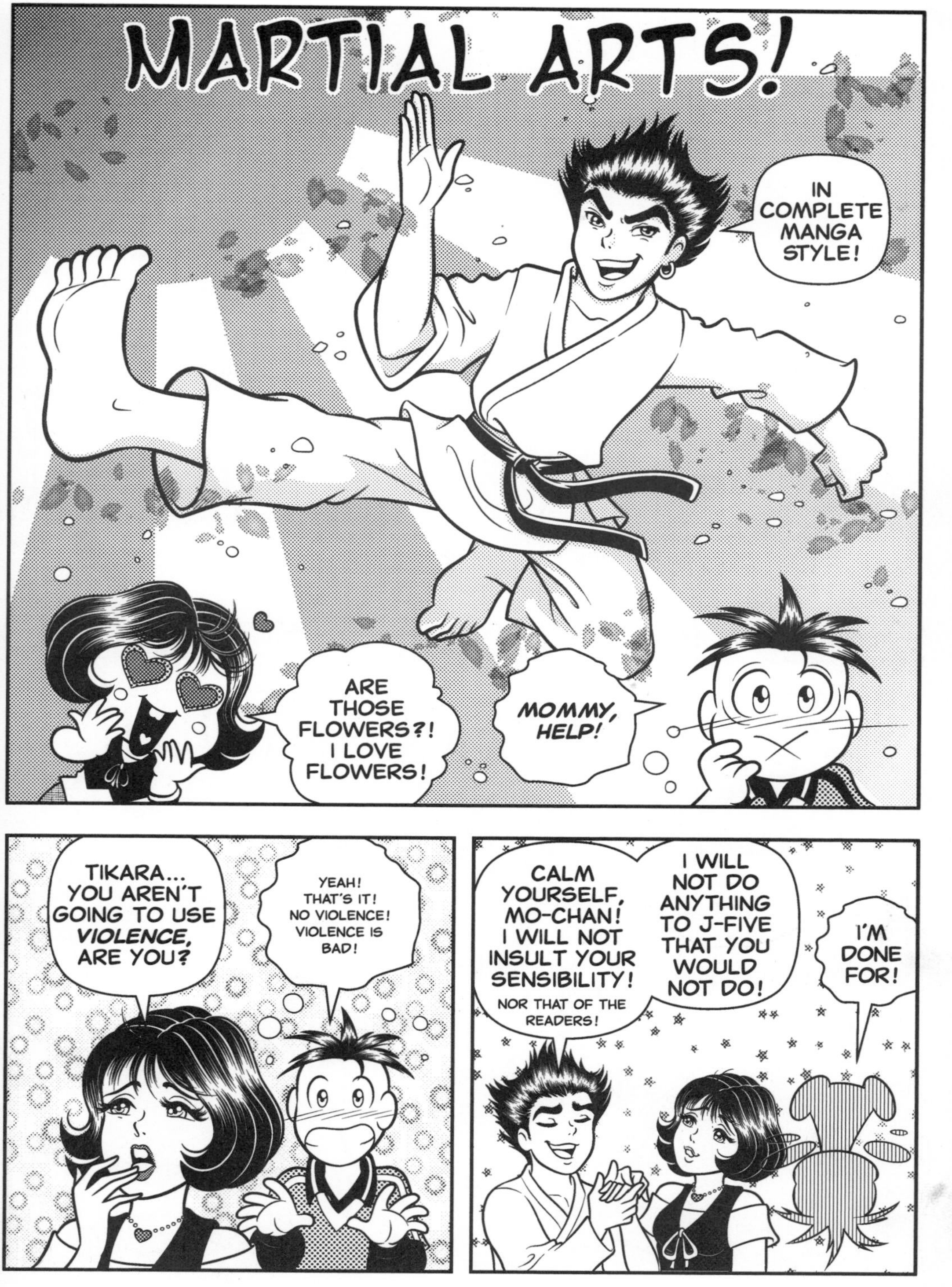
MARTIAL ARTS!
IN COMPLETE MANGA STYLE!
ARE THOSE FLOWERS?! I LOVE FLOWERS!
MOMMY, HELP!
TIKARA... YOU AREN'T GOING TO USE *VIOLENCE*, ARE YOU?
YEAH! THAT'S IT! NO VIOLENCE! VIOLENCE IS BAD!
CALM YOURSELF, MO-CHAN! I WILL NOT INSULT YOUR SENSIBILITY!
NOR THAT OF THE READERS!
I WILL NOT DO ANYTHING TO J-FIVE THAT YOU WOULD NOT DO!
I'M DONE FOR!

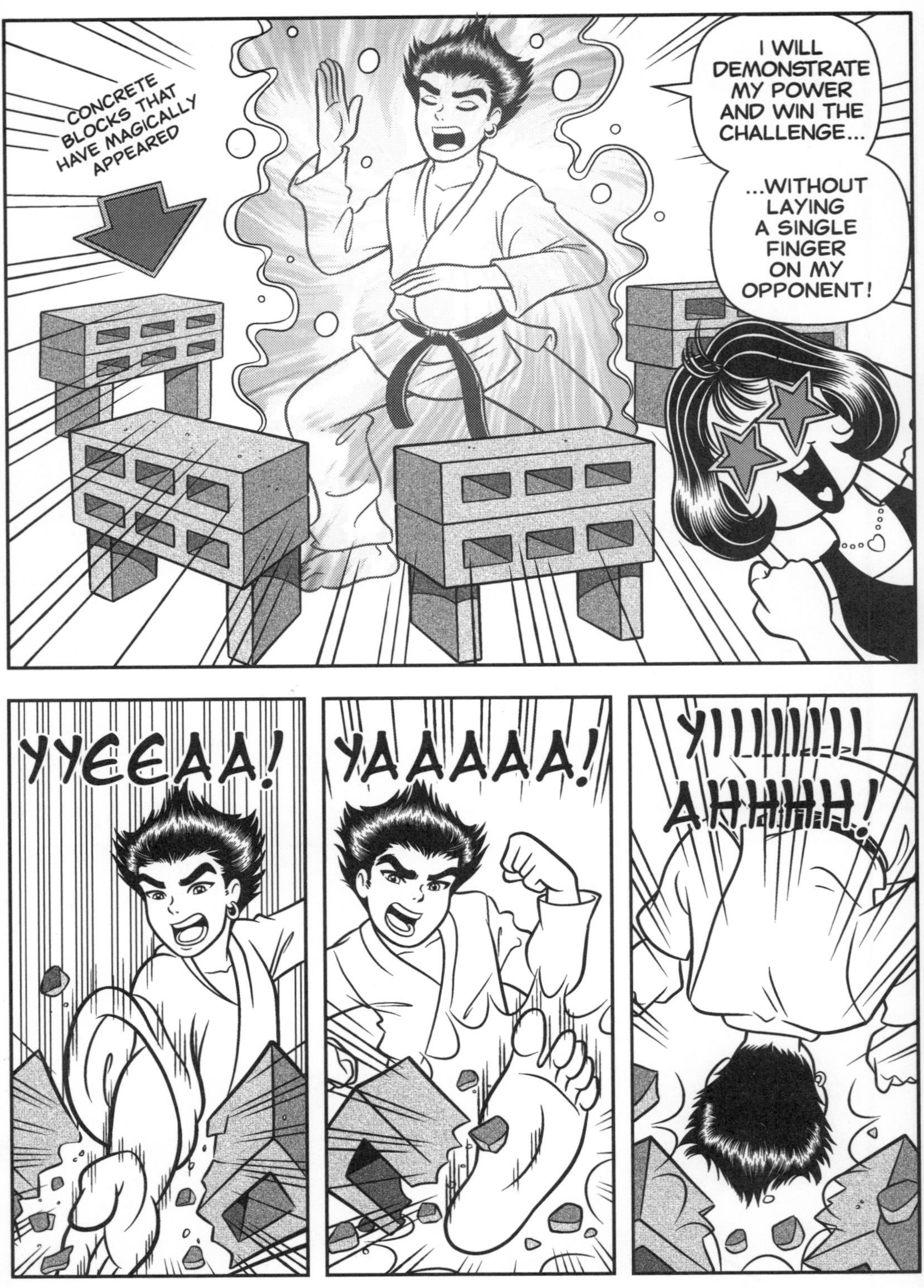
CONCRETE BLOCKS THAT HAVE MAGICALLY APPEARED
I WILL DEMONSTRATE MY POWER AND WIN THE CHALLENGE...
...WITHOUT LAYING A SINGLE FINGER ON MY OPPONENT!
YYEEAA!
YAAAAAA!
YIIIIIIII AHHHHH!

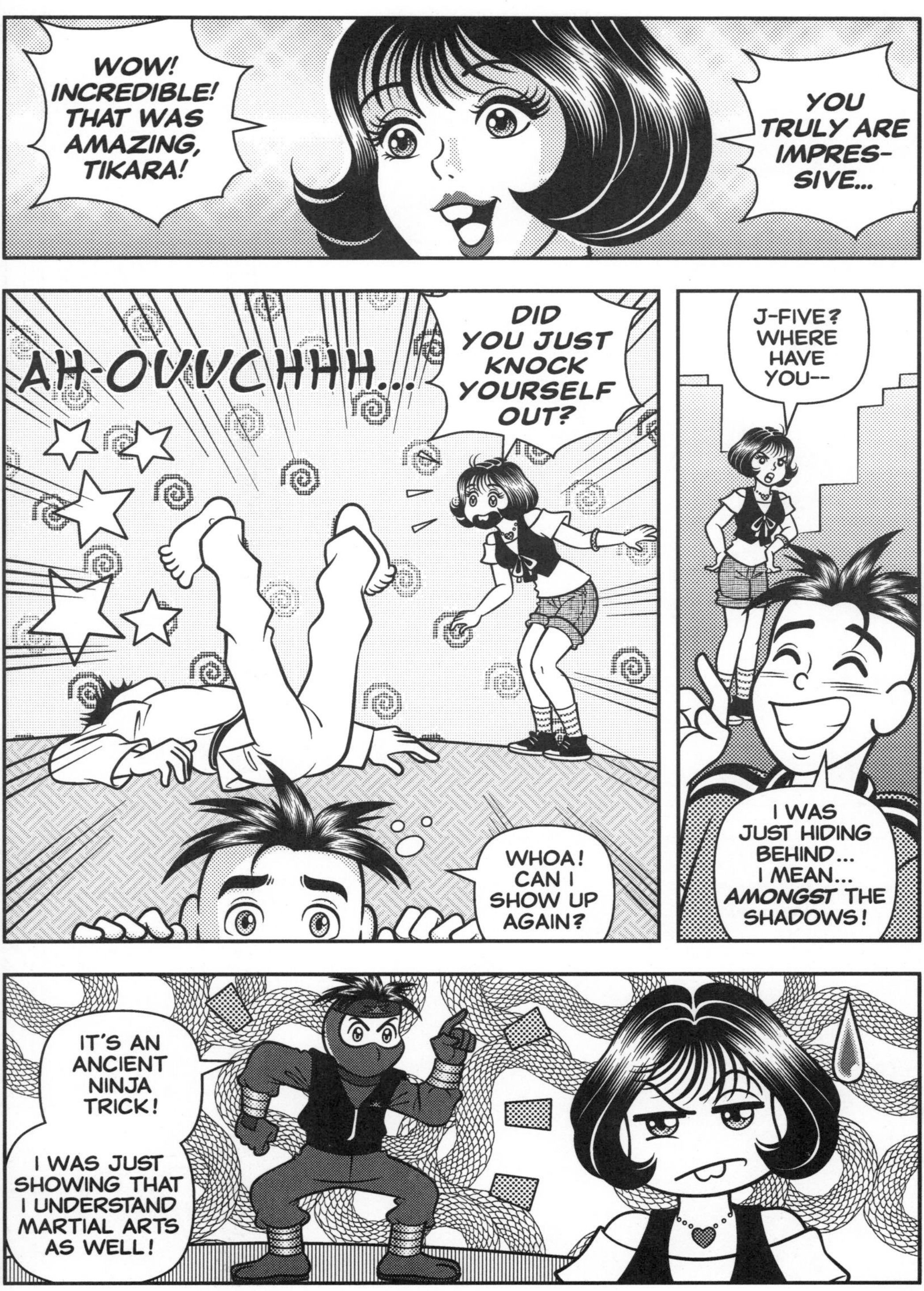
WOW! INCREDIBLE! THAT WAS AMAZING, TIKARA!
YOU TRULY ARE IMPRES-SIVE...
AH-OUUCHHH...
DID YOU JUST KNOCK YOURSELF OUT?
WHOA! CAN I SHOW UP AGAIN?
J-FIVE? WHERE HAVE YOU--
I WAS JUST HIDING BEHIND... I MEAN... AMONGST THE SHADOWS!
IT'S AN ANCIENT NINJA TRICK!
I WAS JUST SHOWING THAT I UNDERSTAND MARTIAL ARTS AS WELL!

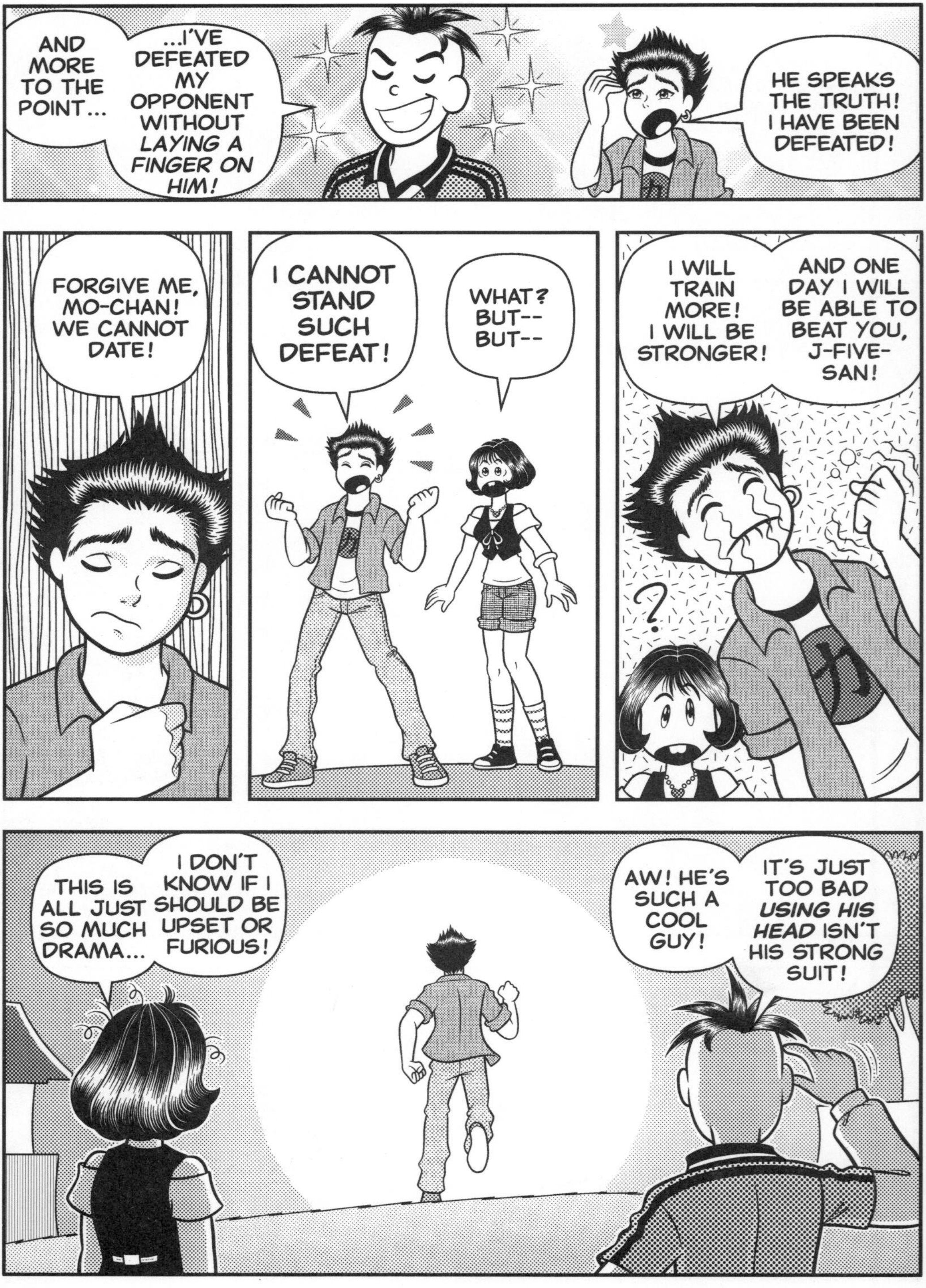
AND MORE TO THE POINT...
...I'VE DEFEATED MY OPPONENT WITHOUT *LAYING A FINGER ON HIM!*
HE SPEAKS THE TRUTH! I HAVE BEEN DEFEATED!
FORGIVE ME, MO-CHAN! WE CANNOT DATE!
I CANNOT STAND SUCH DEFEAT!
WHAT? BUT-- BUT--
I WILL TRAIN MORE! I WILL BE STRONGER!
AND ONE DAY I WILL BE ABLE TO BEAT YOU, J-FIVE-SAN!
THIS IS ALL JUST SO MUCH DRAMA...
I DON'T KNOW IF I SHOULD BE UPSET OR FURIOUS!
AW! HE'S SUCH A COOL GUY!
IT'S JUST TOO BAD *USING HIS HEAD* ISN'T HIS STRONG SUIT!

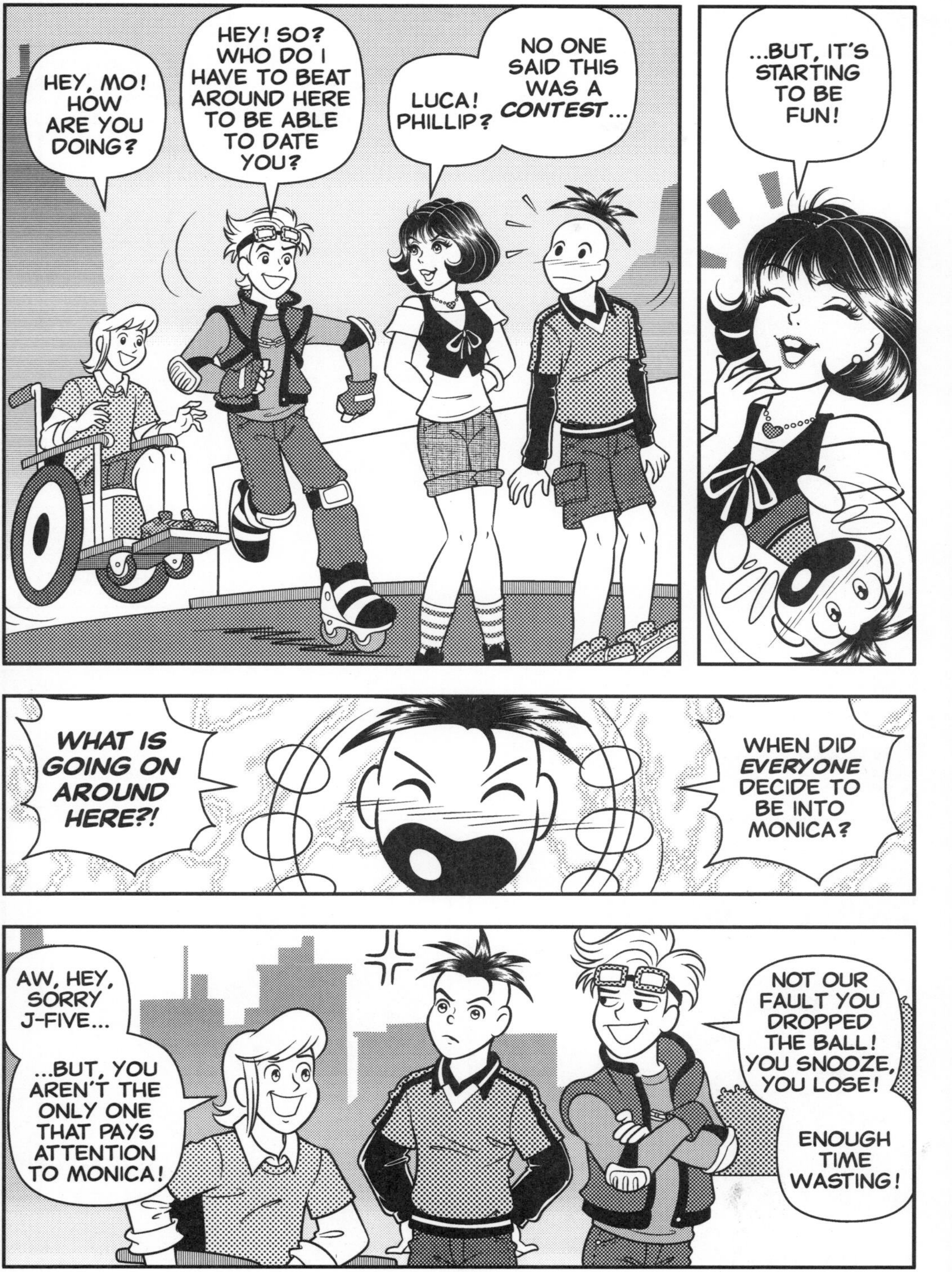
HEY, MO! HOW ARE YOU DOING?
HEY! SO? WHO DO I HAVE TO BEAT AROUND HERE TO BE ABLE TO DATE YOU?
LUCA! PHILLIP?
NO ONE SAID THIS WAS A CONTEST...
...BUT, IT'S STARTING TO BE FUN!
WHAT IS GOING ON AROUND HERE?!
WHEN DID EVERYONE DECIDE TO BE INTO MONICA?
AW, HEY, SORRY J-FIVE...
...BUT, YOU AREN'T THE ONLY ONE THAT PAYS ATTENTION TO MONICA!
NOT OUR FAULT YOU DROPPED THE BALL! YOU SNOOZE, YOU LOSE!
ENOUGH TIME WASTING!

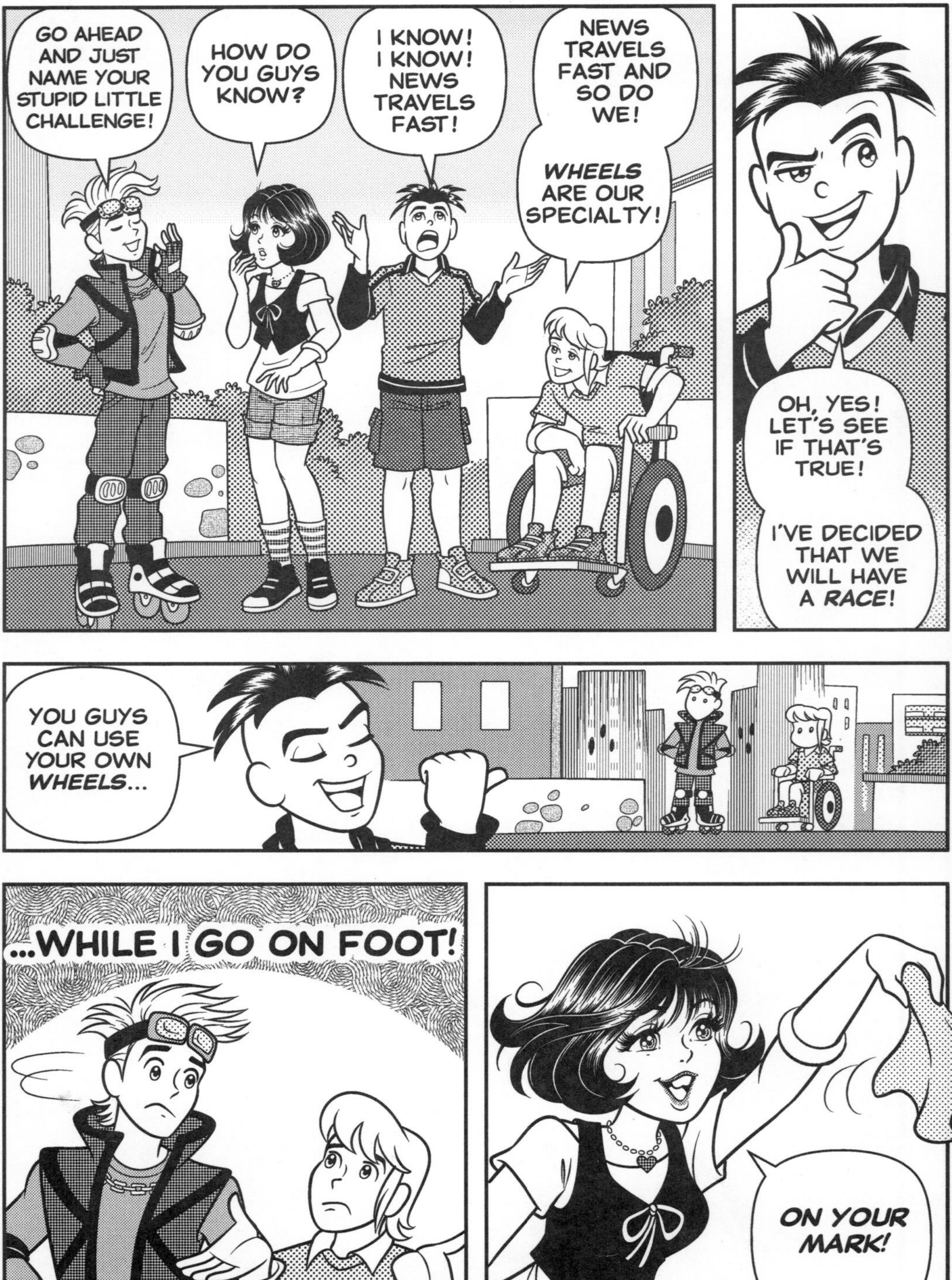
GO AHEAD AND JUST NAME YOUR STUPID LITTLE CHALLENGE!
HOW DO YOU GUYS KNOW?
I KNOW! I KNOW! NEWS TRAVELS FAST!
NEWS TRAVELS FAST AND SO DO WE!
WHEELS ARE OUR SPECIALTY!
OH, YES! LET'S SEE IF THAT'S TRUE!
I'VE DECIDED THAT WE WILL HAVE A *RACE*!
YOU GUYS CAN USE YOUR OWN *WHEELS*...
...WHILE I GO ON FOOT!
ON YOUR MARK!

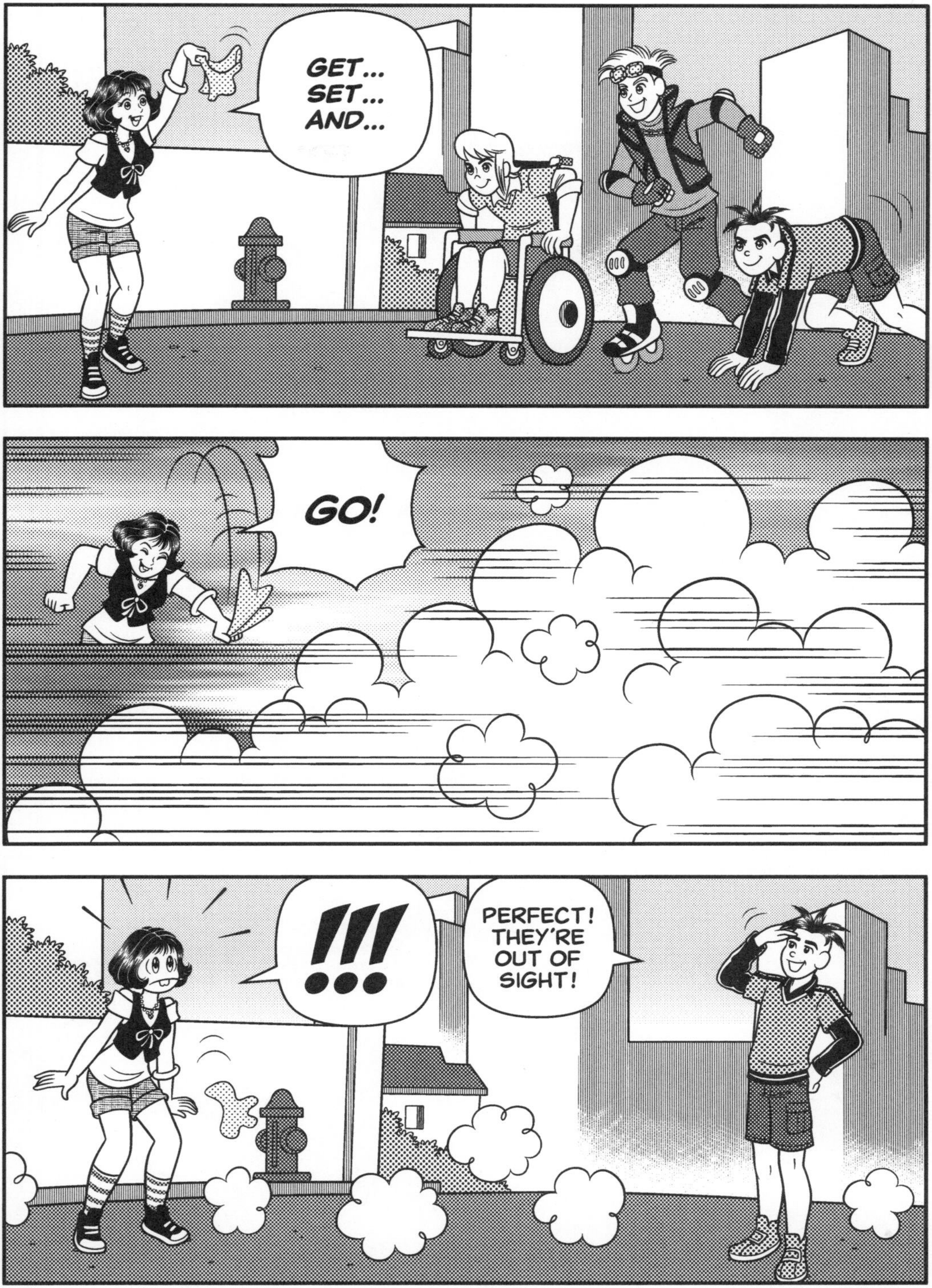
GET... SET... AND...
GO!
!!!
PERFECT! THEY'RE OUT OF SIGHT!

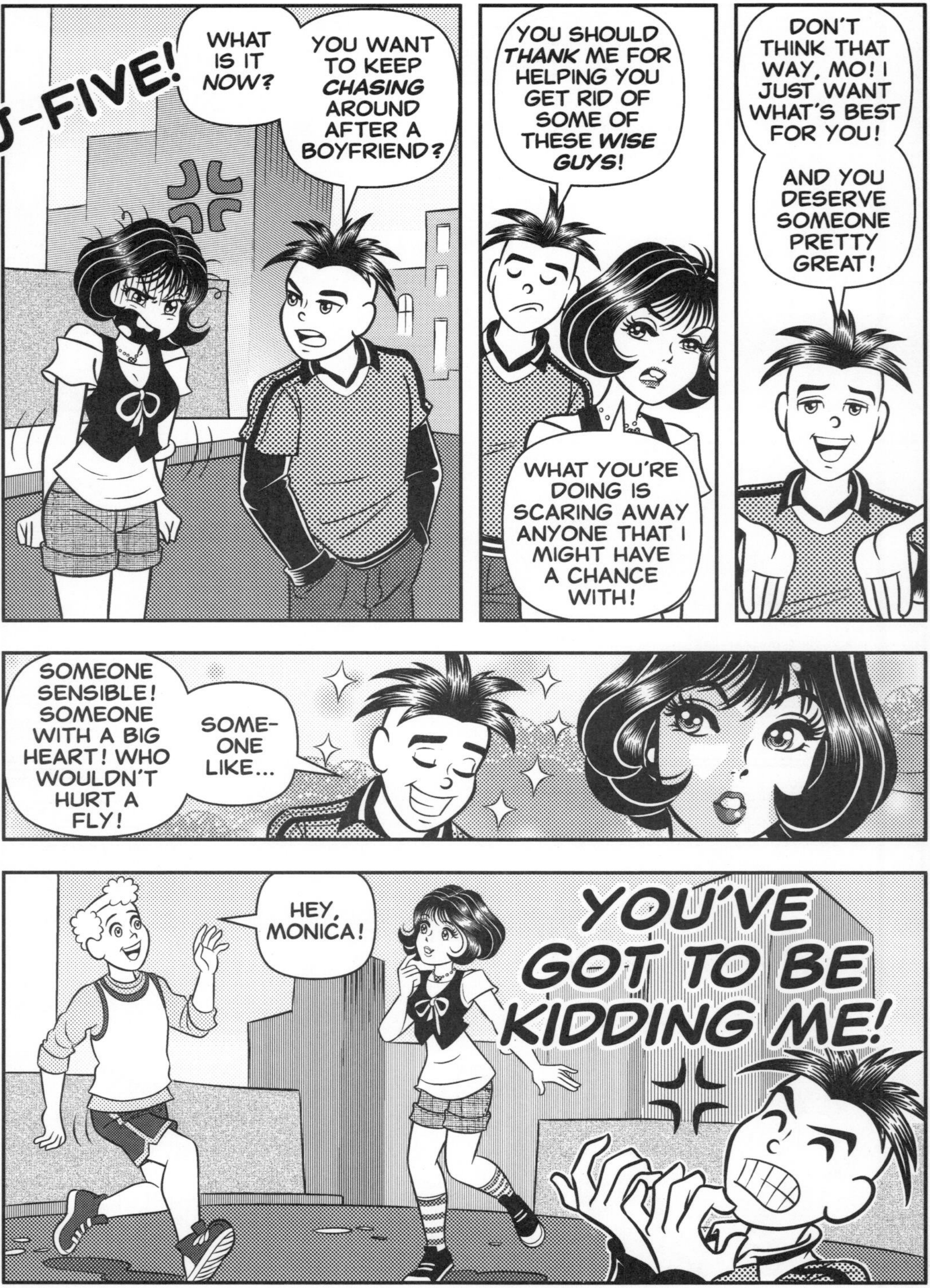
J-FIVE!
WHAT IS IT NOW?
YOU WANT TO KEEP CHASING AROUND AFTER A BOYFRIEND?
YOU SHOULD THANK ME FOR HELPING YOU GET RID OF SOME OF THESE WISE GUYS!
WHAT YOU'RE DOING IS SCARING AWAY ANYONE THAT I MIGHT HAVE A CHANCE WITH!
DON'T THINK THAT WAY, MO! I JUST WANT WHAT'S BEST FOR YOU!
AND YOU DESERVE SOMEONE PRETTY GREAT!
SOMEONE SENSIBLE! SOMEONE WITH A BIG HEART! WHO WOULDN'T HURT A FLY!
SOME-ONE LIKE...
HEY, MONICA!
YOU'VE GOT TO BE KIDDING ME!

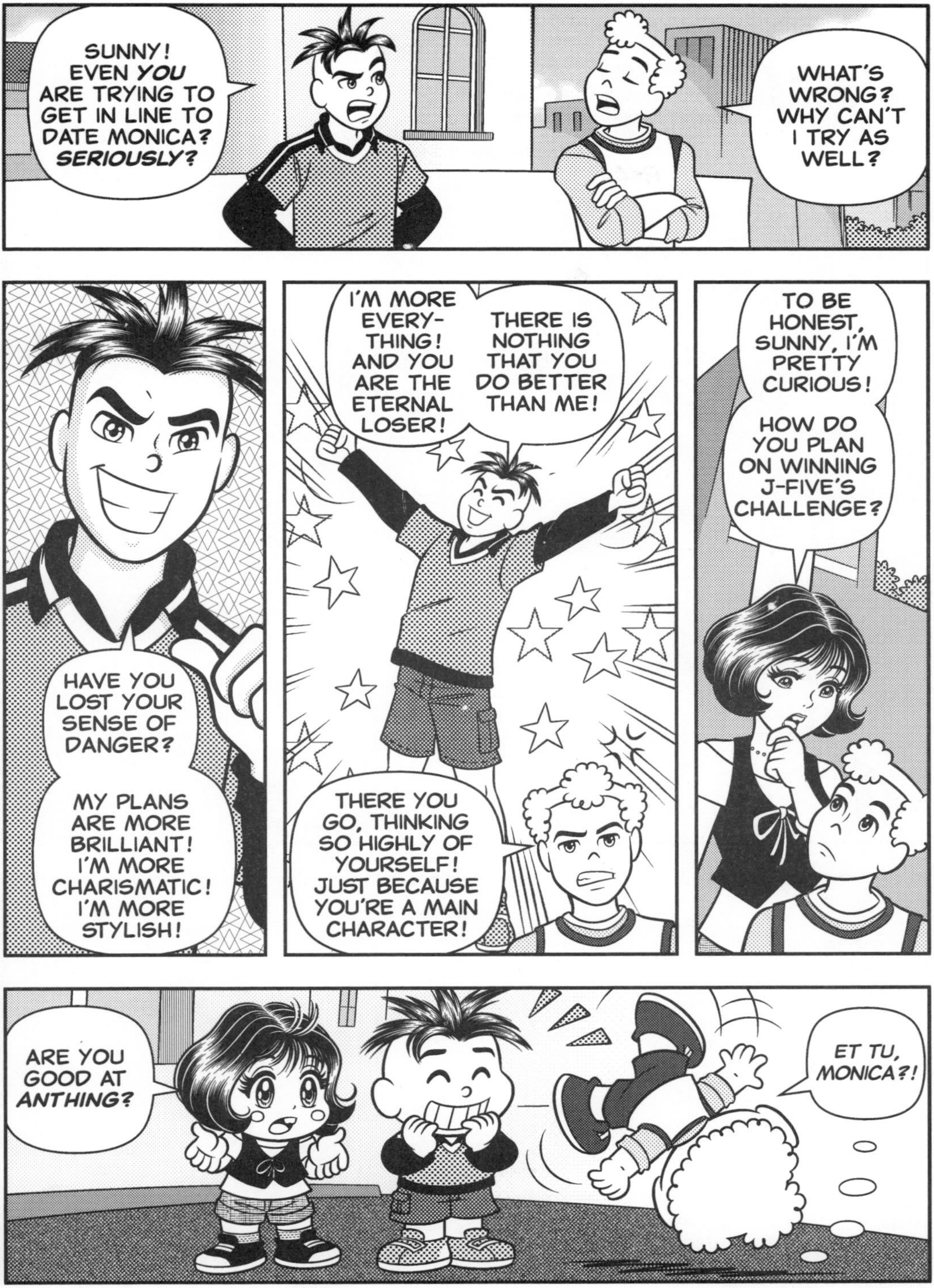

SUNNY! EVEN *YOU* ARE TRYING TO GET IN LINE TO DATE MONICA? ***SERIOUSLY?***
WHAT'S WRONG? WHY CAN'T I TRY AS WELL?
HAVE YOU LOST YOUR SENSE OF DANGER?
MY PLANS ARE MORE BRILLIANT! I'M MORE CHARISMATIC! I'M MORE STYLISH!
I'M MORE EVERY-THING! AND YOU ARE THE ETERNAL LOSER!
THERE IS NOTHING THAT YOU DO BETTER THAN ME!
THERE YOU GO, THINKING SO HIGHLY OF YOURSELF! JUST BECAUSE YOU'RE A MAIN CHARACTER!
TO BE HONEST, SUNNY, I'M PRETTY CURIOUS!
HOW DO YOU PLAN ON WINNING J-FIVE'S CHALLENGE?
ARE YOU GOOD AT *ANTHING?*
ET TU, MONICA?!

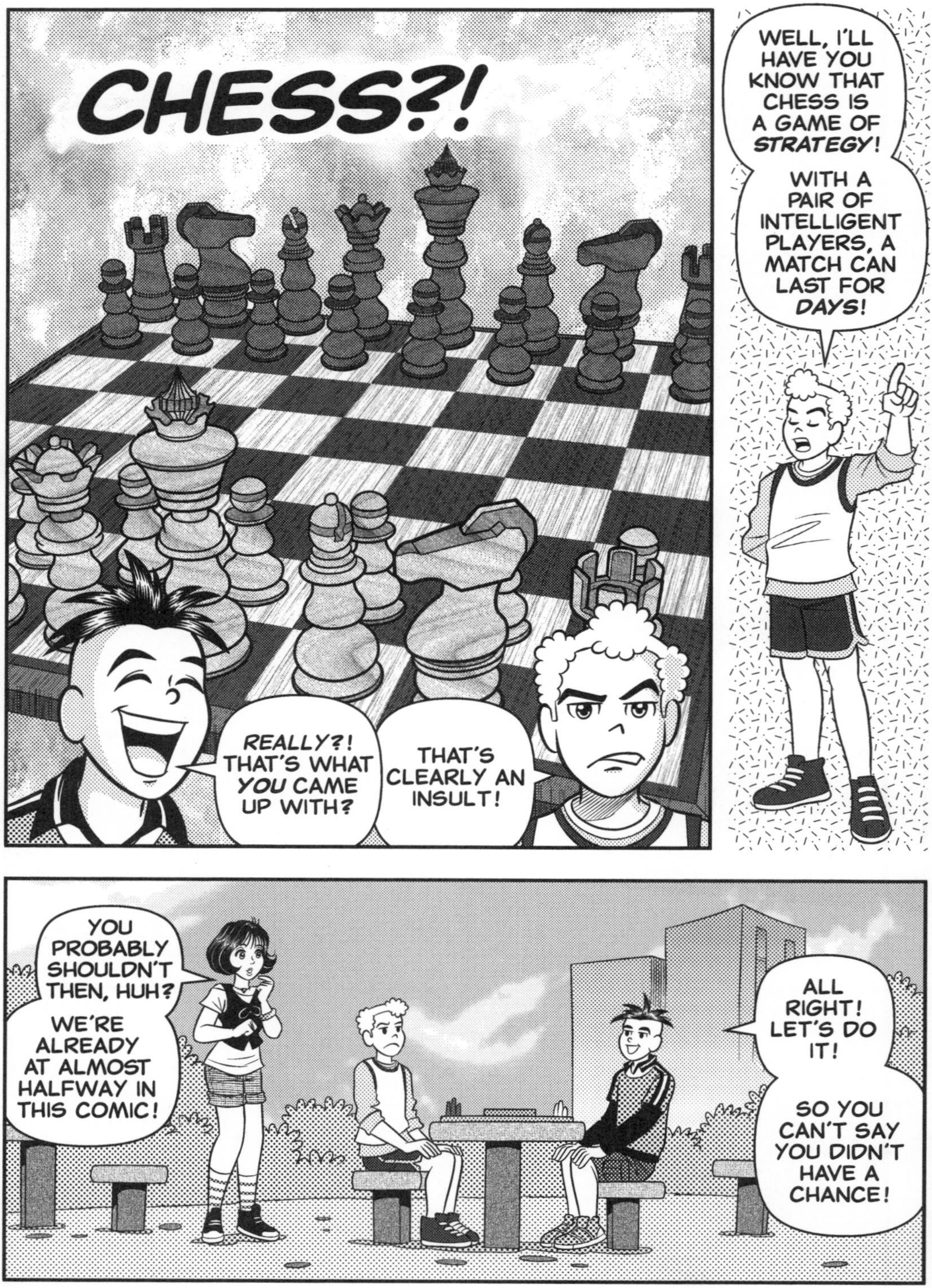
CHESS?!
REALLY?! THAT'S WHAT YOU CAME UP WITH?
THAT'S CLEARLY AN INSULT!
WELL, I'LL HAVE YOU KNOW THAT CHESS IS A GAME OF STRATEGY!
WITH A PAIR OF INTELLIGENT PLAYERS, A MATCH CAN LAST FOR DAYS!
YOU PROBABLY SHOULDN'T THEN, HUH?
WE'RE ALREADY AT ALMOST HALFWAY IN THIS COMIC!
ALL RIGHT! LET'S DO IT!
SO YOU CAN'T SAY YOU DIDN'T HAVE A CHANCE!

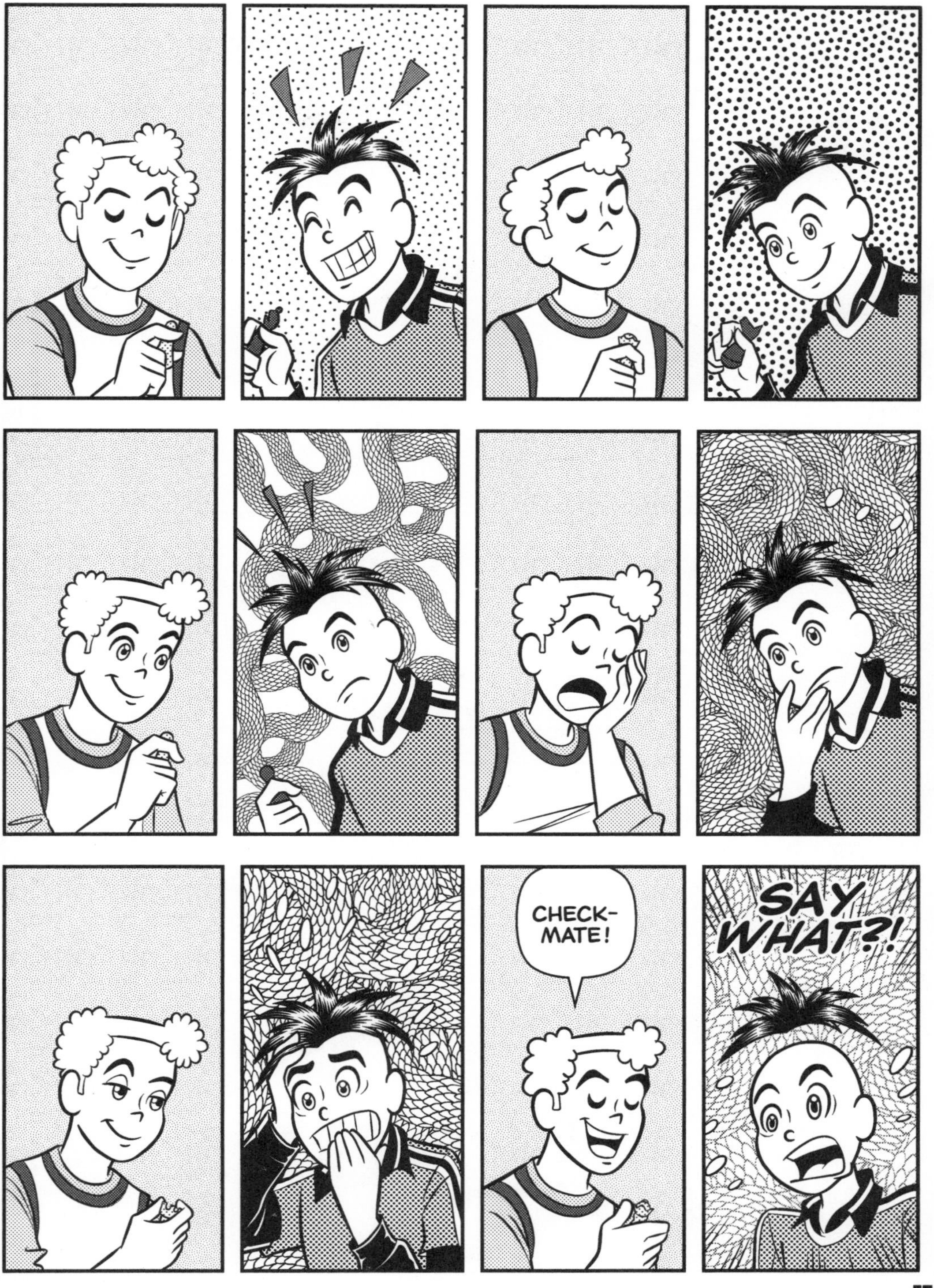
CHECK-MATE!
SAY WHAT?!

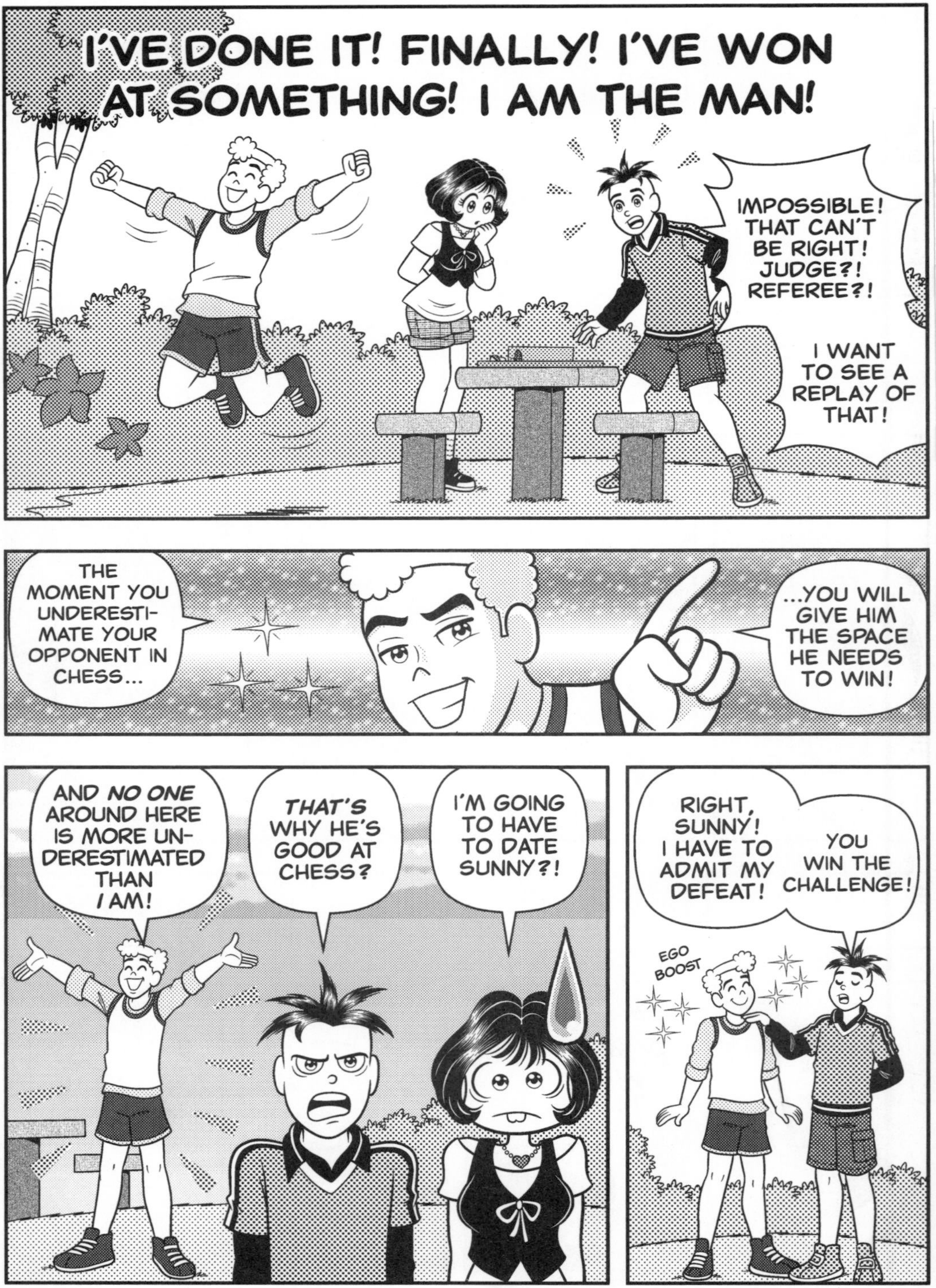

I'VE DONE IT! FINALLY! I'VE WON AT SOMETHING! I AM THE MAN!
IMPOSSIBLE! THAT CAN'T BE RIGHT! JUDGE?! REFEREE?!
I WANT TO SEE A REPLAY OF THAT!
THE MOMENT YOU UNDERESTI-MATE YOUR OPPONENT IN CHESS...
...YOU WILL GIVE HIM THE SPACE HE NEEDS TO WIN!
AND NO ONE AROUND HERE IS MORE UN-DERESTIMATED THAN I AM!
THAT'S WHY HE'S GOOD AT CHESS?
I'M GOING TO HAVE TO DATE SUNNY?!
RIGHT, SUNNY! I HAVE TO ADMIT MY DEFEAT!
YOU WIN THE CHALLENGE!
EGO BOOST

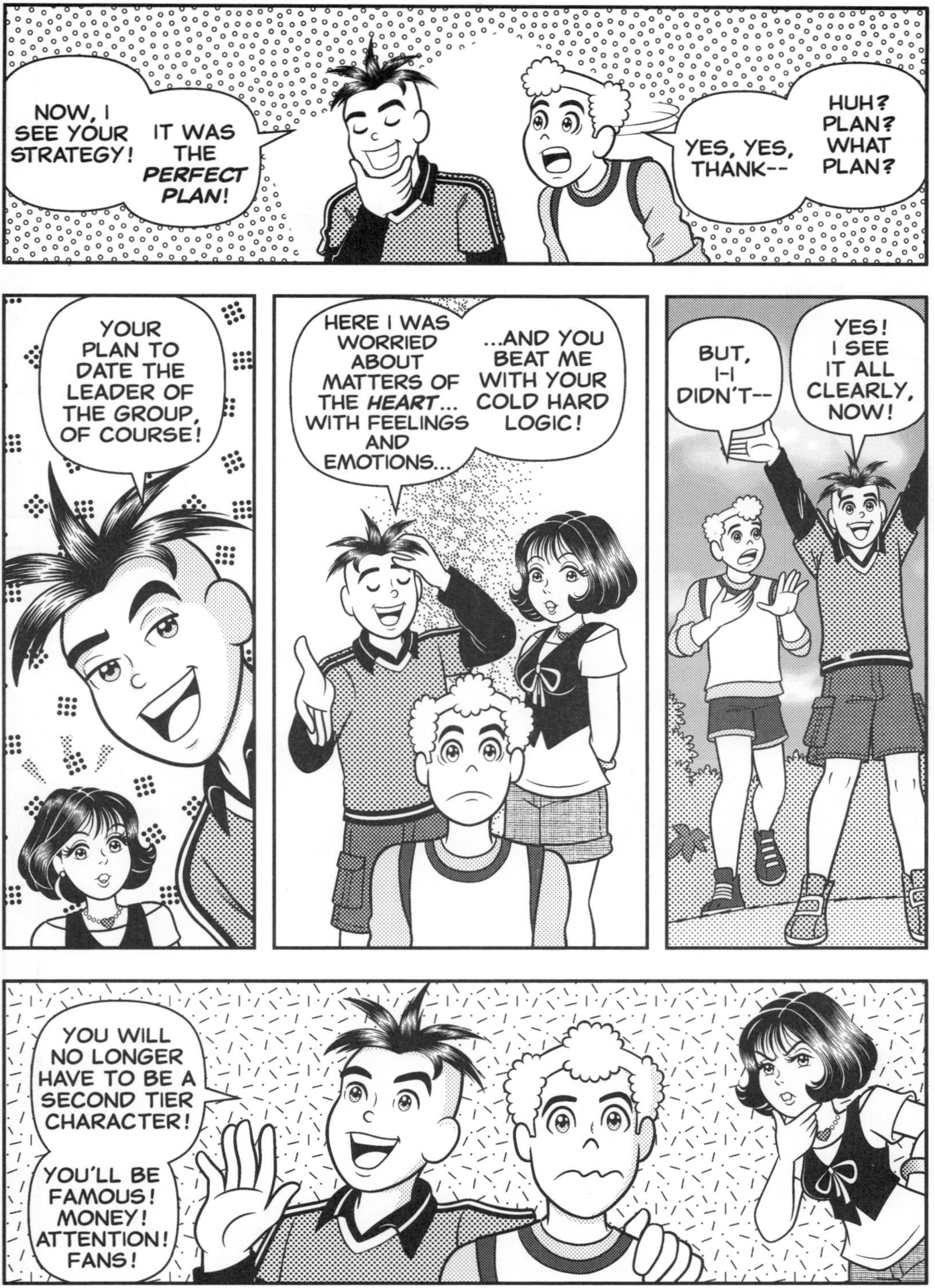
NOW, I SEE YOUR STRATEGY!
IT WAS THE *PERFECT PLAN*!
YES, YES, THANK--
HUH? PLAN? WHAT PLAN?
YOUR PLAN TO DATE THE LEADER OF THE GROUP, OF COURSE!
HERE I WAS WORRIED ABOUT MATTERS OF THE *HEART*... WITH FEELINGS AND EMOTIONS...
...AND YOU BEAT ME WITH YOUR COLD HARD LOGIC!
BUT, I-I DIDN'T--
YES! I SEE IT ALL CLEARLY, NOW!
YOU WILL NO LONGER HAVE TO BE A SECOND TIER CHARACTER!
YOU'LL BE FAMOUS! MONEY! ATTENTION! FANS!

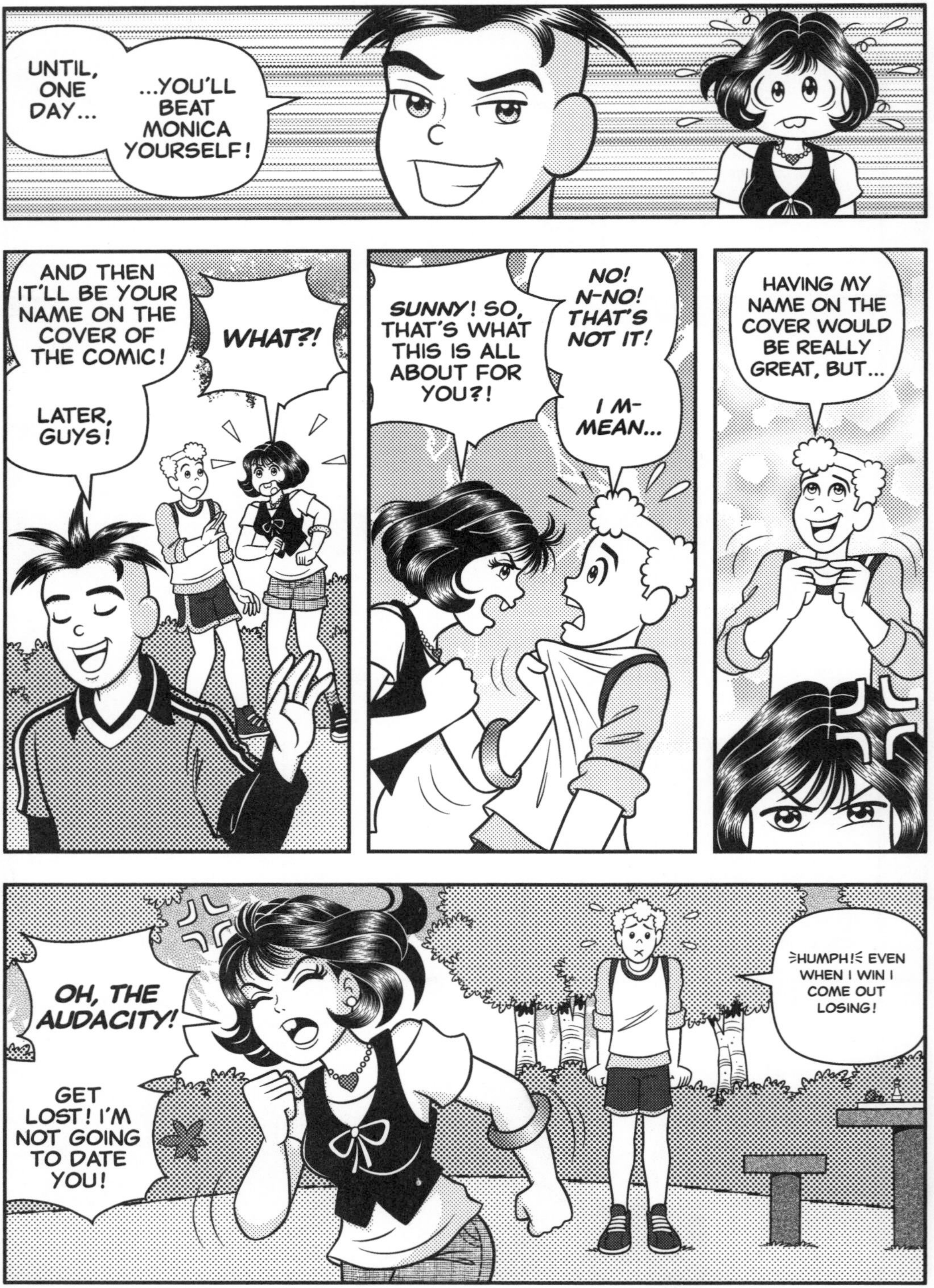
UNTIL, ONE DAY...
...YOU'LL BEAT MONICA YOURSELF!
AND THEN IT'LL BE YOUR NAME ON THE COVER OF THE COMIC!
LATER, GUYS!
WHAT?!
SUNNY! SO, THAT'S WHAT THIS IS ALL ABOUT FOR YOU?!
NO! N-NO! THAT'S NOT IT!
I M-MEAN...
HAVING MY NAME ON THE COVER WOULD BE REALLY GREAT, BUT...
OH, THE AUDACITY!
GET LOST! I'M NOT GOING TO DATE YOU!
HUMPH! EVEN WHEN I WIN I COME OUT LOSING!

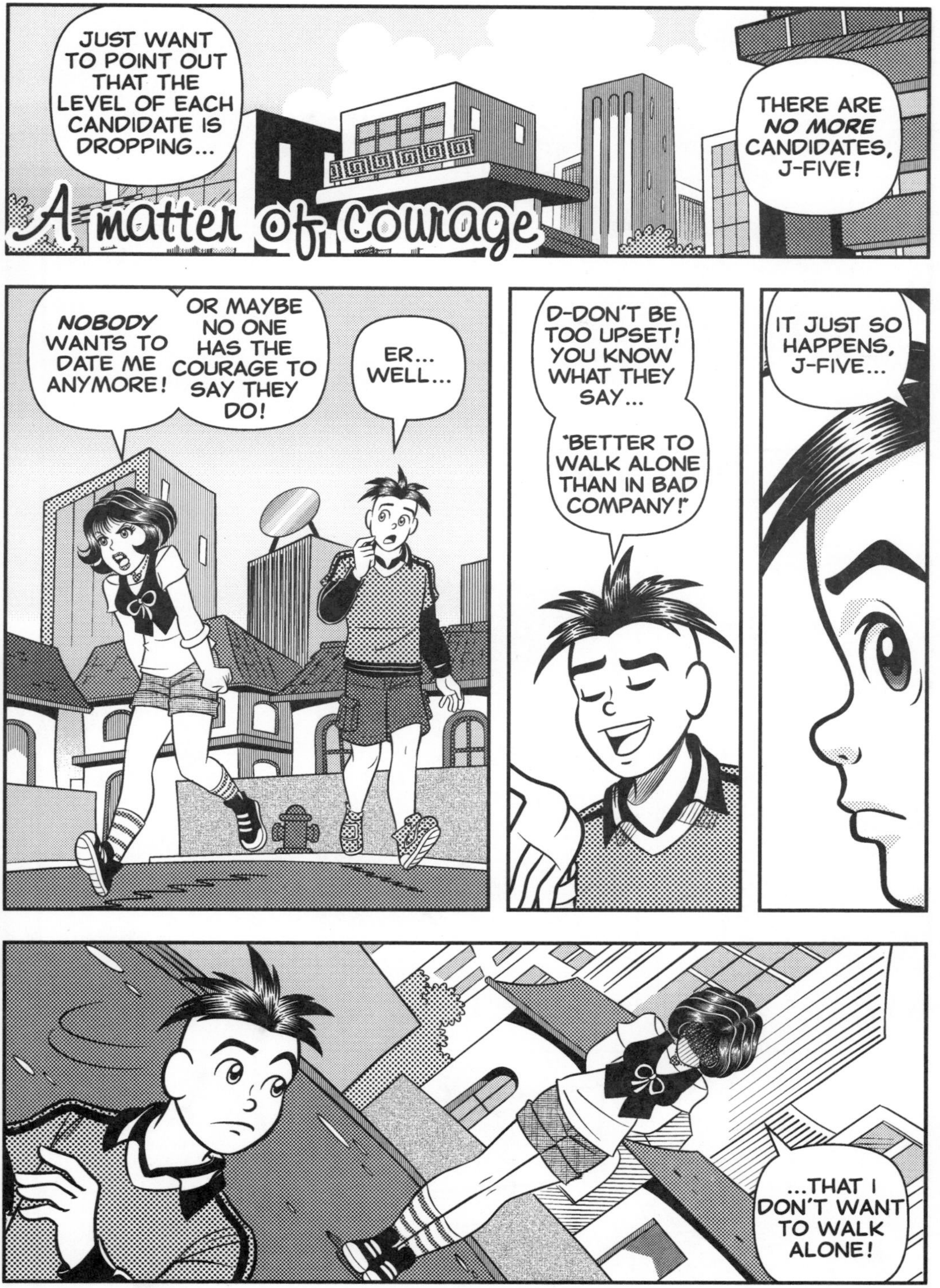
JUST WANT TO POINT OUT THAT THE LEVEL OF EACH CANDIDATE IS DROPPING...
THERE ARE NO MORE CANDIDATES, J-FIVE!
A matter of courage
NOBODY WANTS TO DATE ME ANYMORE!
OR MAYBE NO ONE HAS THE COURAGE TO SAY THEY DO!
ER... WELL...
D-DON'T BE TOO UPSET! YOU KNOW WHAT THEY SAY...
"BETTER TO WALK ALONE THAN IN BAD COMPANY!"
IT JUST SO HAPPENS, J-FIVE...
...THAT I DON'T WANT TO WALK ALONE!

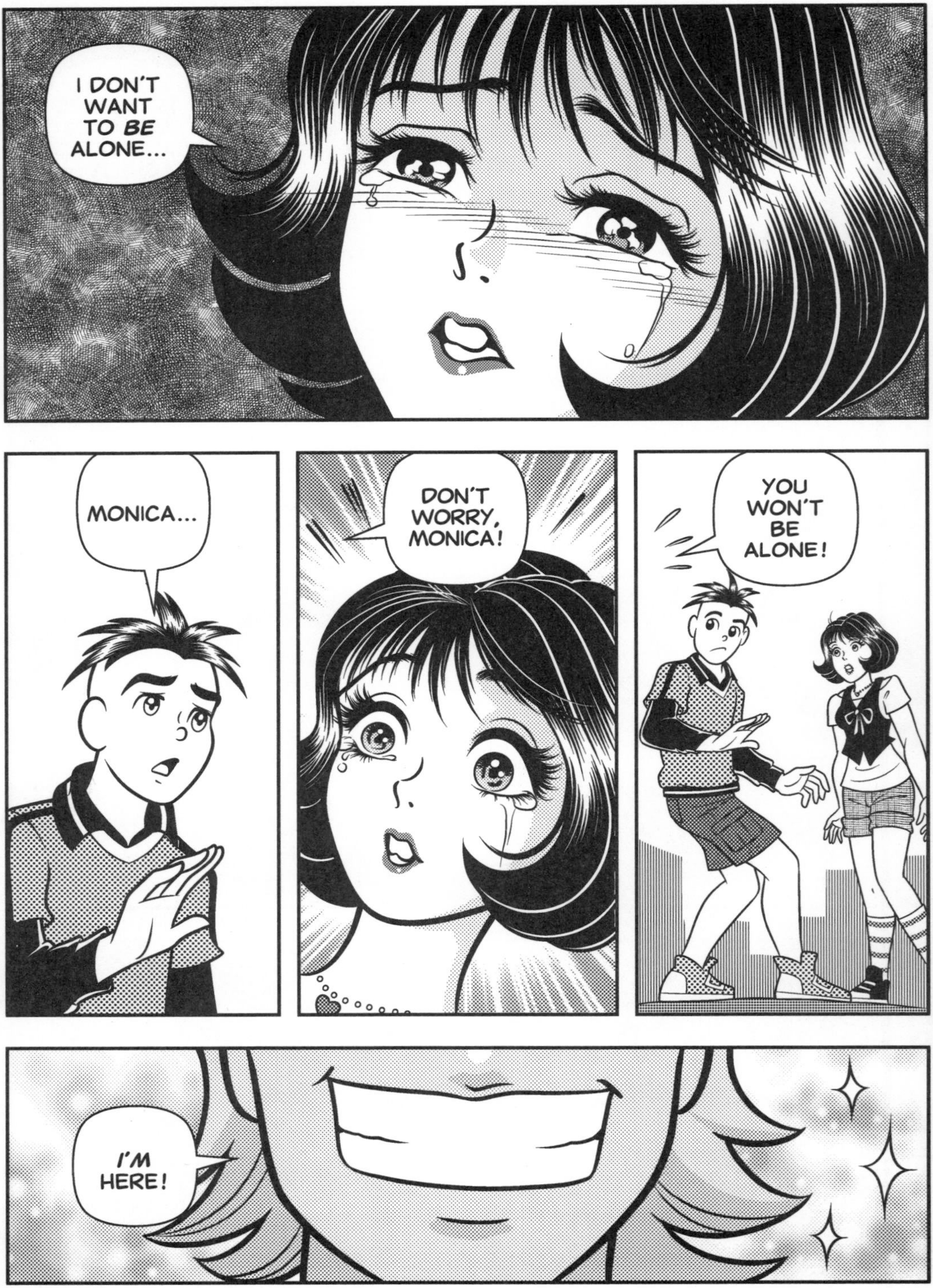
I DON'T WANT TO *BE* ALONE...
MONICA...
DON'T WORRY, MONICA!
YOU WON'T BE ALONE!
I'M HERE!

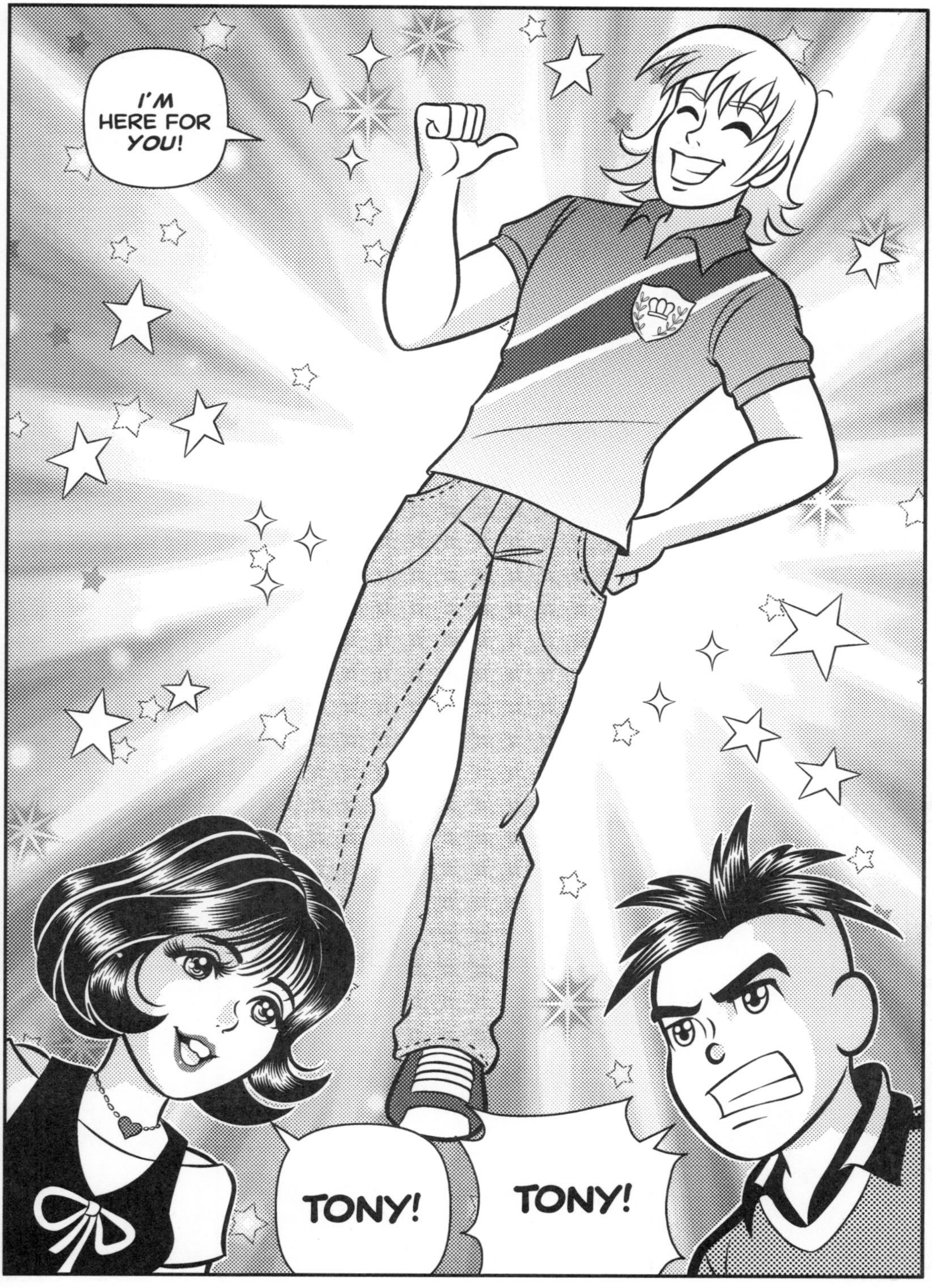
I'M HERE FOR YOU!
TONY!
TONY!

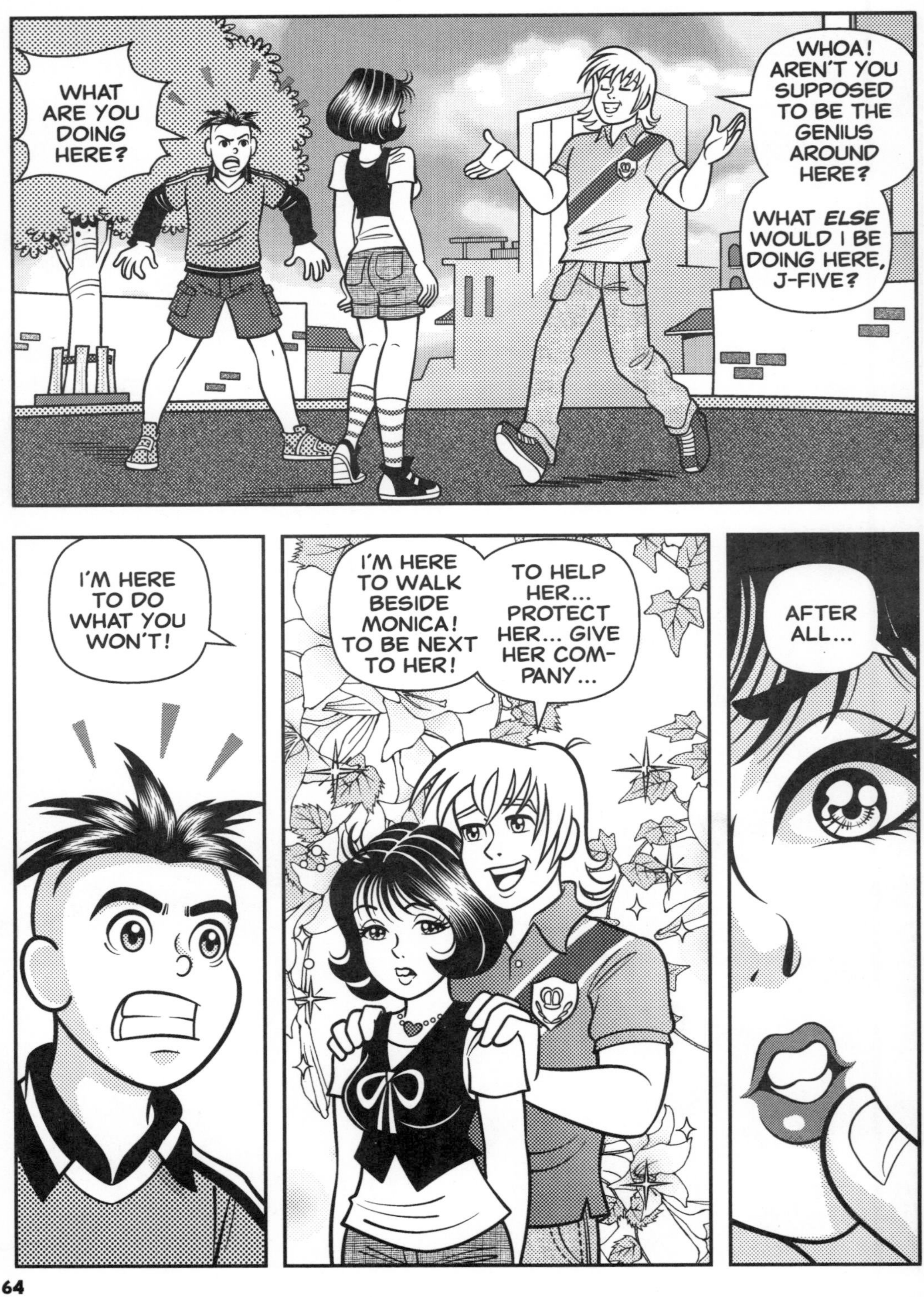
WHAT ARE YOU DOING HERE?
WHOA! AREN'T YOU SUPPOSED TO BE THE GENIUS AROUND HERE?
WHAT *ELSE* WOULD I BE DOING HERE, J-FIVE?
I'M HERE TO DO WHAT YOU WON'T!
I'M HERE TO WALK BESIDE MONICA! TO BE NEXT TO HER!
TO HELP HER... PROTECT HER... GIVE HER COM-PANY...
AFTER ALL...

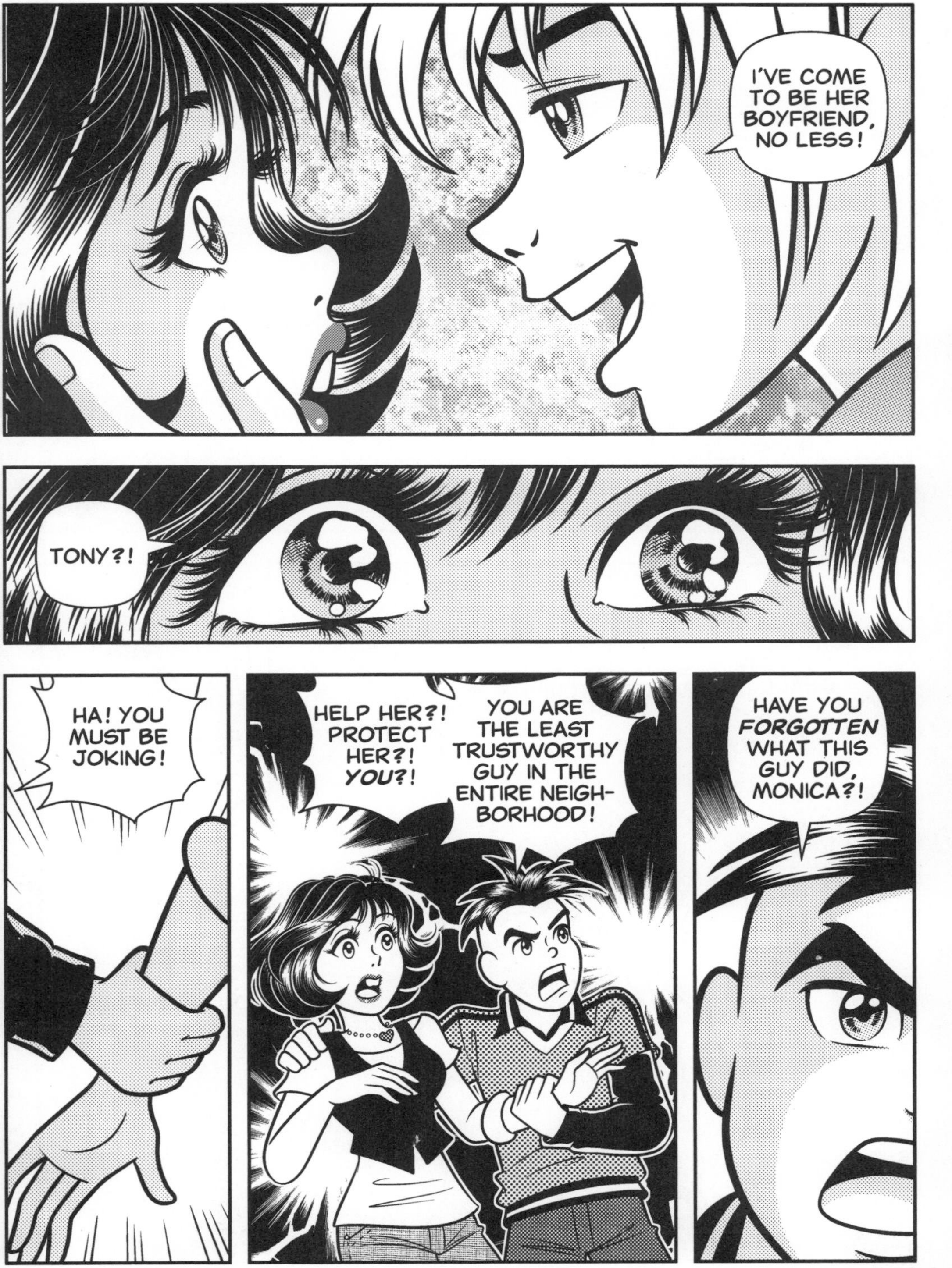
I'VE COME TO BE HER BOYFRIEND, NO LESS!
TONY?!
HA! YOU MUST BE JOKING!
HELP HER?! PROTECT HER?! *YOU*?!
YOU ARE THE LEAST TRUSTWORTHY GUY IN THE ENTIRE NEIGH-BORHOOD!
HAVE YOU *FORGOTTEN* WHAT THIS GUY DID, MONICA?!

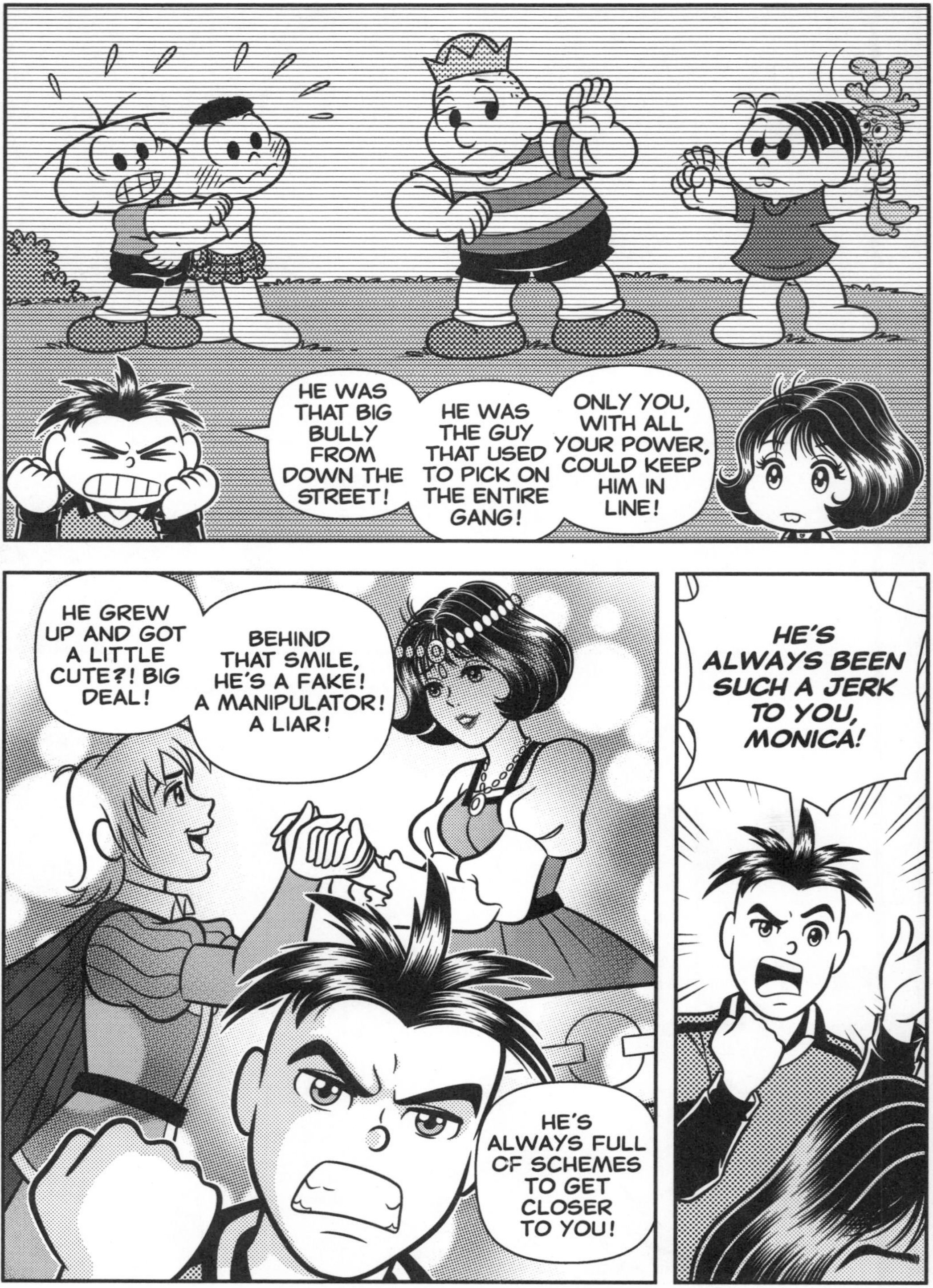
HE WAS THAT BIG BULLY FROM DOWN THE STREET!
HE WAS THE GUY THAT USED TO PICK ON THE ENTIRE GANG!
ONLY YOU, WITH ALL YOUR POWER, COULD KEEP HIM IN LINE!
HE GREW UP AND GOT A LITTLE CUTE?! BIG DEAL!
BEHIND THAT SMILE, HE'S A FAKE! A MANIPULATOR! A LIAR!
HE'S ALWAYS FULL OF SCHEMES TO GET CLOSER TO YOU!
HE'S ALWAYS BEEN SUCH A JERK TO YOU, MONICA!

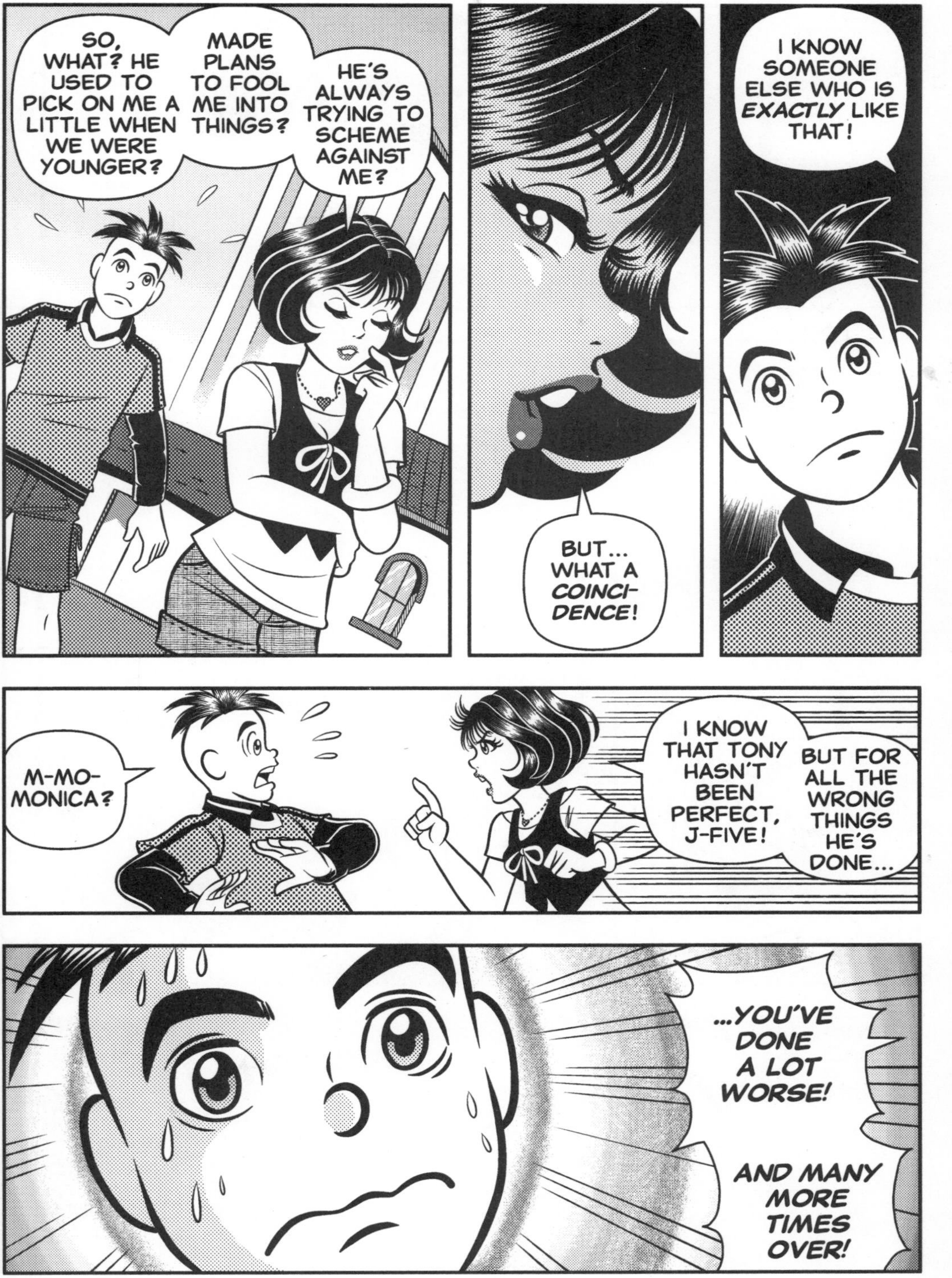
SO, WHAT? HE USED TO PICK ON ME A LITTLE WHEN WE WERE YOUNGER?
MADE PLANS TO FOOL ME INTO THINGS?
HE'S ALWAYS TRYING TO SCHEME AGAINST ME?
BUT... WHAT A *COINCIDENCE*!
I KNOW SOMEONE ELSE WHO IS *EXACTLY* LIKE THAT!
M-MO-MONICA?
I KNOW THAT TONY HASN'T BEEN PERFECT, J-FIVE!
BUT FOR ALL THE WRONG THINGS HE'S DONE...
...YOU'VE DONE A LOT WORSE!
AND MANY MORE TIMES OVER!

I *KNOW VERY WELL* TONY'S FAULTS...

...BECAUSE THEY ARE JUST LIKE YOURS!

BUT, THERE *IS* A GREAT DIFFERENCE BETWEEN THE TWO OF YOU!

TONY HAS THE *COURAGE* TO TAKE RISKS!

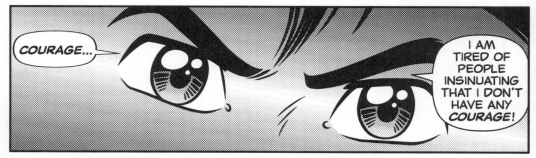

COURAGE...

I AM TIRED OF PEOPLE INSINUATING THAT I DON'T HAVE ANY *COURAGE!*

YOU'RE MISTAKEN, MONICA!

THERE IS *ANOTHER* DIFFERENCE BETWEEN THE TWO OF US!

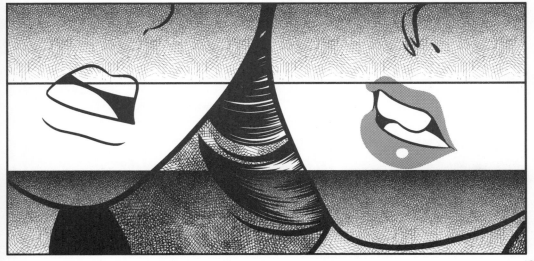

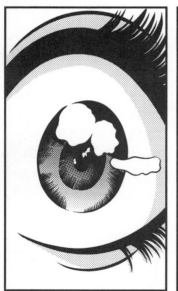

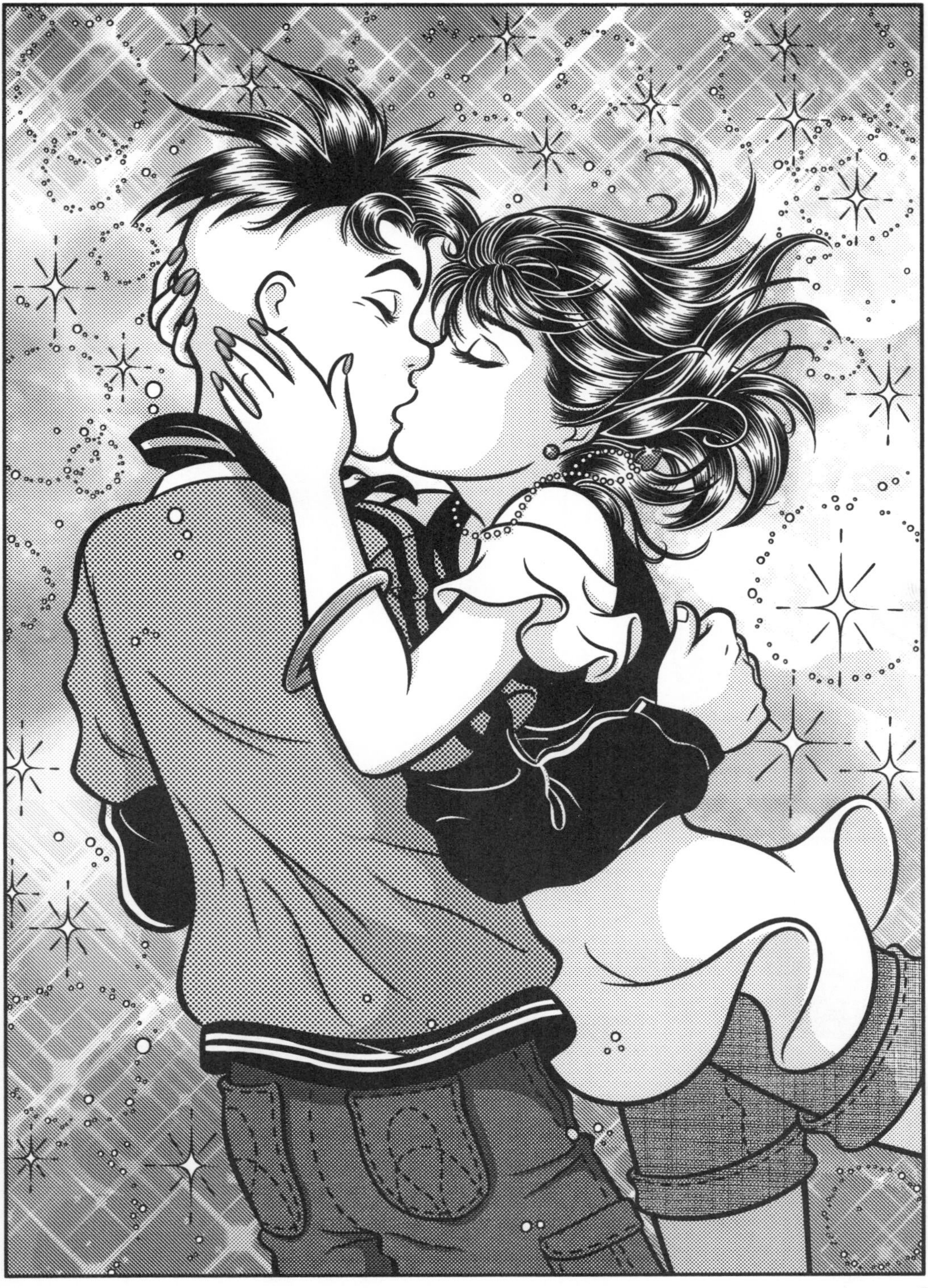

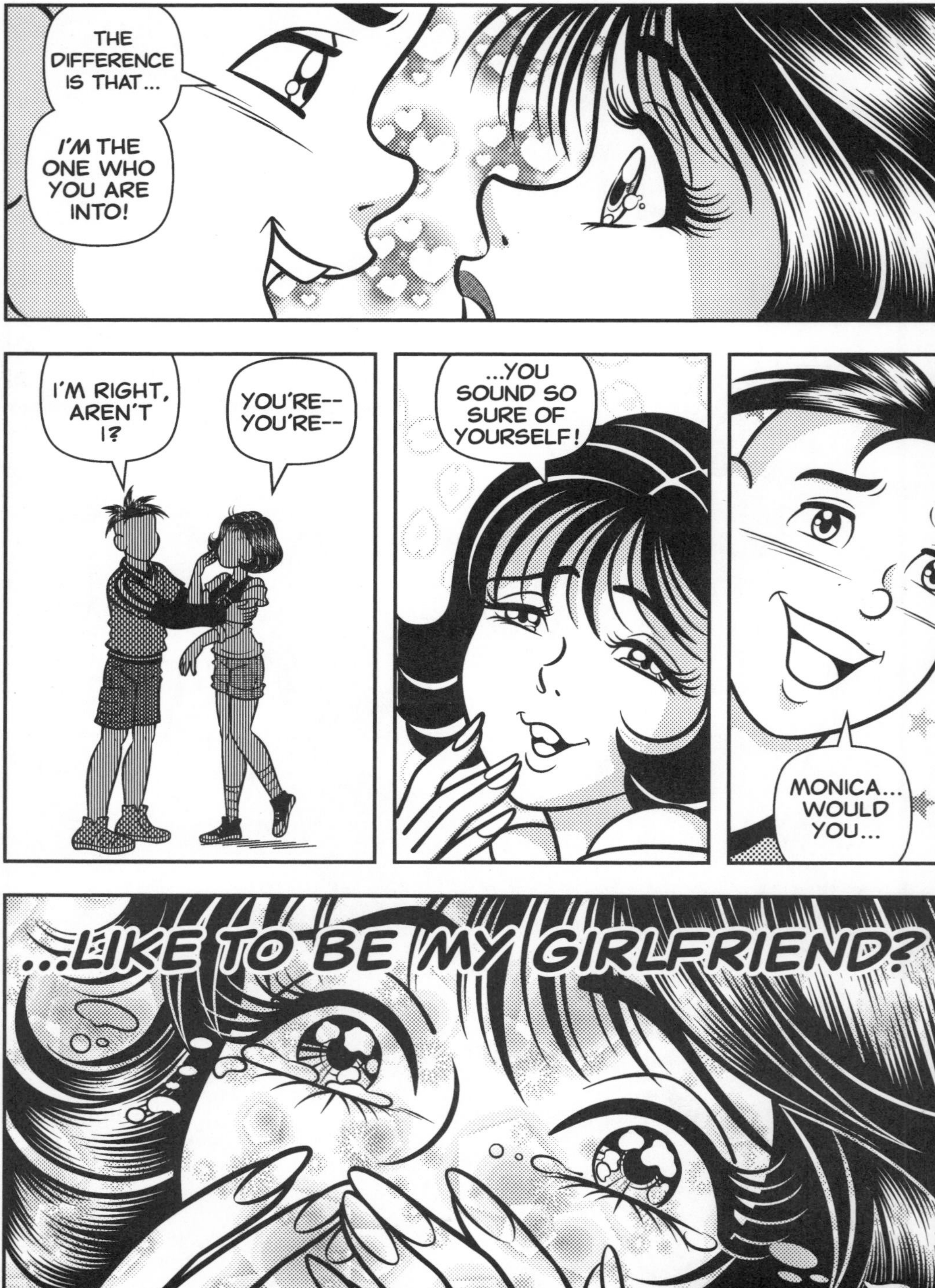
THE DIFFERENCE IS THAT...
I'M THE ONE WHO YOU ARE INTO!
I'M RIGHT, AREN'T I?
YOU'RE-- YOU'RE--
...YOU SOUND SO SURE OF YOURSELF!
MONICA... WOULD YOU...
...LIKE TO BE MY GIRLFRIEND?

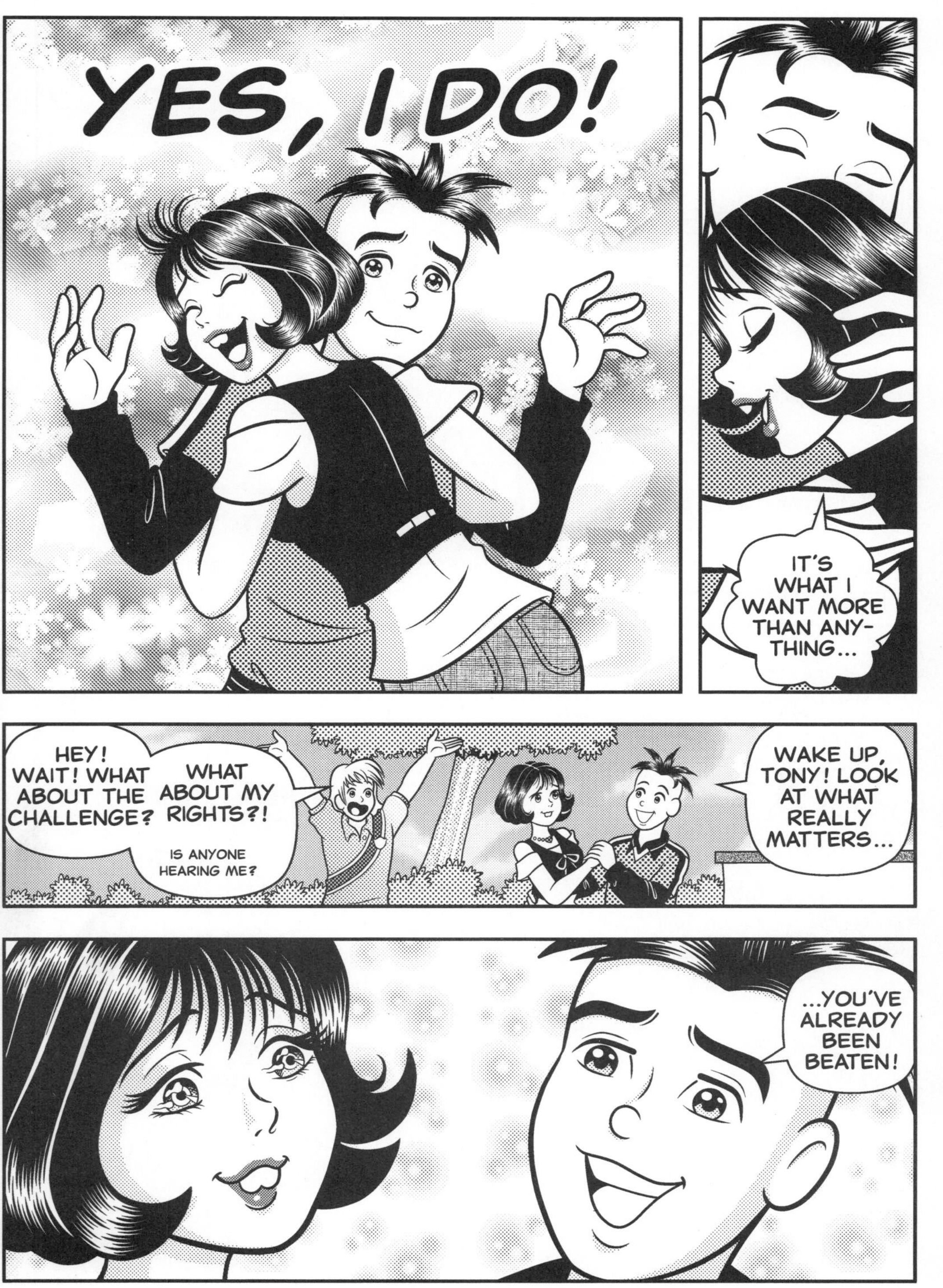
YES, I DO!
IT'S WHAT I WANT MORE THAN ANY-THING...
HEY! WAIT! WHAT ABOUT THE CHALLENGE?
WHAT ABOUT MY RIGHTS?!
IS ANYONE HEARING ME?
WAKE UP, TONY! LOOK AT WHAT REALLY MATTERS...
...YOU'VE ALREADY BEEN BEATEN!

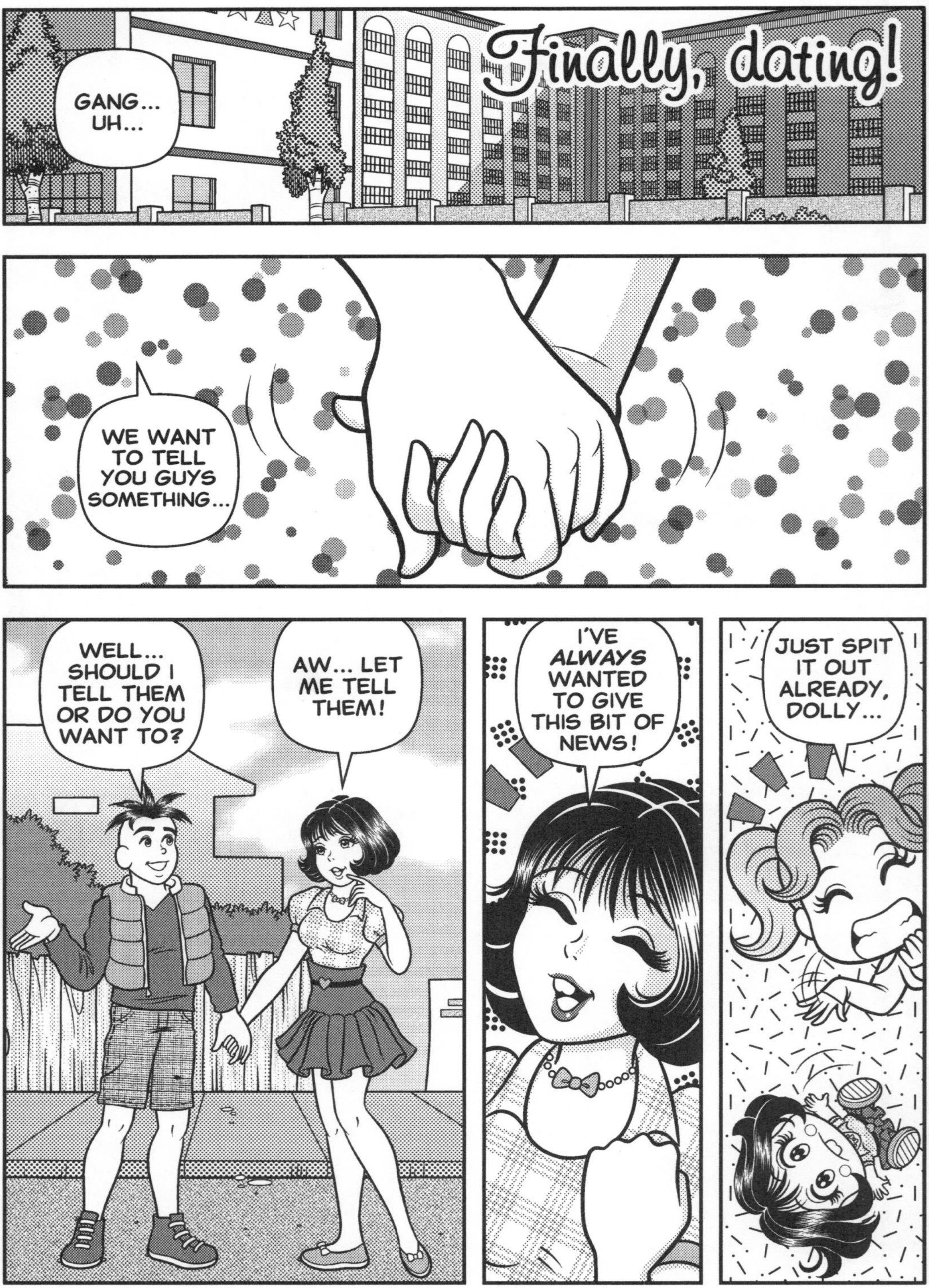
Finally, dating!
GANG... UH...
WE WANT TO TELL YOU GUYS SOMETHING...
WELL... SHOULD I TELL THEM OR DO YOU WANT TO?
AW... LET ME TELL THEM!
I'VE *ALWAYS* WANTED TO GIVE THIS BIT OF NEWS!
JUST SPIT IT OUT ALREADY, DOLLY...

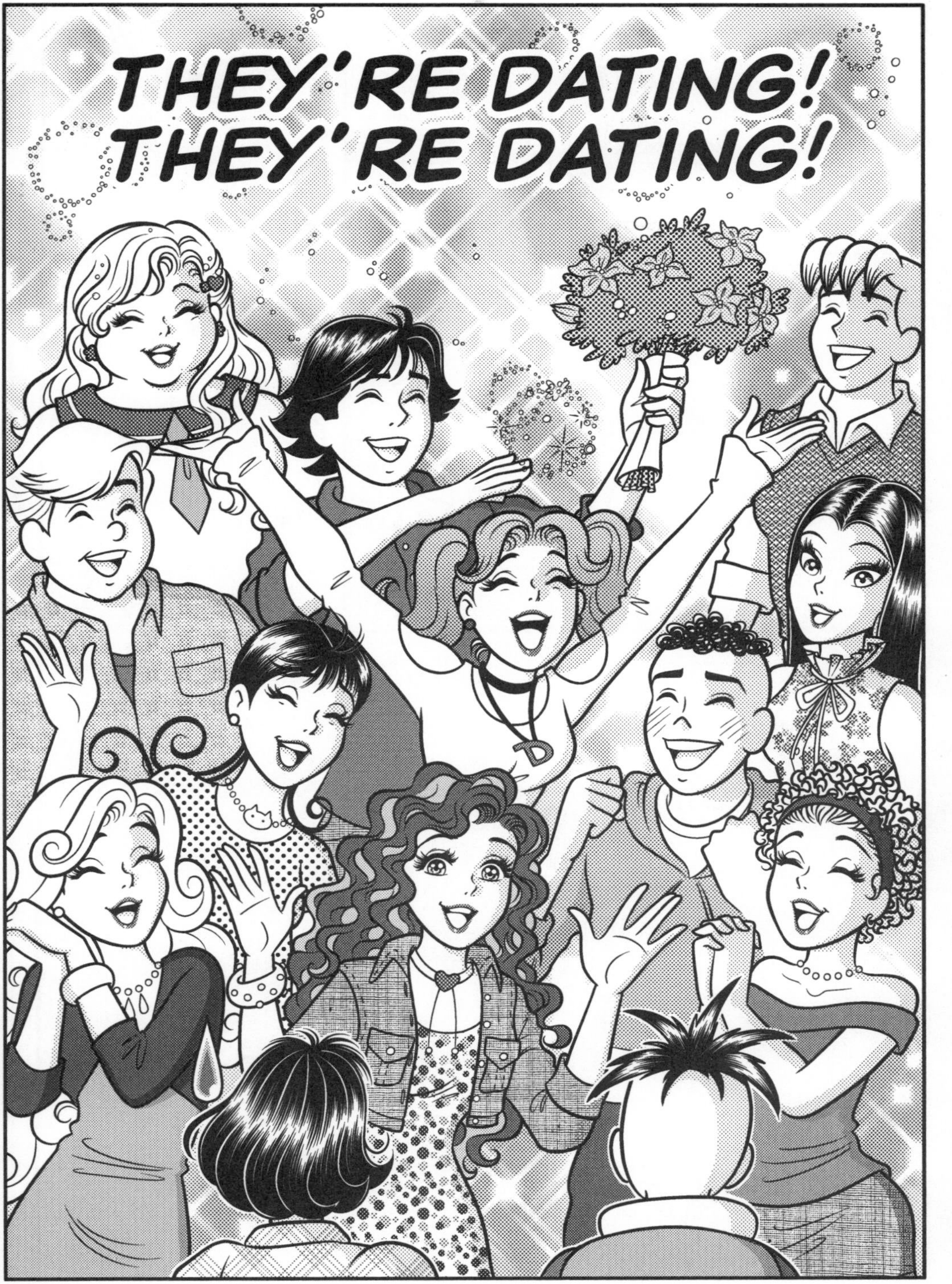
THEY'RE DATING! THEY'RE DATING!

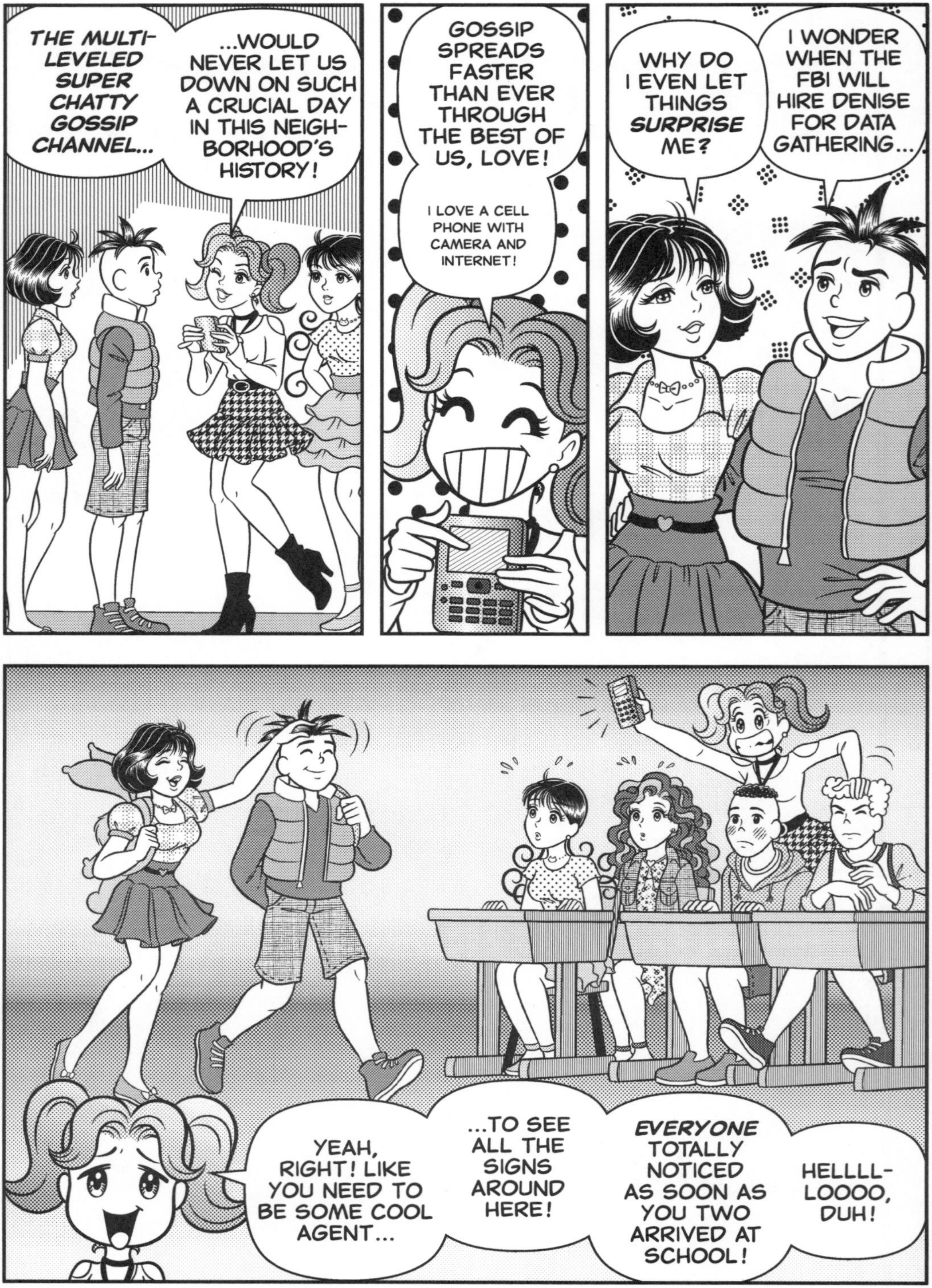
THE MULTI-LEVELED SUPER CHATTY GOSSIP CHANNEL...
...WOULD NEVER LET US DOWN ON SUCH A CRUCIAL DAY IN THIS NEIGHBORHOOD'S HISTORY!
GOSSIP SPREADS FASTER THAN EVER THROUGH THE BEST OF US, LOVE!
I LOVE A CELL PHONE WITH CAMERA AND INTERNET!
WHY DO I EVEN LET THINGS *SURPRISE* ME?
I WONDER WHEN THE FBI WILL HIRE DENISE FOR DATA GATHERING...
YEAH, RIGHT! LIKE YOU NEED TO BE SOME COOL AGENT...
...TO SEE ALL THE SIGNS AROUND HERE!
EVERYONE TOTALLY NOTICED AS SOON AS YOU TWO ARRIVED AT SCHOOL!
HELLLL-LOOOO, DUH!

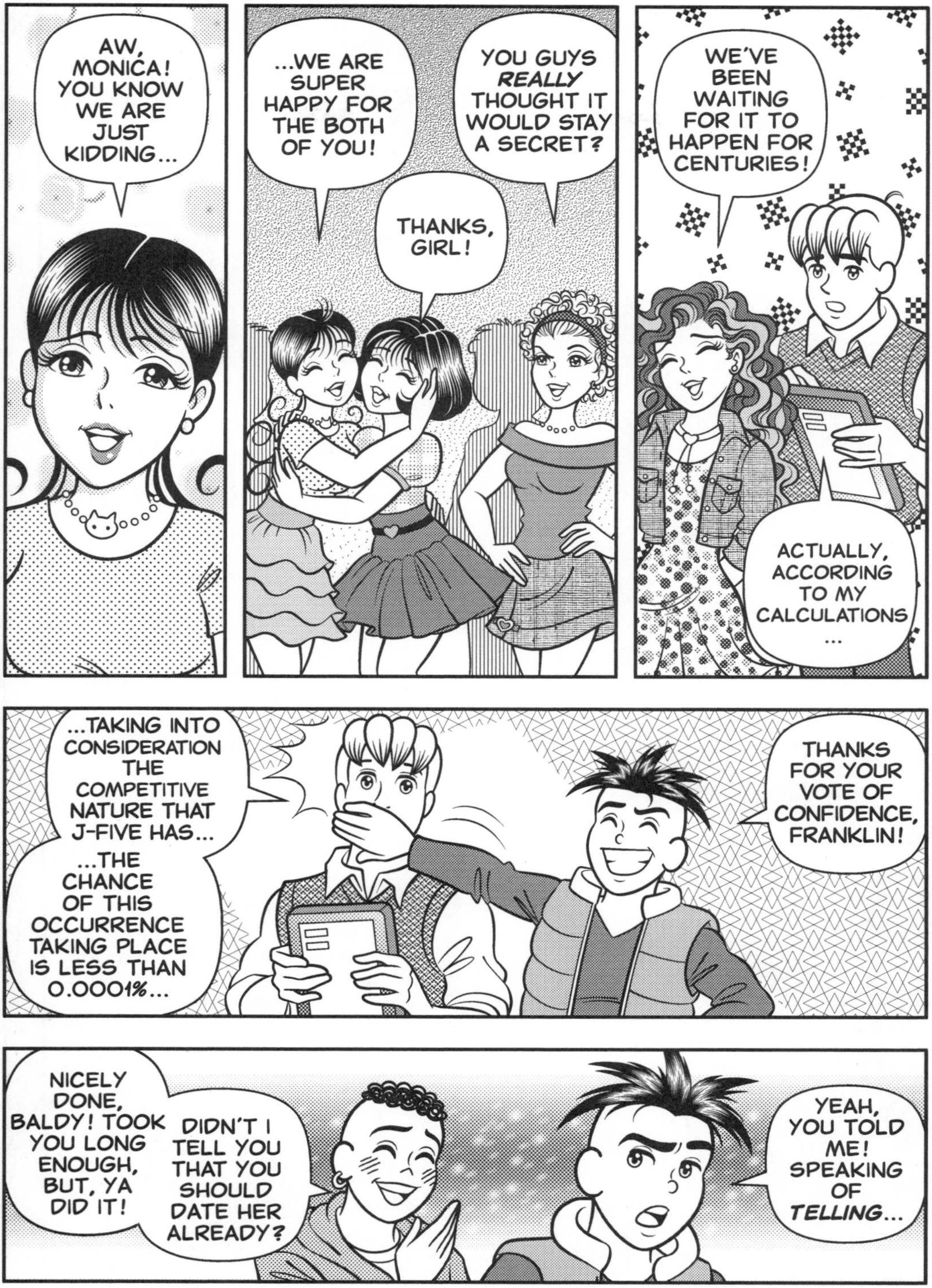
AW, MONICA! YOU KNOW WE ARE JUST KIDDING...
...WE ARE SUPER HAPPY FOR THE BOTH OF YOU!
YOU GUYS *REALLY* THOUGHT IT WOULD STAY A SECRET?
THANKS, GIRL!
WE'VE BEEN WAITING FOR IT TO HAPPEN FOR CENTURIES!
ACTUALLY, ACCORDING TO MY CALCULATIONS ...
...TAKING INTO CONSIDERATION THE COMPETITIVE NATURE THAT J-FIVE HAS...
...THE CHANCE OF THIS OCCURRENCE TAKING PLACE IS LESS THAN 0.0001%...
THANKS FOR YOUR VOTE OF CONFIDENCE, FRANKLIN!
NICELY DONE, BALDY! TOOK YOU LONG ENOUGH, BUT, YA DID IT!
DIDN'T I TELL YOU THAT YOU SHOULD DATE HER ALREADY?
YEAH, YOU TOLD ME! SPEAKING OF *TELLING*...

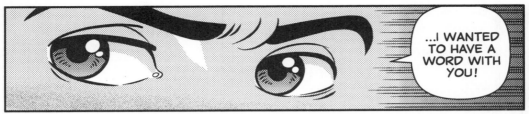

...I WANTED TO HAVE A WORD WITH YOU!

YOU REMEMBER THAT *VERY PERSONAL* CONVERSATION I HAD WITH YOU?

WITH *JUST YOU?*

WELL, YOU WOULDN'T BELIEVE IT... BUT THE *NEXT DAY...*

...THE *ENTIRE GANG* KNEW ABOUT IT!

HOW DO YOU THINK SOMETHING LIKE THAT HAPPENED, HUH?

ER... NEWS TRAVELS FAST?

YOU TALK TOO MUCH! EVER SINCE WE WERE CHILDREN!

STILL, THE SAME BIG MOUTH!

SOME THINGS WILL NEVER EVER CHANGE...

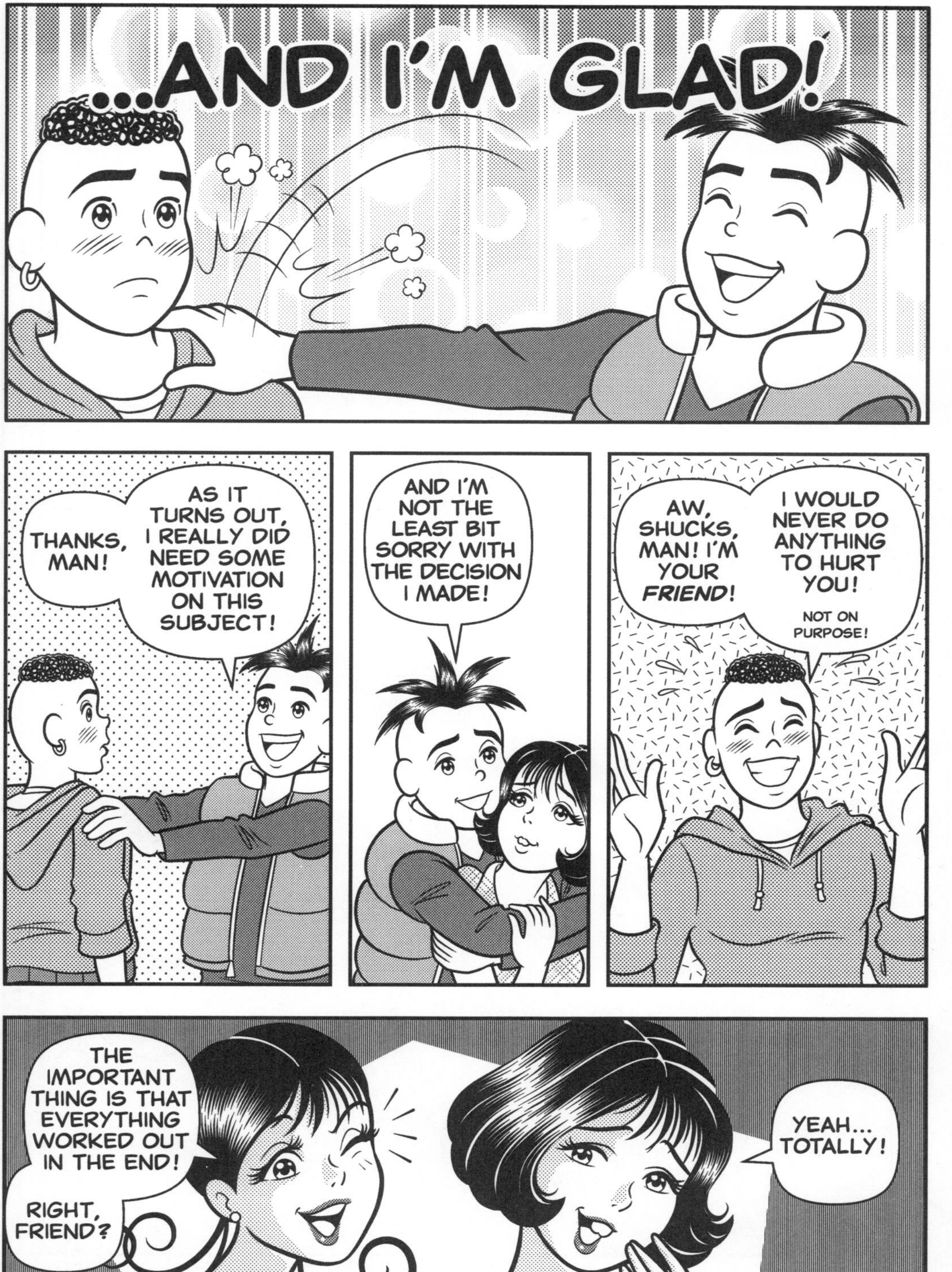
...AND I'M GLAD!
THANKS, MAN!
AS IT TURNS OUT, I REALLY DID NEED SOME MOTIVATION ON THIS SUBJECT!
AND I'M NOT THE LEAST BIT SORRY WITH THE DECISION I MADE!
AW, SHUCKS, MAN! I'M YOUR *FRIEND*!
I WOULD NEVER DO ANYTHING TO HURT YOU!
NOT ON PURPOSE!
THE IMPORTANT THING IS THAT EVERYTHING WORKED OUT IN THE END!
RIGHT, FRIEND?
YEAH... TOTALLY!

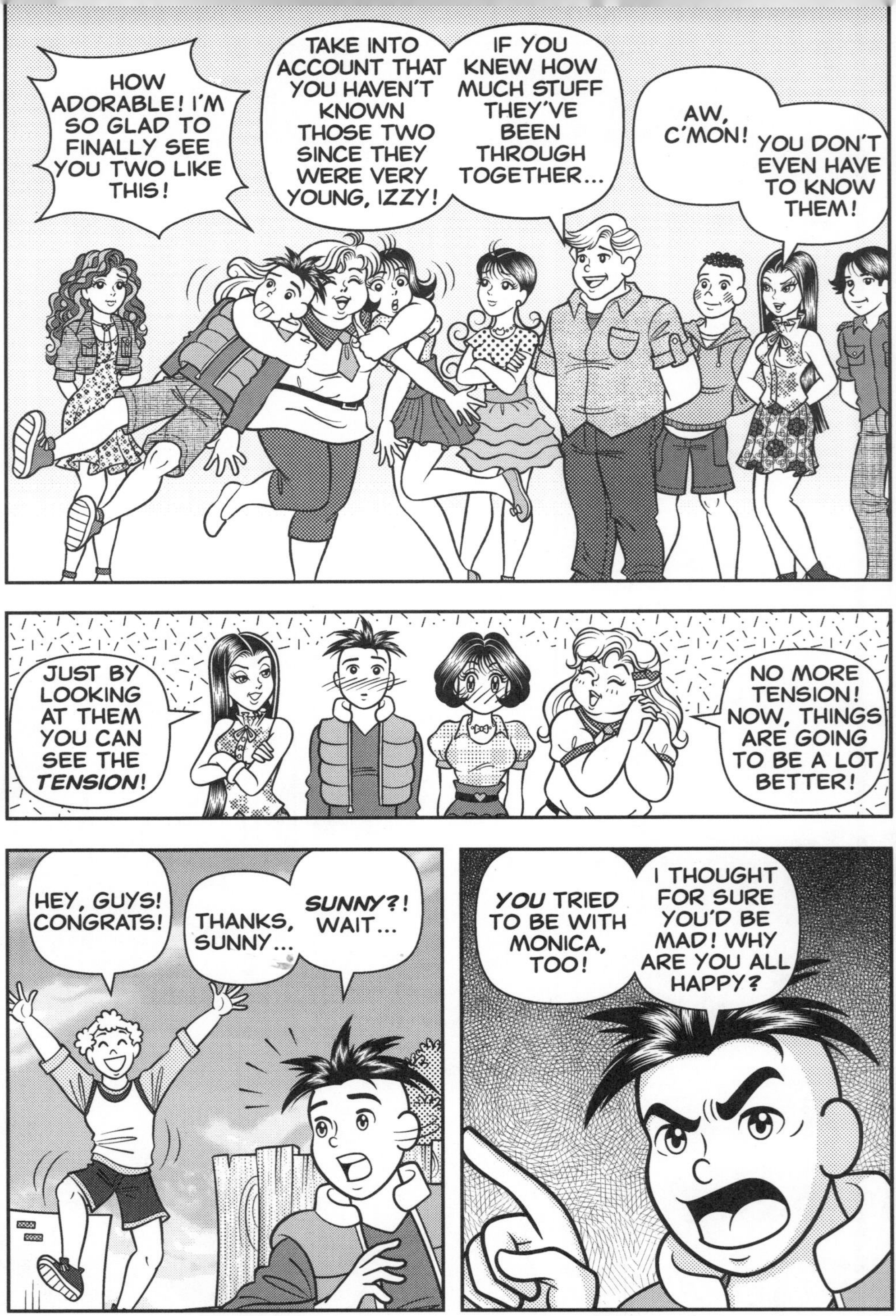
HOW ADORABLE! I'M SO GLAD TO FINALLY SEE YOU TWO LIKE THIS!
TAKE INTO ACCOUNT THAT YOU HAVEN'T KNOWN THOSE TWO SINCE THEY WERE VERY YOUNG, IZZY!
IF YOU KNEW HOW MUCH STUFF THEY'VE BEEN THROUGH TOGETHER...
AW, C'MON!
YOU DON'T EVEN HAVE TO KNOW THEM!
JUST BY LOOKING AT THEM YOU CAN SEE THE *TENSION*!
NO MORE TENSION! NOW, THINGS ARE GOING TO BE A LOT BETTER!
HEY, GUYS! CONGRATS!
THANKS, SUNNY...
SUNNY?! WAIT...
YOU TRIED TO BE WITH MONICA, TOO!
I THOUGHT FOR SURE YOU'D BE MAD! WHY ARE YOU ALL HAPPY?

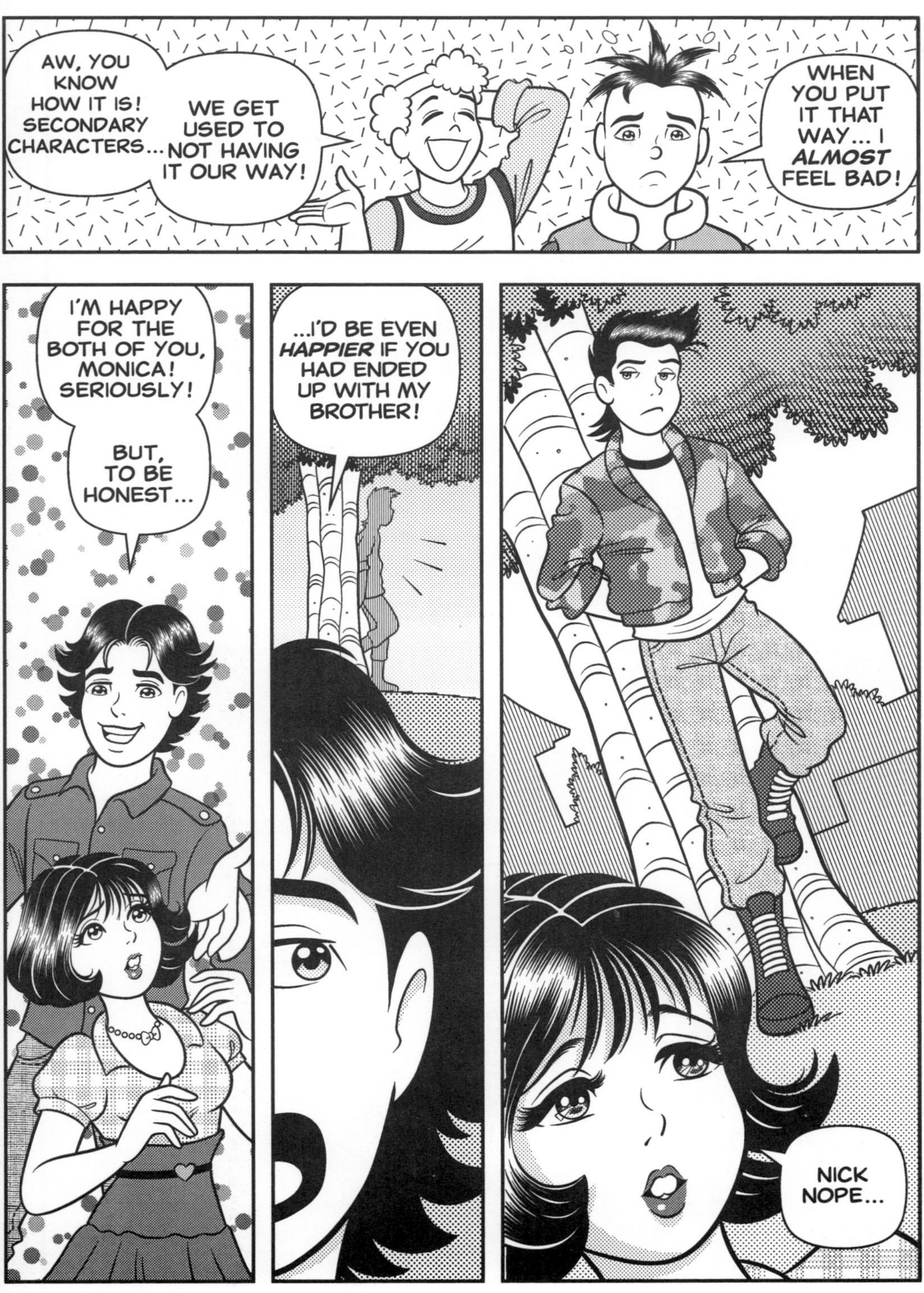
AW, YOU KNOW HOW IT IS! SECONDARY CHARACTERS...
WE GET USED TO NOT HAVING IT OUR WAY!
WHEN YOU PUT IT THAT WAY... I *ALMOST* FEEL BAD!
I'M HAPPY FOR THE BOTH OF YOU, MONICA! SERIOUSLY!
BUT, TO BE HONEST...
...I'D BE EVEN *HAPPIER* IF YOU HAD ENDED UP WITH MY BROTHER!
NICK NOPE...

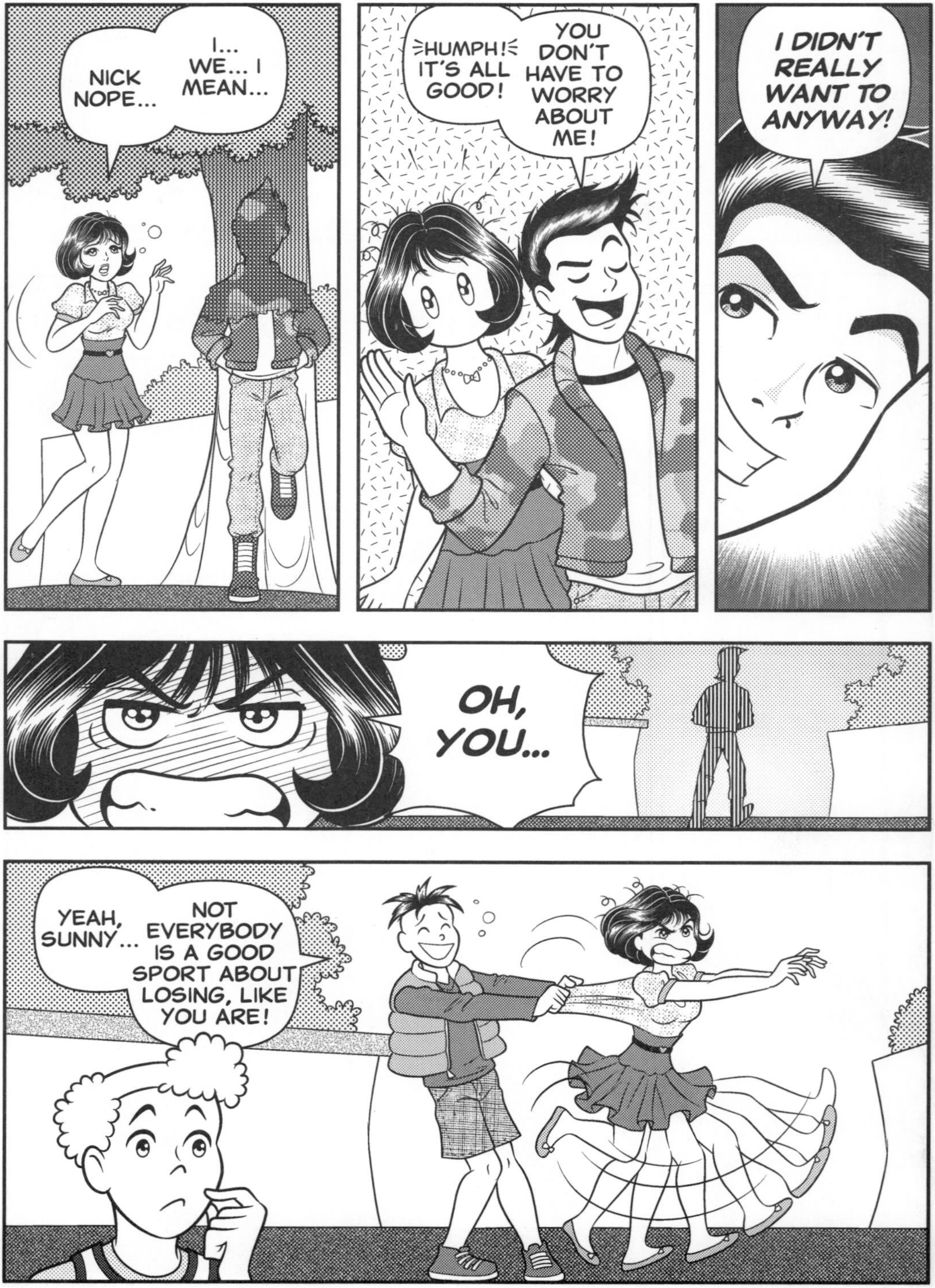
NICK NOPE...
I... WE... I MEAN...
HUMPH! IT'S ALL GOOD!
YOU DON'T HAVE TO WORRY ABOUT ME!
I DIDN'T REALLY WANT TO ANYWAY!
OH, YOU...
YEAH, SUNNY...
NOT EVERYBODY IS A GOOD SPORT ABOUT LOSING, LIKE YOU ARE!

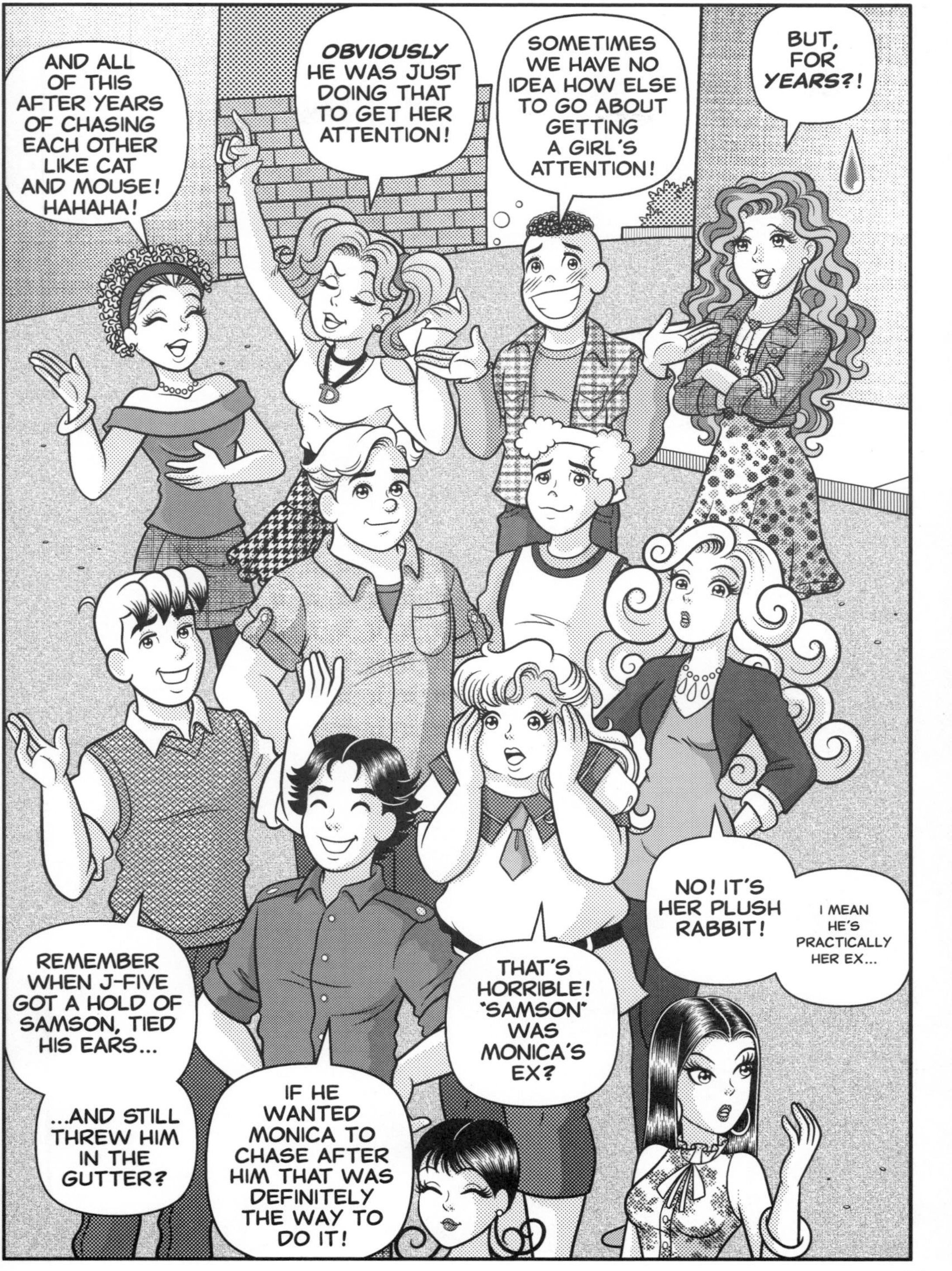
AND ALL OF THIS AFTER YEARS OF CHASING EACH OTHER LIKE CAT AND MOUSE! HAHAHA!
OBVIOUSLY HE WAS JUST DOING THAT TO GET HER ATTENTION!
SOMETIMES WE HAVE NO IDEA HOW ELSE TO GO ABOUT GETTING A GIRL'S ATTENTION!
BUT, FOR *YEARS?!*
REMEMBER WHEN J-FIVE GOT A HOLD OF SAMSON, TIED HIS EARS...
...AND STILL THREW HIM IN THE GUTTER?
IF HE WANTED MONICA TO CHASE AFTER HIM THAT WAS DEFINITELY THE WAY TO DO IT!
THAT'S HORRIBLE! "SAMSON" WAS MONICA'S EX?
NO! IT'S HER PLUSH RABBIT!
I MEAN HE'S PRACTICALLY HER EX...

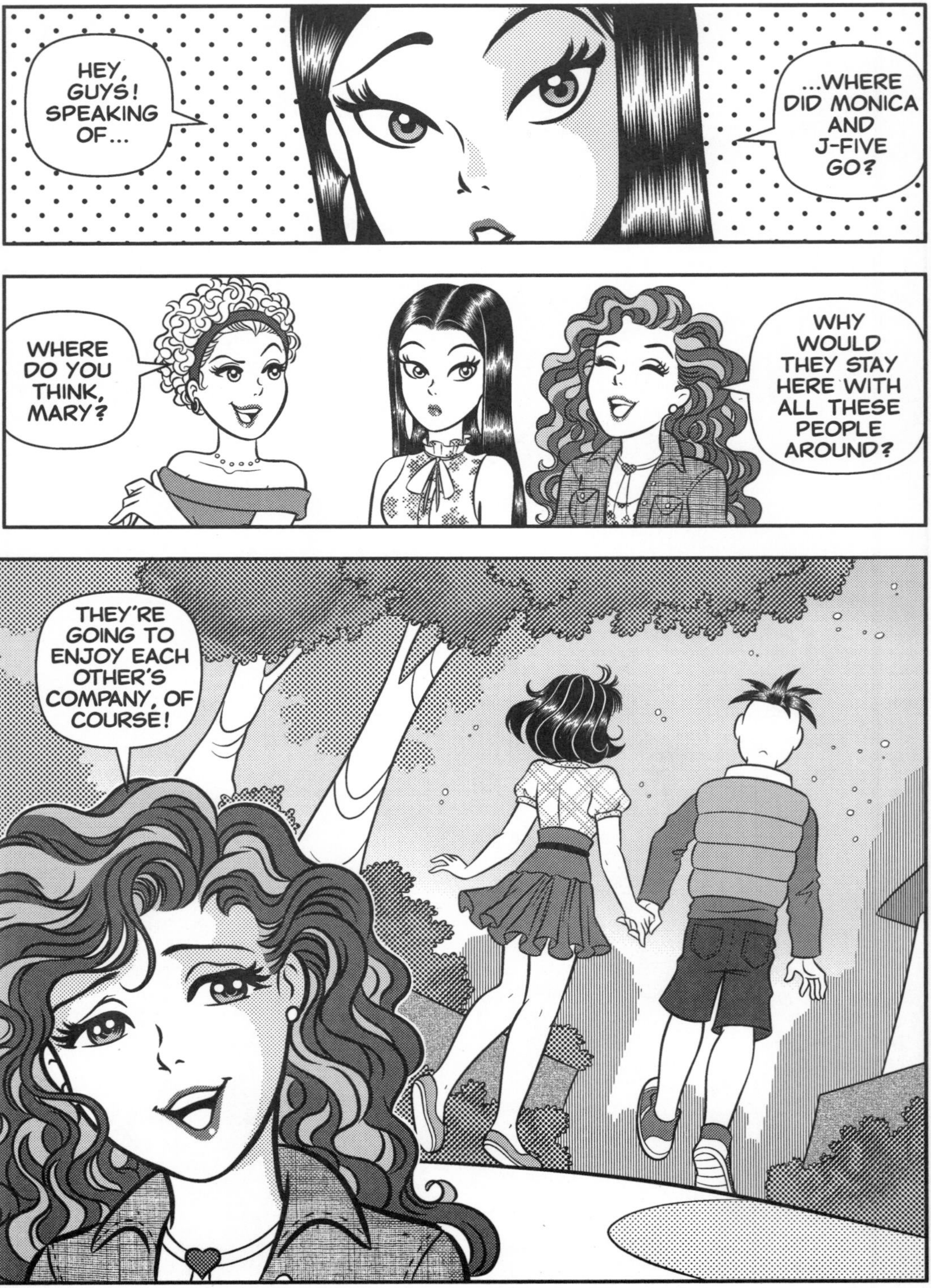
HEY, GUYS! SPEAKING OF...
...WHERE DID MONICA AND J-FIVE GO?
WHERE DO YOU THINK, MARY?
WHY WOULD THEY STAY HERE WITH ALL THESE PEOPLE AROUND?
THEY'RE GOING TO ENJOY EACH OTHER'S COMPANY, OF COURSE!

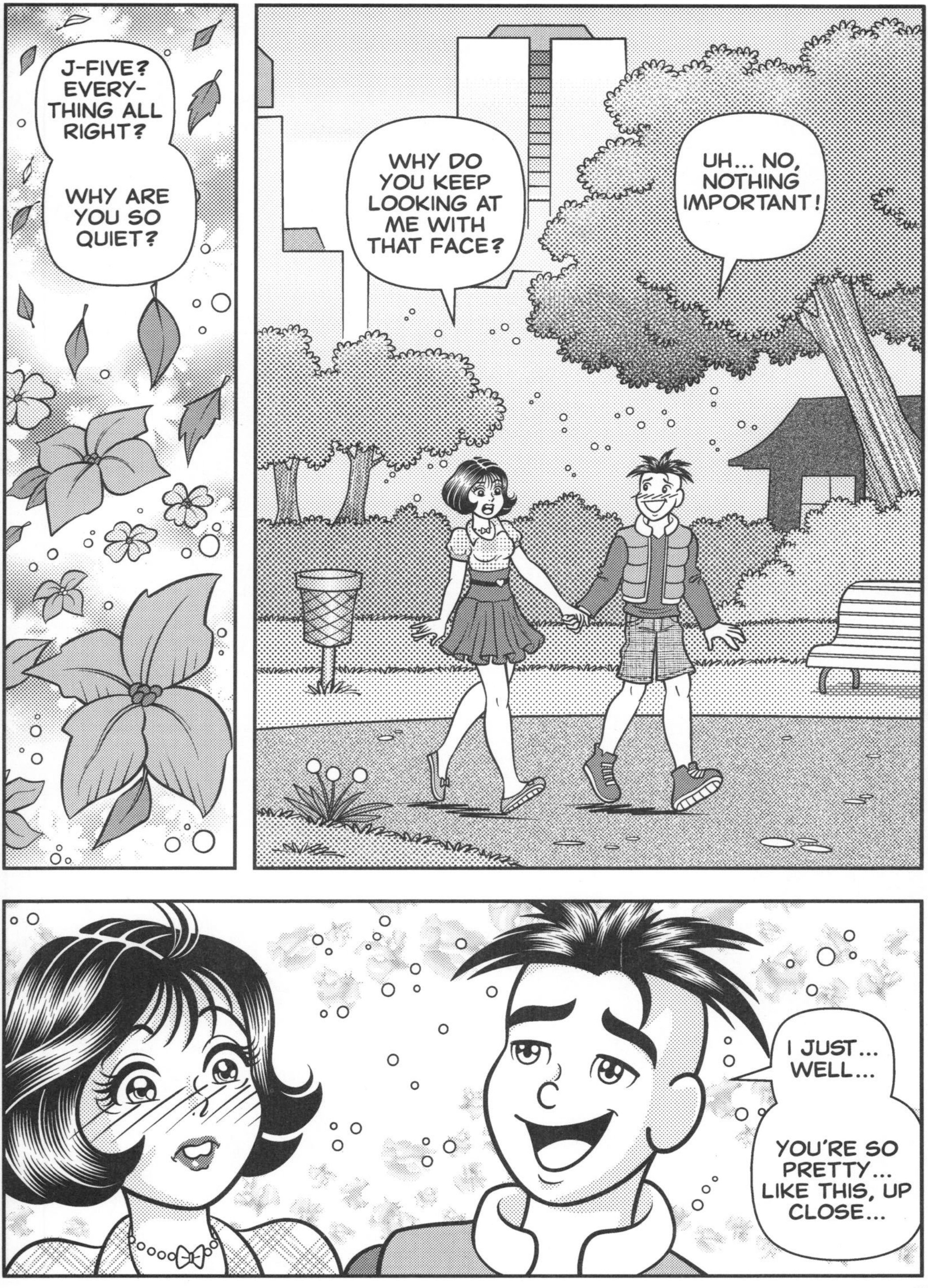
J-FIVE? EVERYTHING ALL RIGHT?
WHY ARE YOU SO QUIET?
WHY DO YOU KEEP LOOKING AT ME WITH THAT FACE?
UH... NO, NOTHING IMPORTANT!
I JUST... WELL...
YOU'RE SO PRETTY... LIKE THIS, UP CLOSE...

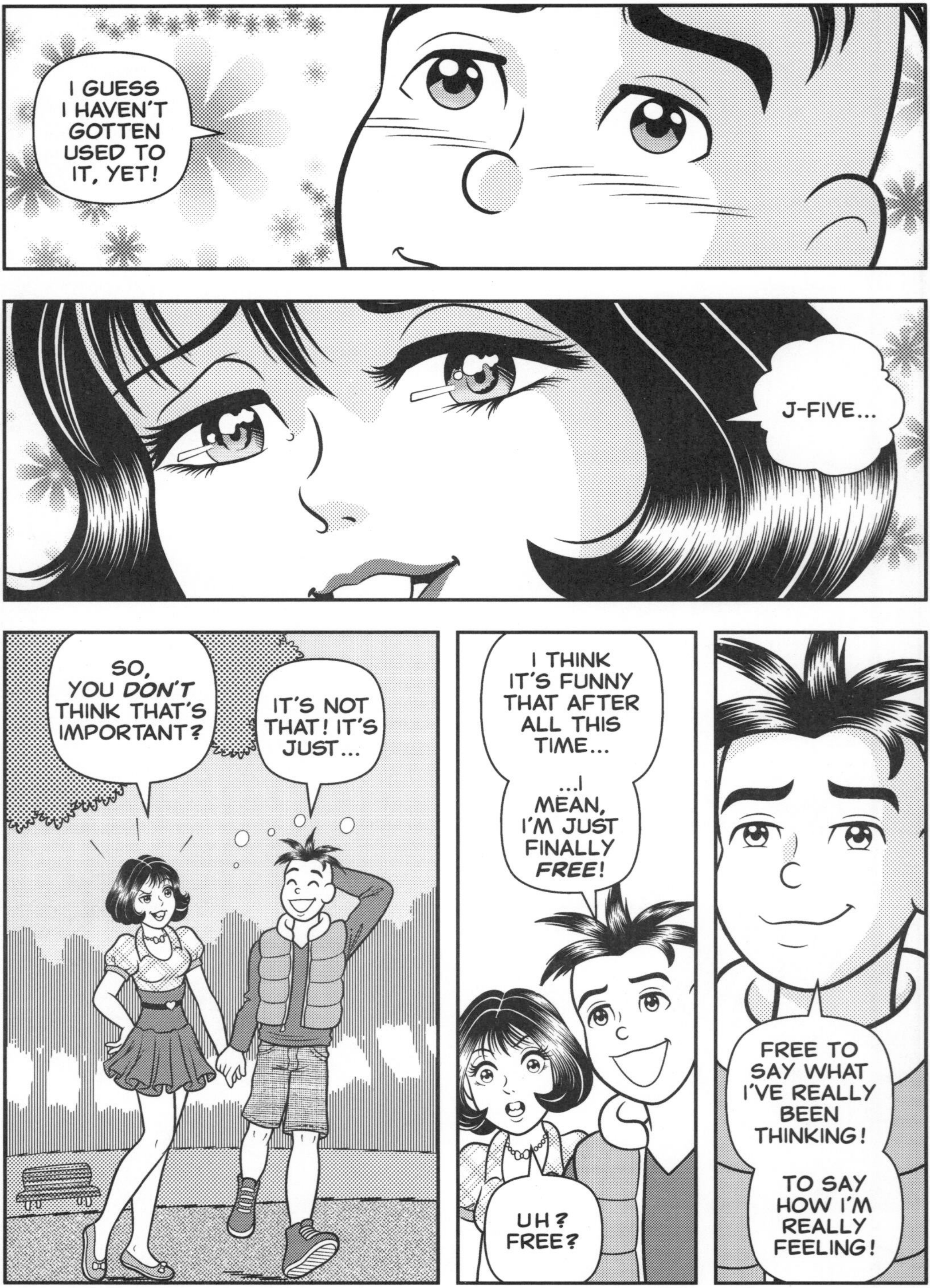
I GUESS I HAVEN'T GOTTEN USED TO IT, YET!
J-FIVE...
SO, YOU *DON'T* THINK THAT'S IMPORTANT?
IT'S NOT THAT! IT'S JUST...
I THINK IT'S FUNNY THAT AFTER ALL THIS TIME...
...I MEAN, I'M JUST FINALLY *FREE*!
UH? FREE?
FREE TO SAY WHAT I'VE REALLY BEEN THINKING!
TO SAY HOW I'M REALLY FEELING!

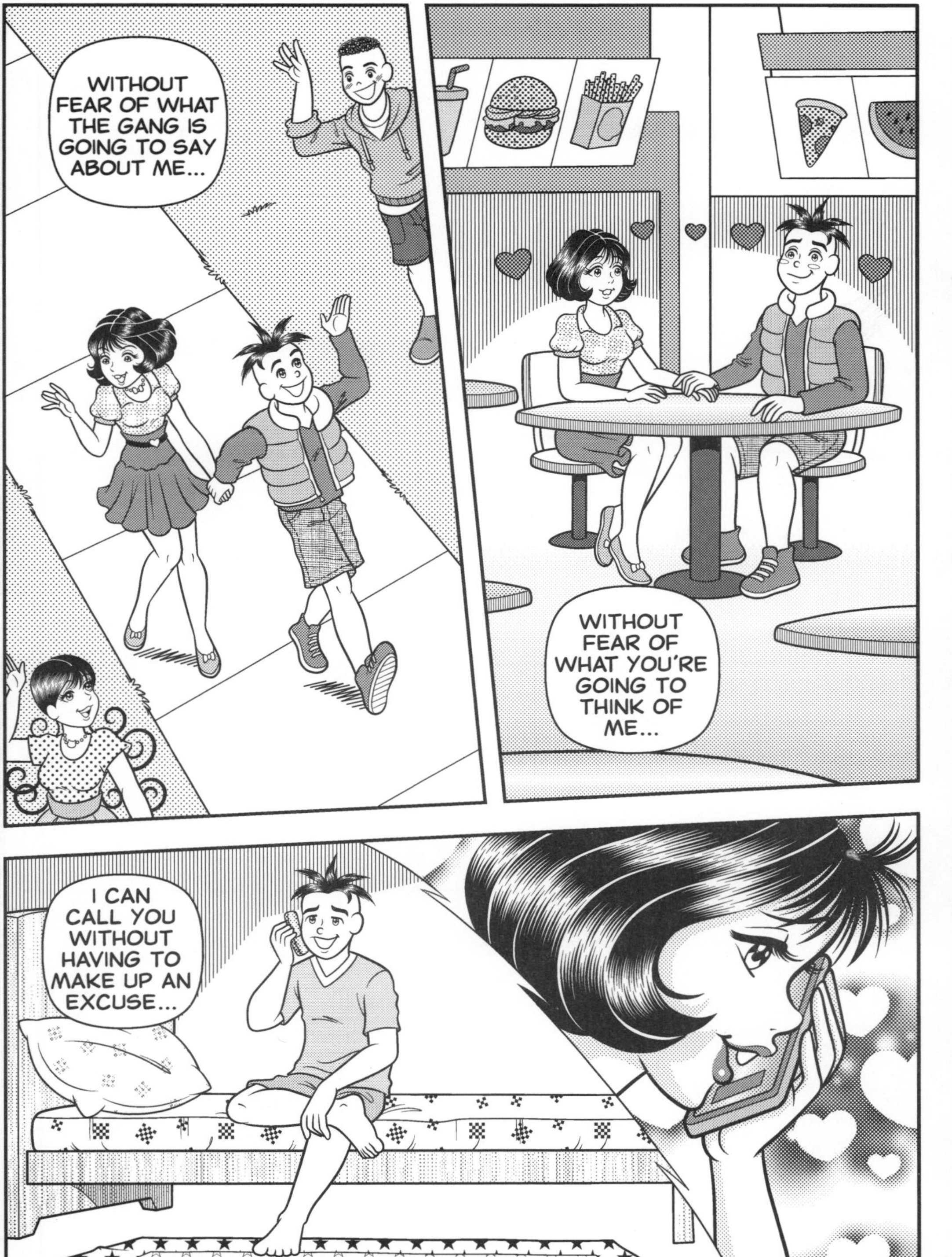
WITHOUT FEAR OF WHAT THE GANG IS GOING TO SAY ABOUT ME...
WITHOUT FEAR OF WHAT YOU'RE GOING TO THINK OF ME...
I CAN CALL YOU WITHOUT HAVING TO MAKE UP AN EXCUSE...

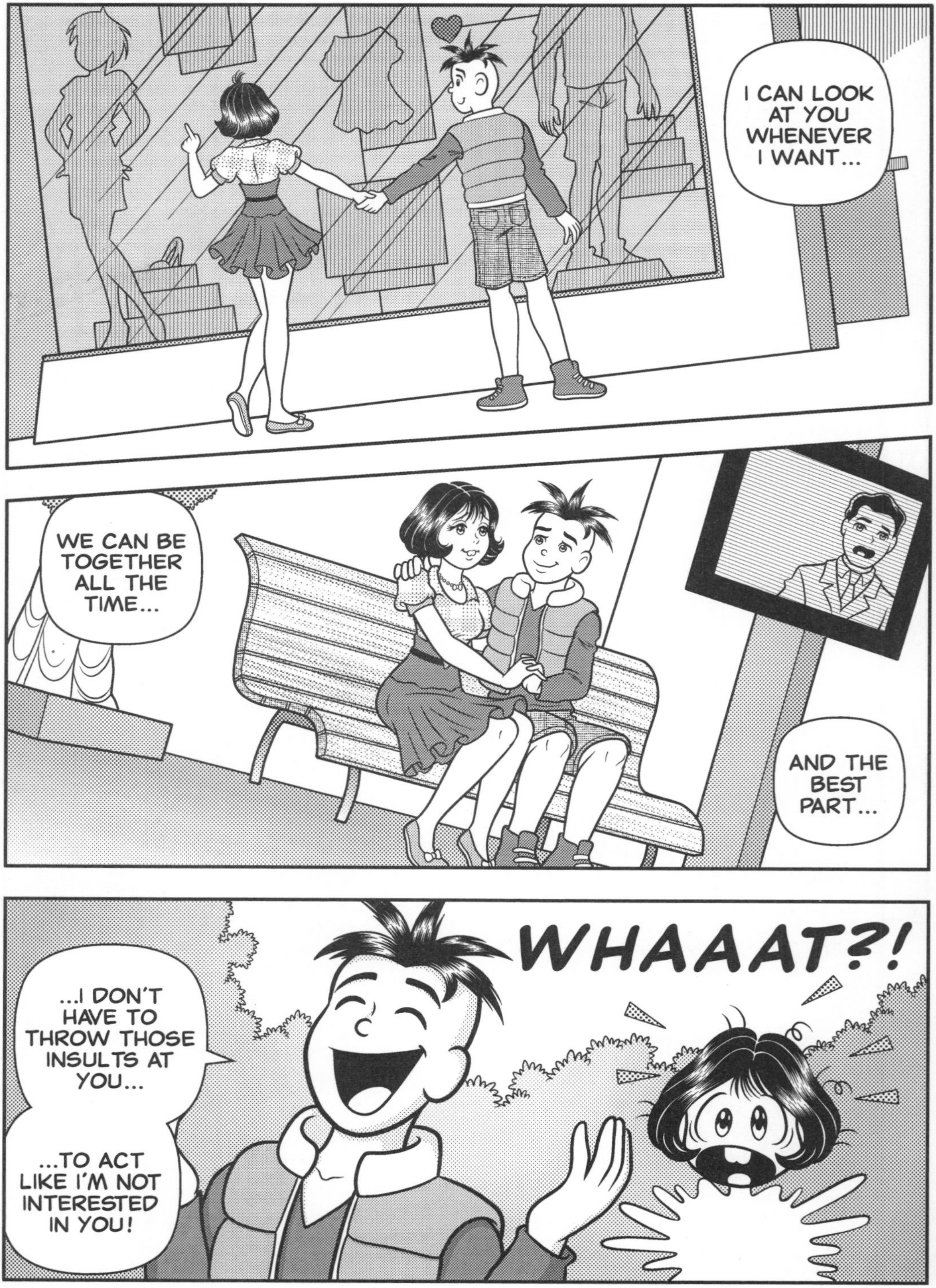

I CAN LOOK AT YOU WHENEVER I WANT...
WE CAN BE TOGETHER ALL THE TIME...
AND THE BEST PART...
...I DON'T HAVE TO THROW THOSE INSULTS AT YOU...
...TO ACT LIKE I'M NOT INTERESTED IN YOU!
WHAAAT?!

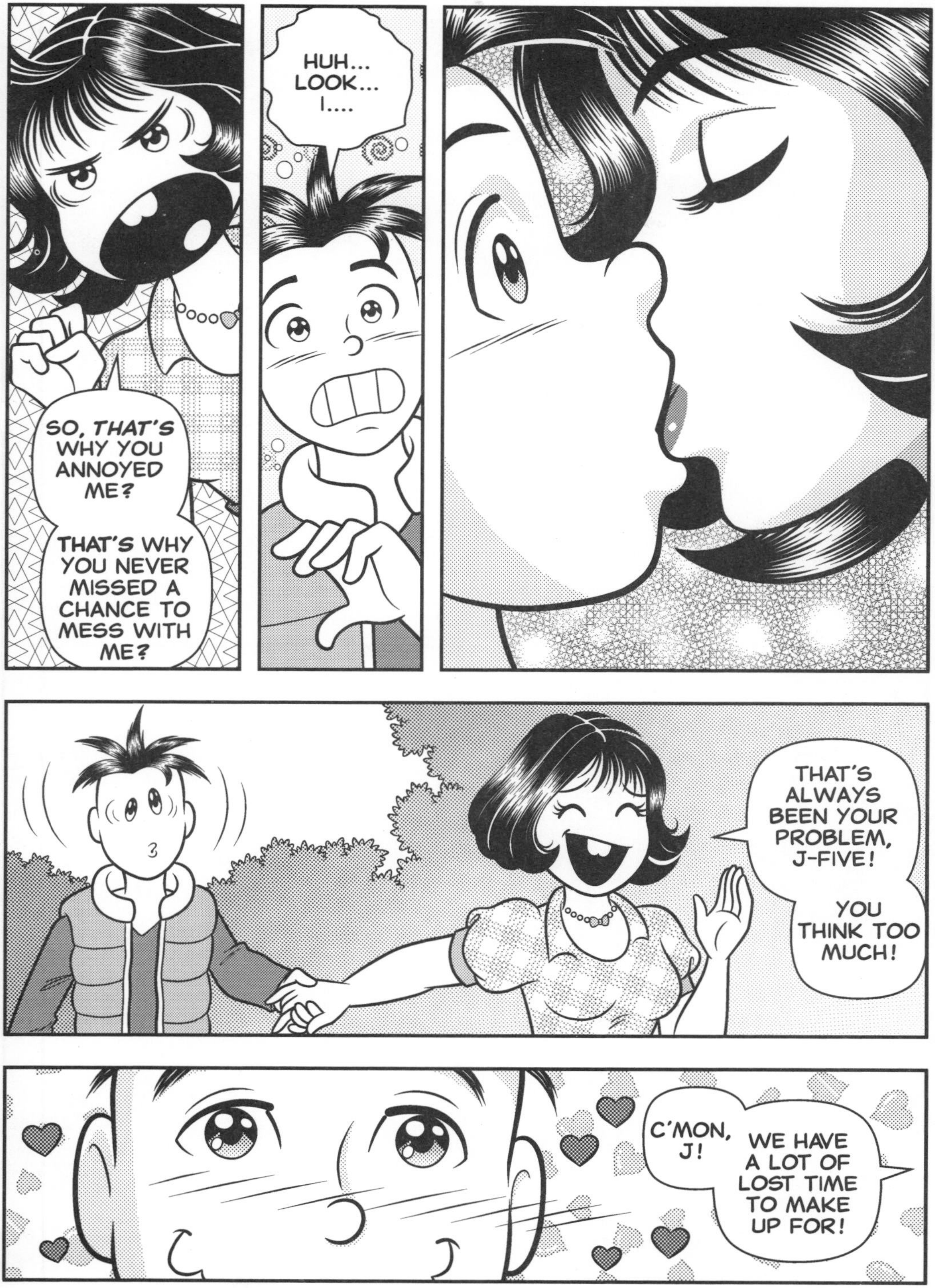
SO, THAT'S WHY YOU ANNOYED ME?
THAT'S WHY YOU NEVER MISSED A CHANCE TO MESS WITH ME?
HUH... LOOK... I....
THAT'S ALWAYS BEEN YOUR PROBLEM, J-FIVE!
YOU THINK TOO MUCH!
C'MON, J!
WE HAVE A LOT OF LOST TIME TO MAKE UP FOR!

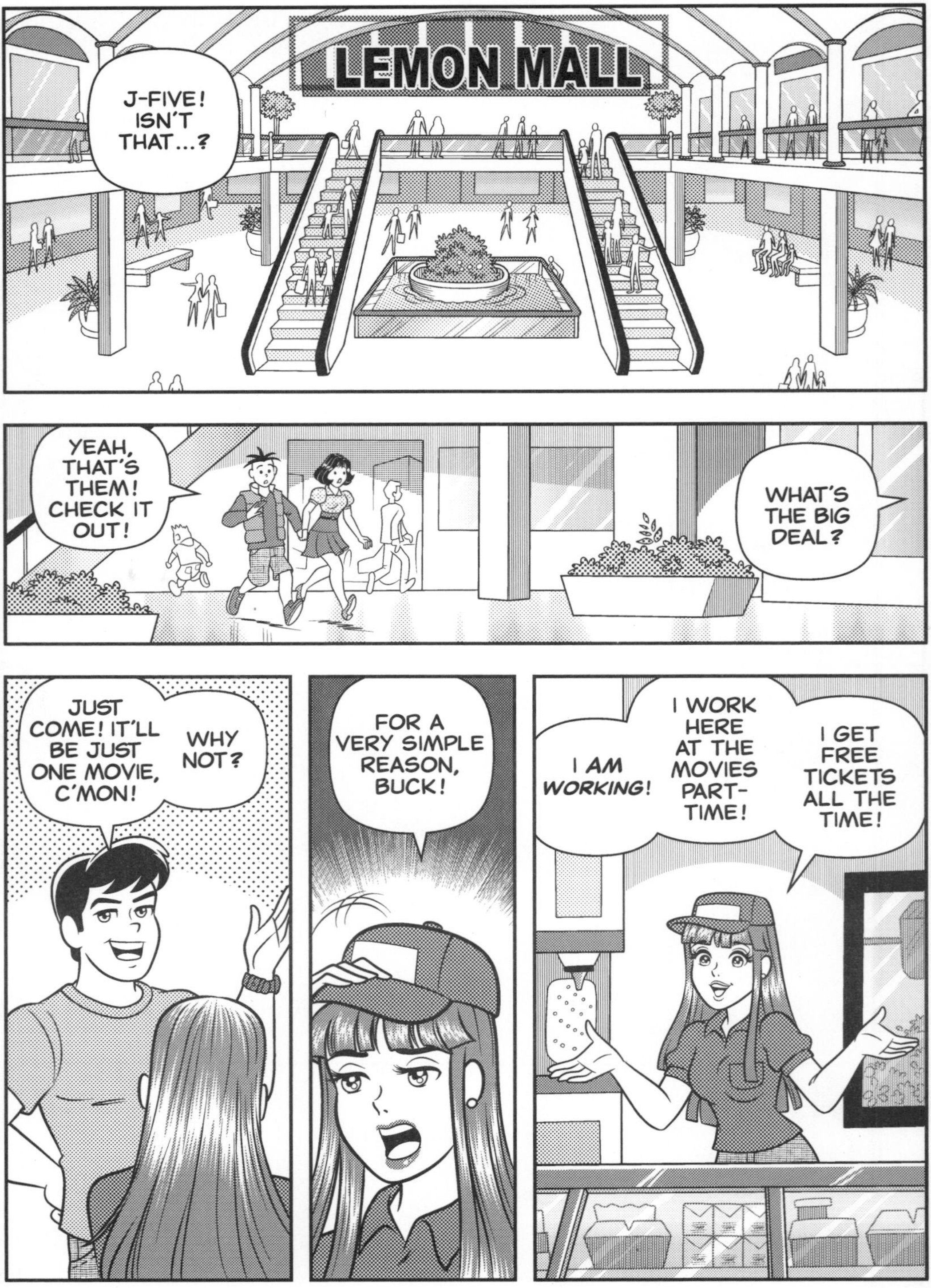
LEMON MALL
J-FIVE! ISN'T THAT...?
YEAH, THAT'S THEM! CHECK IT OUT!
WHAT'S THE BIG DEAL?
JUST COME! IT'LL BE JUST ONE MOVIE, C'MON!
WHY NOT?
FOR A VERY SIMPLE REASON, BUCK!
I *AM WORKING*!
I WORK HERE AT THE MOVIES PART-TIME!
I GET FREE TICKETS ALL THE TIME!

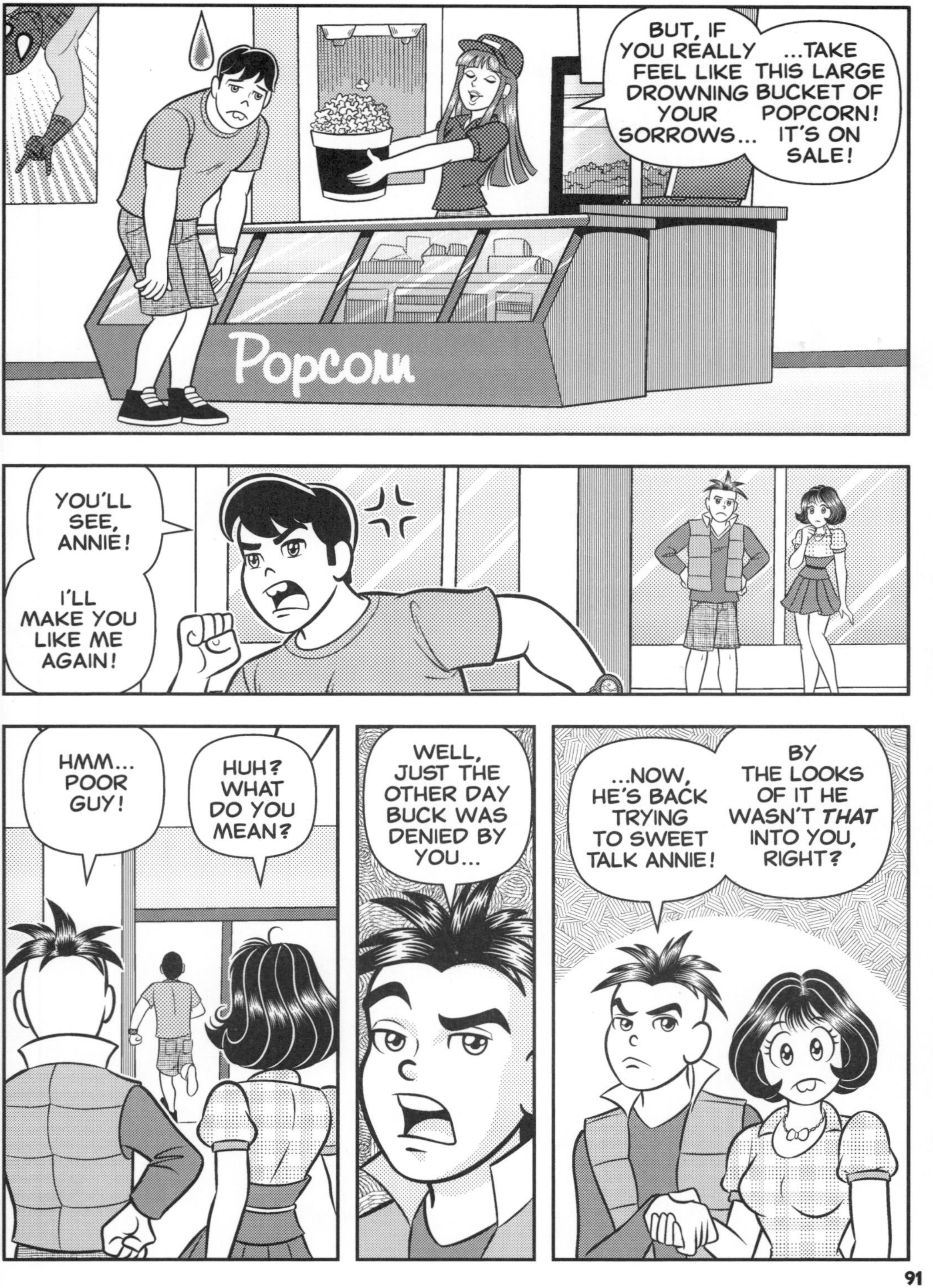
BUT, IF YOU REALLY FEEL LIKE DROWNING YOUR SORROWS...
...TAKE THIS LARGE BUCKET OF POPCORN! IT'S ON SALE!
Popcorn
YOU'LL SEE, ANNIE!
I'LL MAKE YOU LIKE ME AGAIN!
HMM... POOR GUY!
HUH? WHAT DO YOU MEAN?
WELL, JUST THE OTHER DAY BUCK WAS DENIED BY YOU...
...NOW, HE'S BACK TRYING TO SWEET TALK ANNIE!
BY THE LOOKS OF IT HE WASN'T *THAT* INTO YOU, RIGHT?

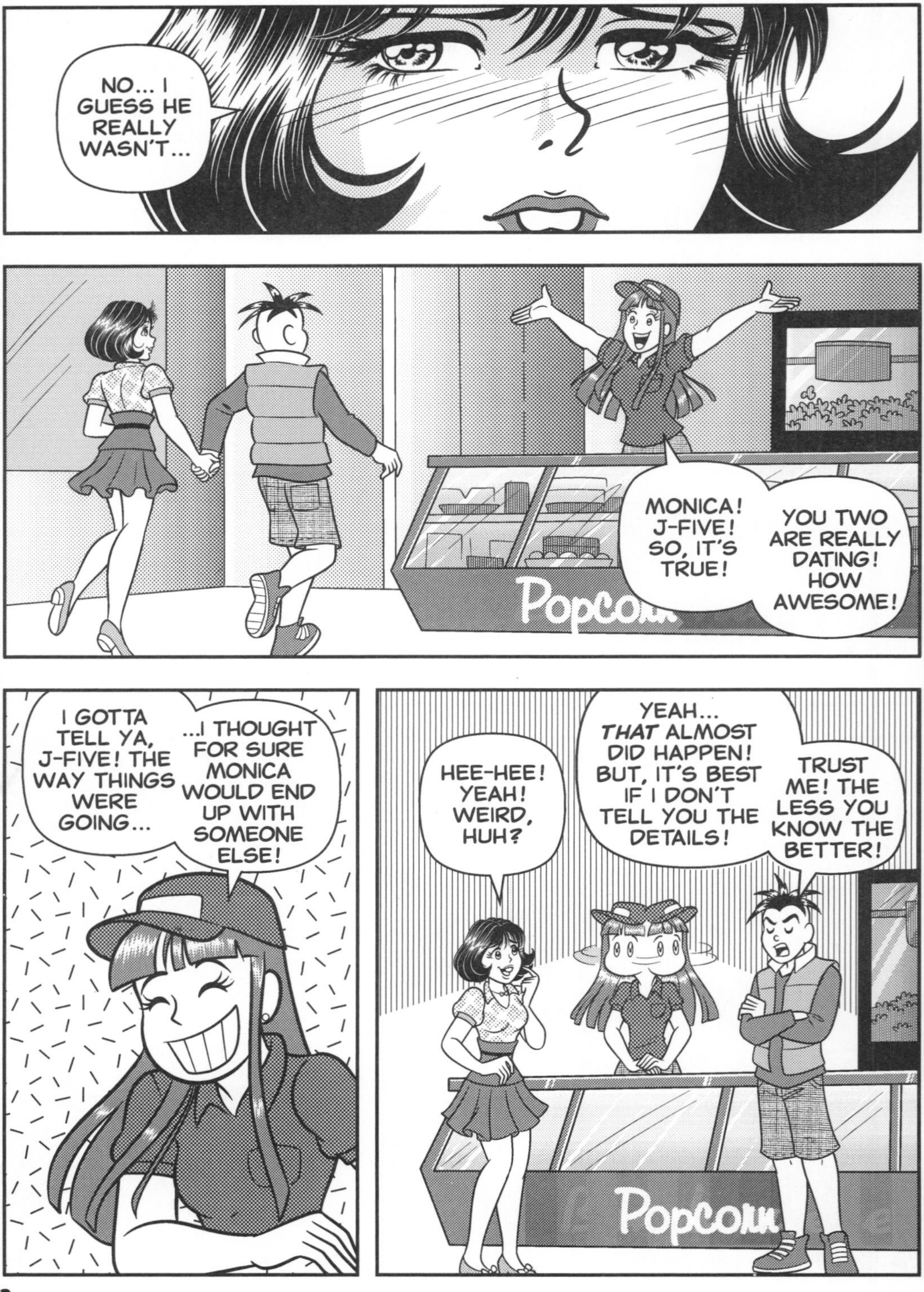
NO... I GUESS HE REALLY WASN'T...
MONICA! J-FIVE! SO, IT'S TRUE!
YOU TWO ARE REALLY DATING! HOW AWESOME!
Popcorn
I GOTTA TELL YA, J-FIVE! THE WAY THINGS WERE GOING...
...I THOUGHT FOR SURE MONICA WOULD END UP WITH SOMEONE ELSE!
HEE-HEE! YEAH! WEIRD, HUH?
YEAH... *THAT* ALMOST DID HAPPEN! BUT, IT'S BEST IF I DON'T TELL YOU THE DETAILS!
TRUST ME! THE LESS YOU KNOW THE BETTER!
Popcorn

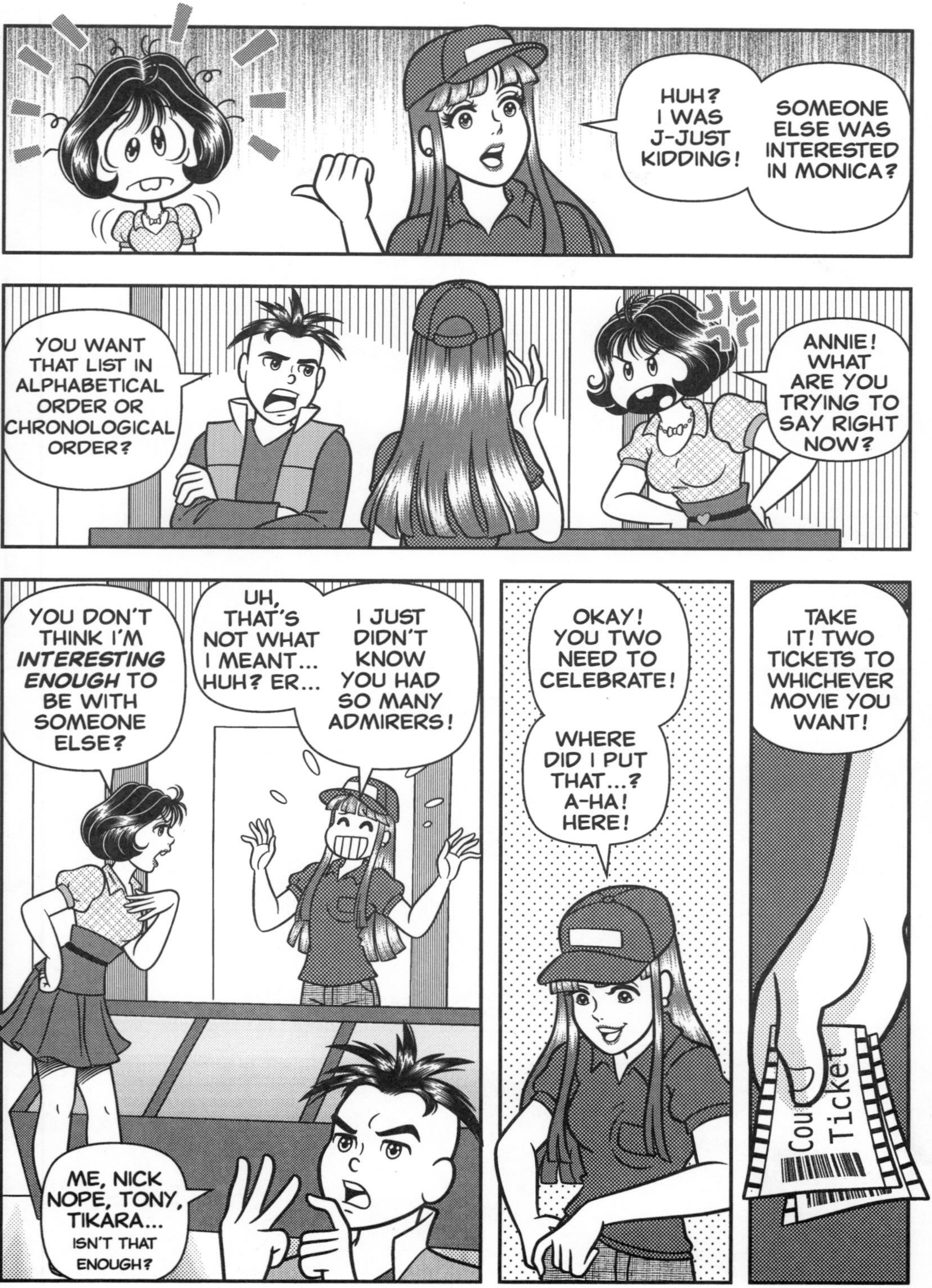
HUH? I WAS J-JUST KIDDING!
SOMEONE ELSE WAS INTERESTED IN MONICA?
YOU WANT THAT LIST IN ALPHABETICAL ORDER OR CHRONOLOGICAL ORDER?
ANNIE! WHAT ARE YOU TRYING TO SAY RIGHT NOW?
YOU DON'T THINK I'M *INTERESTING ENOUGH* TO BE WITH SOMEONE ELSE?
UH, THAT'S NOT WHAT I MEANT... HUH? ER...
I JUST DIDN'T KNOW YOU HAD SO MANY ADMIRERS!
ME, NICK NOPE, TONY, TIKARA... ISN'T THAT ENOUGH?
OKAY! YOU TWO NEED TO CELEBRATE!
WHERE DID I PUT THAT...? A-HA! HERE!
TAKE IT! TWO TICKETS TO WHICHEVER MOVIE YOU WANT!
Ticket

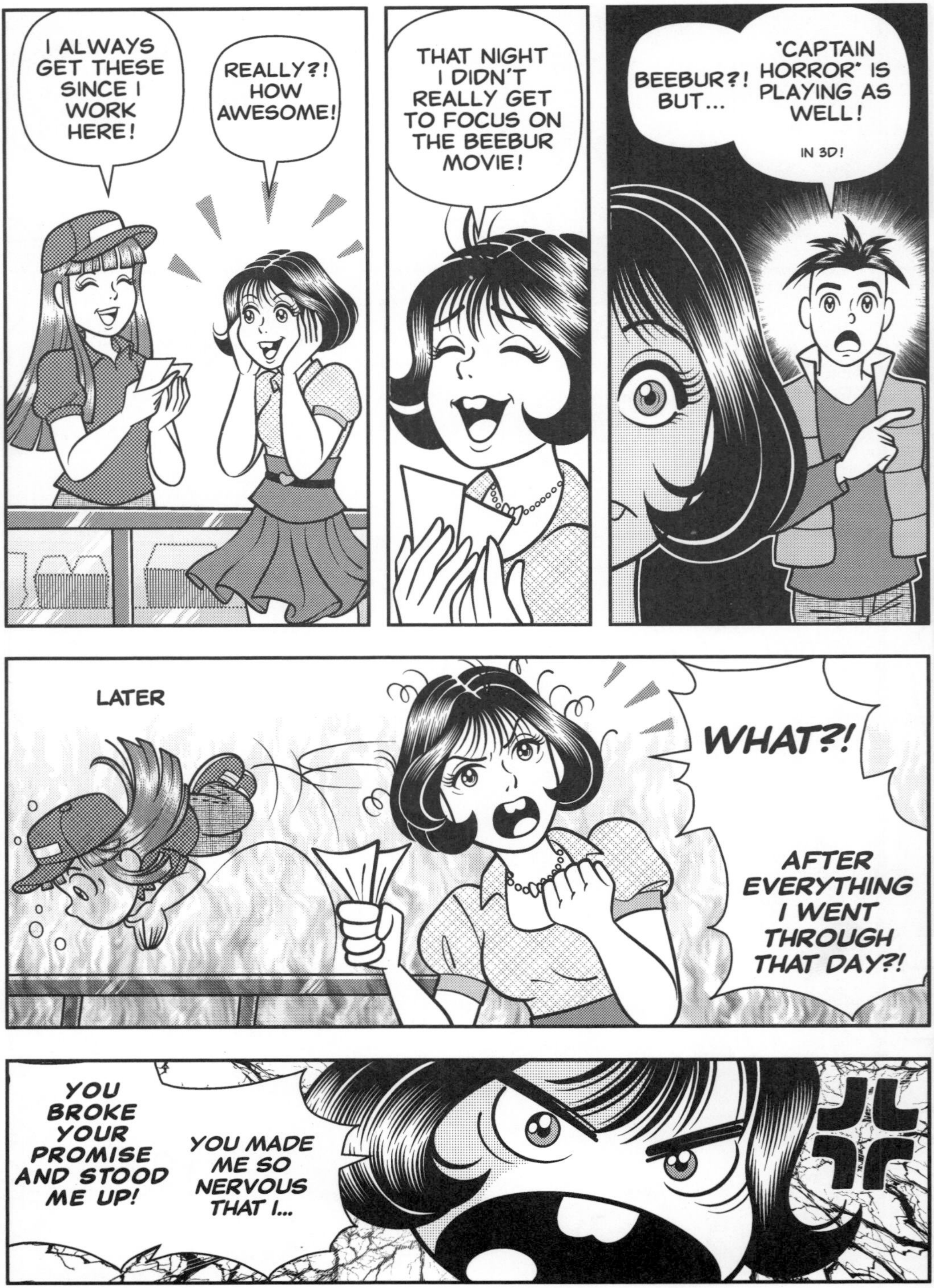
I ALWAYS GET THESE SINCE I WORK HERE!
REALLY?! HOW AWESOME!
THAT NIGHT I DIDN'T REALLY GET TO FOCUS ON THE BEEBUR MOVIE!
BEEBUR?! BUT...
"CAPTAIN HORROR" IS PLAYING AS WELL!
IN 3D!
LATER
WHAT?!
AFTER EVERYTHING I WENT THROUGH THAT DAY?!
YOU BROKE YOUR PROMISE AND STOOD ME UP!
YOU MADE ME SO NERVOUS THAT I...

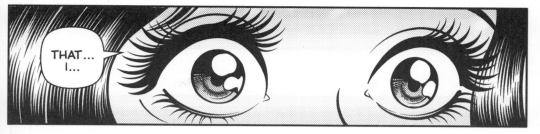

THAT... I...

NO...

IT'S FINE, MO! CALM DOWN!

I DON'T WANT TO FIGHT!

YOU... DON'T WANT TO?

OF COURSE NOT! I WANT TO LEAVE THAT BEHIND US!

YOU'RE RIGHT, I DROPPED THE BALL!

I CAN WATCH "CAPTAIN HORROR" SOME OTHER TIME!

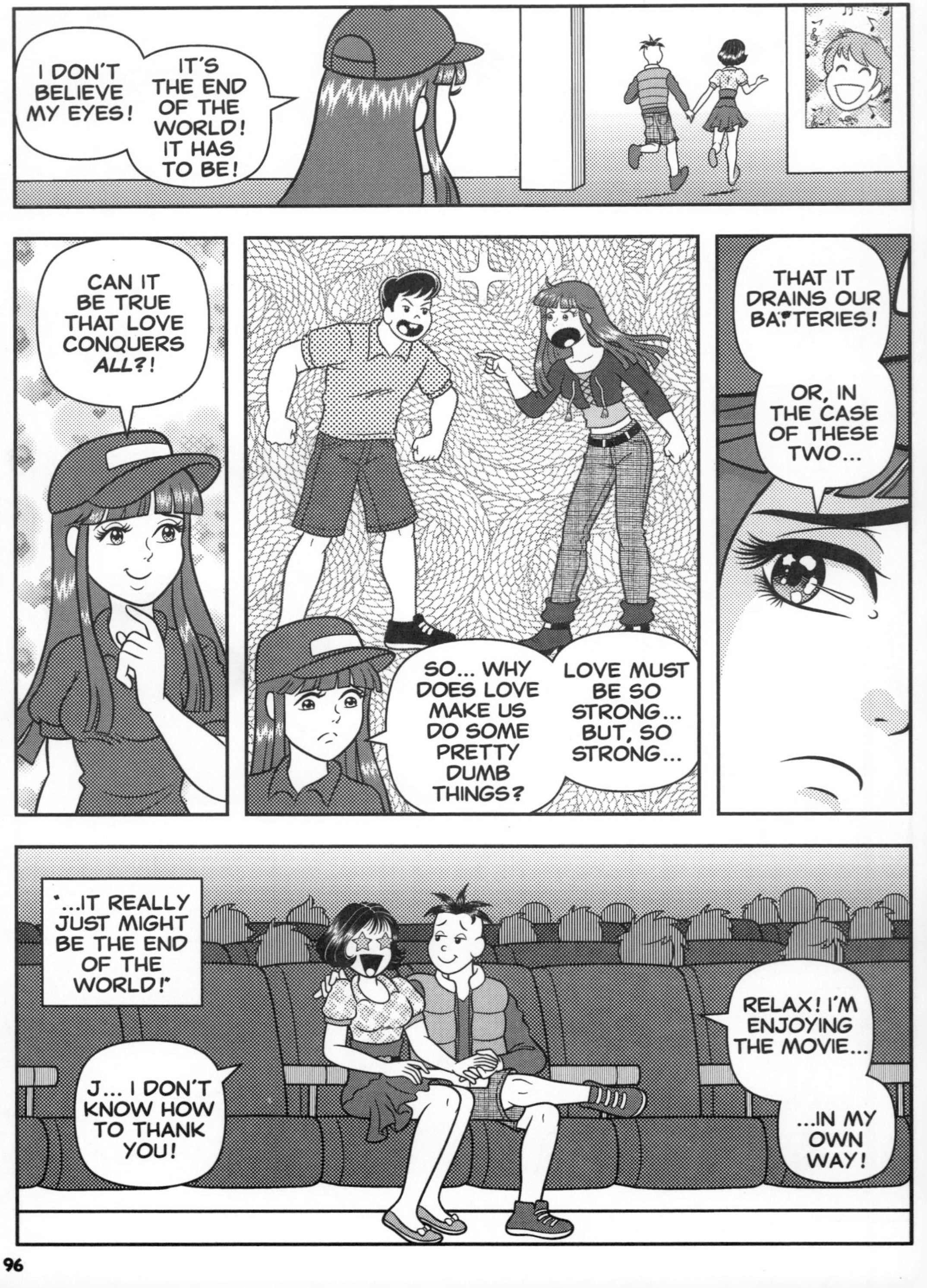
I DON'T BELIEVE MY EYES!
IT'S THE END OF THE WORLD! IT HAS TO BE!
CAN IT BE TRUE THAT LOVE CONQUERS *ALL*?!
SO... WHY DOES LOVE MAKE US DO SOME PRETTY DUMB THINGS?
LOVE MUST BE SO STRONG... BUT, SO STRONG...
THAT IT DRAINS OUR BATTERIES!
OR, IN THE CASE OF THESE TWO...
"...IT REALLY JUST MIGHT BE THE END OF THE WORLD!"
J... I DON'T KNOW HOW TO THANK YOU!
RELAX! I'M ENJOYING THE MOVIE...
...IN MY OWN WAY!

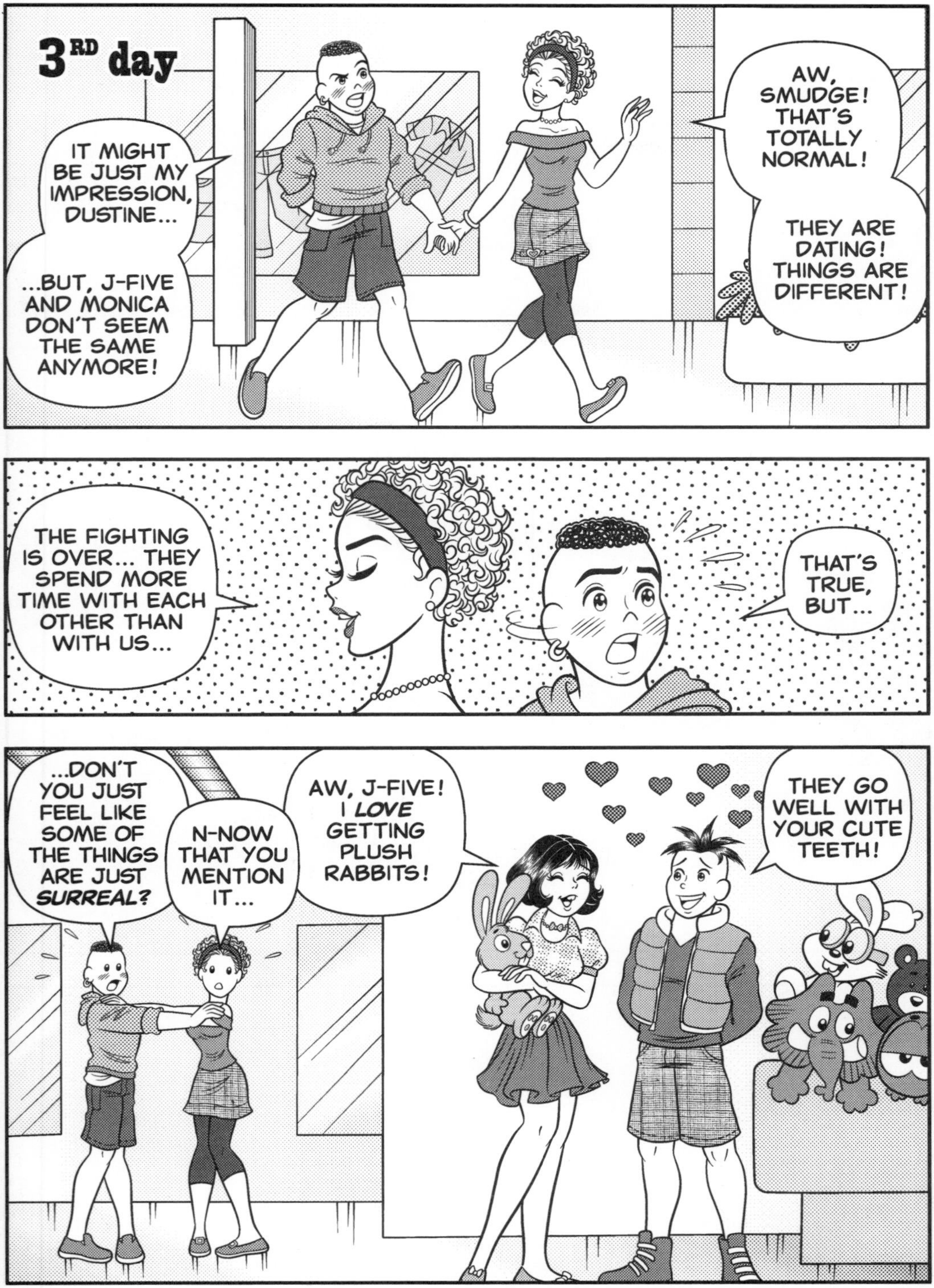
3RD day
IT MIGHT BE JUST MY IMPRESSION, DUSTINE...
...BUT, J-FIVE AND MONICA DON'T SEEM THE SAME ANYMORE!
AW, SMUDGE! THAT'S TOTALLY NORMAL!
THEY ARE DATING! THINGS ARE DIFFERENT!
THE FIGHTING IS OVER... THEY SPEND MORE TIME WITH EACH OTHER THAN WITH US...
THAT'S TRUE, BUT...
...DON'T YOU JUST FEEL LIKE SOME OF THE THINGS ARE JUST *SURREAL?*
N-NOW THAT YOU MENTION IT...
AW, J-FIVE! I *LOVE* GETTING PLUSH RABBITS!
THEY GO WELL WITH YOUR CUTE TEETH!

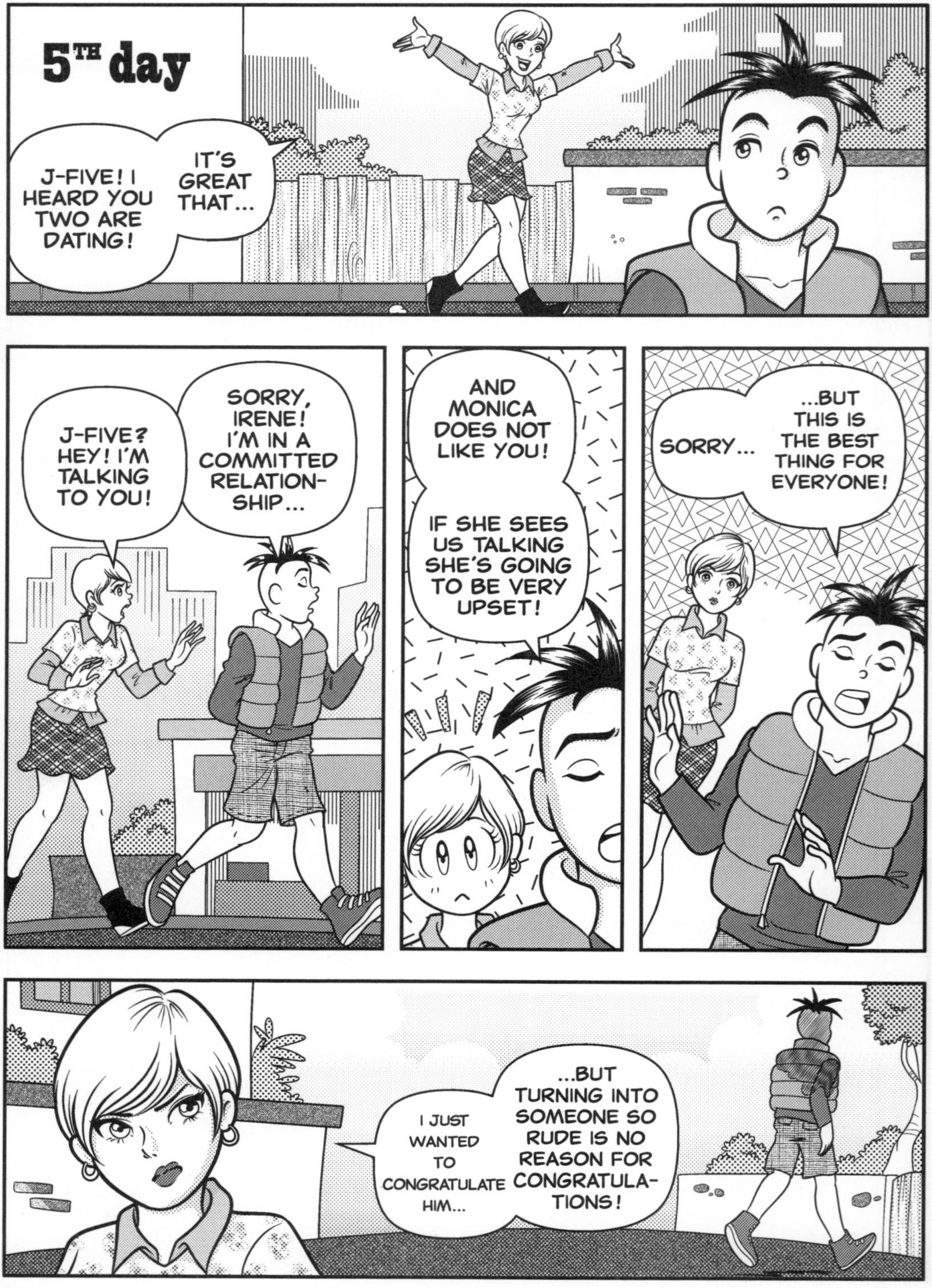
5TH day
J-FIVE! I HEARD YOU TWO ARE DATING!
IT'S GREAT THAT...
J-FIVE? HEY! I'M TALKING TO YOU!
SORRY, IRENE! I'M IN A COMMITTED RELATION-SHIP...
AND MONICA DOES NOT LIKE YOU!
IF SHE SEES US TALKING SHE'S GOING TO BE VERY UPSET!
SORRY...
...BUT THIS IS THE BEST THING FOR EVERYONE!
I JUST WANTED TO CONGRATULATE HIM...
...BUT TURNING INTO SOMEONE SO RUDE IS NO REASON FOR CONGRATULA-TIONS!

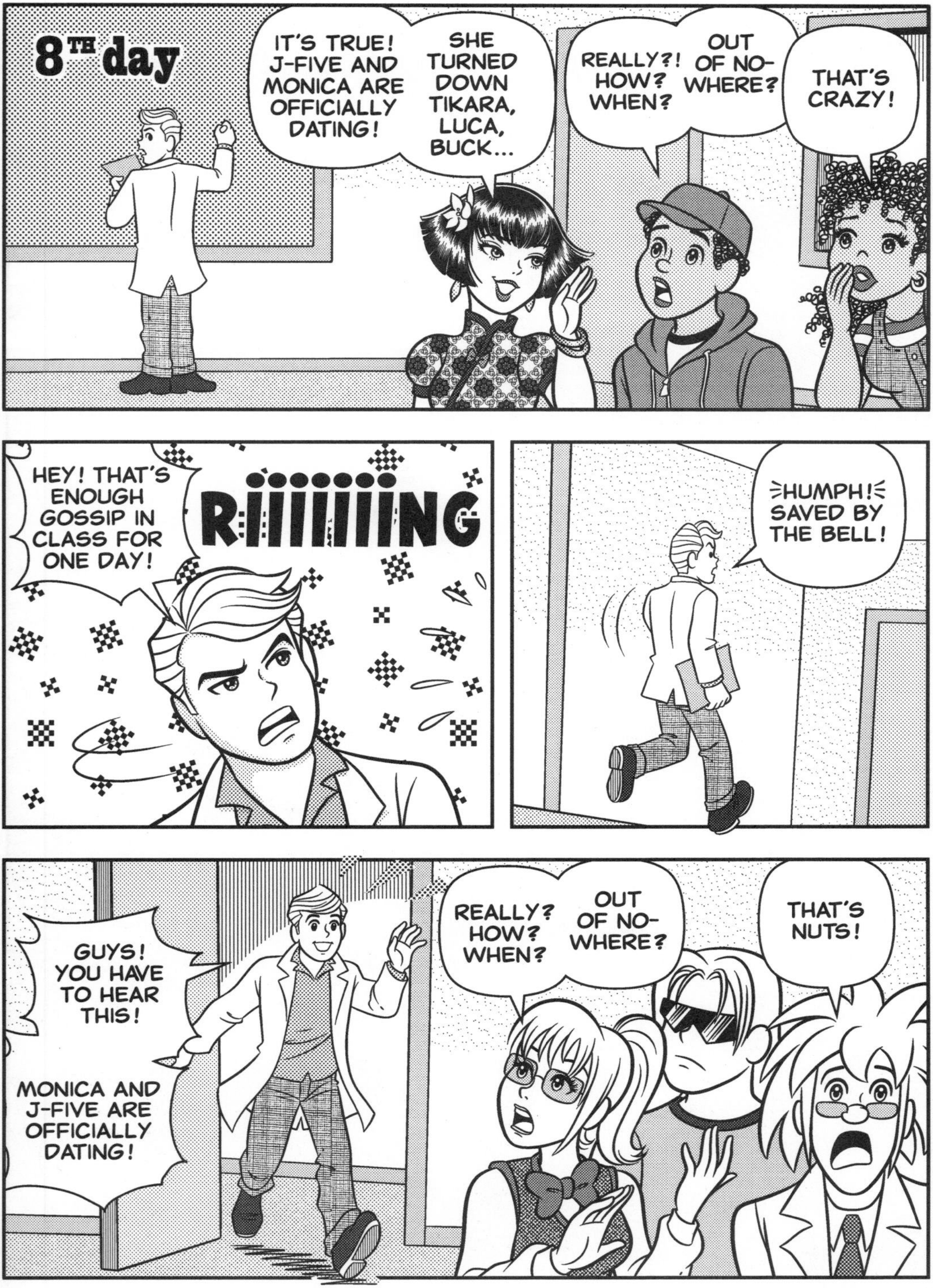
8TH day
IT'S TRUE! J-FIVE AND MONICA ARE OFFICIALLY DATING!
SHE TURNED DOWN TIKARA, LUCA, BUCK...
REALLY?! HOW? WHEN?
OUT OF NO-WHERE?
THAT'S CRAZY!
HEY! THAT'S ENOUGH GOSSIP IN CLASS FOR ONE DAY!
RIIIIIIING
HUMPH! SAVED BY THE BELL!
GUYS! YOU HAVE TO HEAR THIS!
MONICA AND J-FIVE ARE OFFICIALLY DATING!
REALLY? HOW? WHEN?
OUT OF NO-WHERE?
THAT'S NUTS!

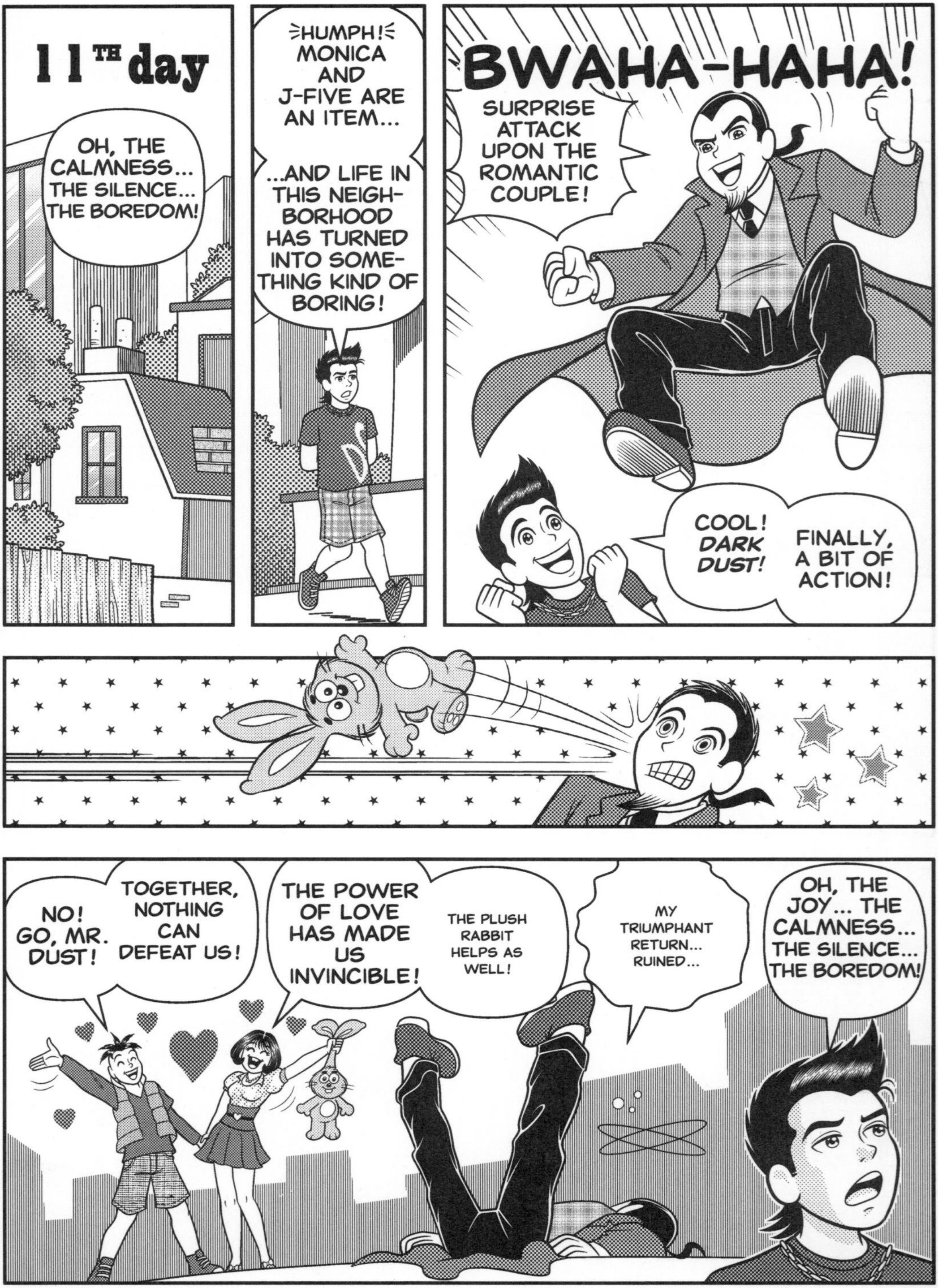
11TH day
OH, THE CALMNESS... THE SILENCE... THE BOREDOM!
HUMPH! MONICA AND J-FIVE ARE AN ITEM...
...AND LIFE IN THIS NEIGHBORHOOD HAS TURNED INTO SOMETHING KIND OF BORING!
BWAHA-HAHA!
SURPRISE ATTACK UPON THE ROMANTIC COUPLE!
COOL! DARK DUST!
FINALLY, A BIT OF ACTION!
NO! GO, MR. DUST!
TOGETHER, NOTHING CAN DEFEAT US!
THE POWER OF LOVE HAS MADE US INVINCIBLE!
THE PLUSH RABBIT HELPS AS WELL!
MY TRIUMPHANT RETURN... RUINED...
OH, THE JOY... THE CALMNESS... THE SILENCE... THE BOREDOM!

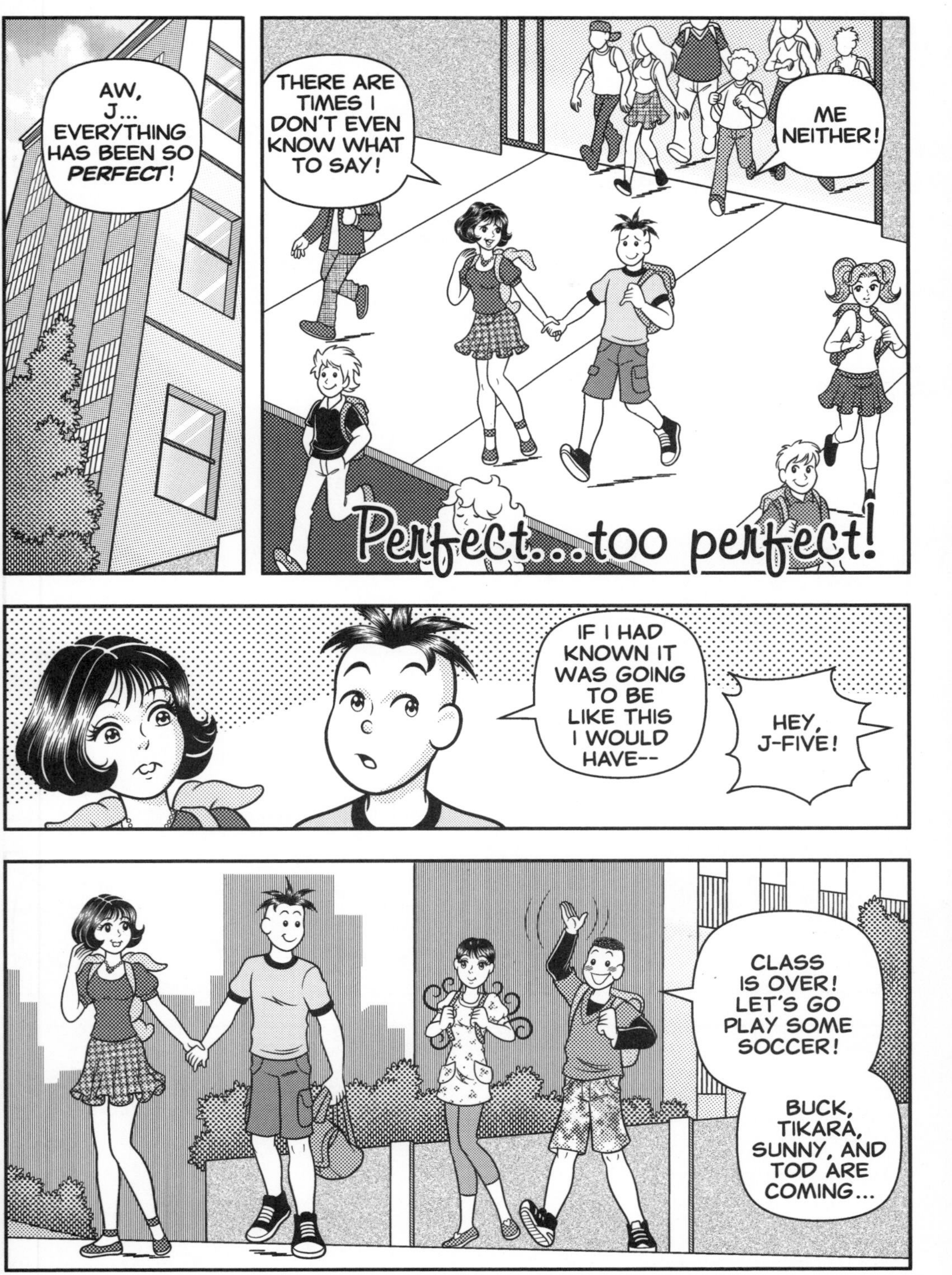
AW, J... EVERYTHING HAS BEEN SO *PERFECT*!
THERE ARE TIMES I DON'T EVEN KNOW WHAT TO SAY!
ME NEITHER!
Perfect...too perfect!
IF I HAD KNOWN IT WAS GOING TO BE LIKE THIS I WOULD HAVE--
HEY, J-FIVE!
CLASS IS OVER! LET'S GO PLAY SOME SOCCER!
BUCK, TIKARA, SUNNY, AND TOD ARE COMING...

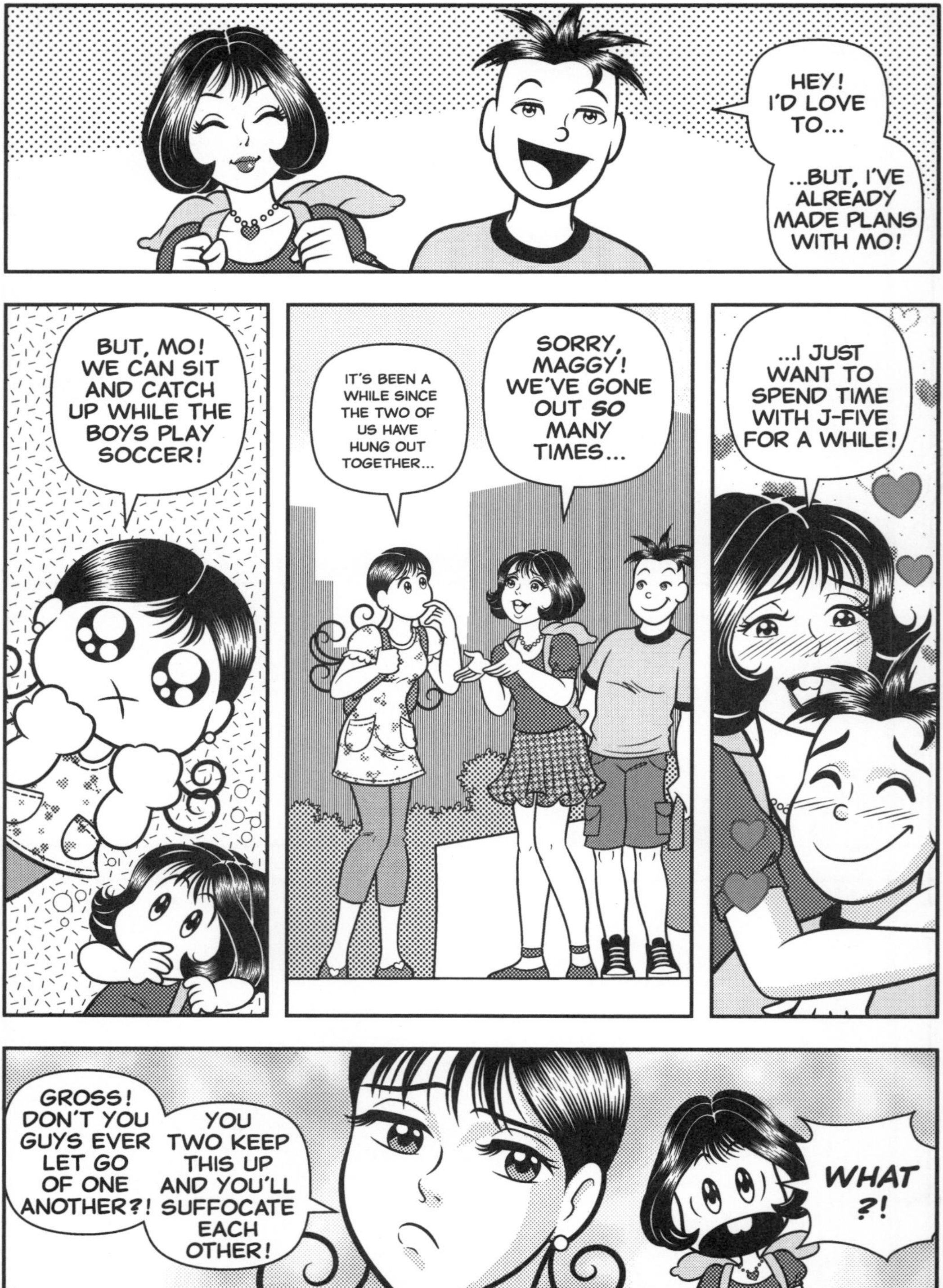
HEY! I'D LOVE TO...
...BUT, I'VE ALREADY MADE PLANS WITH MO!
BUT, MO! WE CAN SIT AND CATCH UP WHILE THE BOYS PLAY SOCCER!
IT'S BEEN A WHILE SINCE THE TWO OF US HAVE HUNG OUT TOGETHER...
SORRY, MAGGY! WE'VE GONE OUT SO MANY TIMES...
...I JUST WANT TO SPEND TIME WITH J-FIVE FOR A WHILE!
GROSS! DON'T YOU GUYS EVER LET GO OF ONE ANOTHER?!
YOU TWO KEEP THIS UP AND YOU'LL SUFFOCATE EACH OTHER!
WHAT ?!

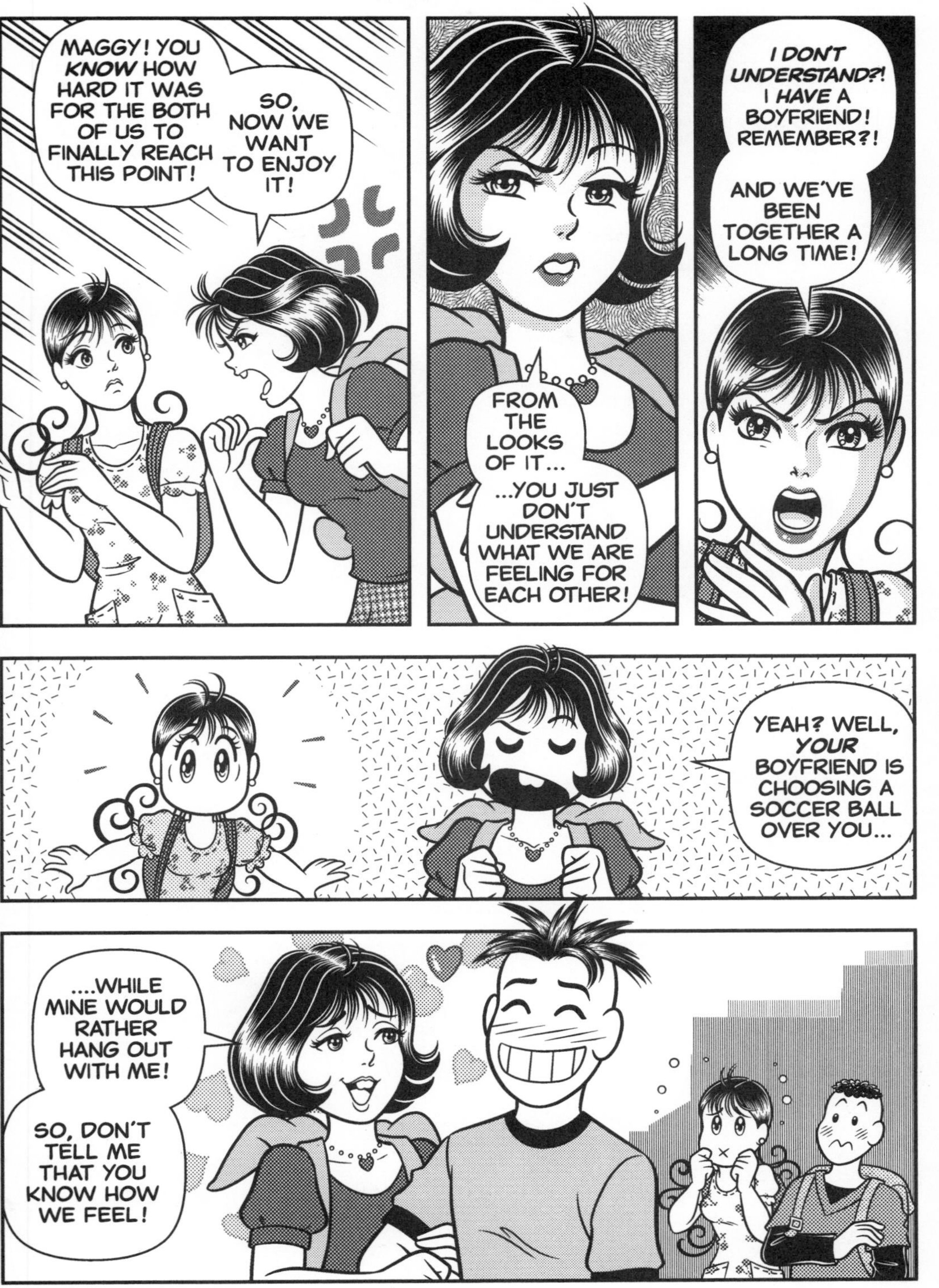

MAGGY! YOU *KNOW* HOW HARD IT WAS FOR THE BOTH OF US TO FINALLY REACH THIS POINT!
SO, NOW WE WANT TO ENJOY IT!
FROM THE LOOKS OF IT...
...YOU JUST DON'T UNDERSTAND WHAT WE ARE FEELING FOR EACH OTHER!
I DON'T UNDERSTAND?! I *HAVE* A BOYFRIEND! REMEMBER?!
AND WE'VE BEEN TOGETHER A LONG TIME!
YEAH? WELL, *YOUR* BOYFRIEND IS CHOOSING A SOCCER BALL OVER YOU...
....WHILE MINE WOULD RATHER HANG OUT WITH ME!
SO, DON'T TELL ME THAT YOU KNOW HOW WE FEEL!

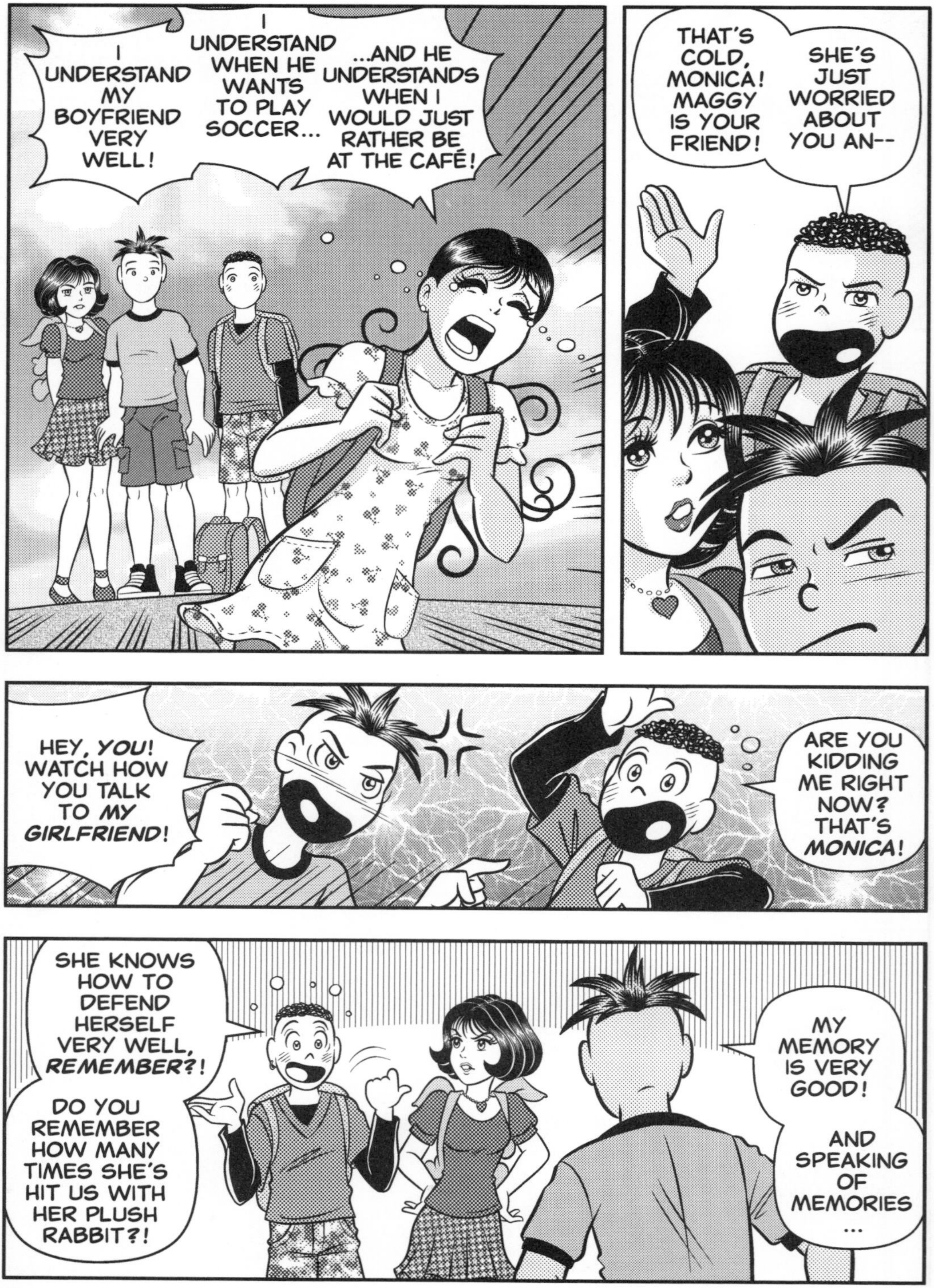
I UNDERSTAND MY BOYFRIEND VERY WELL!
I UNDERSTAND WHEN HE WANTS TO PLAY SOCCER...
...AND HE UNDERSTANDS WHEN I WOULD JUST RATHER BE AT THE CAFÉ!
THAT'S COLD, MONICA! MAGGY IS YOUR FRIEND!
SHE'S JUST WORRIED ABOUT YOU AN--
HEY, *YOU*! WATCH HOW YOU TALK TO *MY GIRLFRIEND*!
ARE YOU KIDDING ME RIGHT NOW? THAT'S *MONICA*!
SHE KNOWS HOW TO DEFEND HERSELF VERY WELL, *REMEMBER?*!
DO YOU REMEMBER HOW MANY TIMES SHE'S HIT US WITH HER PLUSH RABBIT?!
MY MEMORY IS VERY GOOD!
AND SPEAKING OF MEMORIES ...

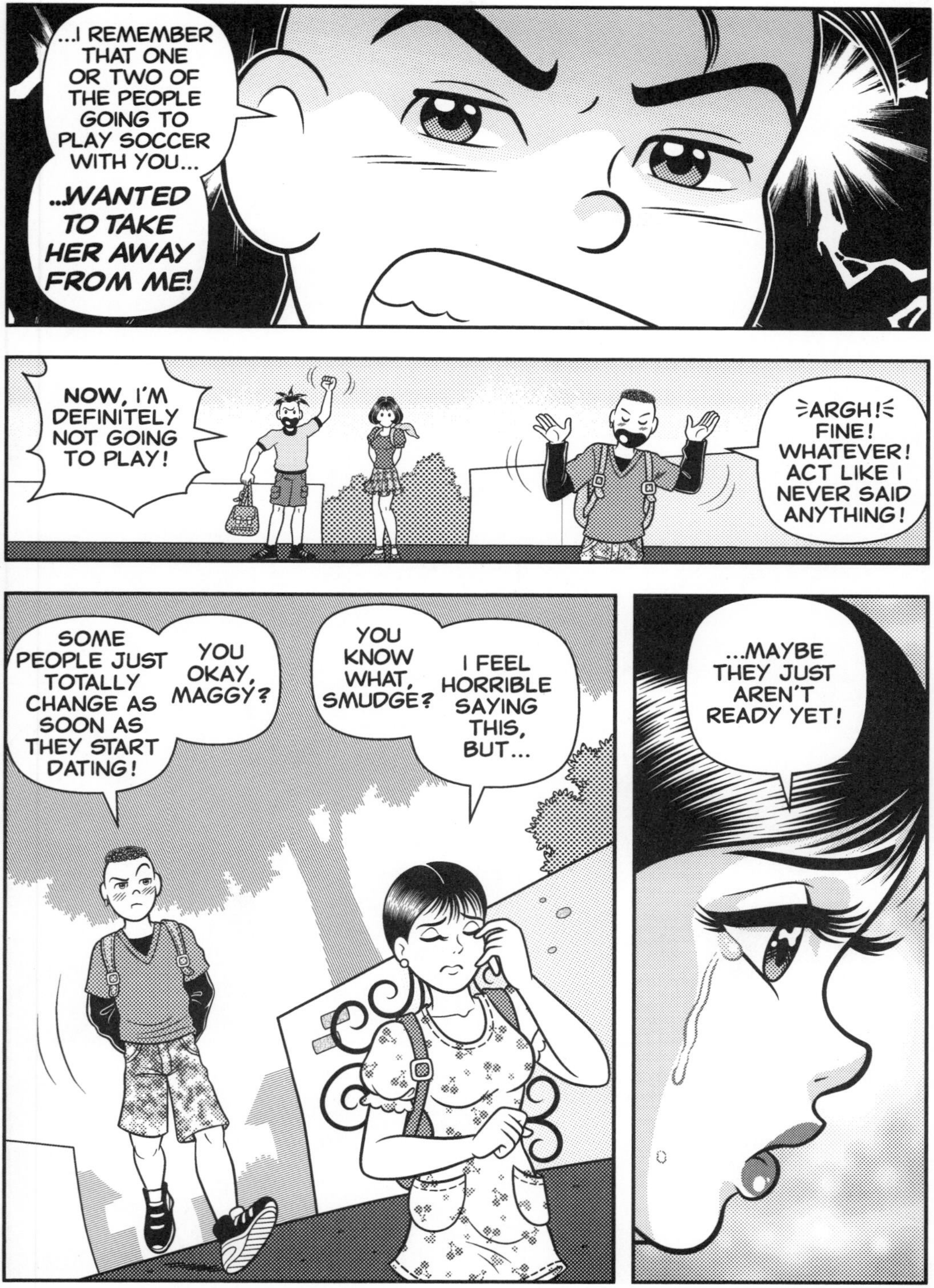
...I REMEMBER THAT ONE OR TWO OF THE PEOPLE GOING TO PLAY SOCCER WITH YOU...
...WANTED TO TAKE HER AWAY FROM ME!
NOW, I'M DEFINITELY NOT GOING TO PLAY!
ARGH! FINE! WHATEVER! ACT LIKE I NEVER SAID ANYTHING!
SOME PEOPLE JUST TOTALLY CHANGE AS SOON AS THEY START DATING!
YOU OKAY, MAGGY?
YOU KNOW WHAT, SMUDGE?
I FEEL HORRIBLE SAYING THIS, BUT...
...MAYBE THEY JUST AREN'T READY YET!

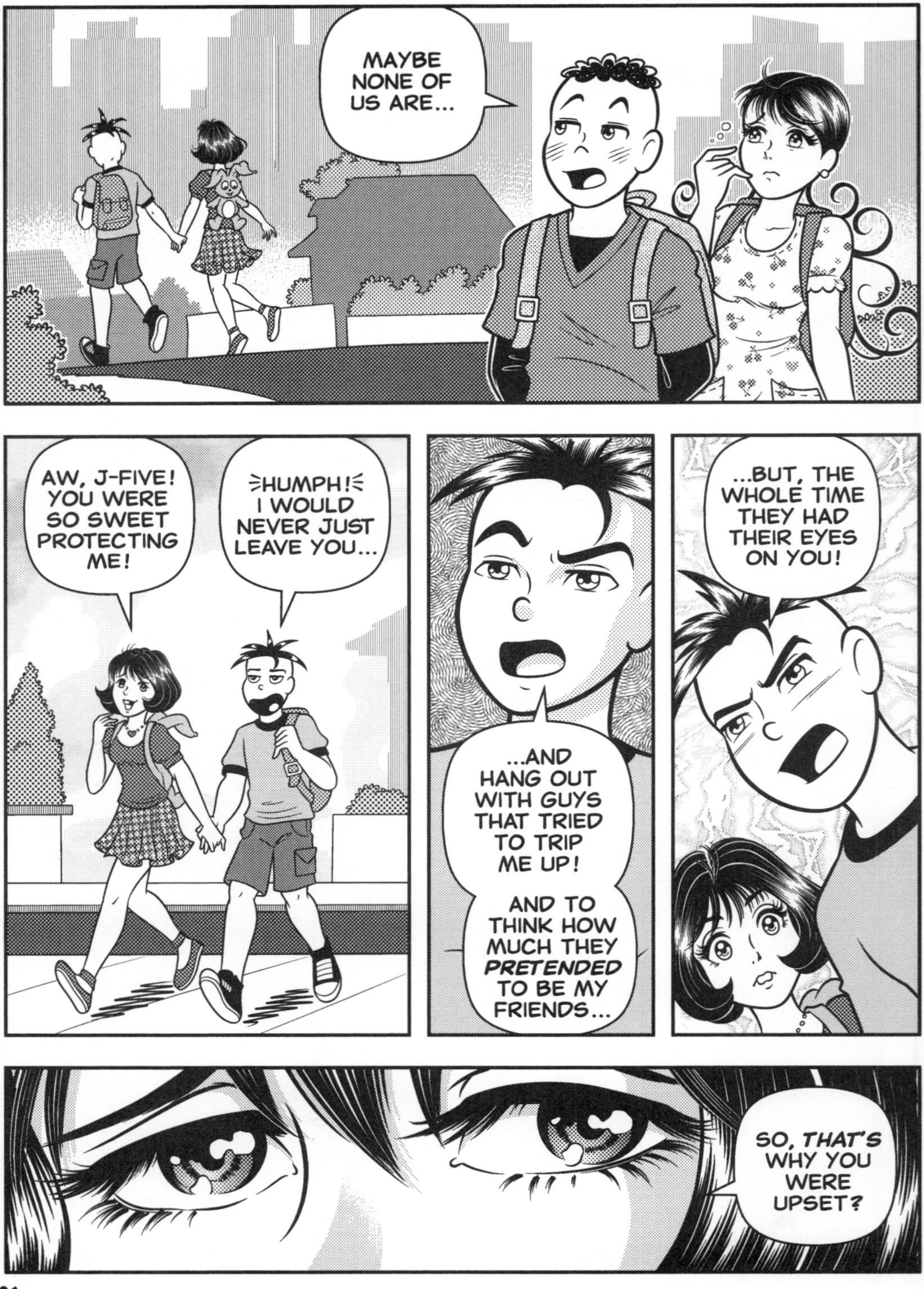
MAYBE NONE OF US ARE...
AW, J-FIVE! YOU WERE SO SWEET PROTECTING ME!
HUMPH! I WOULD NEVER JUST LEAVE YOU...
...AND HANG OUT WITH GUYS THAT TRIED TO TRIP ME UP!
AND TO THINK HOW MUCH THEY *PRETENDED* TO BE MY FRIENDS...
...BUT, THE WHOLE TIME THEY HAD THEIR EYES ON YOU!
SO, *THAT'S* WHY YOU WERE UPSET?

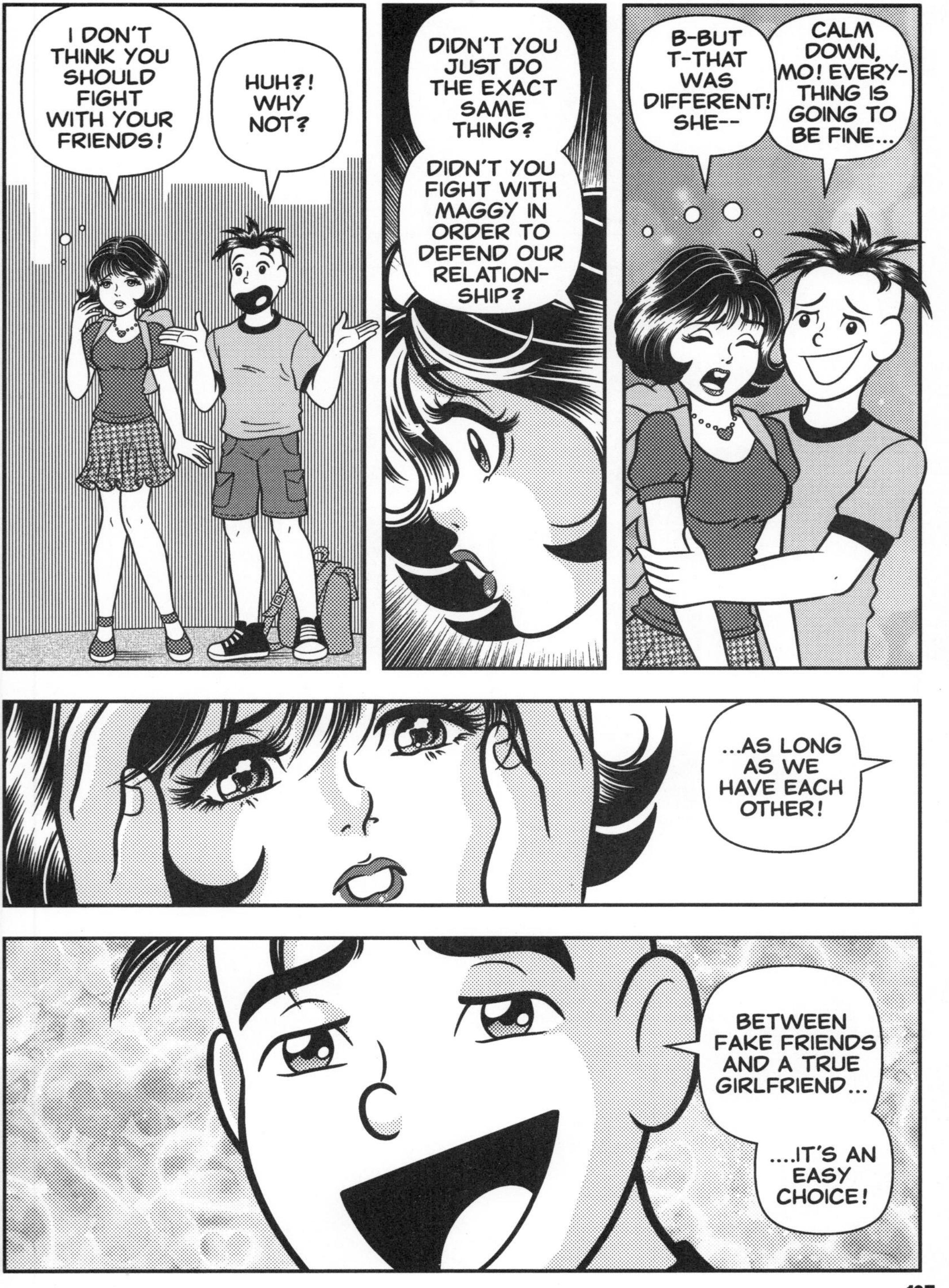
I DON'T THINK YOU SHOULD FIGHT WITH YOUR FRIENDS!
HUH?! WHY NOT?
DIDN'T YOU JUST DO THE EXACT SAME THING?
DIDN'T YOU FIGHT WITH MAGGY IN ORDER TO DEFEND OUR RELATION-SHIP?
B-BUT T-THAT WAS DIFFERENT! SHE--
CALM DOWN, MO! EVERY-THING IS GOING TO BE FINE...
...AS LONG AS WE HAVE EACH OTHER!
BETWEEN FAKE FRIENDS AND A TRUE GIRLFRIEND...
....IT'S AN EASY CHOICE!

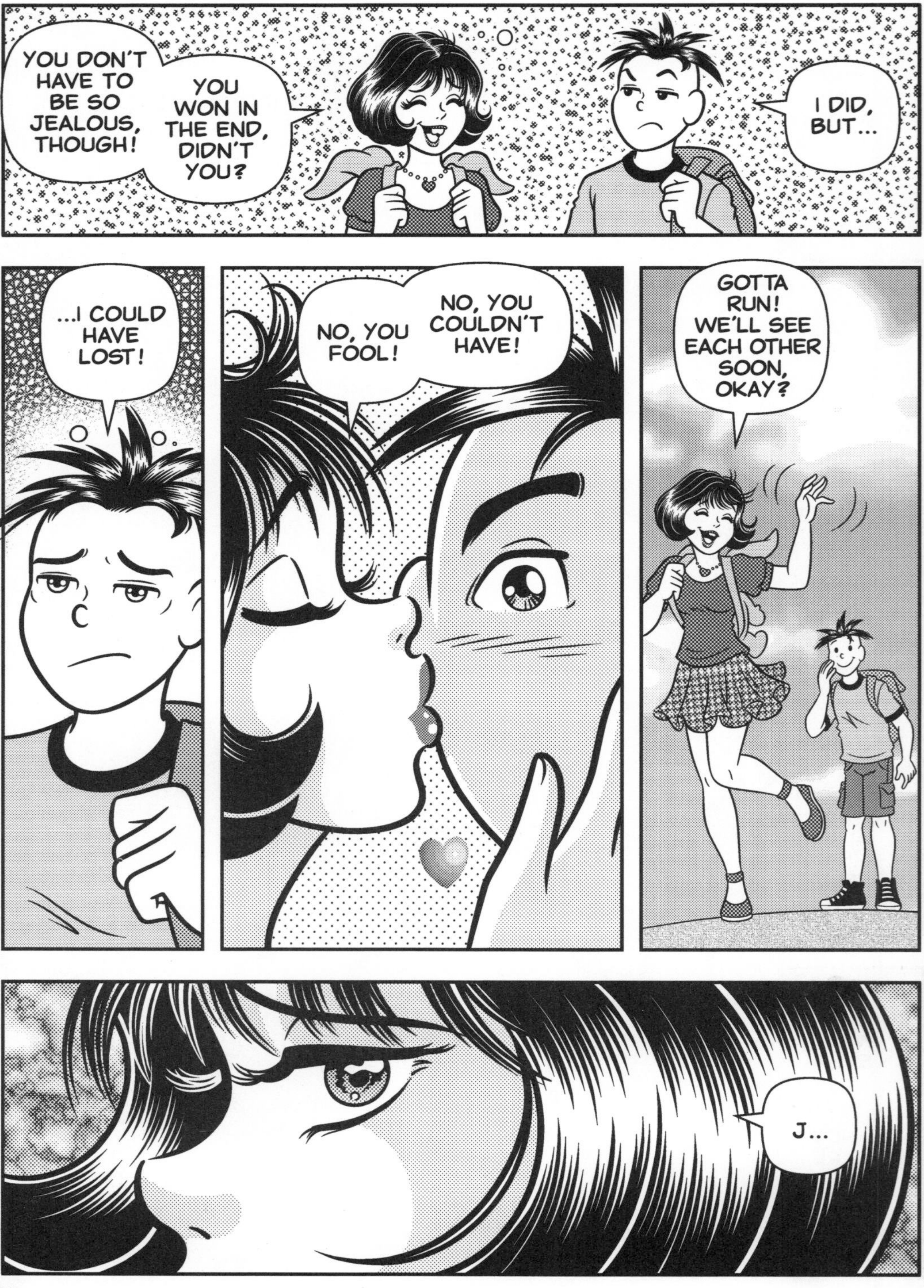
YOU DON'T HAVE TO BE SO JEALOUS, THOUGH!
YOU WON IN THE END, DIDN'T YOU?
I DID, BUT...
...I COULD HAVE LOST!
NO, YOU FOOL!
NO, YOU COULDN'T HAVE!
GOTTA RUN! WE'LL SEE EACH OTHER SOON, OKAY?
J...

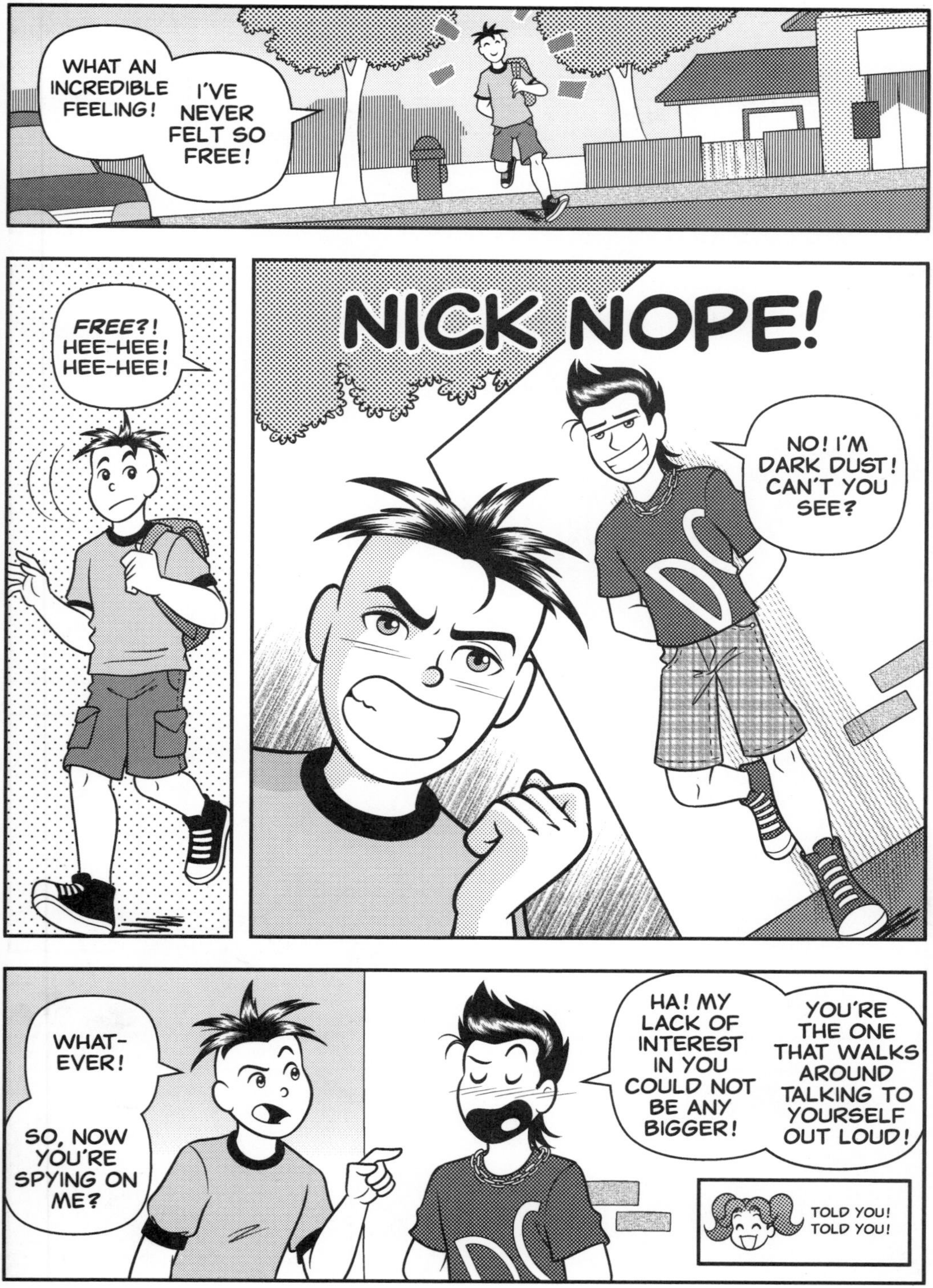
WHAT AN INCREDIBLE FEELING!
I'VE NEVER FELT SO FREE!
FREE?! HEE-HEE! HEE-HEE!
NICK NOPE!
NO! I'M DARK DUST! CAN'T YOU SEE?
WHAT-EVER!
SO, NOW YOU'RE SPYING ON ME?
HA! MY LACK OF INTEREST IN YOU COULD NOT BE ANY BIGGER!
YOU'RE THE ONE THAT WALKS AROUND TALKING TO YOURSELF OUT LOUD!
TOLD YOU! TOLD YOU!

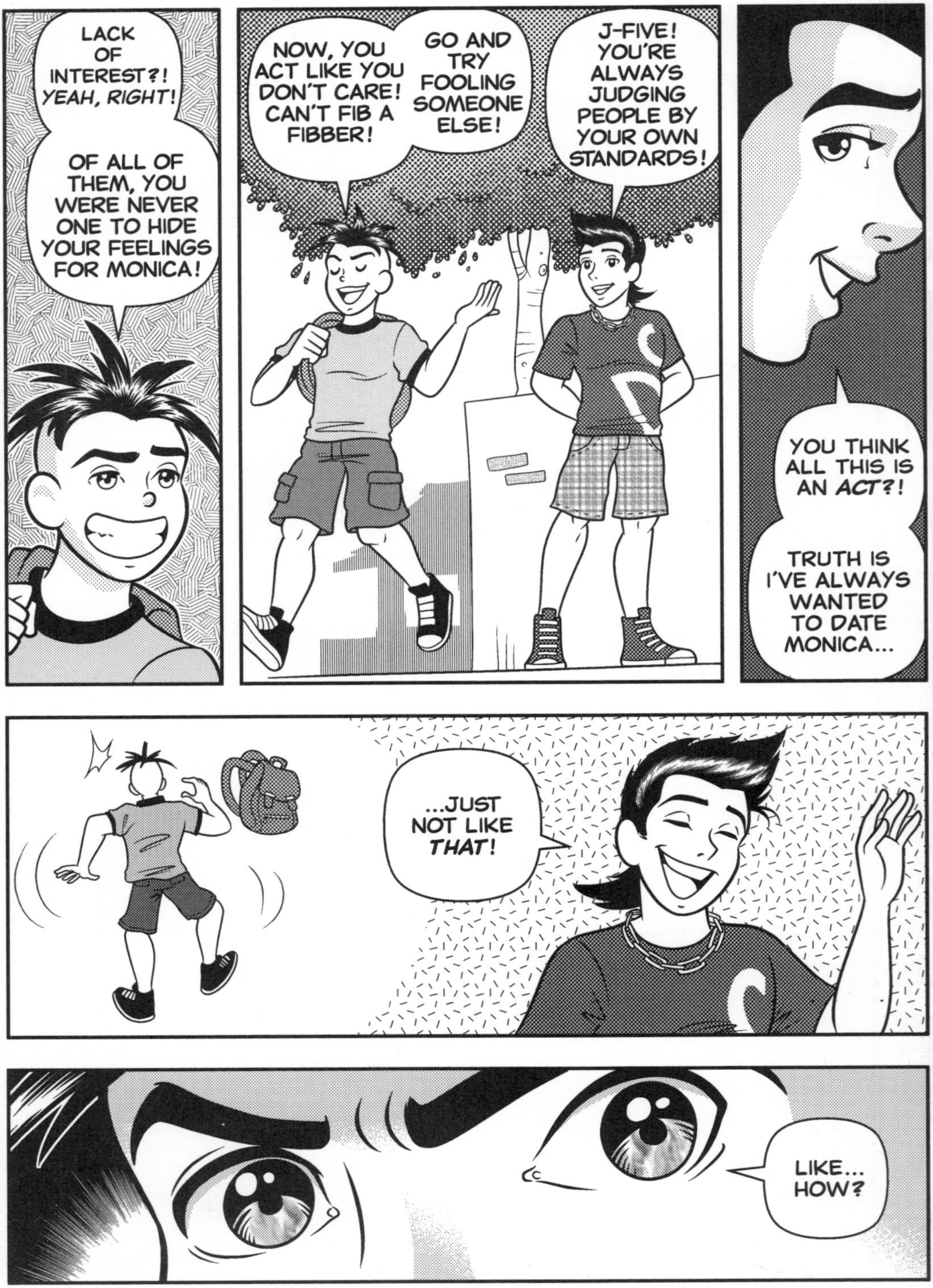
LACK OF INTEREST?! YEAH, RIGHT!
OF ALL OF THEM, YOU WERE NEVER ONE TO HIDE YOUR FEELINGS FOR MONICA!
NOW, YOU ACT LIKE YOU DON'T CARE! CAN'T FIB A FIBBER!
GO AND TRY FOOLING SOMEONE ELSE!
J-FIVE! YOU'RE ALWAYS JUDGING PEOPLE BY YOUR OWN STANDARDS!
YOU THINK ALL THIS IS AN ACT?!
TRUTH IS I'VE ALWAYS WANTED TO DATE MONICA...
...JUST NOT LIKE THAT!
LIKE... HOW?

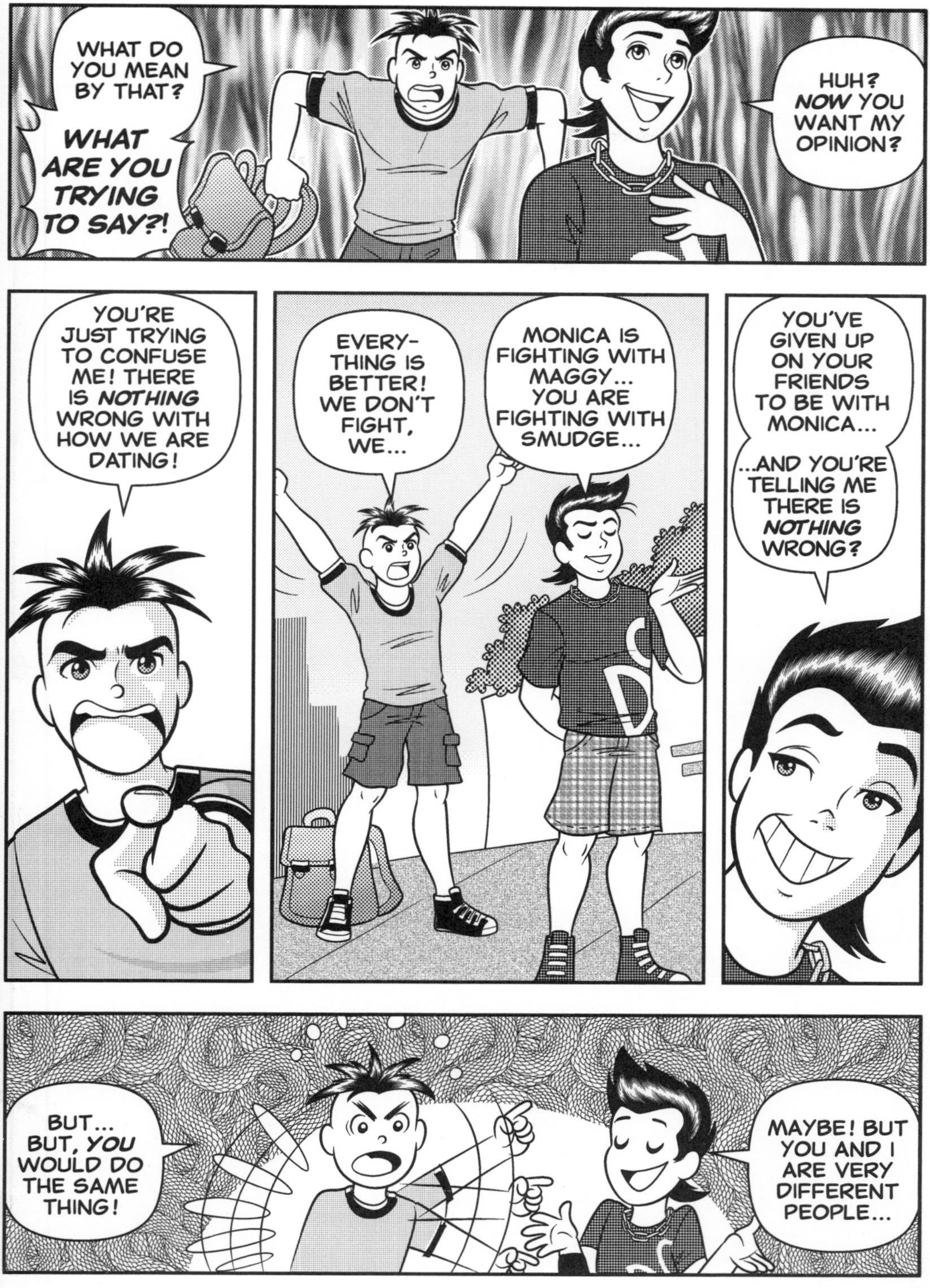
WHAT DO YOU MEAN BY THAT?
WHAT ARE YOU TRYING TO SAY?!
HUH? NOW YOU WANT MY OPINION?
YOU'RE JUST TRYING TO CONFUSE ME! THERE IS NOTHING WRONG WITH HOW WE ARE DATING!
EVERY-THING IS BETTER! WE DON'T FIGHT, WE...
MONICA IS FIGHTING WITH MAGGY... YOU ARE FIGHTING WITH SMUDGE...
YOU'VE GIVEN UP ON YOUR FRIENDS TO BE WITH MONICA...
...AND YOU'RE TELLING ME THERE IS NOTHING WRONG?
BUT... BUT, YOU WOULD DO THE SAME THING!
MAYBE! BUT YOU AND I ARE VERY DIFFERENT PEOPLE...

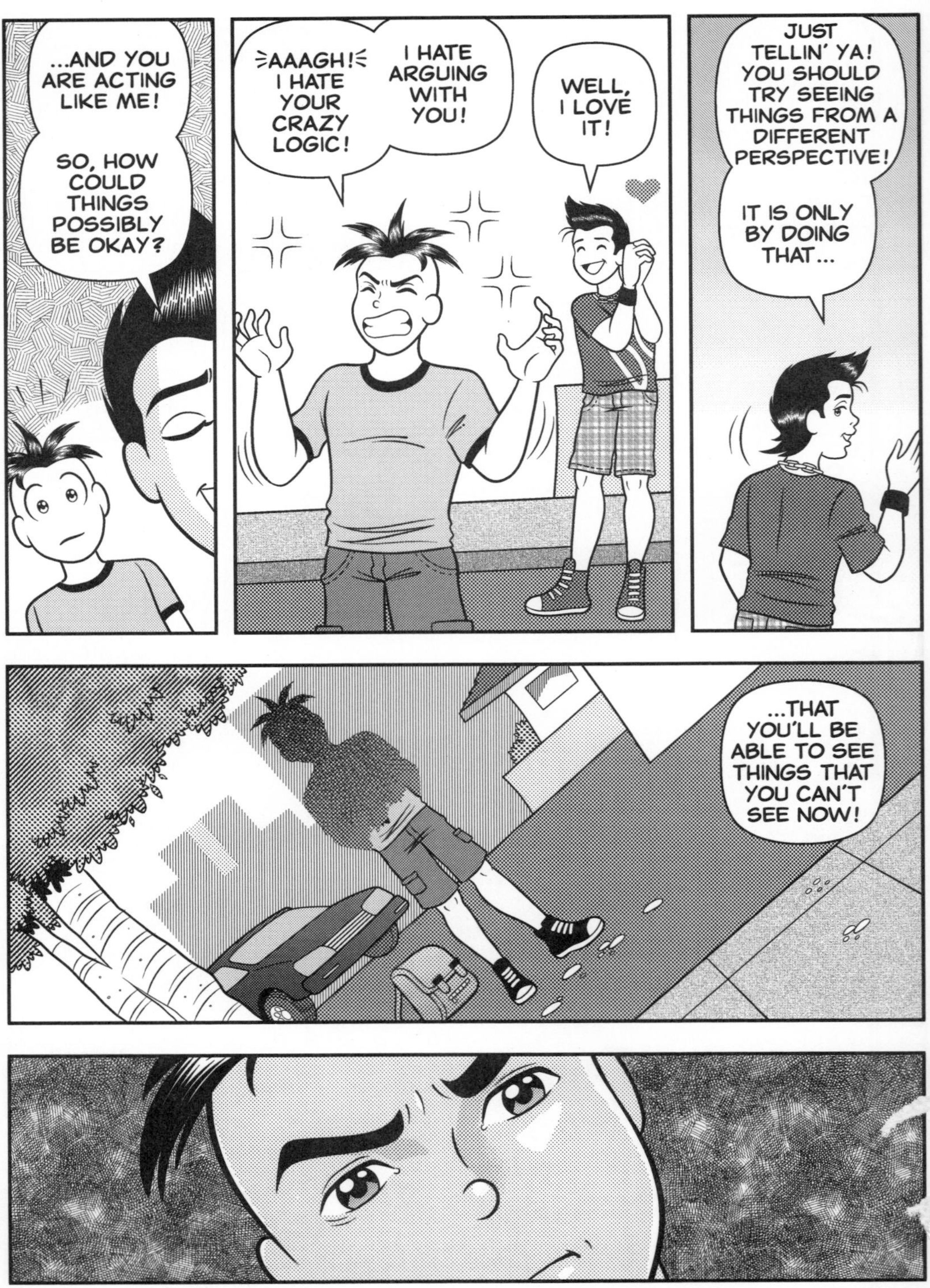
...AND YOU ARE ACTING LIKE ME!
SO, HOW COULD THINGS POSSIBLY BE OKAY?
AAAGH! I HATE YOUR CRAZY LOGIC!
I HATE ARGUING WITH YOU!
WELL, I LOVE IT!
JUST TELLIN' YA! YOU SHOULD TRY SEEING THINGS FROM A DIFFERENT PERSPECTIVE!
IT IS ONLY BY DOING THAT...
...THAT YOU'LL BE ABLE TO SEE THINGS THAT YOU CAN'T SEE NOW!

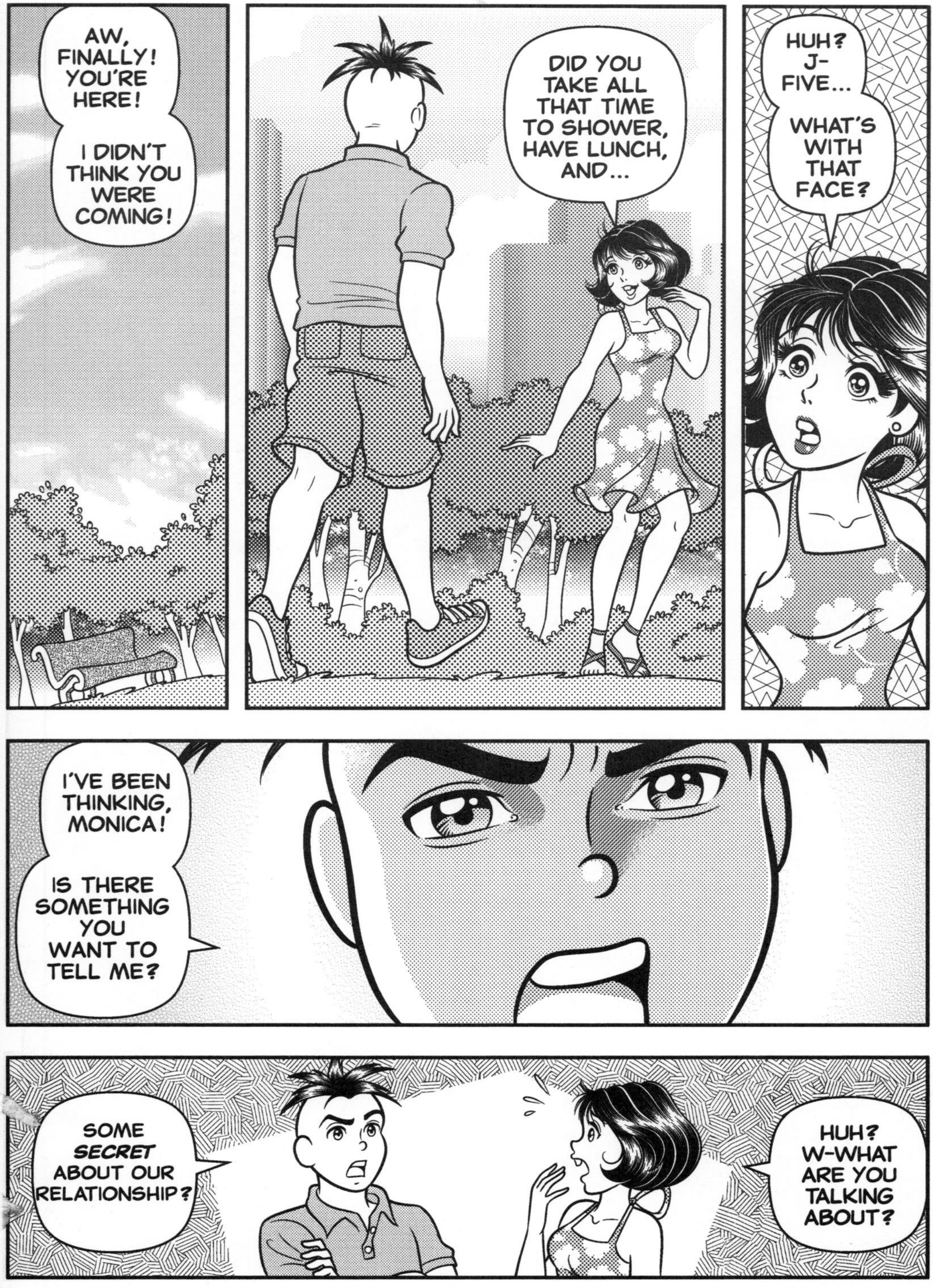
AW, FINALLY! YOU'RE HERE!
I DIDN'T THINK YOU WERE COMING!
DID YOU TAKE ALL THAT TIME TO SHOWER, HAVE LUNCH, AND...
HUH? J-FIVE...
WHAT'S WITH THAT FACE?
I'VE BEEN THINKING, MONICA!
IS THERE SOMETHING YOU WANT TO TELL ME?
SOME *SECRET* ABOUT OUR RELATIONSHIP?
HUH? W-WHAT ARE YOU TALKING ABOUT?

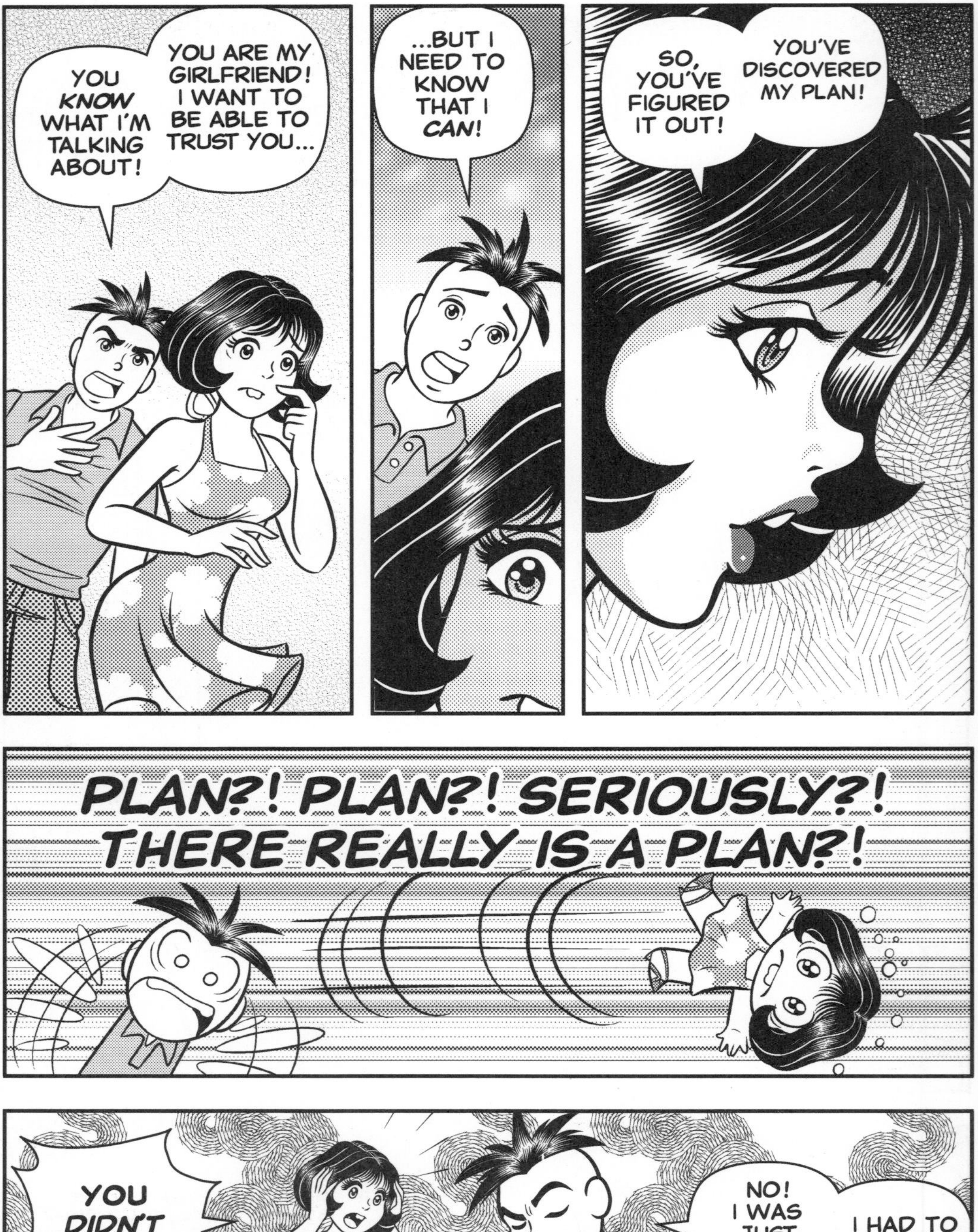
YOU KNOW WHAT I'M TALKING ABOUT!
YOU ARE MY GIRLFRIEND! I WANT TO BE ABLE TO TRUST YOU...
...BUT I NEED TO KNOW THAT I CAN!
SO, YOU'VE FIGURED IT OUT!
YOU'VE DISCOVERED MY PLAN!
PLAN?! PLAN?! SERIOUSLY?! THERE REALLY IS A PLAN?!
YOU DIDN'T KNOW?!
NO! I WAS JUST SUSPICIOUS!
I HAD TO RISK IT AND FIND OUT!

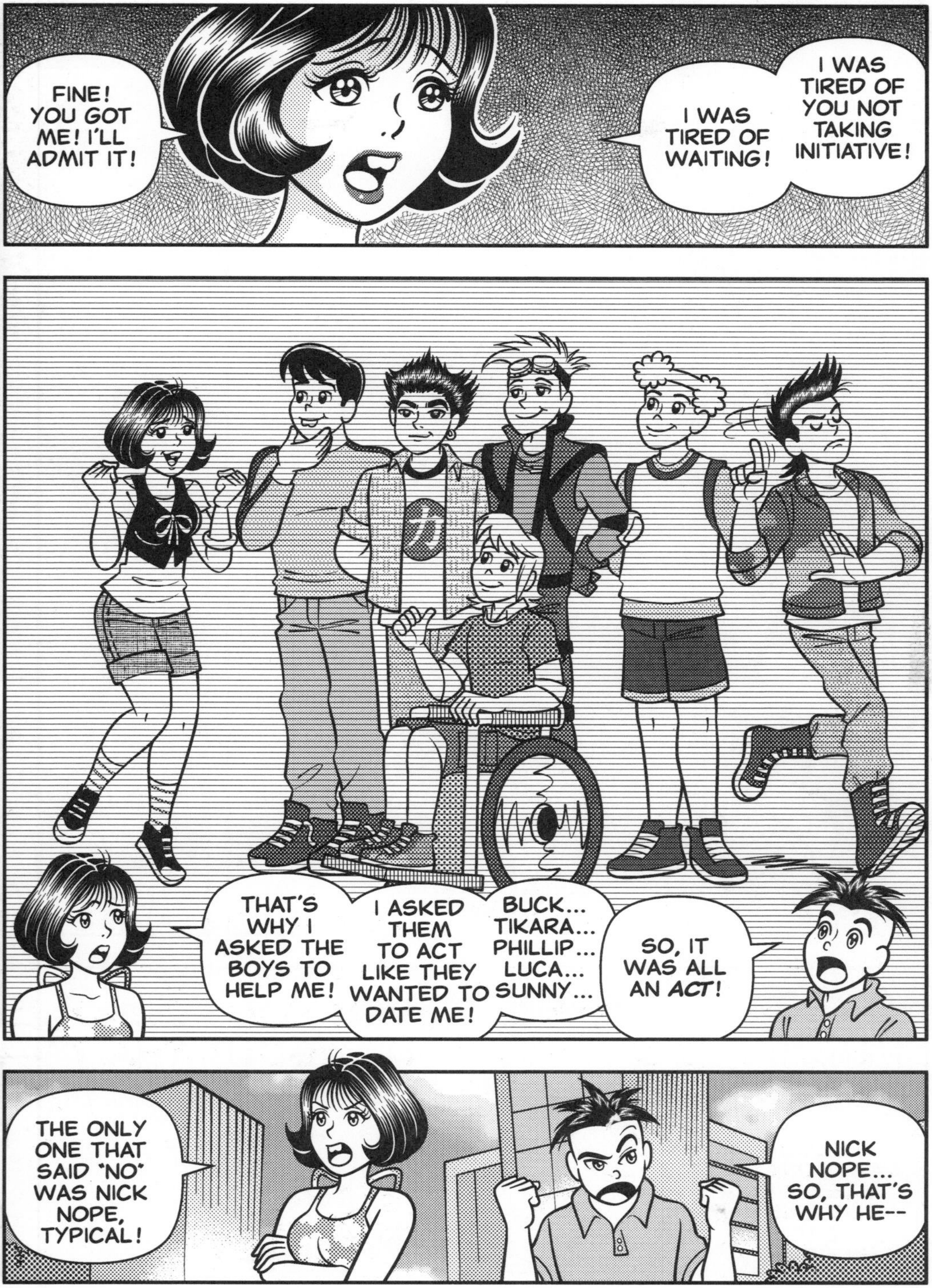
FINE! YOU GOT ME! I'LL ADMIT IT!
I WAS TIRED OF WAITING!
I WAS TIRED OF YOU NOT TAKING INITIATIVE!
THAT'S WHY I ASKED THE BOYS TO HELP ME!
I ASKED THEM TO ACT LIKE THEY WANTED TO DATE ME!
BUCK... TIKARA... PHILLIP... LUCA... SUNNY...
SO, IT WAS ALL AN *ACT*!
THE ONLY ONE THAT SAID "NO" WAS NICK NOPE, TYPICAL!
NICK NOPE... SO, THAT'S WHY HE--

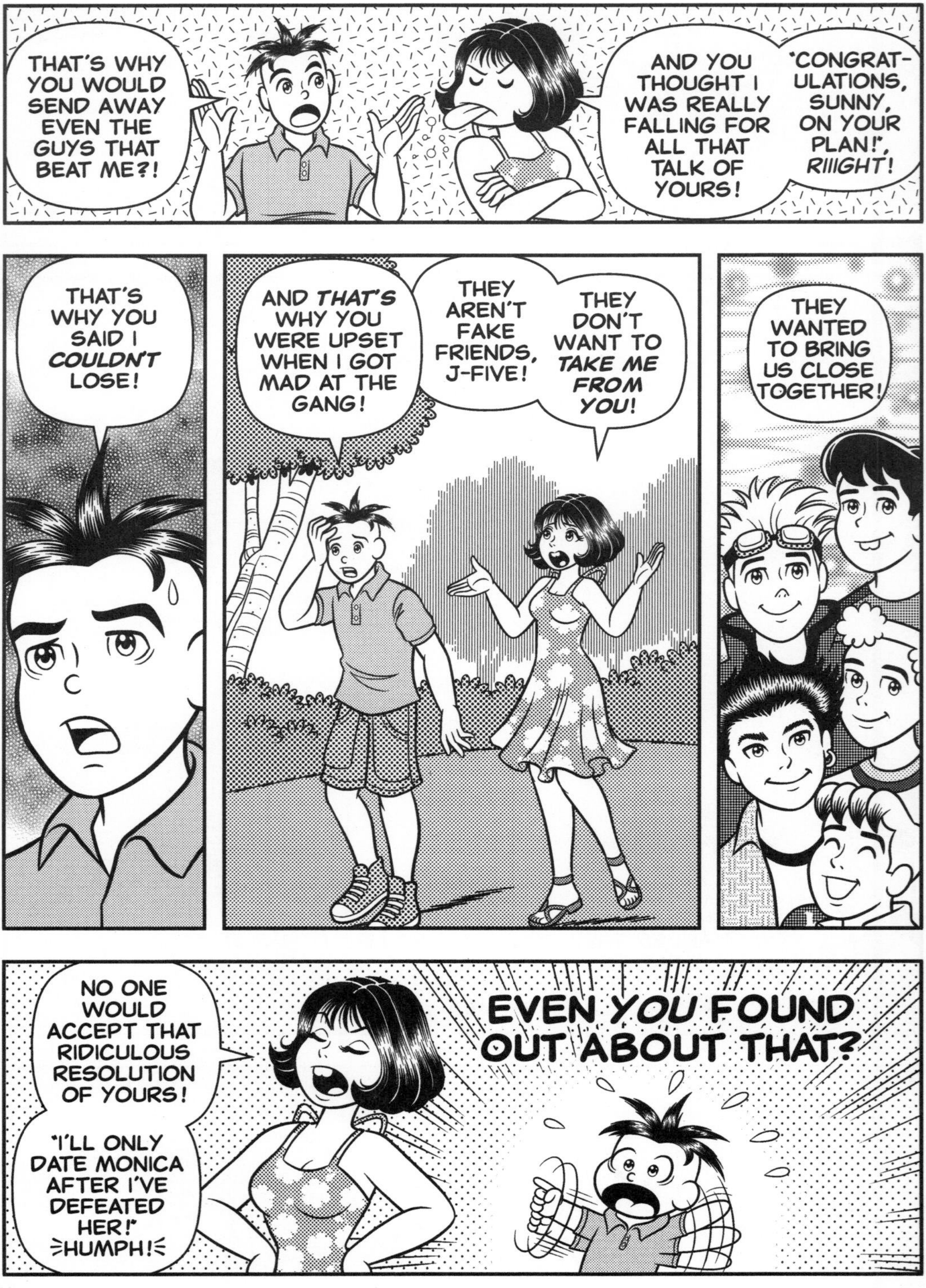
THAT'S WHY YOU WOULD SEND AWAY EVEN THE GUYS THAT BEAT ME?!
AND YOU THOUGHT I WAS REALLY FALLING FOR ALL THAT TALK OF YOURS!
"CONGRATULATIONS, SUNNY, ON YOUR PLAN!", RIIIGHT!
THAT'S WHY YOU SAID I COULDN'T LOSE!
AND THAT'S WHY YOU WERE UPSET WHEN I GOT MAD AT THE GANG!
THEY AREN'T FAKE FRIENDS, J-FIVE!
THEY DON'T WANT TO TAKE ME FROM YOU!
THEY WANTED TO BRING US CLOSE TOGETHER!
NO ONE WOULD ACCEPT THAT RIDICULOUS RESOLUTION OF YOURS!
"I'LL ONLY DATE MONICA AFTER I'VE DEFEATED HER!" HUMPH!
EVEN YOU FOUND OUT ABOUT THAT?

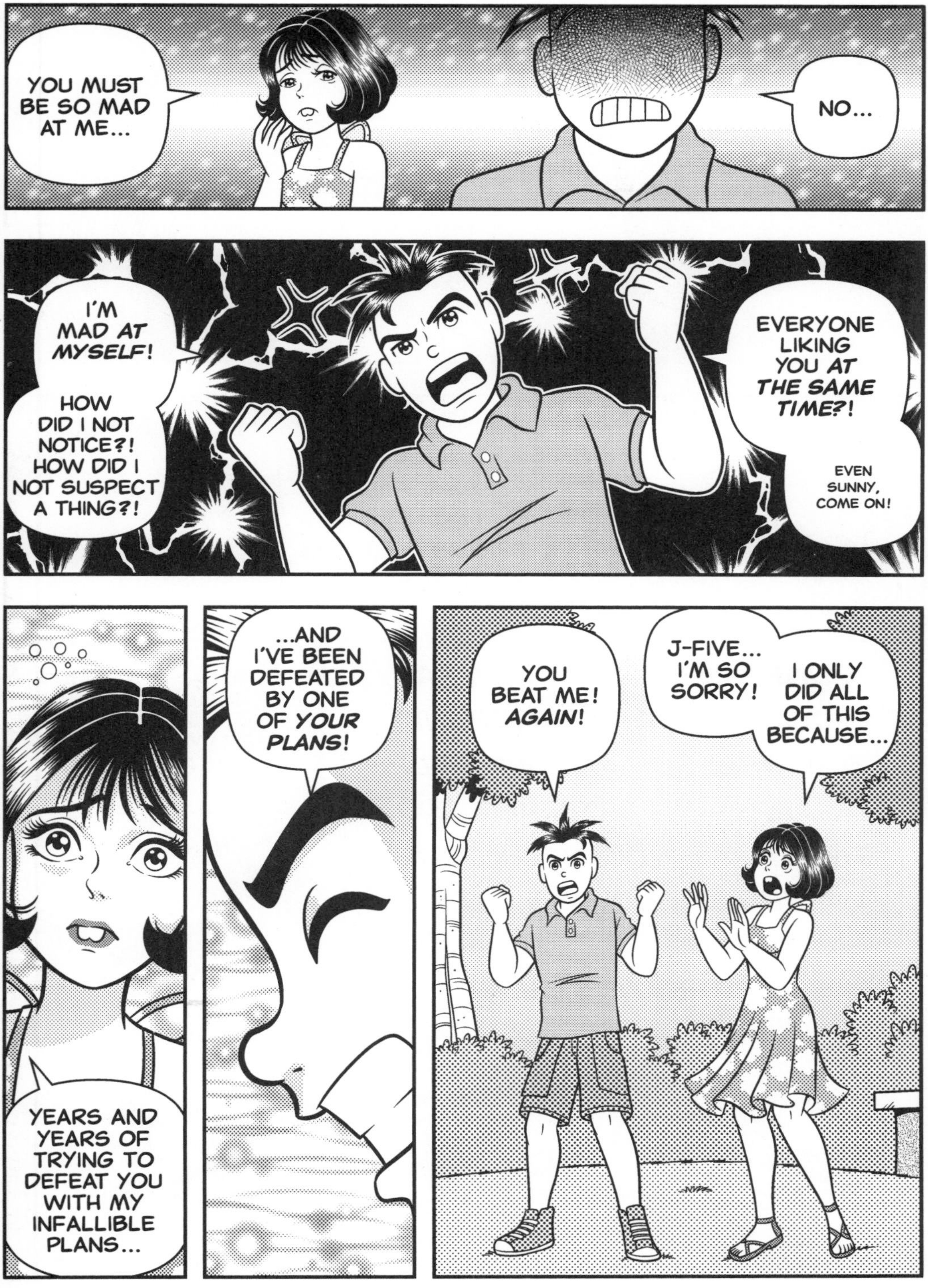
YOU MUST BE SO MAD AT ME...
NO...
I'M MAD AT *MYSELF*!
HOW DID I NOT NOTICE?! HOW DID I NOT SUSPECT A THING?!
EVERYONE LIKING YOU *AT THE SAME TIME?!*
EVEN SUNNY, COME ON!
YEARS AND YEARS OF TRYING TO DEFEAT YOU WITH MY INFALLIBLE PLANS...
...AND I'VE BEEN DEFEATED BY ONE OF *YOUR PLANS*!
YOU BEAT ME! *AGAIN*!
J-FIVE... I'M SO SORRY!
I ONLY DID ALL OF THIS BECAUSE...

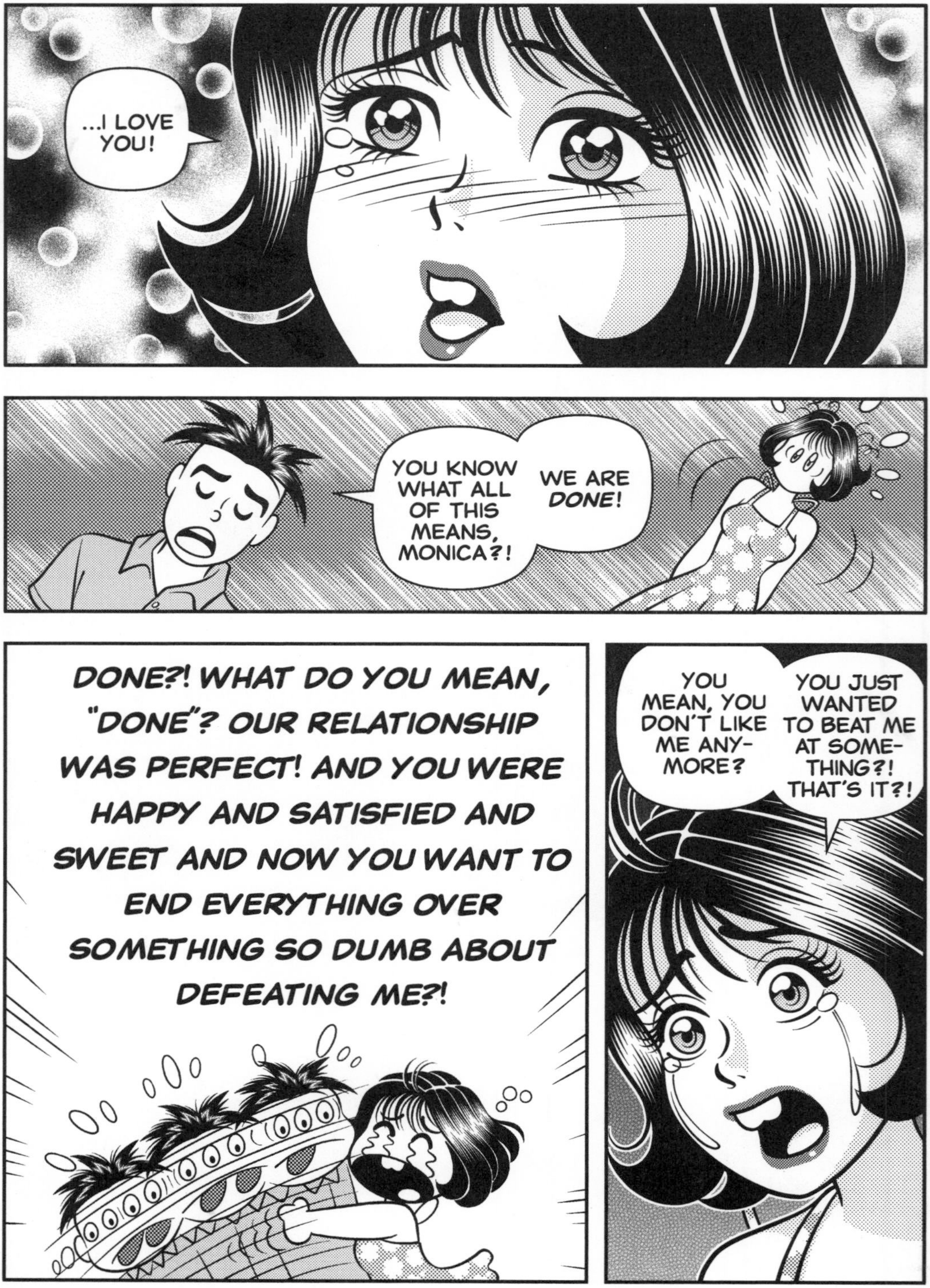
...I LOVE YOU!
YOU KNOW WHAT ALL OF THIS MEANS, MONICA?!
WE ARE DONE!
DONE?! WHAT DO YOU MEAN, "DONE"? OUR RELATIONSHIP WAS PERFECT! AND YOU WERE HAPPY AND SATISFIED AND SWEET AND NOW YOU WANT TO END EVERYTHING OVER SOMETHING SO DUMB ABOUT DEFEATING ME?!
YOU MEAN, YOU DON'T LIKE ME ANY-MORE?
YOU JUST WANTED TO BEAT ME AT SOME-THING?! THAT'S IT?!

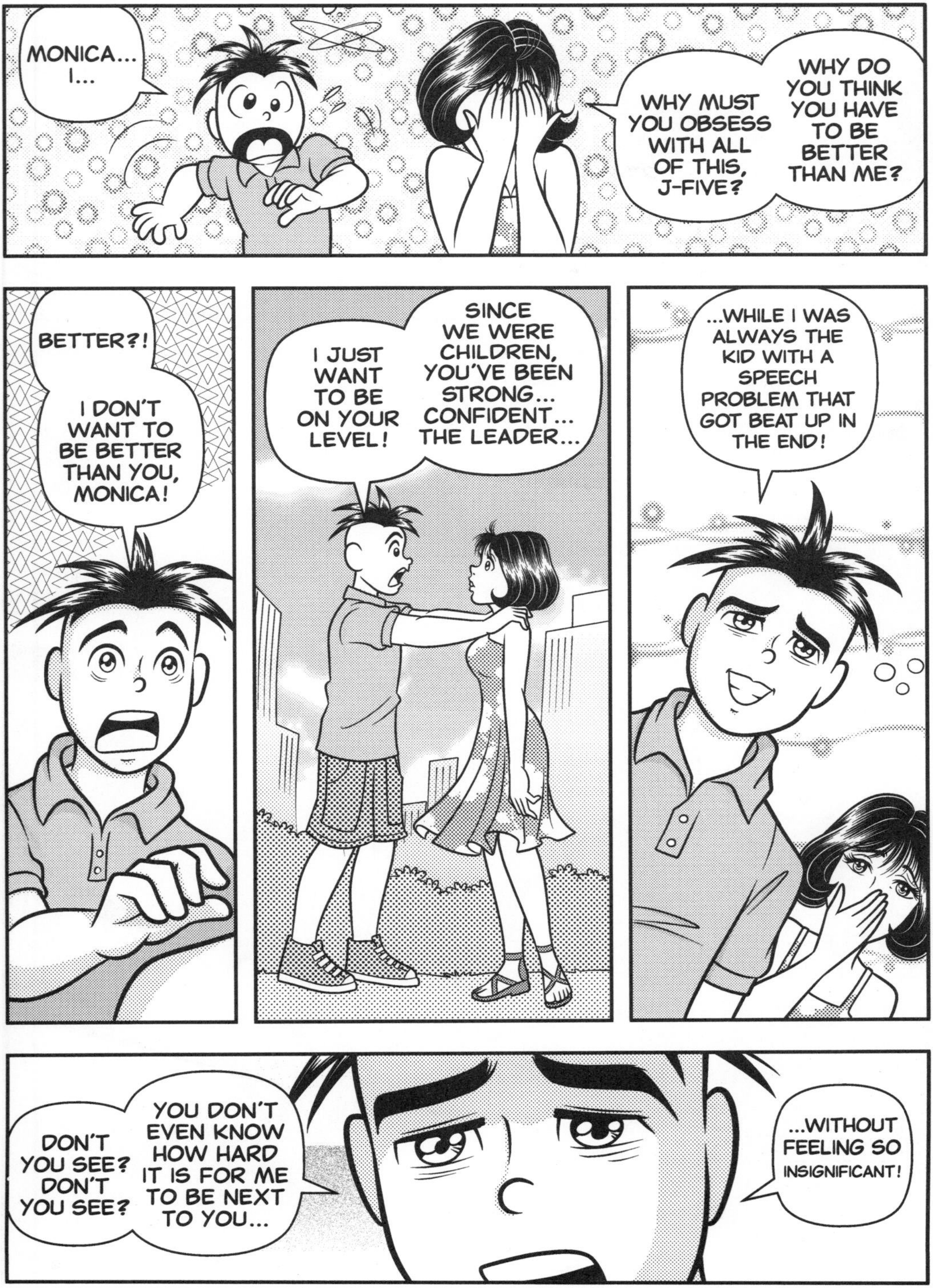
MONICA... I...
WHY MUST YOU OBSESS WITH ALL OF THIS, J-FIVE?
WHY DO YOU THINK YOU HAVE TO BE BETTER THAN ME?
BETTER?!
I DON'T WANT TO BE BETTER THAN YOU, MONICA!
I JUST WANT TO BE ON YOUR LEVEL!
SINCE WE WERE CHILDREN, YOU'VE BEEN STRONG... CONFIDENT... THE LEADER...
...WHILE I WAS ALWAYS THE KID WITH A SPEECH PROBLEM THAT GOT BEAT UP IN THE END!
DON'T YOU SEE? DON'T YOU SEE?
YOU DON'T EVEN KNOW HOW HARD IT IS FOR ME TO BE NEXT TO YOU...
...WITHOUT FEELING SO INSIGNIFICANT!

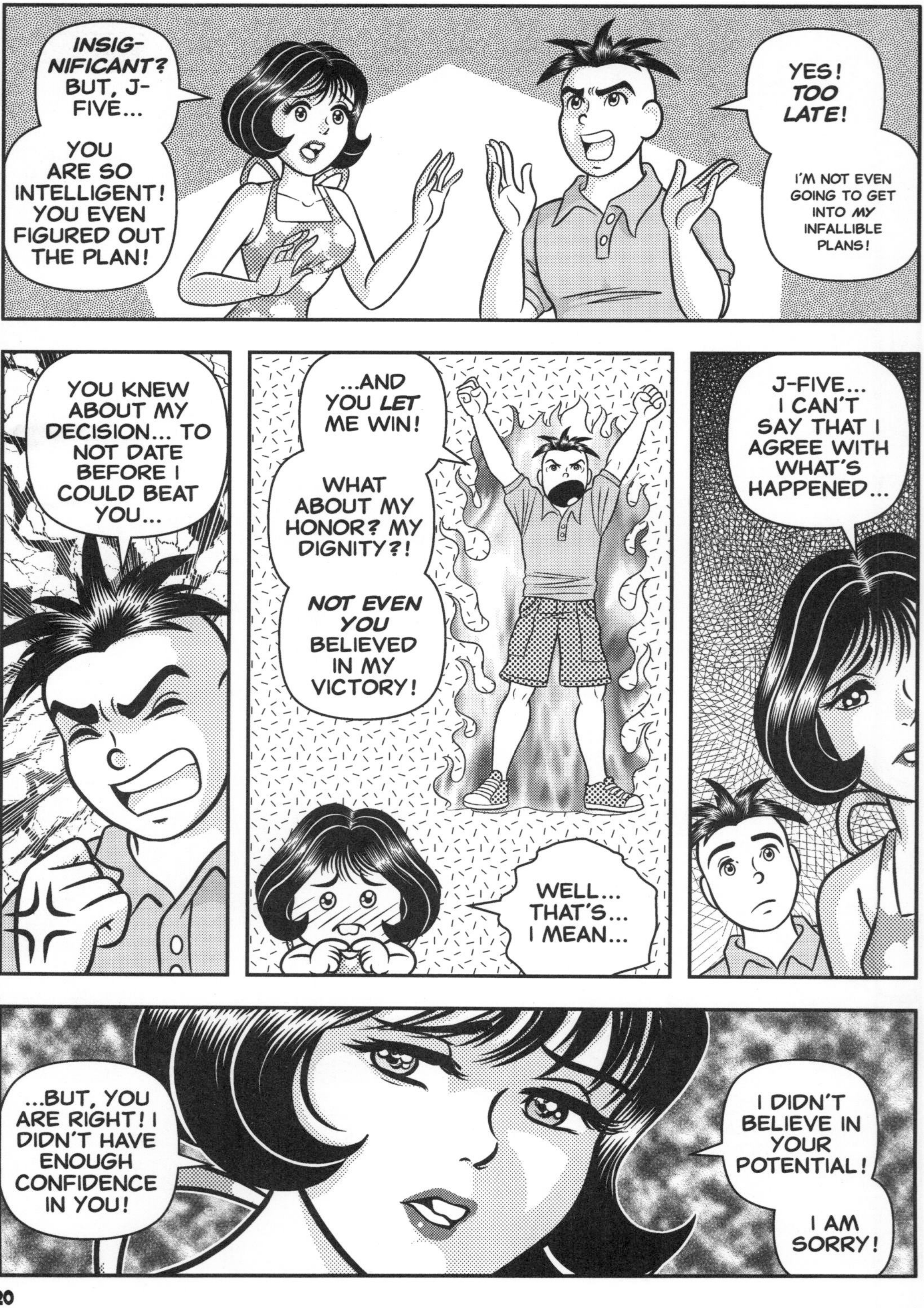
INSIG-NIFICANT? BUT, J-FIVE...
YOU ARE SO INTELLIGENT! YOU EVEN FIGURED OUT THE PLAN!
YES! TOO LATE!
I'M NOT EVEN GOING TO GET INTO MY INFALLIBLE PLANS!
YOU KNEW ABOUT MY DECISION... TO NOT DATE BEFORE I COULD BEAT YOU...
...AND YOU LET ME WIN!
WHAT ABOUT MY HONOR? MY DIGNITY?!
NOT EVEN YOU BELIEVED IN MY VICTORY!
WELL... THAT'S... I MEAN...
J-FIVE... I CAN'T SAY THAT I AGREE WITH WHAT'S HAPPENED...
...BUT, YOU ARE RIGHT! I DIDN'T HAVE ENOUGH CONFIDENCE IN YOU!
I DIDN'T BELIEVE IN YOUR POTENTIAL!
I AM SORRY!

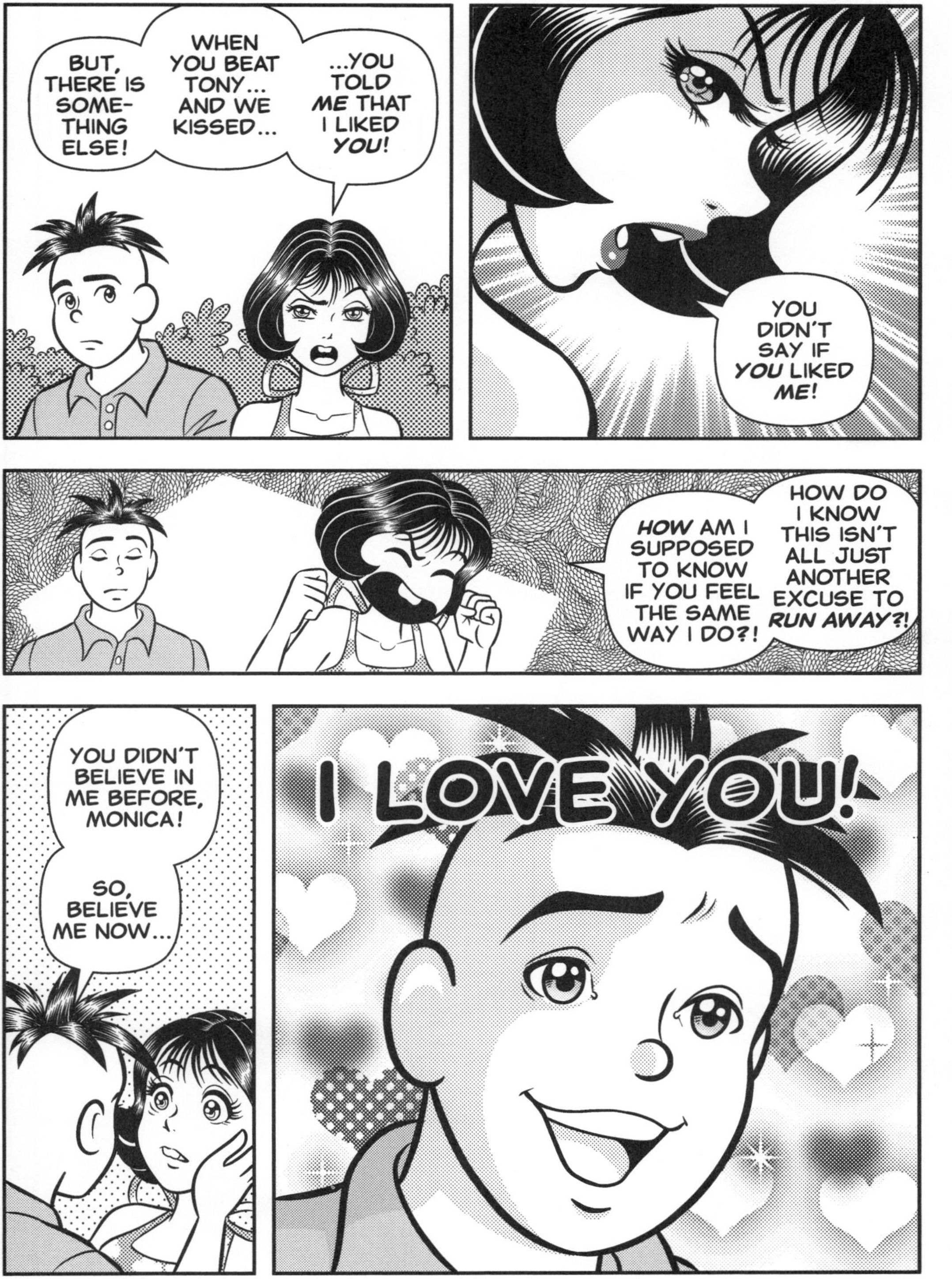
BUT, THERE IS SOME-THING ELSE!
WHEN YOU BEAT TONY... AND WE KISSED...
...YOU TOLD *ME* THAT I LIKED *YOU*!
YOU DIDN'T SAY IF *YOU* LIKED *ME*!
HOW AM I SUPPOSED TO KNOW IF YOU FEEL THE SAME WAY I DO?!
HOW DO I KNOW THIS ISN'T ALL JUST ANOTHER EXCUSE TO *RUN AWAY*?!
YOU DIDN'T BELIEVE IN ME BEFORE, MONICA!
SO, BELIEVE ME NOW...
I LOVE YOU!

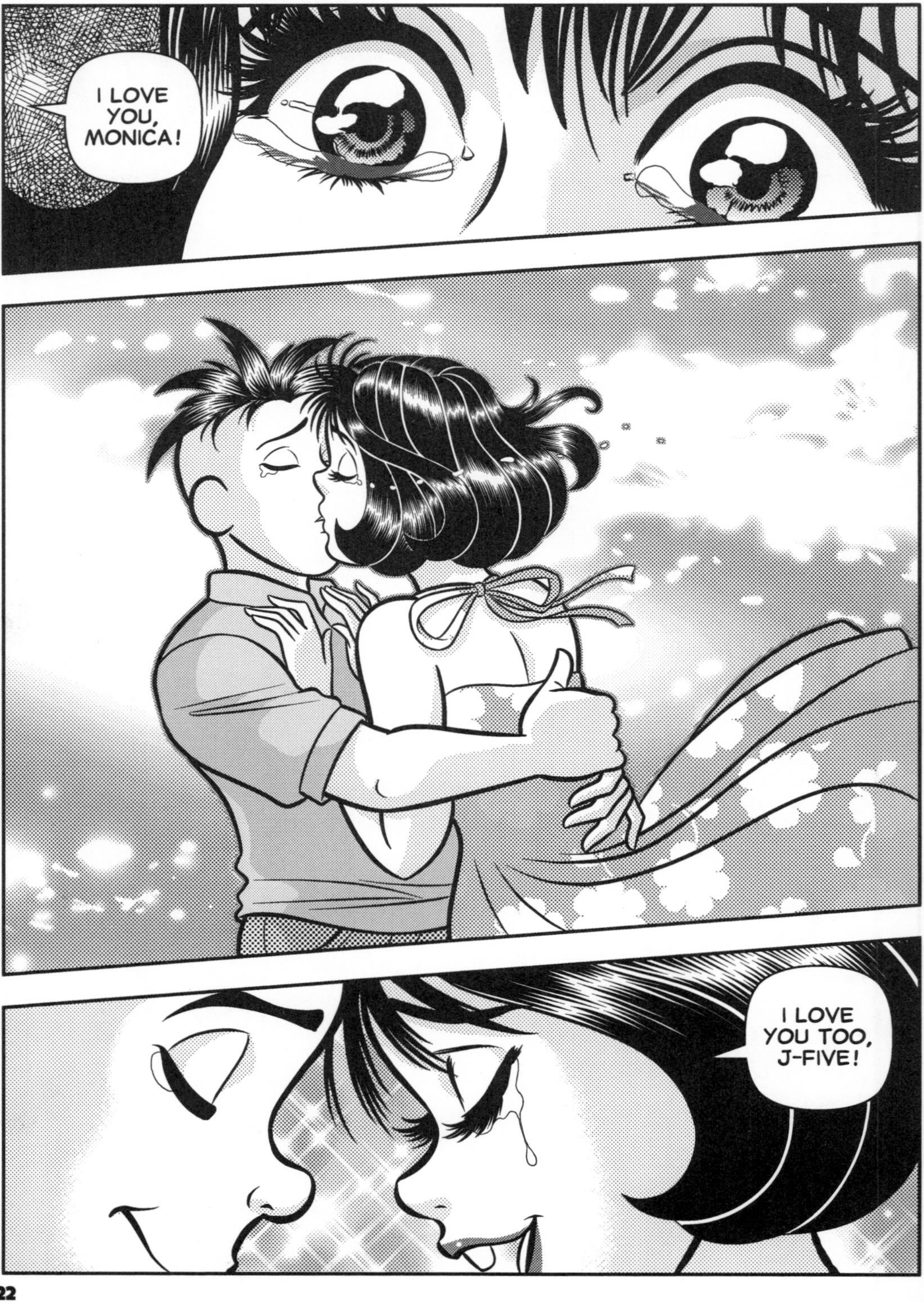
I LOVE YOU, MONICA!
I LOVE YOU TOO, J-FIVE!

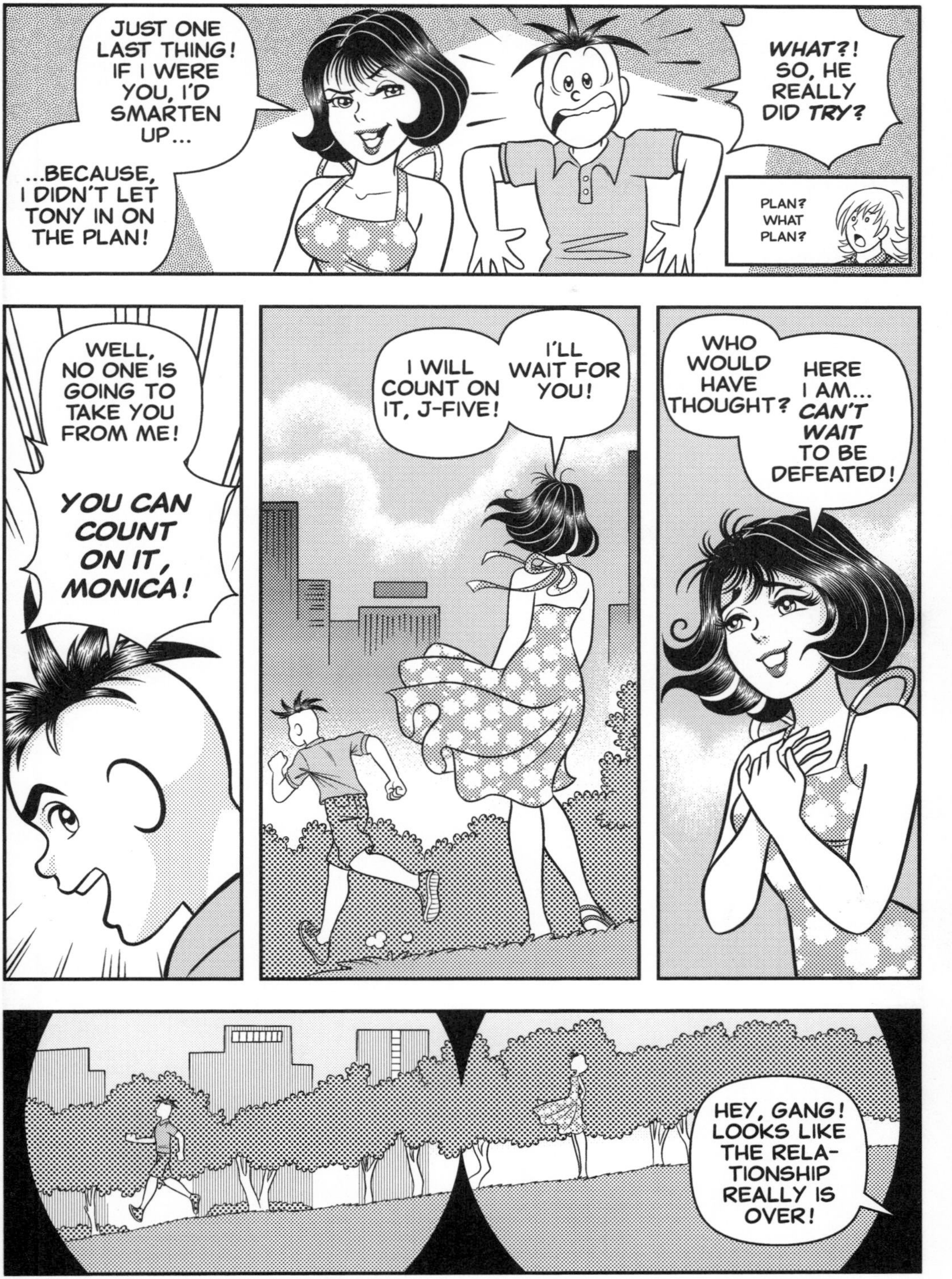
JUST ONE LAST THING! IF I WERE YOU, I'D SMARTEN UP...
...BECAUSE, I DIDN'T LET TONY IN ON THE PLAN!
WHAT?! SO, HE REALLY DID TRY?
PLAN? WHAT PLAN?
WELL, NO ONE IS GOING TO TAKE YOU FROM ME!
YOU CAN COUNT ON IT, MONICA!
I WILL COUNT ON IT, J-FIVE!
I'LL WAIT FOR YOU!
WHO WOULD HAVE THOUGHT?
HERE I AM... CAN'T WAIT TO BE DEFEATED!
HEY, GANG! LOOKS LIKE THE RELA-TIONSHIP REALLY IS OVER!

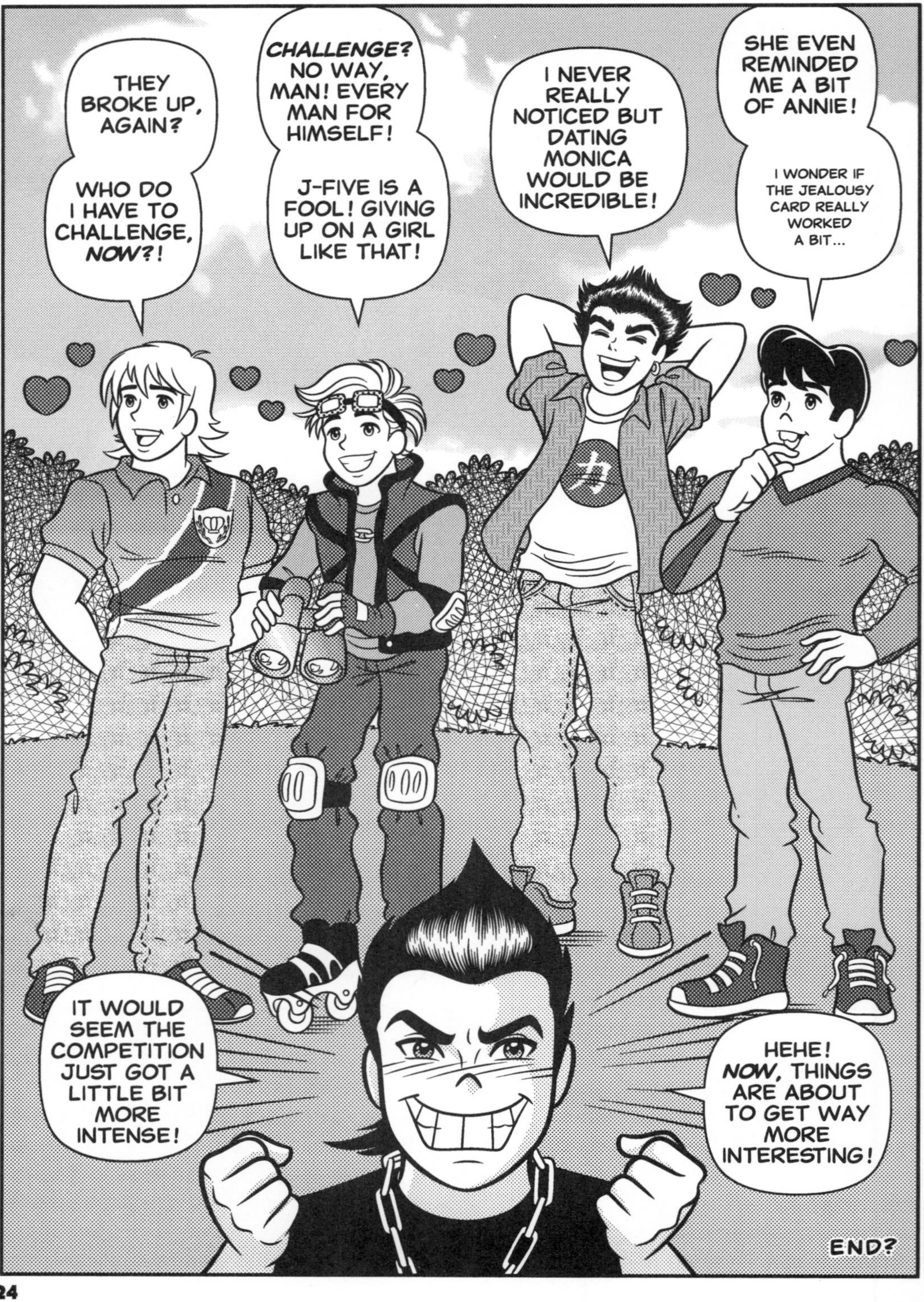
THEY BROKE UP, AGAIN?
WHO DO I HAVE TO CHALLENGE, NOW?!
CHALLENGE? NO WAY, MAN! EVERY MAN FOR HIMSELF!
J-FIVE IS A FOOL! GIVING UP ON A GIRL LIKE THAT!
I NEVER REALLY NOTICED BUT DATING MONICA WOULD BE INCREDIBLE!
SHE EVEN REMINDED ME A BIT OF ANNIE!
I WONDER IF THE JEALOUSY CARD REALLY WORKED A BIT...
IT WOULD SEEM THE COMPETITION JUST GOT A LITTLE BIT MORE INTENSE!
HEHE! NOW, THINGS ARE ABOUT TO GET WAY MORE INTERESTING!
END?

MORE GRAPHIC NOVELS AVAILABLE FROM Charmz™

STITCHED #1
"THE FIRST DAY OF THE
REST OF HER LIFE"

STITCHED #2
"LOVE IN THE TIME
OF ASSUMPTION"

G.F.F.s #1
"MY HEART LIES
IN THE 90s"

G.F.F.s #2
"WITCHES GET
THINGS DONE"

CHLOE #1
"THE NEW GIRL"

CHLOE #2 "THE QUEEN
OF HIGH SCHOOL"

CHLOE #3
"FRENEMIES"

CHLOE #4
"RAINY DAY"

SCARLET ROSE #1
"I KNEW I'D MEET YOU"

SCARLET ROSE #2
"I'LL GO WHERE YOU GO"

SCARLET ROSE #3
"I THINK I LOVE YOU"

SCARLET ROSE #4
"YOU WILL ALWAYS BE MINE"

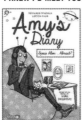

AMY'S DIARY #1
"SPACE ALIEN...
ALMOST?"

SWEETIES #1
"CHERRY SKYE"

MONICA ADVENTURES #1

ANA AND THE
COSMIC RACE #1
"THE RACE BEGINS"

Charmz chat™

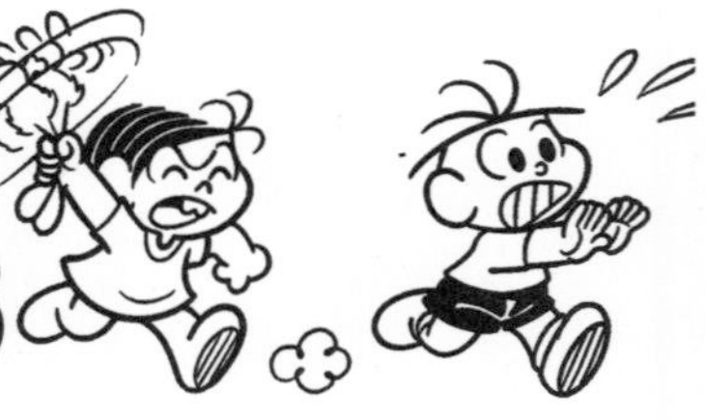

Welcome to MONICA ADVENTURES #2 "We Fought Each Other as Kids… Now We're in Love?!" from the crushing folks at Charmz, the Papercutz imprint devoted to romantic and fun graphic novels. We're thrilled to be able to bring one of the most popular comics characters in the world to North America—MONICA! Created by comics legend Mauricio de Sousa, who was inspired by his own daughter when she was a brash child. Monica the comics character therefore started as a child, and her best-selling comics series is still going strong today. In fact, Monica is still just a kid in her main comics series, but another comic was spun off, called MONICA TEEN, and those are the comics we're presenting here—starring the teenage Monica. Check out MONICA ADVENTURES #1 for a little more background on Mauricio and MONICA.

Here in MONICA ADVENTURES #2, we see longtime childhood rivals Monica and J-Five admitting their feelings for (and their mischievous plans against) one another! It's like watching a tennis match or a really exciting chess match as these two teens battle it out to try and control their hearts and emotions.

Monica and J-Five have been chasing after each other since her introduction in comics back in 1963 in Brazil. Monica appeared in the newspaper strip of J-Five (Cebolinha in Brazil). In that classic comic strip, Jimmy is trying to see how long he can balance on the sidewalk when he comes across Monica. He asks her to move. By the third panel, Monica was already whacking poor Jimmy with her plush bunny. Nursing his new black eye, he laments, "Now I know how women can trip up a guy!" Such was the beginning of a beautiful friendship. For years J-Five continues to try to one up Monica with his infallible plans, and doing silly things like stealing her bunny to tie knots in its ears. But the results would always be Monica returning, pounding Jimmy in fruitless attempts to teach him a lesson. But now that they're teenagers, all that has changed. The story in this landmark MONICA adventure brings their relationship to an important turning point. Everything is now different between these two childhood friends, and we can't wait to see what happens next. Someone who may know exactly what might happen next, offers his insights on all this…

A SPECIAL MESSAGE FROM

MAURICIO DE SOUSA

THE CREATOR OF MONICA

To date or not to date? To marry or not to marry? These are some of the doubts that we've questioned for a long time, especially after the launch of MONICA ADVENTURES. After all, when will J-Five and Monica finally fulfill whatever destiny awaits them? In this graphic novel, we gave a glimpse into what could be around the corner. Which begs the question, is marriage really the best option between these

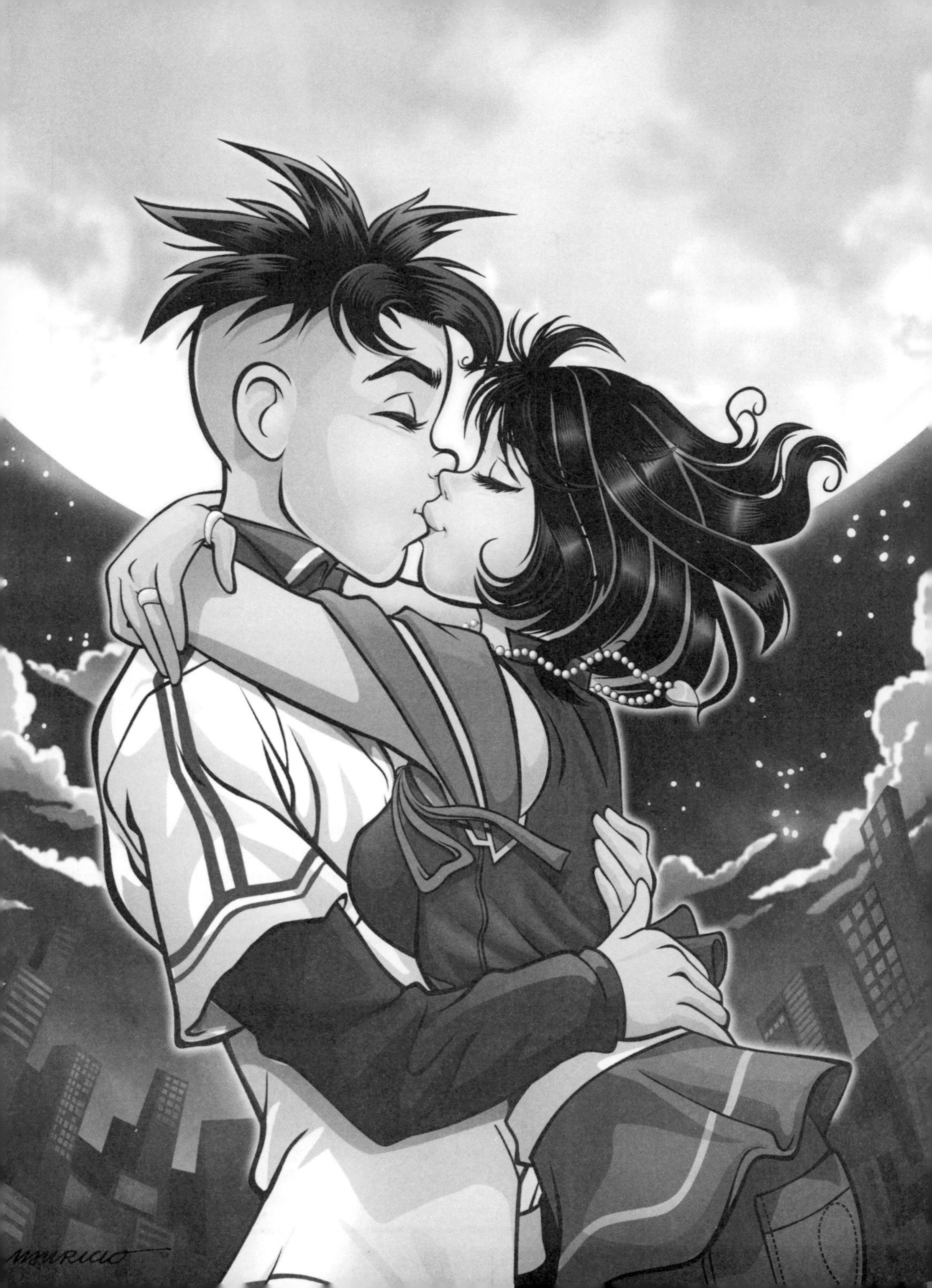
MAURICIO

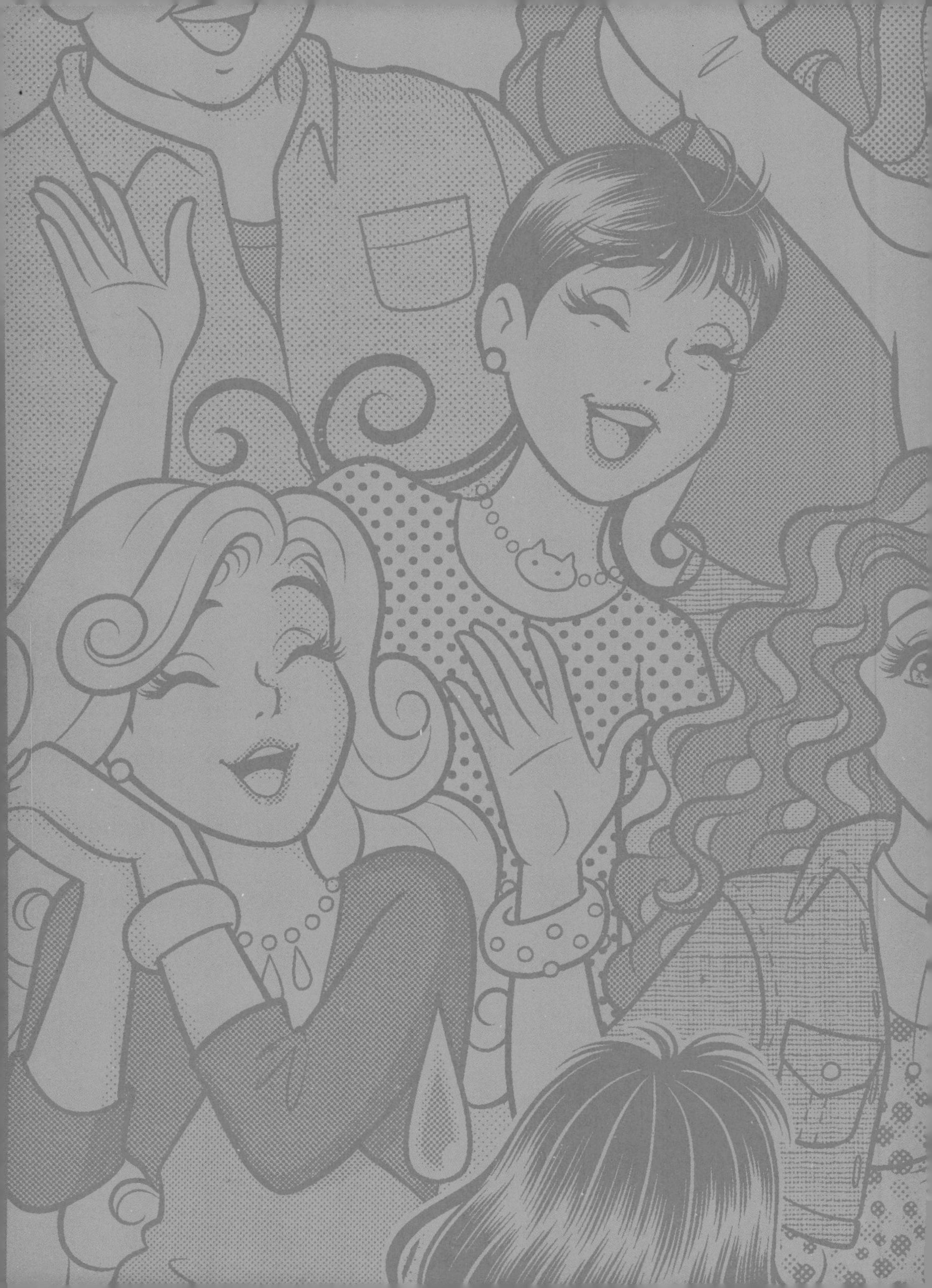